Kylie Ladd is a novelist and freelance writer. She has previously published three novels: *After the Fall, Last Summer,* which was Highly Commended in the FAW Christina Stead Award for fiction, and *Into My Arms,* chosen as one of Get Reading's '50 books you can't put down' for 2013. With Leigh Langtree, she also edited the anthology *Naked: Confessions of Adultery and Infidelity.* Kylie holds a PhD in neuropsychology and lives in Melbourne with her husband and two children.

Praise for *Mothers and Daughters*

'Kylie is a writer of great empathy; that quality is at the heart of her novels . . . a practised and proven storyteller.'

The Wheeler Centre

'Ladd . . . understands the complex relationships between women—and family—incredibly well.'

The Advertiser, Weekend

' a story about . . . women and daughters of privilege. In this territory, Ladd's writing shines.'

Adelaide Review

'A thought-provoking and provocative story'

Booked Out

'. . . a fascinating journey . . . recommended for female readers of quality popular fiction.'

Books + Publishing

'The novel offers lots of touchpoints for midlife mums.'

The Daily Telegraph

Mothers and Daughters

KYLIE LADD

ALLEN&UNWIN

SYDNEY · MELBOURNE · AUCKLAND · LONDON

This edition published in 2015

Copyright © Kylie Ladd 2014

Allen & Unwin
Sydney, Melbourne, Auckland, London

83 Alexander Street
Crows Nest NSW 2065
Australia
Phone: (61 2) 8425 0100
Email: info@allenandunwin.com
Web: www.allenandunwin.com

Cataloguing-in-Publication details are available from the National Library of Australia
trove.nla.gov.au

ISBN 978 1 92526 624 5

Text design by Lisa White
Set in Minion Pro by Bookhouse, Sydney
Printed and bound in Australia by Griffin Press

10 9 8 7 6 5 4 3 2 1

*For my mother, Sue, and my daughter, Cameron,
who have both taught me so much.*

And for Craig, who gave me Broome.

The cruel girls we loved
Are over forty,
Their subtle daughters
Have stolen their beauty;

And with a blue stare
Of cool surprise,
They mock their anxious mothers
With their mothers' eyes.

DAVID CAMPBELL, 'MOTHERS AND DAUGHTERS'

Sunday

'Oh, for fuck's sake, Morag!'

Fiona winced and pushed Morag's case off her big toe, then bent to study it. Thirty bucks she'd paid for her pedicure, and she'd kill Morag if it was chipped before they even left Tullamarine.

'Sorry, sorry,' said Morag, yanking her Samsonite away so abruptly that it almost hit the legs of the man queuing in front of them.

'Christ, that thing weighs a ton,' said Fiona, rubbing her foot. 'What the hell have you got in there—an iron?' Her dark red nail polish was intact, she was pleased to see, but the inspection had revealed that her feet were already swelling in her new sandals, even though it was cool in Melbourne, and nothing like the heat they'd experience up north. Fuck. Fiona sighed. She should have gone with the size ten. Who was she kidding? She hadn't been a nine since before she had Dominic;

since then everything had spread. Her feet were the least of it. She stood back up, surreptitiously hoicking her cargo pants from where they'd snagged between her buttocks.

'Weights, actually,' Morag said.

'Weights?' asked Caro, as the line snaked forward a metre. Everyone picked up their bags and shuffled forward obediently.

'For running,' Morag said. 'Hand weights. I take them with me so my upper body gets a workout too. I don't have time to go to the gym for that.'

'Very efficient.' Caro nodded.

'You're nuts,' said Fiona. 'You already look like a praying mantis with anorexia—you need to eat, not lift weights.'

'I eat!' Morag protested. 'And they're not that heavy, only five kilos. Keeps the tuckshop arms at bay.'

Fiona was glad she hadn't worn a singlet like the other two. 'Whatever, but this is meant to be a holiday. Jeez—you're the only one of us who's completely footloose and fancy-free. You've got a week in the tropics, the boys are with Andrew . . . you should be sipping cocktails, not racing around pumping your skinny arms in the air.'

Caro giggled, then glanced apologetically at Morag, but she was laughing too.

'As if I'd do that. That went out years ago. God forbid you should know anything about exercise, Fiona, other than jumping to conclusions.'

Caro snorted. Fiona smiled too, to show she wasn't bothered. *Yeah, yeah*, she thought. *Mantis arse.*

'Plus I like running,' Morag went on. 'It's not a chore. It

relaxes me. Maybe Janey would like to come with me, Caro? She jogs, doesn't she, as part of her training?'

Caro looked across at her daughter, blonde head bent over her phone, as it had been ever since they'd arrived at the airport, and shrugged. 'Maybe.'

'Well, anything involving sweat isn't my idea of relaxation,' Fiona said, prodding her bag forward as the queue moved up again. 'Unless it's the sweat I'm going to work up sitting on the beach, under an umbrella, waiting for someone to bring me a drink.' She paused for effect. 'Ideally a black man.'

'Fiona!' Caro protested, right on cue. 'You're a shocker.'

'Why? There should be plenty where we're going, shouldn't there? I bet Amira's surrounded by them, lucky bitch. That's probably why she went.'

Morag shook her head. 'You know it isn't, you stirrer. She lowered her voice. 'Keep it down. Bronte's right behind you.'

'Oh, she's off in her own little world as usual,' Fiona scoffed. 'Probably just as well. If she did hear me she'd blush so much she'd lose circulation in the rest of her body.' Fiona's daughter was a mystery to her at times. OK, all the time. Who knew what the hell went on behind those cat-like eyes of hers?

'I can't wait to see Amira again,' Caro said, riffling through her handbag as the check-in counter came into view. 'It's been way too long. Nine months. And Tess too. I wonder if she's enjoyed it? I can't imagine Janey and April living on a mission.'

Fiona was tempted to say that she couldn't imagine Janey doing anything Janey didn't want to do, but Morag spoke first.

'Community,' Morag said. 'It hasn't been a mission for years and years. I looked it up on the net. It's called a community

3

now. Nothing religious. There's still a church there—I saw it on the website—but I don't think it's compulsory.'

Fiona made a show of looking at her watch. 'Damn,' she said, 'and here I was spewing that we'd missed Mass.'

Caro and Morag laughed. Janey looked up from her phone to make sure she hadn't missed anything, then went back to texting.

The Qantas girl who served them was young and bright-eyed. Too bloody bright-eyed, Fiona thought. Was she on drugs? It couldn't be that exciting, waving everyone else off to exotic locations while you sat behind a desk in the outer suburbs and heard the millionth upgrade request of your career.

'And where are you ladies flying to today?' she chirped, holding out a manicured hand for their documents.

'Broome,' Caro replied excitedly. 'We're going to see a friend. She's been working there since the start of the year, and our daughters—' she indicated Janey and Bronte—'are friendly with *her* daughter, so we thought we could all catch up, have a bit of a girls' trip.'

'Oh, I hear Broome's lovely,' the check-in girl trilled mechanically, tapping at her keyboard.

'Well, it's not actually Broome,' Caro went on. 'It's about two hours north. Amira—our friend—is teaching at an Aboriginal school out in the bush there. It used to be a mission. She's always wanted to do that sort of work.'

Shut up, just shut up, Fiona muttered to herself. Didn't Caro know that the girl didn't care? She had only asked them where they were going so she put them on the right plane, for goodness' sake. Now she'd probably seat them by the toilets

4

just for boring her. Fiona looked away in exasperation and caught the eye of Janey, who raised one sarcastic eyebrow.

'God, Mum, you go on,' she said.

Fuck, thought Fiona. *You should have been mine.*

———

Bronte hesitated in the aisle, clutching her backpack to her chest. Should she put it in the overhead locker so that she had more leg room? She could always do with that, and the flight from Melbourne to Broome was over five hours—she didn't want to be any more cramped than was necessary. Then again, it *was* a long flight, and she might need her stuff. She put the bag down on the seat and began to go through it. Magazine, yes, plus her sketchbook and pens. They could all fit in the pocket in front of her. The apple she'd packed in case she got hungry; ditto the rice crackers. *To Kill a Mockingbird*? She had an essay on it due at the start of the term and she was only halfway through, but she hated trying to read anywhere other than in her bedroom at home. There might be a good movie on, anyway, in which case . . .

'Shit, Bronte, you're holding up half the plane,' said Janey, pushing past her to claim the window seat. Bronte turned around and was horrified to discover seven or eight passengers banked up behind her, shifting their own hand luggage from arm to arm. She hurriedly stuffed everything back into her bag and slid into her seat, face burning.

'Idiots,' Janey said as they filed past. 'I wonder how long they would have waited.'

Bronte bent over and wedged the backpack under the seat in front. It fitted, but as she'd suspected there was very little room left over for her feet. Janey watched with interest as she endeavoured to fold it in half.

'Why'd you bring something so big, anyway?' she asked, then sighed. 'Give it to me. I can shove it between my seat and the wall.'

'Thanks,' Bronte said, surprised.

'I guess you need all the space you can get, huh?' Janey remarked as she took the backpack. 'How tall *are* you? Six foot? I reckon you've grown another inch since our game last Saturday.'

'Five eleven,' Bronte said. Not quite six foot, but way too close for her liking. One hundred and eighty-one centimetres, to be precise. Bronte knew the figure because she had begun measuring herself every week before the netball game, horrified at the way her skirt was creeping up her thighs. She was only fourteen, yet she'd already gone past her brother, who'd be eighteen at Christmas; had left her mum in her shadow months ago. Only her father was still taller than her, and she prayed every day that she wouldn't end up six foot four, like him. Bronte sighed. She'd need a new uniform soon, but hated the idea of asking for one, reluctant to draw any more attention to herself.

'You're a freak,' said Janey mildly, placing a tab of bubble gum in her mouth. She offered Bronte the packet. 'D'you want some? My ears always hurt at take-off and landing if I'm not chewing on something.'

'No, thanks,' Bronte said. She had no idea if her ears would hurt. This was only the second flight of her life. The first, seven years ago, was when her parents had taken them to Sydney one Easter. Dom had got some sort of tummy bug and vomited all over their hotel room; when he was finally well enough to do a tour of the Opera House, their father had been so appalled at the cost of the tickets that he'd stormed out of the building, claiming they could look at it for free from the harbour. Since then any family holidays had taken place at her grandmother's house in Rosebud, with its splintery decking and seagrass matting. It was different for Janey, Bronte thought as the plane began to vibrate, then started rolling slowly along the tarmac. She flew all the time—most term breaks, it seemed, with her parents and sister to Noosa or Port Douglas; with her swimming team to their various meets around the country. She was fiddling with her phone again now, not even listening as the flight attendant carefully lifted a banana-yellow lifejacket over her hairdo, then gestured, arms stiff, towards the exits. This was all old hat for Janey, as boring as a maths class, or a cafe with no wi-fi.

Not for her mother, though. Bronte leaned forward, peering between the seats for a glimpse of the three women in the row in front of her. Morag's fair head was buried in either a magazine or the safety guide; Caro was watching the attendant and absently playing with the strand of pearls around her neck. Bronte watched as her hand lifted automatically to smooth her silvery-blonde bob, then, satisfied that everything was in place, returned to her throat. Pearls to Broome. Coals to Newcastle. Bronte smiled to herself, but she knew Caro couldn't help it.

She was wedded to those pearls, to always looking immaculate. In contrast, her own mother's dark hair stuck out from her head. She had her eyes tightly closed, hands clenched in her lap. She probably wanted the others to think she was napping, but Bronte knew the truth. For all her bravado, her mother was ridiculously afraid of flying. Bronte had watched her growing steadily more tense as their bags were weighed and check-in was completed; had stood with her in the public toilet next to the boarding gate and held her purse while her mum took a swig of water straight from the tap and washed down a sleeping tablet, then two Valium. She'd offered Bronte one, but Bronte had refused. Maybe she shouldn't have, she thought. She probably could have sold it to Janey.

The engines roared and the plane shot forward. Behind them, in the galley, bottles burst into tinkling conversation, as if exclaiming over the sudden movement; Caro's carefully coiffed hair defied its coating of lacquer and swung momentarily free around her face. Bronte grabbed the armrest and felt her stomach contract. Up, up . . . the brown Tullamarine paddocks tilted outside her window and fell away, replaced by blue. The plane lurched, shuddered, and hauled itself into the air. Beside her, Janey blew a large purple bubble and then popped it with her tongue.

'Are your ears OK?' Bronte asked.

'Fine,' said Janey, licking shards of gum from her lips. She stared despondently at the silenced phone in her lap. 'But it's such a drag to have to turn my mobile off. I wanted to text Caitlin. She gave me a card to give Tess, but I left it at home.'

'Do you miss Tess since she left?'

Janey looked surprised, as if this was the first time the idea had occurred to her.

'I guess so, but it's not as if she's my BFF or anything.'

'But you were, weren't you?' Bronte persisted. 'All through primary school, and in year seven too, I thought.' She'd spent every one of those primary school years in the same class as Janey and Tess—it was how their mothers had met. Morag too, though she had twin boys, Callum and Finn, who liked to pull Bronte's ponytail when she was looking at the board, then blame the other when she turned around. Bronte had often been jealous of Janey and Tess's friendship, their contrasting blonde and black heads always bent together over the desk or whispering furiously in a corner. It wasn't that she liked Janey, especially—being with Janey was like sleeping with an echidna, her mum had once said: no matter how careful you were, you were bound to get hurt—but what she did envy was their closeness. Bronte had friends, but not ones that called her every night to talk for two hours about nothing, or who nagged their mothers into buying the much-coveted heart-shaped charms sold at Bevilles in the city. Gold and shiny, the charms split down the middle into two matching halves, to be worn ostentatiously by besties wanting to flaunt their allegiance.

Tess and Janey, of course, had taken it even further than that. One day in grade four they had gone into the toilets at lunchtime and swapped underwear, proudly lifting their dresses in the playground to show the rest of the girls what they'd done.

'You'll get germs,' Bronte had ventured, to which Tess had replied, 'No we won't, because we're *best friends*.' The underwear swapping had continued daily, a ritual of devotion and exclusion, till almost the end of grade five, when Janey had suddenly declared it 'gay' and the whole thing had stopped. Six months later, when Bronte won a scholarship to a private school, her main emotion was one of relief. Tess and Janey would be going to the local secondary school. She wouldn't have to endure another six years of watching them together. Bronte pulled at a cuticle. But a week would be OK, she told herself. She could manage a week.

Janey yawned, and pulled her gum out of her mouth with two fingers. Daintily, she rolled it into a ball, then stuck the wad to the side of her seat, dangerously close to Bronte's bag.

'It's different at high school,' she said. 'Everyone's replaceable.' She looked restlessly out the window, then pulled some earbuds out of jeans so tight Bronte didn't know how she could even get her fingers in the pocket. 'How's St Anne's?' she asked grudgingly.

'Great,' Bronte replied. 'I've got this fabulous art teacher, Ms Drummond.' She blushed and stared at her lap. Would Janey understand about Ms Drummond? 'She thinks my drawings are really good. I mean, she probably says that to everyone, but still . . .' Bronte took a deep breath and rushed on. 'She wants me to take her fashion design class next year. We have all these electives for art in year nine—fashion's one, but there's also ceramics and woodcraft . . . and I really want to, but I'm not sure what Mum will say. I think she wants me to stick with French. What would you do?'

She turned to Janey, but Janey wasn't listening. She had her earbuds in and was mouthing the words of a Rhianna song.

———

Caro shifted in her seat, uneasy. To her right, Fiona sat with her eyes closed and her body frozen in position, turned away towards the wing; to her left, Morag was reading a guidebook, highlighting every second or third paragraph. Behind them Janey stared out the window nodding along to her music while Bronte flicked through a magazine. Had this been a mistake?

When she'd first come up with the idea for the trip, she'd imagined Fiona, Morag and herself giggling together on the flight, feet curled beneath them, leaning in to exchange confidences about the bikinis they'd packed or the waxing they'd endured. She'd pictured Janey and Bronte reconnecting, chatting about their schools or their nail polish, whatever it was fourteen-year-olds were interested in. Instead, they were already an hour out of Melbourne, and barely anyone had said a word to each other.

It would be alright once they were there, she told herself. Amira would put them all at ease, would enfold and include them. She was the one who had brought them together, after all. Eight years, Caro thought, leaning back in her seat. Nearly nine. You knew you were middle-aged when you found yourself wondering where the time had gone. But where *had* it gone? She still remembered that morning—the humid February drizzle, remnant of a cool change; Janey in a too-big uniform, starched and pleated, her hair in plaits. All summer she'd been excited about going to school, boasting about being a big girl, but when the day actually arrived she'd gripped Caro's hand so tightly that her fingernails almost drew blood.

Amira had noticed. Amira, a total stranger, had seen Caro hesitate, seen Janey's face quiver, and had swooped down and complimented the girl on her bright blue ribbons. 'They match your eyes,' she'd said, the perfect praise for a girl like Janey, who even at six couldn't walk past a mirror without assessing her reflection.

'I like your hair,' Janey said in return, reaching out to touch it. 'It's all fuzzy.'

Amira had laughed. 'That's because of the rain.' She tried to smooth it down, but the black curls sprang back undeterred. 'Actually, it's always pretty crazy. My daughter Tess thinks I look like a sheep. Would you like to meet her? She's in this class too.'

'OK,' said Janey, dropping Caro's hand and allowing herself to be led to a table where a dark-eyed child sat quietly colouring in a picture of a koala.

'Thank you,' Caro said once the two girls were exchanging textas.

'Sorry—I hope you didn't think I was rude, or interfering,' Amira replied. 'It was just that I could see she had her hands full.' She nodded towards the teacher by the blackboard, one crying child clinging to her hip, another sitting at her feet calling for its mother.

'Rude? I thought you were brilliant.'

Amira smiled. 'Thanks. I'm a teacher myself. I know what first days are like, but most of the kids just need to be distracted.' She held out a soft brown hand. 'I'm Amira. Nice to meet you. They look fine, don't they?'

Tess was peering over Janey's shoulder offering encouragement while Janey carefully coloured the animal pink. A sliver of tongue protruded from her mouth, and her eyes were fierce with concentration.

'They do,' Caro said and shook Amira's hand, feeling herself relax. 'Caroline. And thank God. I don't know who was more nervous about this morning, me or Janey, particularly when Alex couldn't come. That's my husband,' she explained. 'He's away for work. He travels a lot. Is yours here?'

Amira shook her head. 'Single parent. It's just me and Tess.'

'Oh. Sorry,' Caro said.

'Don't be,' said Amira. 'The best thing he ever did was leave.' She'd smiled, her white teeth a bright flash of light in her face.

Caro had liked Amira immediately, she recalled now: her confidence, her warmth, the way her gold hoop earrings gleamed against her hair. When Fiona bowled up, demanding to know if this was Prep L, Caro had wanted to shoo her away, to keep this lovely woman all for herself, but Amira had welcomed and soothed her too, positioning Bronte on the other side of Tess. Fiona was also by herself. 'I didn't even think of asking Todd to come,' she'd murmured, looking around the classroom at all the fathers there to see their children launched upon the seas of formal education. She shrugged. 'He probably wouldn't have wanted to anyway.' Then Morag had struggled into the room with a tow-headed boy tugging at each arm and a belly that arrived a full minute before the rest of her. Morag's husband Andrew was there, Caro remembered, but it was Amira who had detached the twins and shown them where to put their bags, had urged Morag to sit down lest she go into labour on the spot, had quietly handed them all tissues when Prep L's teacher finally told them it was time to go and the small faces of their children had turned towards them wreathed in doubt and anticipation and a perfect blank innocence that would never be there again.

It was strange, Caro thought. Theoretically, Amira was the one who needed help, the single parent with the useless ex—trying to get by on a teacher's pay cheque and whatever else she could scrape together from the jewellery she made and sold at local markets. The rest of them had husbands, superannuation funds, mortgages that were almost paid off . . . Yet it was Amira who looked after them, Amira who was always there. She picked up Bronte and took her home on the days Fiona had to work late; she reassured Caro when Janey was hauled before the principal for hitting another child in the playground; she organised a class meals roster after Morag gave birth to Torran the day after the sports carnival.

'She's got three kids,' Amira had demurred when Caro had commended her for her initiative. 'It's the least I could do.'

'Three and a half,' Fiona had said, because by then they all knew about Macy.

Caro peered down the aisle, hoping to spot the drinks trolley. It would be wonderful to be with Amira again. She'd missed her. That was why she'd organised this week, for them all to see Amira, and for Janey to see Tess. True, Janey didn't exactly seem to have been pining for her friend, but maybe that was just Janey. She didn't give much away. The trip would be valuable for all of them. It would be good to spend some proper time with her eldest daughter, rather than just ferrying her to training or nagging her about the mess on her bedroom floor; it would be good for Tess, Janey and Bronte to be together again, as they had been in primary school. And there were her own friends too—Morag must need a break from all those boys and the upheaval that came with Macy two weeks a month, while Fiona . . . Caro shook her head. Fiona definitely needed to get out of that house. Not that you could tell her, especially now Bronte was going to St Anne's and Caro and Fiona didn't run into each other every day at pick-up. The girls were still in the same netball team, of course, playing every Saturday morning from nine to ten thirty, but Fiona rarely came to watch, dropping Bronte at the last possible minute without getting out of her car, then racing off to rush through her supermarket shopping before the game had finished.

The truth was that they'd drifted. It was inevitable, wasn't it? Bronte at a different school, Tess off in the back of beyond, Callum and Finn preoccupied with their skateboards and the latest surf report . . . with the children all moving in different directions, what hope did the mothers have? Still, it bothered Caro. Just a few years ago they'd been thrown together almost every day: at drop-off, on tuckshop duty or classroom reading, at the innumerable sports days and recorder recitals and choir concerts, at the gate every afternoon where they gossiped and bitched while they waited for the bell to ring. Fiona hadn't made every event and neither had Caro, but back then there was always another one coming up behind. The school, it turned out, had organised their social lives for them, had knitted them together. Caro sighed. It was a relief to attend one less class assembly, it was only right that their children were growing up and able to make their own way home from school, but she missed those daily meetings with her friends: hearing about Morag's latest saga with Macy, all the more entertaining for Morag's droll, dry delivery; Fiona sniping at another mother's outfit and making them all laugh; Amira asking them back to her place for a drink, because it was Friday afternoon and that was what they always did.

'I'd forgotten Australia was so big.' Morag remarked. She closed her guidebook, tucking the highlighter into its spine. 'I can't believe we still aren't even halfway there.'

Caro turned to her, relieved. She needed to talk to someone. She was getting maudlin.

'You've never been up north before, have you?' she asked.

Morag shook her head.

'No further than the Gold Coast. We took the boys there a few years ago to do the Worlds, remember? Only Torran was still too small to go on half the rides, and Callum and Finn spent the whole time teasing him about it. Fun for all the family.'

Caro laughed.

'I'm really glad to be going, though,' Morag continued. 'I can't quite believe I've been here so long and have never seen the top end.'

'I haven't either,' Caro said. 'The closest I've got is a school trip to Ayers Rock thirty years ago now, and I don't think that counts. They don't even call it that anymore.' Her legs were getting cramped and she stretched them out in front of her, kicking off her shoes. 'You take it all for granted, I think. You just assume you'll get there someday, but I bet most don't. I wouldn't be doing this if Amira hadn't moved.'

'It'll be good to see her, won't it? It must be such a different life . . .'

There was a pause, and Caro looked around again. Where the hell was the drinks trolley?

'So how'd you go getting away?' she asked. 'Andrew's taking the boys to Tasmania, isn't he? Did you have to pack their bags for them?'

'Hell, no,' Morag said. 'If they've forgotten anything, that's their lookout. They won't forget it again.'

'Even Torran?' Caro asked.

'Even Torran. He's nine now. That's quite old enough to throw together some socks and jocks and t-shirts. I did have to talk him out of taking his Nintendo, though. He'd probably leave it by the river.'

'I wouldn't have even attempted to separate Janey from her phone,' said Caro. 'She would have found a way to smuggle it in anyway. I assume there'll be somewhere we can charge them?'

Morag shot her a look. 'I don't think it's *that* primitive.' She picked at the price sticker on the cover of her book, pushing back a corner. 'It was amazing, actually. I didn't have to do anything—Andrew organised it all. It helps that it's Macy's week with Janice, of course, but he's really been looking forward to the trip. You know, four men against the elements—hiking, fishing, cooking over an open fire . . .'

'Ugh. Sounds disgusting. I bet none of them change their jocks all week.'

Morag laughed. 'I thought it sounded great. I would've liked to have gone too. Maybe another time.' She bent over the guidebook, working at the sticker, her fair hair hiding her face. The sticker came away, taking a segment of the cover with it.

'What about you?' she asked, looking up. 'Is Alex taking care of April?'

Caro shook her head. 'Not a chance. He's in Italy again, left yesterday.' Alex was away even more now than he had been when Janey started school. Caro understood that he needed to travel for his job, but she'd never truly got used to it. It was always a shock and a nuisance to have him gone once more, disappearing from their lives just when she'd adjusted to him being at home.

'So April's with Maria?'

Caro nodded. 'She could have gone to stay with a friend, but Maria insisted. I didn't have a chance. She rang Alex at work and told him she wouldn't hear of anything else, that April should be with family. Anyone would think I was leaving her for a month, not eight days.' She sighed. 'Then when I dropped her off Maria said something to April in Italian about how lucky I was to be having a holiday. She doesn't think I understand her, but I do. All those bloody family dinners I've had to sit through—you'd think she'd realise that I must have picked up some of the language by now.'

Morag laughed. 'You *are* lucky,' she said simply.

'I know, but I've earned this, and I'm taking Janey—it's not as if I'm flitting off and abandoning everybody. Alex is away half of every month, but she never says anything to him.'

'Ah, but that's different.'

'Why?' asked Caro. 'Because he's working?'

The drinks trolley finally lumbered, clanking, to their seats. Morag waited as Caro gratefully ordered a gin and tonic.

'Because he's her son,' she said.

———

The flat was a mess. Older people's homes often were, crammed with old jam jars and catalogues, plastic bags and odd bits of string, the collections seemingly first hoarded, then curated. Morag knew that it gave her clients a sense of security, offered some sort of buffer against destitution, but it made her job that much harder. She had to bite her lip as she came into the tiny kitchen and nearly tripped over a stack of newspapers just inside the door.

'Mrs Griggs,' she said, when she'd recovered her balance, 'these are dangerous. How do you get your walker around them?'

'Och, I just lift it up and then put it on the other side,' said her client, unperturbed.

'But what about if it's dark or you're in a hurry?' asked Morag. The lino was uneven too, she noticed; she reached into her bag for Mrs Griggs' file, so she could write it all down. 'You shouldn't be lifting your frame anyway, should you?' she scolded. The older woman had already fractured one neck of femur. If she did it again she wouldn't be coming back here other than to collect her things for the nursing home.

'Ahh, you all fret so,' said Mrs Griggs, shuffling—without her walker—towards the sink. 'Would you like some tea? You look a bit peaky.'

If she looked a bit peaky it was because of cases like this, Morag thought. How she hated basement flats: damp stone, not enough natural light and far too many steps. Mrs Griggs' were outside, leading down from the street, which made things even worse in a climate like Scotland's. How on earth did she get her walker up and down them, or her shopping, come to that? Morag winced at the image of her teetering on the slippery stone with heavy bags. Rails, she thought, lots of them—on the stairs, above the step between the front door and the hallway, next to the toilet. Then non-slip mats, and the lino nailed down, a new light in the bedroom . . .

Mrs Griggs placed the kettle on the stove, her sleeve brushing a hot plate as she did so. *Cordless kettle*, wrote Morag, though would the old woman be able to learn how to use it?

'Sugar, love?' asked Mrs Griggs. In the distance there was a muffled thump. Out of habit, Morag glanced at her watch. The one o'clock gun. Amazing how you could hear it even all the way out here in Portobello. She needed to be getting back to the Royal Infirmary—she had a family meeting at two, and Mrs Griggs to write up before that. The details would be lost if she didn't, the dangerous stairs, the cramped kitchen merging into all the other stairs and kitchens and dank, dark flats she'd visited and despaired over.

'There you go,' said Mrs Griggs, placing a chipped floral teacup before her. 'Please raise your seat and put your tray in the upright position.'

Morag woke with a start. She wasn't in Edinburgh, she didn't have a meeting to get back to—she must have drifted off during the movie. Covertly she wiped some drool from her chin and quickly checked to see if anyone had noticed, but Fiona was still asleep and Caro's seat was empty.

How strange to dream of her old job like that, she thought. She supposed it must have been because she'd mentioned Edinburgh earlier, to Caro, but it had seemed so real. She closed her eyes again, clutching at the fading remnants . . . she could almost see herself hurrying across the Meadows, awash with students and tourists; feel the Castle, ever-present, hovering over her above the trees; see the grey stone of the Royal Infirmary looming ahead, the man who sold coffee in the old police booth out the front nodding to her as she came past. Only, the Royal Infirmary was gone, she remembered, fully awake now, torn down to make way for boutique apartments, the doctors and nurses and other allied health workers like herself moved to a soulless new building out in Little France. She'd almost been pleased when she'd heard that, a few years after she'd moved to Australia. She missed Edinburgh, missed it keenly, and the Royal Infirmary was one less thing to mourn. Still, it was almost impossible to imagine it gone, it had been such an important part of her life—with her work, of course, as deputy head of the occupational therapy department, but even moreso when she was pregnant with the twins. She'd first seen Finn and Callum at her twelve-week scan on a tiny black and white screen in the obstetrics department in the basement of the hospital; she'd given birth to them on an August evening three floors up in the Simpson Pavilion. *Pavilion*, she thought, smiling. Such an odd name for a maternity ward, as if the occupants were playing cricket, not moaning through labour. And moaned she had, though hardly anyone had heard her. It was the last night of the Festival, with the fireworks from the Princes Street Gardens going off so loudly outside the window that at the first barrage the midwife had sworn and dropped her stethoscope.

Caro reappeared in the aisle. Morag pulled in her knees so that her friend could get back to her seat in the centre of the row. White pants, she thought as Caro squeezed past, her bottom inches from Morag's face. Linen, just to top it off. Only Caro could get away with that—almost five hours of travel, drinks, a meal, and they were still spotless. Morag glanced down at her own navy-blue tracksuit, feeling vaguely embarrassed. Some women had the knack of wearing the right thing at the right time. She didn't.

'We've started our descent,' Caro said. 'Did you hear the pilot? You were asleep. I thought I'd fix my make-up before we arrive.'

'Won't it just melt as soon as we're out of the plane?' Morag asked, then added, 'That's a pretty lipstick,' so she didn't sound like a bitch, and because the soft coral colour really did look good against Caro's creamy skin.

'Thanks,' said Caro. 'Janey picked it out actually, a few weeks ago, when we were shopping. I think she only wanted me to get it so she could borrow it, but at least we've got the same colouring.' Fiona stirred slightly in her seat against the window. 'Do you ever do that with Macy? Go shopping, I mean.'

22

Morag snorted. 'Not a chance. As far as Macy's concerned, I'm just there to provide meals and drive her to rehearsals. Besides, the only lipstick she ever wears is black.' Her step-daughter was going through a goth phase. That was how she'd reassured Andrew when Macy had started dyeing her hair and had her nose pierced, though in reality it was well over a year now. Was that still a phase, or had she turned professional?

'God, how depressing,' said Caro. 'I don't know how Janice puts up with it. And you too,' she amended, 'but that's different, isn't it? At least you can always tell people she isn't yours.'

The sentiment was a bit harsh, but Caro was right, Morag thought. It *was* different. She liked Macy, and would never disown her. Loved her, in fact, on those occasions when she let Finn play her guitar, or helped Torran organise his rock collection—but no, she wasn't hers. Years ago, Morag had longed for a daughter. Pregnant with the twins, she was sure one of them must be a girl. When she discovered she was wrong she'd talked Andrew into trying again. He didn't care—he already had a daughter, of course—but he'd gone along with it because he could see what it meant to her. When Torran was born fat and pink and with an undeniable scrotum, the disappointment had lodged in her throat like something she hadn't ordered and couldn't quite choke down. Yet within a week he had captivated her, just like his brothers before him, and she put away her longing. Callum, Finn and Torran were healthy and gorgeous and their blue eyes shone when they saw her. This was her lot, and it was a damn fine one.

Anyway, she no longer felt as though she was missing out. She wouldn't have been any good at those shopping trips, with her track pants and her hair always pulled back, not blow-dried artfully around her face like Caro's. Besides, from what she could see, girls were much harder: Janey with her mind games and her obsession with her phone; Macy with her black boots, her ridiculous dreams of being a rock star, and the packet of the pill Morag had once found in her schoolbag but hadn't told Andrew about. She was better off with her boys. At the airport, Caro had said something to the woman behind the check-in desk about them travelling with their daughters, but even that hadn't stung. Not too much, anyway. Fiona had Bronte, Caro had Janey, and Amira had Tess, but she, Morag, had a whole week off, free from any parental responsibilities whatsoever. If nothing else, it was worth it for that.

The fasten seatbelts sign came on. Morag did so almost gleefully. It had been ages since she had been alone, with no one to please but herself. Amira had said she could have her own room at Kalangalla, if she liked. If she liked?! Morag hadn't had her own room since she was twelve, when she left Fort William, where she'd grown up, for boarding school in Edinburgh. After that it was university, and a tiny bedsit with a roommate who smelled of wet dog and sausages. She'd later moved to a share house, but even there it felt as though she was always surrounded. There were parties that lasted all weekend and on into Tuesday, people asleep in the bath or the boxroom or, once, flaked out in her wardrobe; there was always a friend of a friend camped out on the couch or helping themselves to her museli when they thought she was in the shower. And there was Andrew. For a few sweet months there was Andrew: sharing a cigarette with her on the front steps on a summer's evening, the sky still light at eleven o'clock, or in the kitchen with a tea towel over his shoulder, coaxing the ancient Aga into staying alight long enough to cook spaghetti . . . but mostly, mostly in her bed. Morag shifted in her seat. She hadn't wanted to be alone then, had she?

They'd given up the cigarettes, of course, but without realising it she'd given up time alone too. Barely a day now went by when she had more than ten minutes to herself—usually while driving to see a client or using the toilet, though even that could be interrupted at any moment if Torran had a problem that he needed her to solve. But she loved it, she told herself, the mess and scramble of family life—Macy on the phone, Finn with his head in the fridge, Callum's RipStik in the hallway, Andrew and Torran wrestling on the rug. She loved her job too, particularly since discovering that while the homes of the elderly were no less cluttered in Australia, they were at least warmer and drier. She'd chosen this; it was what she wanted—but oh, how liberating it was to flee it for a while.

'Hey,' called Janey from behind her, uncharacteristically animated. 'Look! Out the window.'

The cabin had begun to tilt. Morag leaned across Caro, felt the landing gear drop. Fiona woke up, blinked at them both in surprise, then turned to see what they were staring at.

Below them was the coast, a cerulean ocean stretching out to the horizon from a golden half-moon of sand, the land before it red and green and glinting like an opal. For a second it reminded Morag of the Highlands, though she hadn't been there in a decade: all that space, all that sky. A lump rose in her throat and she forced it down. As the plane dropped lower she could see that the place wasn't completely uninhabited. There were some people sunning themselves on the beach; further along, where russet cliffs jutted into the sea, there was a lone swimmer just off the point, head down and arms slicing neatly through the water as if to quickly put some distance between himself and the land. She knew how he felt.

<hr />

Amira stood by the gate, one foot jiggling impatiently. The sun was prickling her scalp—amazing how rapidly it could penetrate the thick bush of her hair, even matted together with salt as it was from the swim that she'd had to break up the long drive into town. She should go inside, wait in the tiny shed that Broome airport liked to call a terminal, but she didn't want to miss seeing them coming off the plane. Despite the heat, she hugged herself, excited. She and Tess had left Melbourne in January, just after New Year, so they could be settled and organised before term one began. It was October now, the second week of the school holidays, and term four was almost upon them. Ten months, they'd been away, ten amazing months when so often she'd wanted to turn to one of her girlfriends and tell them everything she was seeing and experiencing. Soon she could.

The white jet she'd been watching came to the end of the runway and slowly wheeled towards her, rolling to a stop. Amira had been anticipating this moment for days: as she lay in bed last night, watching the gecko that lived in one corner of the ceiling; when she woke this morning, the sun already strong and hot at six am; across every bump and corrugation of the Cape Leveque road. She fought down a giggle. Caro wasn't going to like the Cape Leveque road. None of them would, but the road was a fact of life, the only cleared stretch of earth between the community and Broome. And at least it was open—in a month or so, when the first rains of the wet washed across the Dampier Peninsula, it might be closed for weeks, waterlogged and impassable. If that happened, she and Tess would be cut off from the world, marooned in the community. The thought sent a frisson of fear and excitement through her.

The plane was stopped now, only a couple of hundred metres away. Amira watched as two sweating men in fluoro vests pushed a set of stairs under its tail, grunting as they locked them into place. At how many airports in the world did that still happen, Amira wondered, passengers forced to confront their new environment immediately, rather than gliding into the shelter of an air-conditioned terminal? She liked that about the north: there was no pretence, no artifice. What you saw was what you got.

The door of the plane was pushed open and passengers emerged, squinting and reaching for their sunglasses. Amira held her breath. A dozen disembarked, fifteen, twenty . . . and then there they were, coming down the stairs. Morag was first, her strawberry-blonde hair catching the light. The first time they'd been introduced, Amira had had to fight the urge to reach out and touch it, it was so fine and delicately coloured, so unlike her own. A few weeks later she'd mentioned the moment to Morag, who had laughed. 'Really? Everyone has hair like this in Scotland. It's common as muck.' But Amira had never stopped noticing it, somehow both auburn and gold, the first thing her eyes were drawn to every time they met.

Next came Caro, looking cool and unruffled, a stylish leather tote over one shoulder. Did Caro sweat? Amira didn't think so, but she'd soon find out. Caro was blonde too, though a different sort of blonde, the kind that came from a salon and needed regular maintenance. Then Janey, trailing her mother down the stairs, head lowered, checking her phone, and . . . was that Bronte? It had to be, but how she'd grown! She swayed like a giraffe next to Janey, and Janey wasn't short. Tess would barely be up to Bronte's shoulders.

An elderly couple appeared at the top of the stairs, followed by Fiona. Though furthest away and wearing dark glasses, she was the first to spot Amira and waved wildly with both arms. Amira returned the gesture, her face breaking into a grin. The woman in front of Fiona hesitated, made nervous by the descent, and Fiona mimed pushing the pair down the steps, then smiled sweetly when the man turned around to apologise for how long they were taking. As soon as he returned his attention to his wife, Fiona was at it again, this time throwing in some stabbing motions for good measure. Amira giggled. Oh, she was wicked, Fiona. She did and said things the rest of them would scarcely dare think. She was their collective id.

'Helloooooo!' cried Caro, striding towards her across the tarmac. Her bag slipped and she dumped it unceremoniously, running the last few metres to throw her arms around Amira.

'Careful,' Amira laughed, returning the embrace. 'I've been

driving for hours. I'm probably a bit smelly.' Caro's grasp only tightened in response, warm, almost frantic.

Amira kissed her friend's cheek and gently disentangled herself.

'It's fabulous to see you,' she said, holding Caro's hands.

To her surprise, her friend's eyes were damp. Caro blinked self-consciously, her mascara smudging.

'I've gone all emotional,' she said, pulling one hand away to wave it in front of her face. 'Or maybe it's menopause.'

'You wish,' said Fiona, barging between them. 'My period's due this week. It's a fucking pain in the arse. I can't wait to be done with all that. The sooner it's over the better.' She leaned in for her own kiss, then stepped back to look at Amira appraisingly. 'You look good,' she said. 'You're so bloody brown! God, you could get land rights.'

'She's always brown, Fiona,' Morag said. She took in Amira with a smile and added, 'Though now you look black next to me.' She raised one pale arm to Amira's in comparison, then touched her lightly. 'Hello,' she said. 'We made it. I've been looking forward to this for ages.'

No kiss, thought Amira, squeezing her wrist. That was OK. Morag needed her space. She turned to Bronte and Janey, who were loitering a few steps behind their mothers. 'Look at you two! You've grown up so much.' Amira grimaced. 'That makes me sound so old, doesn't it?'

'Yes,' said Janey, raising a hand in greeting. Bronte smiled and shuffled forward to hug her.

The girl stooped down, but even so Amira had to strain to reach up around her neck. 'Where's Tess?' Bronte asked.

'I left her up at Kalangalla. I didn't think I'd get you all in the car otherwise, particularly with your bags.'

'Particularly with *Caro's* bags,' Fiona said. 'She's got about six. I'm guessing there's one just for her night cream.'

'I only brought three!' Caro protested. 'One's full of towels. And my pillow,' she added, looking across at Amira for support. 'I hate using someone else's pillow, you know that. It never feels right.'

'I know,' Amira soothed, then started ushering them towards the building before Fiona could make another remark. 'Let's go get them anyway. The bags, then a drink.'

She'd been right to leave Tess at home, Amira thought as they pulled out of the airport. Even with the community's troop carrier it was a tight squeeze—tighter still tomorrow, once she'd done the shopping.

'I thought we'd spend the night in Broome,' she said. 'I've booked us rooms at one of the resorts. The Mangrove. It's right on Roebuck Bay. You'll like it.'

Caro was fiddling with the air-conditioning vent, trying to direct the cold air onto her face. 'Fine. How come?' she asked without looking up.

'I need to go to Coles and get some groceries,' Amira said. 'There's a tiny supermarket at One Arm Point, fifteen minutes from where we live, but everything's much cheaper down here. As soon as people find out you're going to town they all want to give you a list.' She turned onto the main road, waving at a dark-skinned man raking seedpods in the courthouse gardens. Ned. He'd moved from Kalangalla a month or so ago now. It was good to see him in work. 'By the time I finish that it'll be getting a bit late to leave. I thought it would be better to stay here and hit the road first thing in the morning.'

'How long's the trip?' asked Morag from the middle seat.

'About three hours. We could do it, just, if we left now, but no one takes that road around dusk. It gets too dangerous.'

'No streetlights?'

Amira laughed. 'Well, yeah, but actually it's the animals. Roos, donkeys—they wander out, and you don't see them until the last minute. One of the older men almost hit a camel last week.'

'So you're just going to leave Tess up there with the savages, then?' said Fiona.

'Fiona!' Caro exclaimed.

'What?' said Fiona, feigning innocence. 'The savage camels, I meant. They could do some damage. All those humps.'

'Tess will be fine,' said Amira calmly, swinging the troop carrier through another roundabout—Broome was full of them, but not yet, thank God, any traffic lights. 'She's having a sleepover at a friend's, but I'd also have been happy to leave her at our place. It's safer there than Melbourne.'

They came over a slight rise in the road, and Roebuck Bay appeared before them, its turquoise water fringed with green mangroves. Without thinking, she slowed, feasting her eyes. She could never grow tired of that view.

'Oh, stop, stop!' said Caro. 'It's incredible. I want to get a photo.'

'We're almost there,' said Amira. 'You'll see it from the hotel. From your room, if you're lucky, but definitely the bar.'

A small silver dinghy chugged out across the bay, its lone occupant sitting back in the boat, one hand on the motor. Probably going fishing, Amira thought. Lucky sod. Solitude actually meant something up here, she had found; it was deeper, richer, more textured. The silence opened up and let you in in a way that never happened in the city. She pulled up outside The Mangrove as Janey shrieked from the back seat that her reception had dropped out.

An hour later, Amira was seated at a table on the lawn over-looking the water, waiting for the others to shower and then join her. Check-in had been a trial. The stay was her treat, she'd told them—the owner of the resort had once worked at Kalangalla and always gave them reduced rates—but Caro had insisted they'd all pay for themselves. Then Fiona had got annoyed and asked why should they if Amira was happy to foot the bill, while Morag stood between them, looking from one to the other, conspicuously quiet. Somehow they'd ended up with Fiona, Caro and the two girls sharing a family suite, while she and Morag had a twin room. Amira was grateful for that, at least. Fiona snored, but she wouldn't want to be the one to tell her.

Predictably, Morag was the first to arrive, her hair still wet and scraped into a ponytail.

'That feels better,' she said. 'I was dying in those tracksuit pants. Do you even wear them up here?'

Amira laughed. 'Not so far. The locals pull out jumpers and act all affronted if it gets below twenty-two degrees . . . Tess and I just shake our heads. I guess it's all relative. Wine?' She lifted the bottle, dripping, from its ice bucket.

Morag shook her head.

'Not yet. Just some water to start. I'm a bit light-headed.'

'Too long on the plane with Fiona?'

Morag smiled. 'No, it's the heat, and the light. It's incredible, isn't it? It's clearer, somehow . . . sharper.' She began to rummage through her bag on the table in front of her. 'Before I forget, I've got something for Tess. I'll give it to you and you can pass it on. It's a letter. From Callum.'

'Callum?' Amira asked, raising her eyebrows. 'For Tess? I didn't think they'd spoken since primary school. Were they even in any classes together last year?'

'Who knows?' said Morag. 'I was surprised too. French, maybe—if Tess even did French?'

'Amira had to think. 'Yes, she did, though I don't think she got past *croissant* and *merde*, and she hasn't opened her textbook since we've been here.'

Morag passed across a long yellow envelope. 'How's that going? She's doing School of the Air, isn't she? Does she like it?'

'Yeah, she does. Where I teach only goes to year seven, so it was that or nothing. And it's "school of the net" these days—it all comes by email. She's at work on it every morning when I leave, but she always seems to be finished and off at the beach by the time I get back.' Amira shrugged. 'I'm not sure if the material's too easy or if she's just much quicker because she's not being distracted by classmates.' She held up the envelope. 'Or boys.'

'Shit, I'm ready for a drink.' Fiona slid into the seat next to Morag. Amira quickly tucked the letter into her backpack.

'Caro, you too?' she asked, picking up the bottle.

'Thanks,' said Caro, sitting down and holding out her glass. 'The girls have gone for a swim. I said I'd come and grab them before dinner.'

Amira poured the wine. 'I booked early—six o'clock. I thought I'd better, seeing as your stomachs are still three hours ahead. We're just going to a local place, the Aarli Bar. It's down the hill, in town.'

'So we can walk?' Fiona asked. 'You don't have to drive?'

Amira nodded.

'Excellent.' Fiona pulled Amira's glass to her and sloshed in more wine, draining the bottle. 'Drink up, then. We've got ten months of Friday nights to catch up on. Cheers!'

'Cheers,' said Caro, lifting her glass high. 'To the week ahead. To friendship. To us.'

'To us,' echoed Morag and Amira. Fiona was already taking her first long swallow.

'You're so sentimental,' she said to Caro as she put down the half-empty glass. 'To wine,' she toasted instead, then burped loudly, neglecting to cover her mouth.

'Oh, Fiona,' Caro complained.

'I'll really enjoy having a drink tonight, actually,' Amira said. 'Kalangalla's dry—you know that, don't you?'

'You're kidding,' said Fiona, pausing with her glass halfway to her mouth. 'We're on holiday, without our husbands, and it's fucking dry?'

'I'm positive I told you. I assumed you'd realise, anyway. Most communities are, at least those like Kalangalla.'

'The boring ones, you mean?' said Fiona.

'The ones where everyone's trying to make a go of it. No grog, no domestic violence, no sniffing . . .' Amira took a deep breath and made a conscious effort to relax her tone. 'Look, you can have a drink, but you'll have to buy it and bring it up yourself, then keep it in your room. No sem sauv on the beach. Some of the people there are recovering alcoholics. They don't need the temptation.'

'Faaaark,' exhaled Fiona. 'What about smoking? I may have to take it up again if I can't drink.'

'Plenty of smokers,' said Amira. 'You'll fit in well.'

'Do you miss it?' Caro asked. 'Drinking, that is.'

'Oh, I still have one occasionally, with dinner. Some days I need it after work. As I said, it's fine if it's not a public thing.' Amira toyed with the stem of her glass. 'What I do miss—at least, I used to—is my mobile phone. There's hardly any coverage on the Dampier Peninsula. That's why I've been emailing you all so much, and I let Tess go on Facebook. We needed to stay in touch somehow.'

Fiona rose from her seat, clutching her purse. 'I think I better buy another bottle, pronto. No booze, no mobiles—and I'm guessing there won't be a Krispy Kreme either?' Amira laughed and shook her head. Fiona let out a low whistle. 'I'd better come back with a bloody good tan, then.'

When dusk fell they hauled Janey and Bronte out of the pool and set off for the restaurant. Amira pulled two frangipanis from a tree at the side of the road and tucked one behind her ear, handing the other to Janey.

The girl buried her nose in it and inhaled deeply.

'Thanks. I was wondering what that scent was.'

'It's always stronger at night,' Amira said. 'Lovely, isn't it? I put them on my pillow sometimes.'

The afternoon had been a lot of fun. It was great to see her friends again, to fall back so easily into their teasing banter. Amira and Tess had both settled into Kalangalla quite quickly, but it felt different to be with people who really knew you, she thought, people who'd minded your kids, slept at your house; people from whom there were no secrets. The night air was warm, and she was looking forward to eating out—there were no restaurants in the community. She'd order two threadfin salmon, maybe three, and they could pull off the flesh with their fingers . . .

'Ya fuckin' moll! Ya cunt!'

An Aboriginal man was standing, swaying, in the road just ten metres in front of them, barefoot, his blue singlet torn and damp. Before Amira could react he reached out and hit a woman cowering next to him, the blow spinning her around and sending her sprawling to the bitumen. There was a dull crack as her head hit the road. A third Aborigine emerged out of the darkness, bent down and prised the bottle she'd been holding from her fingers, then disappeared back into the sandy scrub between the town and the bay.

Caro clutched Janey to her, rooted to the spot. Behind them, Fiona, Bronte and Morag looked on in horror. The first man nudged the woman with his toe, then ambled off after his friend. 'Fuckin' moll,' he repeated as he left.

———

It had all been . . . exciting, Janey thought as she sat in the Aarli Bar reliving the scene. She knew that wasn't how she was supposed to feel—she was meant to be scared, horrified, preferably both, but there you had it. She just felt thrilled. She'd never seen someone knocked out before. On the TV, sure, all the time, but it was different in real life; it was in your face. A small jolt of adrenalin buzzed through her as she recalled it again: the smell of the man—beer, urine, BO; the crunching sound his fist had made as it connected with the woman's jaw; the way her knees had folded together, like a deckchair, as she sank to the ground. Janey's mum had grabbed her after that, buried Janey's face in her chest—something she hadn't done for a good ten years, thank you very much—but it was too late. Janey had seen what had happened, and part of her had enjoyed it.

Sadly, though, that was where it had ended. Almost as soon as the woman had hit the road, the air rushing out of her with a grunt, Fiona had seized Bronte's wrist and hauled her to the restaurant, its burgundy sign glowing up ahead. Her own mother had followed suit, of course, continuing to shield Janey's eyes as if she was five. Caro only let go when she had Janey seated and was pushing a barley sugar from her bag into Janey's hand, no doubt in case she was suffering shock. Morag and Amira were nowhere to be seen.

'How was the arm on that guy?' Fiona asked, her voice slightly too loud. She caught the eye of a waiter, who picked up some menus and came towards them. 'Bloody Mike Tyson. Or Lionel Rose, really. *He* was a boong too.'

Her mum didn't even try to shush Fiona this time, Janey noticed, just ducked her head and fiddled with her cutlery.

'A bottle of red, please,' Fiona said to the waiter. He went to open the wine list and she shooed him away. 'Just red. I don't care what sort. Whichever one you can get here quickest.' Bronte blushed.

'Someone's going to have a sore head tomorrow,' Fiona went on. 'God. Welcome to Broome. Beware of the locals.'

'Do you think she took his grog?' Janey asked.

Her mother looked up.

'Janey!' she warned.

'It's a fair question,' said Fiona. 'They're always fighting over something—booze, women, land.'

'I don't know how Amira stands it.' Caro sighed. 'Imagine living with that all the time.'

Bronte cleared her throat, a puny sound, like a kitten sneezing. 'She said her community was dry, remember? That's probably what they're trying to prevent. I'm sure it's different there.'

'Yeah, well, it would be better if they just learned to hold their drink, like the rest of us,' said Fiona, 'or got a job, so they didn't just sit around, pissing on. That's our taxes, you know. We're paying for their dole and their beer.'

The waiter returned with the wine. Fiona held out her glass insistently, then moved it away before the waiter had finished pouring, ruby liquid spilling onto the table. Though it had been her fault, he apologised and pulled out a cloth.

'Can I have one too, Mum?' Janey asked.

'Don't be ridiculous,' said Caro. 'Of course not.'

'I do at home. Dad always lets me. You know that.'

'We're not at home now, and you're in training. Two mineral waters please,' her mother instructed the waiter without consulting either Bronte or Janey.

'Diet Coke,' Janey called after him, but she was too late. She sank back in her chair. They were supposed to be on holiday, weren't they? Couldn't her mum cut her some slack for one night?

Amira and Morag arrived, looking flustered.

'I'm starving. Have you ordered?' Amira asked, squeezing herself into the seat next to Janey. She could use some Diet Coke too, Janey thought.

'Not yet,' replied Caro. 'We wanted to wait until we knew that everything was OK. You were alright, I mean. What happened?'

'I didn't want to just leave the woman lying in the street,' Amira said. 'I stayed with her while Morag ran down to the police station. It's not far. Everything's close in this town.'

'Weren't you scared?' asked Janey.

'Not really. I didn't think the men would come back. They had what they wanted. I was more afraid the woman would stop breathing.'

'Well, *I* was scared,' said Morag from the other end of the table. 'I didn't want to be there in the dark, near all those bushes. I kept thinking about snakes.'

Amira laughed. 'Not at night. Not the legless variety, anyway.' She turned to address the others. 'She did a great job though—had the cops back there in less than ten minutes, and by the time they arrived the woman was starting to come round.'

'I should have stayed,' Janey's mother said to no one in particular. 'I didn't realise she was unconscious. I was just worried, you know? I wanted to get Janey out of there.'

'What did the police do?' asked Bronte. 'Did they find the man who hit her?'

Amira shrugged. 'They didn't really look. They were more concerned with getting the woman to hospital. She'll know who it is—she can tell them later. They probably know too.'

'So you went back to the station and made a statement?' Fiona was leaning forward, wine in hand.

'No,' said Amira. 'I told the sergeant I was working up at Kalangalla, in case he needed to get in touch, but it won't go to court. It never does. They couldn't get through all the cases.'

Fiona drained her glass and put it down. 'Well, well, well,' she said slowly. 'I thought you would have been prosecuting it yourself. That's why you came here, isn't it, to save the darkie? Are you giving up that easily, or have you gone off them now you actually have to live with them?'

Amira picked up a menu and opened it, speaking without looking at Fiona. 'It's far more complicated than you could ever imagine. I've learned to pick my battles. Let's eat.'

Later, when they'd finished their dinner and were heading back to The Mangrove, they passed the spot on the road where the man had punched the woman. Janey examined it as carefully as she could in the dim light, looking for blood, a clump of hair or maybe even a tooth, but there was nothing, no evidence of what had transpired.

'Does that sort of thing happen a lot?' she asked Amira.

It had been a few hours, but Amira knew immediately what she was referring to. She sighed.

'A bit. I wish you hadn't had to see it.' She turned and smiled at Bronte. 'Your mum is going to be dining out on it all week.'

Bronte just stared at her feet. 'Hopefully she'll get so pissed tonight she forgets all about it.'

Amira laughed. 'There's a fair chance of that, I'd say.'

After they'd finished eating, Fiona had pushed back her chair and insisted that the adults kick on.

'Cocktails, dancing . . . Is there a nightclub here, Amira?'

Amira had nodded. 'The Bungalow, on Dampier Terrace. It's a bit dodgy, though.'

Morag wasn't keen, Janey noticed, but Fiona was adamant. 'It's the first night of our holiday! And,' she added, sneaking a sly glance at Amira, 'our last in civilisation. Don't be pathetic.'

'What about the girls?' Janey's mother had asked, but Fiona had an answer to that too.

'Amira can walk them back while we have another drink. They'll be fine, as long as they keep the door locked and stay away from the porn channel. It'll come up on the bill, you know,' she said, wagging a finger at Bronte, who had flushed to the roots of her hair.

'There you go,' said Amira now, pushing open the door to the room Janey and Bronte were sharing. She handed the key to Bronte. 'You heard your mother. Keep it locked.' She stepped back to let them go in, impulsively touching Janey on the arm as she passed. 'It's lovely to see you again. Tess has been so looking forward to this week.'

'Me too,' mumbled Janey, because she knew it was expected of her, and ducked inside before Amira could get any ideas about kissing her goodnight.

'You'll be fine then?' Amira asked, turning to go. 'You've got our mobile numbers. We won't be late. I hope. Sleep well.' She disappeared back into the night, her footsteps fading after her.

Bronte carefully turned the key in the lock, then drew the chain across for good measure.

'You scared?' asked Janey.

'A little,' admitted Bronte. 'Mum was saying that a girl got raped up here a month or so ago. A tourist, like us.'

'Tourists get raped in Melbourne, too,' Janey said. 'Lots of people do.'

Bronte grabbed some stuff from her bag and went into the bathroom without replying. When she came out again she was wearing a t-shirt and pyjama pants with a motif of two pink teddy bears tucked up in bed, a line of Zs above their heads.

Janey smirked.

'Nice,' she said. 'Did your mum pick those out for you?'

'My grandmother,' Bronte muttered, reaching for her hairbrush. 'I like them. They're comfortable.'

'They're too hot for up here,' Janey said, pulling off her own clothes and kicking them under the bed. 'I'm going to sleep nude.' She moved so she could see herself in the mirror attached to the wardrobe door. Bronte went red and turned away, furiously dragging the bristles through her long dark hair. Janey smiled to herself. Little prude.

She looked into the mirror, admiring her reflection. She liked her body. Long blonde hair, flat stomach, tight arse. She ticked off her attributes one by one. Good legs, firm and shapely from all those laps in the pool. They weren't as long as Bronte's, sure, but Bronte was a mutant. Great tits. That's what Darren in year ten had called out anyway, when he passed her in the corridor before school broke up. Janey's hands reached to cup them. They *were* nice. Round and high, the nipples a dusky pink, not brown and used-looking like her mother's. Her mum had caught her peeking at them once as they got changed for the beach, and pulled a face. 'Children,' she'd said. 'That's what you get from pregnancy and breastfeeding.' If that was the case, Janey was going to adopt.

The light snapped out.

'Hey!' Janey said.

'I want to go to sleep. It's after midnight in Melbourne.' Bronte's voice was muffled. She probably had the covers pulled up to her nose, hiding from all the rapists. 'Go into the bathroom if you want to stare at yourself.'

She was just jealous, Janey thought, but slid into the second bed anyway.

An hour later she was still awake. It was too hot. The air pressed against her face like a warm wet sponge, congealed beneath her knees and in her armpits. She sat up and turned on the bedside lamp, then went over to switch on the air-conditioner, but it shook itself to life with such a combination of clanking and wheezing that Bronte woke up and complained. Fine, Janey decided, shutting everything off and grabbing her bikini from where she'd left it in a damp heap on a chair. If she couldn't sleep she'd go for a swim. Fiona had only told them to keep the door locked, after all. She hadn't said anything about actually staying in the room.

A small green frog hopped away from her feet as she followed the pathway outside her door. The sky was a deep navy blue dusted with stars; the pool when she came to it was still and serene. Janey dived in and swam underwater, revelling in the luxury of not counting her strokes or rushing to the surface as she usually did, mind fixed on the session or the race ahead of her. Guided by a blue underwater beacon, she made it to the far end, turned and got halfway back before coming up for air. She rolled onto her back and floated, catching her breath. A bat wheeled past overhead, lit briefly by the light reflected from the water.

'Are you part mermaid?' someone called, and Janey stood up, looking around.

'Over here,' came the voice again, and then Janey saw him, sitting on the edge of the pool, half hidden in the shadows, his feet dangling in the water. 'I was lying on the banana lounge when you dived in. Sorry to scare you.'

'You didn't,' Janey said. She lay back in the water again, annoyed at being disturbed.

'My mates are all in the bar,' the man continued. 'I was sick of the smoke; came out here for a breather and a bit of a lie-down. Didn't know I was going to get woken by a mermaid. Show us your tail.' He grinned, white teeth and gleaming eyes all she could see in the darkness. Seventeen, Janey thought, judging by his voice. Maybe eighteen. It was hard to tell, but she liked his smile.

'No way,' she said, holding her legs tightly together and splashing water towards him. 'You'll sell me to a museum.'

'Do mermaids fetch a good price?' he asked. 'I've been hunting for a bunyip, but maybe I should change my tack.'

'Heaps,' Janey said. 'Even more if you can catch one alive.'

'OK, then,' he replied, then stood up and dived into the water, still clothed, before she could blink. Janey struck out for the shallow end but he was onto her in a moment, reaching for her feet. She shrieked and giggled, kicking spray into his face and wriggling away.

'Powerful, too,' he said, wiping his eyes. 'You'll make me a fortune!' He took a deep breath and dived under again. Janey felt his hands on her ankles, on her calves, sliding up towards her thighs . . . and then heard a new voice, a loud and very angry one.

'Janey!' her mother bellowed from the paved area at the far end of the pool. Fiona, Morag and Amira stood beside her, Fiona swaying slightly. 'Janey, *what* are you doing? You're meant to be in bed!'

Janey's companion surfaced beside her, took in the situation and slowly breaststroked away.

'See you, mermaid,' he whispered.

'Janey, come here right now,' said Caro. 'I'm very disappointed in you. This trip was meant to be a treat, but you've already let me down.'

Janey sighed and pushed her hands through her hair, squeezing out the moisture. Silver drops ran glistening down her fingers and back into the water. She trudged towards the steps, wishing she could join them.

'You could have hit your head,' her mother was saying. 'You could have drowned! Where's Bronte? And who was that boy? Do you even know his name?'

She was only getting started, but thankfully Janey was spared the full tirade; at that moment Fiona groaned, bent over, and vomited all her cocktails into the pool.

Monday

Fiona pressed her head against the glass of the troop-carrier window and wished everybody would just shut up. Amira had gone all tour guide on them and was pointing out the paltry sights of Broome, Bronte was dutifully nodding and asking questions, and Caro was still exclaiming—when she could get a word in—over the fucking mango she'd had for breakfast. Fiona stifled a groan. The memory of watching Caro shovelling it into her mouth, juices dripping onto the table, fingers sticky and gleaming, made her stomach contract. All Fiona had been able to force down was a lukewarm coffee, and at every bump in the road she feared that she would soon be seeing it once more.

She belched cautiously. It had been good of Amira to make sure she had the front seat, though with the fumes coming off her the others would probably have offered it quick smart anyway. Amira had also got her into the shower last night after she'd thrown up by the pool; had hunted around for a skimmer and removed the worst of the floating vomit. Fiona closed her eyes. Sadly, that wasn't even her most humiliating memory of the evening. That honour belonged to the moment after her third cocktail when it had seemed a good idea to invite one of the locals propping up the bar to dance with her. He must have been about twenty-three, with shoulders as broad as his accent, and he'd certainly been friendly enough when she'd sidled up beside him and ordered a Sex on the Beach.

'Pretty exotic, eh,' he'd grunted when the bartender had no idea what she was talking about. She'd pouted and cooed that she was on holiday, and there was a beach here, wasn't there, so with any luck she'd get it anyway. He'd laughed at that, but later, when a Michael Jackson song came on and she approached him again he turned her down flat.

'I'm too bloody young for that shit,' he'd said, cocking his sun-bleached head at 'Blame It on the Boogie'. Then, giving her a once-over, he added, 'And you.'

Fiona had felt heat and rage rise inside her. How *dare* he?

'Your loss,' she'd slurred, yanking down her strappy singlet top to give him a quick flash of her tits, which were still in pretty good shape. Then she'd stormed back to their table and got riotously, recklessly drunk.

It hadn't taken long. She'd barely eaten all day, and it was so hot in The Bungalow—the lack of air-conditioning no doubt a ploy to encourage the patrons to spend more on drinks. Fiona didn't remember much after that, just Amira and Morag trying to keep her upright as she stumbled back to The Mangrove, and the look on Janey's face when she'd almost chundered over her in the pool. It would have to be Princess Janey, wouldn't it? Always so perfect, the golden girl . . . not so perfect now though, she thought, smiling for the first time all morning. That look on Caro's face when she'd realised her precious daughter was breaking the rules—and with a boy, what's more. Welcome to the real world, Caroline. It sucks, doesn't it?

The troop carrier shuddered to a halt and Amira tapped her lightly on the shoulder.

'Are you awake? We're going into Coles. Do you want anything?'

Fiona shook her head. All she wanted was to be left alone, and a nice cool bed. Predictably, she'd hardly slept last night, resorting to a sleeping tablet around three am. Having to take it pissed her off—she was trying to cut down—but enduring the way she was feeling for another minute was a far worse option. Besides, she wouldn't need any at Kalangalla. There wasn't any chance of getting drunk there every night.

'Last Liquorland for a thousand kilometres,' Amira teased, as if reading her mind.

'Go away,' Fiona said, then, when Amira did, called after her, 'Coke. Get me some Coke and some chips—crinkle cut, plain. And Berocca,' she added, head falling back against the seat. She already had a tube of B vitamins in her case, but that was buried somewhere in the back of the vehicle, no doubt wedged between the spare tyre and Caro's fucking pillow. The thought of standing out in the heat in the middle of the supermarket car park, sorting through all their bags to get at it, made her want to heave all over again.

She must have nodded off, because the next thing she knew Amira was once more tugging on the handbrake before the carrier had completely stopped, jolting Fiona forward.

'All out!' Amira announced jauntily.

Fiona pushed her sunglasses back up her nose and resolutely turned her shoulder away, trying to tug her slumber back around her as if it was a blanket that had just slipped off.

'Come on, Fiona,' Amira said, shaking her. 'You've got to see Cable Beach. You'll feel better if you get out of the car, anyway.'

Fiona was inclined to disagree, but Bronte had come around to her door and was pulling it open, so she had no choice. Reluctantly she lowered herself from the car. They had driven right down onto the sand, which stretched golden and vast in both directions as far as she could see. Tiny crabs scurried away from her feet, their bodies translucent.

'It's beautiful,' said Morag. 'This is what we saw from the plane, isn't it? Do we have time for a swim?'

'Sure,' Amira said. 'The water's gorgeous at this time of year—twenty-seven, twenty-eight degrees or so. Tess and I saw two huge mantas just off shore when we were last here, in September.'

'Are they dangerous?' asked Bronte.

'Nah. They look like they should be, but they don't have a barb like stingrays do. They're gentle giants—stunning to watch. People pay to swim with them further down the coast, at Ningaloo.'

'I haven't got my bathers on,' complained Caro.

'So go naked,' suggested Amira, smiling. 'This part of the beach is for nudists, anyway.'

Fiona glanced around. There were only two other cars besides theirs, but sure enough the elderly couple sitting back in their deckchairs a hundred metres away didn't appear to have any clothes on. The woman's large breasts lolled almost to her lap, like deflated airbags. Fiona winced. Sunburnt nipples. Nice.

'It is lovely,' she conceded, 'but I've got to go to the loo. I'll meet you back at the car.'

She hurried away before they could protest. Yes, it was pretty, but her bladder was bursting and the glare was giving her a migraine. A small plane flew overhead, shattering the stillness. *Coast Watch*, Fiona read on the side of the plane, and thought of whales, then saw the smaller lettering on the tail: *Customs*. It was watching for people, not animals; refugees, illegal immigrants. *Keep up the good work*, she thought silently. Australia was already too crowded. Well, not here, maybe, but it was.

The public toilets were empty, save for a backpacker rinsing her plates directly under a sign that read, *Please do not wash dishes in the hand basin*. She smiled blithely when she saw Fiona and continued rinsing. Fiona went into a cubicle and pulled down her cargo pants, the phone in her back pocket falling to the floor. As she stooped for it, head pounding, it occurred to her that she should probably ring Todd. She hadn't called yesterday, and they were about to disappear up into the Dreamtime or something, where there was apparently no reception . . . Fiona sat down on the toilet, relaxed her bladder and punched in the numbers. Who cared if the backpacker heard her; she probably couldn't even speak English.

Todd sounded flustered when he answered. 'Hello?' he barked.

'Hey, it's me,' Fiona said, urine still flowing between her legs. God, it was a relief to let go.

'Oh, you've remembered us, have you?' he asked in that half-joking, half-sniping tone she knew so well.

'Of course,' she said. 'Sorry I didn't get a chance to call yesterday. The plane was delayed,' she lied, 'then I knew you were going to be out all afternoon. Did you have a good time?'

'Yeah, it was alright,' Todd said. 'Got a bit of a hangover now, but. Dom too.'

'I hope you didn't let him drive home.' The words were out before she could stop them.

'Jeez, you're unreal. You piss off on holiday, spending a fortune, then ring up to nag. Go back to your chardonnay, Fiona. We're doing just fine.'

Fiona took a deep breath. *Please dispose of sanitary items in the bin provided*, said a sign on the back of the door in front of her. The euphemism had always amused her. The items weren't that sanitary by the time you disposed of them.

'Sorry,' she said. 'I just worry about him after last time. And I miss you both. Caro's already driving me nuts.' She wasn't really, but she said it for Todd, who had never liked her friend.

'Well, it was your choice,' he replied, still miffed. 'I've gotta go. Some of us have to work. Have a good time.'

He hung up, and she sat there fuming. She hadn't had a chance to tell him about Kalangalla, that she wouldn't be able to call . . . he hadn't even asked her what she was doing, or if she was having fun. Arsehole. Fiona wiped herself, then stood up to flush, tempted to throw the damn phone down the toilet as well. When she went out to wash her hands the backpacker had gone, but the sink was full of gristle and soggy shreds of lettuce.

'Here we are,' said Amira as she spotted the sign for the turn-off to Kalangalla. 'Almost there.'

'Thank fucking Christ,' moaned Fiona, stirring herself from where she'd slumped back against the window the minute they'd left Cable Beach. She wouldn't be the only one who'd be glad to get out, Amira thought. The others had chattered and laughed as they'd headed along the bitumen road out of Broome, but had fallen silent as soon as they turned onto the red dirt of the Cape Leveque track and the corrugations began. It was too hard to talk when your teeth were jolting together and your head kept threatening to hit the roof of the car.

'That took *forever*,' Janey complained from the back seat. 'I wouldn't come here again unless I could fly.'

'Some people do fly in,' Amira said. In the rear-view mirror she could see Janey checking her reflection in a compact, lips pursed critically. Like mother, like daughter. 'There's an airstrip at the Wajarrgi resort, ten or so minutes away. Tourists sometimes fly up from Broome to spend the day there.'

Janey snapped the compact shut. 'That's how I'm getting back then.'

'Is it worth visiting the resort?' Morag asked.

'Definitely,' said Amira, slowing as she came through the gate into the community. 'I've already booked us in for lunch on Wednesday. The restaurant's fabulous, and there's some really lovely snorkelling areas. Mind you,' she added, bringing the troop-carrier to a halt beside the administration building, 'our own beach is none too shabby either. I'll take you down once you've unpacked and got settled.'

She looked out in pride and satisfaction at Kalangalla: green lawns, sprinklers, fences. True, the grass was dusty and tough underfoot—it had to be to survive in this climate—and the sprinkler water stained your clothes if you got too close, but no other community she had seen up here looked anything like this. Elsewhere, the fences were rusted and broken, the ground strewn with burnt-out cars and worm-ridden dogs; they didn't have schools or bakeries or medical centres. Kalangalla was an oasis, she thought, a model of the way things could be done—*should* be done.

'Wow,' said Caro, opening her door. 'It's pretty primitive, isn't it?'

Amira felt a flash of anger. She'd expected such a comment from Fiona, but Caro? She thought Caro had understood why she'd applied for the teacher exchange—because her life was too bland, too safe, too predictable; because she wanted to do something with her skills, make a difference somehow, and that wasn't going to happen in a place where there was a Starbucks on every corner or an Xbox in every home. 'It's not the Gold Coast, no,' she replied. 'Then again, I wouldn't want it to be.'

'Sorry,' said Caro, colouring. 'I didn't mean it like that. I just sort of had these visions of you living in a hut on the beach, with coconut trees and a hammock . . .' Her voice trailed off. 'That was pretty stupid, wasn't it?'

Amira had to laugh. 'Beach huts are overrated. No air-conditioning, and I couldn't watch *MasterChef*. It may not look like it but we're actually pretty up with it. We've got a shop and the clinic, plus there's internet access at the school and the office.'

'Positively cutting edge,' Fiona said, but smiled at her. She hauled herself out of the car, landing beside it in a fine spray of red dirt. 'Shit, it's hot.'

Amira looked again at the scene in front of her, suddenly seeing it through her friends' eyes. It was true, the community did look primitive. The squat fibro houses had peeling paint; the roads were dirt, not paved. Two children ran past barefoot and barely clothed. Everything sagged in the heat. Oddly though, it hadn't struck her that way when she first arrived. Instead, there had been this enormous sense of something new, something beginning . . . something real, somehow. For years—ever since Davis had walked out, and he'd left before Tess's first birthday—she had done what was expected of her. She had established a routine, she had found a part-time job, she had swallowed her pride and asked her parents for a loan so she could buy Davis out of his share of their flat. She had, in short, done everything in her power to provide Tess with stability: financial certainly but emotional too. There had been no passionate love affairs that might distract her from her daughter; and nothing had been decided—new carpet, a holiday—without considering, then, in later years, consulting, Tess. And it had worked, hadn't it? At fourteen Tess was a lovely girl, thoughtful and funny, smart and sensitive. When the flyer for the exchange had gone up on the noticeboard in the staffroom Amira had immediately felt drawn to it. *Tess is fine*, it seemed to whisper to her. *It's your turn now.*

'Mum, Mum!'

Amira turned to see her daughter racing towards her, brown legs flying. She loved that about Tess, loved that she still wore her heart on her sleeve, showed her enthusiasm; that puberty hadn't yet rendered her too cool or too jaded to get excited about things. And she was barefoot too, Amira noticed, at home in her skin and this place . . . She smiled. Tess was thriving. Tess would always thrive.

'Hello, angel girl,' she said, throwing her arms around her daughter and burying her face in Tess's hair. The thick dark strands tickled her nose. Tess complained about her unruly mane, about the knots and the weight of it, just as Amira had done when she was younger, but thank God she'd inherited it rather than Davis's thin hair, now receding. Anyone could tell at a glance that Tess was Amira's daughter. As a single parent, that mattered somehow. She squeezed her tightly. 'Did you enjoy yourself with Tia?'

'Yep,' said Tess. 'We went crabbing. I got three and we cooked them, but I kept one for you. Janey!' she exclaimed, spotting her friend. 'And Bronte! It's amazing to have you here. I can't wait to show you everything.' She pulled away from Amira and enfolded both the girls in a violent hug, at which Janey winced slightly. 'Come on,' Tess said, tugging Janey by the hand. 'I want to show you my room, and the beach, and the church.'

'The church?' said Janey dubiously.

'It's all lined with pearl shell. The missionaries who first came here just picked it up off the beach. Everything glows . . . it's like being under the sea, or inside an oyster.'

'Great,' said Janey. 'Just what I've always dreamed of.'

'I think it sounds beautiful,' said Bronte, taking Tess's other hand. 'And I want to see your house too. Let's go.'

'Take your hats,' called Caro, reaching into the car for them. 'You'll need to watch your skin this week—especially you, Bronte.'

Janey held out her hand for the cap, then thrust it into a back pocket. 'We'll be inside in a moment,' she said, turning away. Bronte hesitated, pulled hers on and ran after the other two.

The four women watched them go.

'It's nice to see them together again,' said Amira. 'Tess has been so excited.'

'I can tell!' laughed Caro. 'She's looking great—so fit and healthy.'

Morag gazed around. 'It's so quiet here. Where is everybody?'

'At work,' Amira replied. 'There's no unemployment—everyone has jobs with the garage or in maintenance, or the shop or in tourism. It's so different to Broome and the Kimberley, where at least half of the Indigenous population is on benefits.'

'Why?' asked Morag simply.

Amira shrugged. 'Lots of things. Being dry helps, but it's more than that. I think it's simply that there *is* work here, and work that feels like it matters—keeping the place running, showing visitors some of the old crafts and traditions, taking care of the children. The people here still have a connection to the land, a sense of history.' She corrected herself. 'Not history. Continuity. Life going on. It's important to them. There are songlines here that are thousands of years old.'

That's enough, she thought, noticing Fiona stifling a yawn. Amira felt strongly about the way the community worked, protective and impassioned, but there was no point lecturing. People either got it or they didn't—anyway, her friends had only just arrived. She smiled at them. 'Let me show you where you're sleeping, and then we'll hit the beach.'

It wasn't the Gold Coast, Amira was right about that. It wasn't even The Mangrove, and that had hardly been the last word in luxury. Caro looked around the room that she and Janey had been assigned, one of four side by side in a drab concrete block marked *Visitors*. Threadbare curtains, worn carpet, an ancient ceiling fan slowly rotating overhead, as if unable to work up any more effort. Everything was scrupulously clean, thank God, but it was so small. She'd stayed in youth hostels with more space than this. Where the hell was she going to put all her stuff? Caro sank down on the bed to take stock. The springs squeaked, so she got up and tested the other one, which was against the opposite wall. May as well have her choice before Janey arrived from wherever she was, though neither appealed. Single beds! She hated single beds. One of the benefits to Caro of Alex's never-ending travel—and heaven knows there weren't many—was spreading out across their king-size mattress, making herself as comfortable as she could, compromising for no one. She hadn't slept in a single bed since the youth hostels, well before they met. She'd thought those days were behind her.

Caro sighed and opened the first of her bags. She needed to hang up her clothes before they got any more creased. There didn't seem much chance of finding an iron here. The bedroom situation could have been worse, she told herself. At least she didn't have to share with Fiona again, who'd snored and moaned throughout the previous night, and it would be nice for her and Janey to be roommates. She needed to make more of an effort with Janey, Caro thought, maybe actually stay at training and watch her swim, so they had something to talk about in the car on the way home afterwards, instead of Janey jamming in her earbuds and Caro returning the calls she hadn't got to during the day. The trouble was that there was never any time, with the business to run and the house to look after, April always needing help with her homework . . .

She shook out a pair of capri pants. In her walk-in robe at home they'd seemed perfect, just the sort of thing for afternoon drinks and evenings out, but now she threw them back in her case. She'd had her evening out. There weren't going to be any more, and everything she'd packed was far too dressy for Kalangalla. It was all wrong, all of it, the structured sundresses and the white linen shirts, the wedges and the silk wrap. She'd look like an idiot parading around in that stuff. Caro felt a tightness across her chest. What she needed were plain shorts and singlets like Amira was wearing. She'd brought some, hadn't she? She was sure she had, positive . . . She tipped the bag upside down on the bed, ferreting through its contents, then did the same with the next. Her breath came in gasps as she searched. Just two casual t-shirts, a singlet and three pairs of shorts. That wasn't enough. Were there washing facilities here? Could she buy powder? Maybe she could get Amira to take her back into Broome so she could go to the shops there and buy the right sort of clothes.

Caro forced herself to leave the mess on the bed and walk over to the small handbasin in the corner of the room. She splashed her face with water and stood there, dripping, holding tightly to the sink and taking deep breaths until she could face her reflection in the mirror that hung above it. *You're OK*, she told herself. *Everything's OK. It'll be fine.* There was a faded blue hand towel hanging next to the basin and she patted her face dry with it, then brushed her hair and reapplied her lipstick.

Caro believed in surfaces. Feeling in control began with looking in control. It was why she did what she did, why her interior design business was so successful; not just because she made things look nice, but because she understood that imposing order—a colour scheme, a design—relaxed the eye, and from there the heart. She had no idea how Alex managed to work at his desk in their study, obscured as it was by a litter of papers and catalogues, drawers half open and spilling their contents onto the floor. She couldn't walk into a room without wanting to line up the cushions on the couch or straighten the curtains. It wasn't neurotic, no matter what Fiona said; it was practical. Chaos screamed. Order soothed, and it was much easier to get things done when you were calm.

She turned back to the clothes on the bed and began to go through them methodically, folding the garments she didn't intend to wear and placing them back in her bag; hanging those she did. She would take these into the bathroom later when she had a shower, and the hot steam would remove the wrinkles. She wouldn't need an iron. Her mother used to do the same thing. Caro's hands fell to her sides, momentarily stilled. Her mother. How stupid that she could remember that—her mother carrying a white dress patterned with tiny blue flowers into her ensuite, hanging it on the shower rail, then turning on the hot tap—but she couldn't remember her mother's face. Not stupid: awful. If she closed her eyes and tried to remember, all she saw was a rictus grin, her mother's mouth hanging open as if in surprise, cheek flattened against the kitchen lino, the back of her head bloody from where she'd hit the corner of the oven as she fell. Yet she couldn't recall her mother's smile, or her eyes as she leaned in to kiss her goodnight every evening. Caro clenched her fists, swallowed the pain, made herself return to unpacking. She'd only been eight when her mother had the aneurysm. No wonder she didn't remember. April was nine and she still forgot her lunchbox most days. It made Caro wonder though . . . would she have been the same sort of person if her mother had lived? If she'd been there to talk to as Caro grew up, to argue with, to push against? Not that Caro had turned out so terribly. She had her anxious moments, sure, but she also had a successful business, a loving husband, two beautiful daughters . . .

Janey banged through the door.

'Shit, this is tiny,' she said, looking around. 'Have you got my bag? I need my bikini. Tess said to get ready for the beach.'

'Janey, don't swear,' Caro said automatically, then noticed that her daughter was holding a packet of chips. 'And don't eat that rubbish! Come on, Janey, you've got the state meet in two months. I know we're not at home, but officially you're still in training.'

Janey dipped her fingers into the bag, licked them, then screwed it up. 'I've finished anyway. And I kept them from lunch at Cable Beach, so you don't have to fret. It's all part of my recommended daily allowance.' She tossed the empty packet at a wastepaper basket under the handbasin. It hit the edge and bounced off onto the floor.

'Chips still aren't a great idea,' Caro persisted. 'If you're hungry I'll find you some fruit.' That meet was important, she wanted to add. Secretly she was hoping that good results would win Janey a sports scholarship to the private school that Bronte attended. They offered them at year nine; she'd checked the website and then rung the bursar, just to be sure. Not that she'd mentioned that to Janey or, indeed, Alex. Janey was happy where she was, he would say to Caro, so why move her? And that was all very well, but Caro was sure that Janey could be happy at St Anne's too, and benefit from everything it offered. Caro had wanted her to go there from the start, after primary school. They could certainly afford it, but Alex had overruled her. 'Janey chooses,' he'd said. 'If she works hard and keeps her marks up she can stay. If she mucks around we move her. Deal?'

'Deal!' Janey had agreed delightedly, but Caro had been less than ecstatic. Where was her say in this? She'd always dreamed of seeing Janey in that navy-blue blazer with the white edging and the embroidered crest, not the hideous striped rugby jumper of the local high school. And her school didn't even have a swim team! It was crazy. At St Anne's she could be training at lunchtime.

'Chill out, Mum,' said Janey. 'It's not the Olympics, though you've probably got a plan for those too.' She spied her pack lying on the bed and tugged at the zip. 'Oh, and Tess wants me to sleep there tonight, at her place. I said it would be OK.'

'Do you have to?' asked Caro. 'I thought we could be together. It's our first day here. Maybe tomorrow.'

'Mum! I haven't seen her in ages. You're the one always going on about how lovely it would be for us to'—Janey turned and drew quotation marks in the air—'"reconnect". So I wanna reconnect, OK?'

Caro gave in. 'Oh, I suppose so. Is Bronte going too?'

'Yes. Unfortunately. She's sooooo boring. She's brought her homework with her! What a dork.' Janey yanked her t-shirt over her head and undid her bra, which was pink with small cherries on the cups. She shrugged it off and reached for her bikini top, lifting her hair away from her neck and presenting her bare back to Caro so she could tie the strings. God, she was lovely, Caro thought. Her hair like a sheaf of wheat, her skin silky and olive, inherited from her Mediterranean-born father, her strong, supple shoulders . . . hideous, Janey had said when she gave up butterfly, fearing they were becoming too broad.

Impulsively, Caro dropped her lips onto the girl's right shoulder blade, kissed her, then drew back.

'You look fabulous, Janey. Enjoy it while you can.'

'Thanks,' Janey muttered, grabbed her towel and banged back out the door. Caro bent and retrieved the chip packet.

Fifteen minutes later, when she'd unpacked Janey's things and changed into her own bathers, Caro ventured outside. Now to the beach—but where was it? All she could see were some grey-green trees, a yellow sheet flapping on a clothesline, ochre tracks meandering off into the scrub. She began to follow one, moving in the opposite direction from the way they'd come in. It couldn't be too far, surely. She hoped not. The sun was already beating through her hat, prising sweat from her brow.

'You right? Are you lookin' for something?'

Caro jumped. She hadn't noticed the man standing in the shade of the boab tree next to the path. He was clad only in shorts, a bandana tied around his neck, the red fabric standing out against his dark skin.

'The beach,' she said, breathing quickly. 'Sorry, you startled me. I'm here with Amira. She's a teacher at the school.'

The man smiled, revealing the pink flesh of his lips. 'I know who Amira is. We all do, and we knew she had friends coming. Nothin' much that's a secret around here.' He pointed back over his shoulder. 'You're goin' the right way. The beach is down there, about five minutes.'

Caro watched his chest rise and fall, a lone drop of sweat or seawater snaking down his stomach.

'Do you want to come too?' she asked, then coloured. What a stupid thing to say.

The man just smiled again.

'Already been.' He gestured to a bucket containing some silver fish, one still twitching and opening its mouth. 'Promised the missus I'd get her some boab nuts on the way back. She carves them. They're in the gallery.'

'Oh. I'll have to go see them then,' Caro said, shifting her straw bag from one shoulder to the other.

'Enjoy the beach.' The man turned back to the tree and crouched down, foraging at its base. Caro stood there for a second, watching the play of shadows on the muscles of his back, then continued down the track. She felt quite light-headed.

———

Dear Tess,

Thanks for your postcard. I put it on the shelf next to my bed, but Finn teased me so much that I took it down and put it in my homework diary instead. The only time I ever look in there is to read it again. I think Finn's jealous. Maybe you better send him one too!

I didn't know your address, so I had to send this with my mum, but she's pretty cool. I don't think she'll open it, and if she does SHAME ON YOU MUM! I put masking tape on the envelope as a test. If it's gone, she's read it and you should make sure you put a spider in her bed, or hide her running shoes. That will kill her.

How are you enjoying it up there? It must be so different to Melbourne. Do you go to the beach all the time? Is there any surf? And what about the food? I bet you miss Subway.

I remember how you always went there on a Friday after school with Janey and the rest of your gang. Stevie and Finn and I always acted like we bumped into you by accident, but we actually went there just to see you all. You probably worked that out. It was fun though.

School is OK. There's more homework than last year, and my form teacher isn't as nice. I got a detention at the start of the term because I did a book report on Kelly Slater's autobiography. I thought that was a bit rough. They said we could pick any book! Mr Birmingham said it should have been a novel, or at least something with a few less pictures, but I reckon he's just jealous because he doesn't look like Kelly. I mean, they're both bald, but that's about it.

That's pretty much all the news. Nothing has really changed here, I just wanted to check how you are and to say that I still think about the year seven disco and that you're pretty cool. I won't say anymore in case Mum is reading this (STOP IT MUM!). I hope you can write back sometime, but put it in an envelope because Finn's a snoop, and he tells Torran everything.

Have fun,

Callum

Tess folded up the letter, heart racing, and shoved it back in its envelope. She pulled her legs up to her chest and hugged herself, at the same time pushing back against the door. Her mum was getting into her bathers, and she'd never barge in on her without knocking anyway, but somehow it had felt important not just to shut the door while she read the letter, but to sit against it too.

She went to stand up, then changed her mind and pulled out the single sheet of paper again, unable to resist reading it once more. It looked as if it had been torn from an exercise book, the foolscap sort they'd started using once they'd moved to high school. Had Callum written it in class? She could picture him hunched over one of the old wooden benches in the science lab, arm curled protectively around the page while Stevie farted or did something dangerous with a Bunsen burner nearby . . . He wouldn't have written it at home, she was sure of that. Not in the bedroom he had to share with Finn.

Tess smoothed out the blue-lined paper, noticing that her hands were damp. *I put it on the shelf next to my bed*. So he'd kept her postcard, valued it, even . . . *The only time I ever look in there is to read it again*.

It had felt so daring sending it to him. She'd wanted to write to him almost since the first day she and her mother had arrived in Kalangalla, but she'd waited two months to carry it out. It wasn't good to look too eager. She'd learned that at Subway. Lack of interest interested them every time. Eventually she'd chosen a few postcards from the general store—scenes of the beach, turquoise and white. Anyone who hadn't been here would assume that the colours must have been adjusted, tarted up to impress the recipient and encourage tourism, but they hadn't; it really did look like that. She'd written as much on the back of each of the cards—to Callum, to Janey, to a few other kids at school. If Callum mentioned that he'd heard from her he'd learn that others had too. That was good. That protected her.

I put masking tape on the envelope as a test. The tape had been untouched when her mother gave her the letter. Morag wasn't a snoop, and neither was her own mother, who had handed it to her without a word once she'd got back from showing Fiona, Caro and Morag to their rooms, and Janey and Bronte had left to find them. Nonetheless, Tess hadn't trusted her with the postcards, instead handing them directly to the postman when he called into the office on one of his twice-weekly stops. It wasn't that there was anything on them that she didn't want her mum to see—everything she had written was as bland and cheery as a holiday brochure—it was just that she didn't *need* to see them, either. That was part of growing up, wasn't it? Taking care of your own business.

How are you enjoying it up there? Tess tipped back her head, staring at the ceiling as she framed an answer in her mind. *I really love it,* she would write back. *When we first arrived it was so humid and hot that I could barely move. I needed a sleep every afternoon like a toddler! And I missed everyone too—Janey and Bron and the school and you. I even missed French! Well, not really, but I missed how we used to pass each other notes, and sometimes you'd write yours in 'French' except it wasn't really French, you just put 'le' in front of everything.* Was that too much, she wondered, admitting she'd missed him? Maybe she wouldn't mention that. *After a couple of months I got used to it though. By April it wasn't so humid, and I loved that once I'd done my lessons I could do what I liked—read or nap or go to the beach. There are three or four other kids here that are also too old for the school and do their work by correspondence like me. Sometimes we sit together in the community hall and help each other out. No one supervises us so we get to muck around a lot, though Mum checks every night that I'm up to date and she goes off if I'm not. My best friend is called Tia. She's Aboriginal, with a bit of Japanese in her too. You should see how deep she can dive to get abalone! I still don't like eating it, but she gives me the shells and they're really pretty.* Tess paused and reconsidered. *My best friend here*, she amended in her mind. Janey was her real best friend, though it annoyed her that Janey hadn't made the effort to write her a letter like Callum had. Maybe it was because she was coming up to see her anyway? Still, it had been a long time . . .

I just wanted to see how you are and to say that I still think about the year seven disco and that you're pretty cool. That was it. That was the sentence she had been reading for. Tess took a deep breath and went over the words again, committing them to memory. She still thought about it too, usually at night when she was drifting off to sleep. The year seven disco had been held not long before they'd left for Kalangalla, as an end-of-year celebration. The principal had insisted it take place during the day, so that no one could sneak off into the darkness and teachers didn't have to be bribed or forced to return out of hours to supervise the students, and at first Tess had thought it was a bit of a joke. The multipurpose room still looked like a multipurpose room, even with cellophane on the windows and a glitter ball hanging from the ceiling. The boys that were so keen to flirt at Subway or in PE had suddenly gone aloof and reserved, clumping together at the far end of the room like adolescent algae. The girls bitched about what everyone was wearing or stood around similarly feigning boredom and indifference. Tess's eye was throbbing where Janey had accidentally jabbed her with a mascara wand while they were getting ready, and she was thinking about going home, when someone put on 'Dancing Queen' by ABBA. Her mother loved that song. From as far back as Tess could remember, as soon as her mum had heard the distinctive opening piano flourish and Benny's breathy *Ah Ah Ahhh*s she would drop what she was doing and shimmy around the room, or, if she was waiting at traffic lights, throw her head back and shake her shoulders until the car behind them honked to indicate that the lights had changed. Without thinking about it, unaware of the stares of the boys and Janey's tight frown, Tess moved out into the centre of the floor, lured by the music, and began to dance. For the first verse she was all alone, but then someone appeared beside her. Callum. 'You look pretty good,' he'd said, leaning in as she dipped and swirled, and matching his own movements to hers. 'Mind if I join you?'

It had broken the ice. Everyone began dancing after that—girls, boys, even the teachers, and as long as the old songs kept coming they stayed on the floor. He and his mates had been idiots, Callum said later when they were out by the bubblers, getting a drink and catching their breath. They had thought they were so cool, requesting a playlist of Jay-Z and Limp Bizkit, but the trouble was no one could actually dance to that stuff. All you could do was stand around violently nodding your head until someone thought you were having a fit and made you lie down with a pencil between your teeth. Tess was laughing so much that she didn't notice him leaning towards her until his mouth was on her own, warm and soft.

'Thank goodness for ABBA, hey?' he'd said, drawing back with a smile, and when she didn't protest he leaned in and kissed her again, longer this time.

She'd been kissed before, of course she had, though mainly in public spin-the-bottle-type clinches at parties or as the result of some sort of dare. But she'd never been kissed like this . . . Callum's lips pressed against hers, more insistent this time, yet still gentle. Before she knew what she was doing her mouth was open, and his was too; an electric shock went right through her as their tongues met, retreated, then touched again. Callum had his hands on her shoulders, then deep in her hair, pulling her even closer to him . . . and then they'd heard Stevie whistling as he came towards them and had sprung apart instinctively.

Still, Callum had danced with her for the rest of the afternoon, and had kissed her again too, when the bell had gone and she was meant to be walking home. She lingered with him at the back of the science block for as long as she could, until she knew her mother would be starting to worry and Janey would have stormed off, furious. Sure enough, when she finally checked her phone there was a text from her friend asking where the hell she was, and hadn't they agreed to go to Westfield after the disco to do their Christmas shopping and hang out? Tess had texted back with a lie, saying that she hadn't felt well and had had to leave the disco. She couldn't tell Janey about Callum, couldn't hold him out for her scrutiny. Callum was one of their classmates, someone they'd known since prep, and year seven boys were beneath Janey. She'd just laugh and tell Tess to get a grip or, worse, ridicule her choice. Anyway, it was only two weeks until she was moving to Kalangalla . . .

'Tess!' called her mother. 'Are you ready yet? You're taking ages in there.'

Tess dreamily reread the last paragraph. *Write back.* She would. She might even show Callum's letter to Tia. Tia got it, she thought. Tia was a year older than her and had a boyfriend, an eighteen-year-old, Jago, who was doing an apprenticeship in Broome but visited her on weekends whenever he could hitch a lift. Tia understood. Not that Tess would call Callum her boyfriend, but maybe when she was back in Melbourne . . .

'*Tess!*' came a shout, this time with an edge to it. Tess shoved the letter under her mattress and grabbed her bathers.

———

Bronte trudged behind Morag, concentrating on where she was putting her feet. She didn't want to trip over something and have them all laughing at her, but more to the point she was watching for snakes. Bronte hated snakes, and there were sure to be plenty here, it was so hot and grassy. She just hoped that Amira would know what to do if any of them got bitten, or could call in the Flying Doctor before the poison took hold.

The sun was stinging the back of her neck, and she pulled up her shirt collar to protect it. Caro had been right. She was going to have to watch it this week—she'd burn in a second up here. Morag too, she thought, studying the pale freckled calves striding away in front of her. Did Morag also detest it, all the mucking around with sunscreen, always having people asking if you felt OK or needed a blood test? Maybe she'd gone unnoticed in Scotland, but it was different here. Having a fair complexion in Australia was positively a disability.

Morag stopped so suddenly that Bronte almost walked into her. 'Wow,' Morag breathed, tugging off her daypack and reaching inside for her camera. 'This is just amazing. I thought Cable Beach was incredible, but this . . .'

Bronte followed her gaze. She wasn't a huge fan of beaches— too many visits had ended in pain and peeling shoulders—but Morag was right. This was something special. A crescent of white sand swept around a lagoon the colour of the sky; at the horizon it was impossible to tell where one finished and the other began. The water was so clear she could see something moving in it from twenty metres away. Something large . . . not a dolphin, but too big to be just a fish. Bronte ran forward to investigate; the tiny waves lapping at her toes were as warm as bathwater. 'It's a turtle!' she cried, enchanted. She'd never seen one in the wild.

'Shh, keep it down or it'll be dinner,' Amira laughed, appearing beside her. Bronte looked at her, not understanding. 'Turtles are part of the diet here,' explained Amira. 'Pretty much everything is that comes from the sea, but turtle's a particular delicacy. Don't worry,' she added, noticing Bronte's frown. 'No-one's here to get this one. See if you can swim with it.'

'Really?' Bronte asked.

'Sure,' nodded Amira. 'It's gorgeous in . . . Give me your shirt and your hat. I'll take them up to the shelter. But be careful—it gets addictive in there. Don't be too long.'

'I know—my skin.' Bronte peeled off her shirt and dived in quickly before anyone could see her in her bathers. Silver fish darted by as she swam towards the turtle. It was even bigger than she'd thought—it probably weighed as much as she did. She trod water, watching it feed on seagrass.

'Go on!' yelled Amira from the shore. 'Grab onto it. It won't bite you.'

With her heart in her mouth, Bronte reached out for the turtle. The shell felt solid but also velvety soft, like a boulder swathed in moss. The turtle's long neck craned around and it peered at her, seemingly in disdain. They stared at each other for a moment, then the creature slowly beat its flippers, moving through the water with Bronte trailing behind.

'Wheeeeeeeee!' she called out, as if she was a kid at Disneyland, holding on until the sea below her darkened and the turtle began to dive. 'Bye,' she said, watching it go, then slowly swam back to the beach.

By the time she stood up in the shallows, the others had spread out their gear under the two brush shelters further along the sand. Bronte shook the water from her hair and began walking towards them, wishing Amira hadn't taken her towel. She hated the thought of them all looking at her body, at her ridiculous legs, her flat chest, the way her knees knocked together when she walked. She hadn't even realised they did that until her mother had pointed it out. That was on the day Bronte had told her about the agent who'd approached her outside the school gates and asked her if she'd ever thought of modelling. The woman had handed her a card, which Bronte, thrilled, had shyly passed to Fiona as soon as she got home, but Fiona had just laughed and dropped it in the bin.

'Probably some scam to get us to pay for pictures,' she'd said. 'Who'd want a model with pigeon toes and no tits? I can just see that on the catwalk.' She'd smiled at her to soften the blow, but the memory still made Bronte burn with embarrassment. Her mother was right. It probably was just a scam.

She reached her towel and collapsed onto it in relief, pulling her shirt back on before she lay down on her stomach, her face turned away from the group. She was too tall and too skinny, that was the problem. A freak, just as Janey had said, a stick insect, a pipe cleaner. Funny how you weren't allowed to call people fat anymore, but no holds were barred at the other end of the scale. *God, Bronte, put some weight on*, Janey had drawled when they'd met to go to the beach. *You look like one of those kids in the World Vision ads, only taller.* Bronte blinked, tears stinging her eyes. Dr Bennison at her mum's work had told her that she'd stop growing once she got her period. Surely, at fourteen, that would be soon? She liked Dr Bennison; she was kind and approachable, she didn't laugh at you or rush you out of the room. Ms Drummond was the same. She listened; they both did. Bronte felt better just thinking about them. A thought occurred to her—maybe she was gay? Boys did nothing for her—they did nothing *to* her except tease and stare—but she often thought she loved Ms Drummond. She rolled onto her side. Great. Another way to stand out. She would be a lesbian stick insect.

'Tess really is looking fantastic, Amira,' said Caro. 'Living here clearly agrees with her.'

Bronte lay still, careful to keep her eyes closed. Tess and Janey had run off to swim not long after she'd come out of the water. Maybe the mothers didn't think Bronte was awake or could hear them. Maybe they didn't care.

'Thanks. It does, but she's also at that great stage just before she starts getting fat like me.'

'You're not fat!' Fiona protested. 'You're . . . comfortable. I'm the one who's fat.'

Amira laughed. 'Comfortable. Well, I'm comfortable with it, anyway, but there's no escaping the Leb thighs. Tess will find that out.' There was the tremulous sound of flesh being slapped.

'Tess is only half Lebanese, though,' Caro pointed out. 'If she keeps exercising she'll be fine. Look what it's done for Janey.'

'Ah, everyone admires Janey,' said Fiona archly.

'Tess is gorgeous,' Morag quickly interjected. 'You must be proud. They're all lovely, every one of them—Tess, Janey, Bronte. They're like . . . nymphs or something at this age, aren't they? Ethereal. So beautiful they're almost otherworldly.'

Fiona snorted.

'Macy too?' Amira asked.

'I can't tell under all that eyeliner,' sighed Morag.

'God, you give them everything, and that's what you get in return,' Fiona said. 'They grow up and want to get their nose pierced.'

Bronte knew she was talking about Dom, Bronte's brother. He'd mentioned it just before they left—his latest girlfriend had piercings in one nostril and her bottom lip, and Dom had said that he was thinking of getting one too. 'Don't be so stupid,' Fiona had snapped, which of course got Dom's back up. He'd told her it was none of her business, and she'd retorted that it damn well was—he still lived in her house, didn't he, so she had to look at his ugly mug every day. 'I'll move then,' Dom said, slamming out of the room without finishing his dinner, but they all knew he was too lazy for that. Now Bronte held her breath, silently praying that her mother wouldn't share the story with everyone. She had a tendency to do that, laying bare the private details of their lives, laughing as if it was all some great joke. It wasn't. It was awful—not just for Bronte and Dom and their father, but for anyone else who had to listen to it.

'That's Dom's latest idea, anyway—did I tell you?'

Bronte pulled her hat down over her ears, but to no avail. Fiona's voice always carried.

'It's his bogan girlfriend's fault. She should have been given away at birth. Mind you, I almost wanted to do the same with him. He split me from arsehole to breakfast.'

Someone shut her up, Bronte thought, push a towel in her mouth or offer her a drink.

But to her surprise, Amira sounded interested.

'How many stitches? I had twelve with Tess. I had to sit on one of those donut things for a week.'

'Sixteen,' Fiona replied, clearly proud to have bested her. 'It was so bad I didn't just have the donut. They also gave me a condom full of ice.'

'Huh? A condom? What on earth for?' asked Morag.

Caro joined in, her voice lit with glee. 'Easy to see that you had C-secs. It's to soothe the inflammation. You put it on your sore bits, you know, inside your . . . oh, I can't say it!'

'Prude,' Fiona remarked, though fondly. 'You shove it up your vajayjay. The ice cools everything down, makes you feel better. Or so I'm told. I threw mine in the bin. After all nine and a half pounds of Dom pushing his way out, the last thing I was going to do was put anything back in there. I told Todd that too.'

The four women erupted with laughter. Bronte stifled a groan. They were carrying on like idiots. Worse, teenagers.

'You must have, though,' said Caro slyly. 'You had Bronte, didn't you?'

'Immaculate conception,' Fiona answered. 'I wasn't there for it, anyway. I must have been asleep.'

'Was Todd with you when you had them?' Amira asked, then went on without waiting for a response, 'Davis stayed, which was all well and good, but then he insisted on coaching me through labour. That was fine in the early stages when he could rub my back and get me cups of tea, but by the time I reached transition I just wanted to shove his CD of humpback whale songs down his throat. And forget the condom. When it was all over he handed me this jade crystal and told me that if I focused on it all my pain would be gone.'

Morag giggled. 'Fat lot of good it was then. If it was so powerful, why didn't he give it to you when you were still pushing?'

'Exactly!' shrieked Amira. 'Probably because he was too busy waving herbs under my nose. I mean, yes, we had discussed it at antenatal classes, that we were both going to be calm and say no to drugs and just sort of draw the baby towards our energy . . . but I don't think anyone told the baby that.' Her voice sobered. Bronte could picture her looking around at them all, brown eyes serious. 'I had no idea. Neither of us did. I mean you don't, do you? No one would go through with it if they knew what it was like.'

There was a silence, predictably broken by Bronte's mother.

'I reckon one day scientists are going to work out what those whales are saying and all you hippy types are going to be disappointed. It's probably just: "This water's cold" and "Christ, I could go some krill right now".' She chuckled to herself. 'Or, if they really do have higher intelligence, it'll be: "Get the hell away from me. I might be a humpback, but I don't want to hump you."'

Bronte jumped to her feet and ran towards the water, looking for Janey and Tess. She couldn't take any more. She'd rather be subjected to Janey's snarky prattle than have to hear her mother talking about sex for a moment longer.

———

Morag rinsed the conditioner from her hair, but then stayed there, under the shower, with her head tipped back and her eyes closed. Were there water restrictions at Kalangalla? Surely not, given Amira had said that their wet season lasted three or four months. She sighed gratefully. There was no hurry to get out, and she luxuriated in the moment, in the rare experience of not having anyone to please but herself. It had been fun on the beach that afternoon. The four of them had shared their birth stories when they first met, a bonding ritual women seemed unable to resist, but that had been years ago. Morag counted them up in her head: eight, nearly nine. No doubt the details were the same, but the telling had changed . . . Amira letting loose about Davis; Fiona and her iced condoms; Caro confiding that her greatest fear regarding childbirth wasn't the pain but that she might defecate on the bed while she was pushing. Then she'd leaned in and whispered, 'And I did! I nearly died. As soon as I knew it had happened I sent Alex out of the room so the nurse could clean me up, and I didn't let him back in again until Janey's head was crowning and I knew there was nothing left in me except her.' Caro's cheeks had been red but her eyes sparkled, high on the thrill of sharing a confidence. Oh yes, their birth stories had definitely improved with age, Morag thought, their defences worn down by years of shared tuckshop duty and Friday night drinks and checking each other's children for lice.

Ten minutes later she was combing her hair, towel wrapped around her, when there was a knock on the door.

'It's me,' Fiona sang out. 'I need a favour. Can I come in?'

'Sure,' Morag called back. 'It's unlocked.' Amira hadn't even given them each a key when she'd shown them to their rooms earlier that afternoon. 'No-one locks their doors here,' she'd said, 'though I'm sure I could find keys in the office if you wanted to.' Morag had said she was fine. She hadn't brought much that was valuable, other than her camera, and she expected that that would mostly be with her. Besides, her room was between Fiona's and Caro's. If anyone did want to steal anything there'd be much richer pickings in those.

Fiona shuffled in, also wrapped in a towel, clutching a plastic bottle to her chest. 'I think I got burnt,' she said, 'on my back, but I can't see it. Can you rub some moisturiser on for me?' She handed the container to Morag and turned around. The skin from her shoulders to her lower back was a bright angry pink.

'Ouch,' Morag said, tipping some cream into her hand. 'How did that happen? We spent pretty much all of the afternoon under the shelter.'

'Swimming,' Fiona said glumly. 'I didn't expect to stay in that long, and I thought I'd be OK if I kept my shoulders underwater. It's not as if I'm as fair as Bronte.' She groaned. 'I'm an idiot—and there I was thinking what a berk you looked for wearing that rash vest.'

Morag smirked. She'd noticed Fiona's disparaging glance when she'd pulled on the vest before their dip, but it hadn't bothered her. If Fiona thought her rashie was daggy, so be it. Morag would be wearing it regardless—and she wouldn't be the one miserably dealing with first-degree burns. She gently put the back of one hand to her friend's scapula. Fiona winced.

'This looks really sore,' Morag said.

'You're telling me,' moaned Fiona. 'It goes with my head.'

'Spread out your towel and lie down on the bed. I've got a spray in the fridge that always helps when I get burnt. It's even better when it's cold.'

Fiona hesitated. 'I haven't got anything on,' she said.

Morag laughed. 'You, going all coy? Is this the same woman who was flashing her breasts to half of Broome last night?'

Fiona coloured, but only from the neck up, where she had applied sunscreen.

'I just don't want to subject you to the sight of my great big arse. Do you think you can cope?'

'I'll try not to ravage you,' Morag said, moving across to the wardrobe in the corner of the room. She shed her own towel and pulled on a singlet top and undies. Though the light was fading, it was still too hot for anything else. Next she opened the small bar fridge beside the handbasin, glad she had filled the jug in there earlier. She poured two large glasses of water, grabbed the burn spray and returned to the bed.

Fiona was lying face down, her back appearing even redder in contrast to those areas of her body that had been covered by her swimsuit. Morag put the glasses of water on the bedside table next to her.

'Drink up,' she said. 'Both of them. You're bound to be dehydrated.'

Fiona obediently reached for a glass, drained it, coughed a bit and lay back down.

'I'll have the other one when you've finished. Otherwise I'll need to piss straight away, and you probably don't want that on your bed.'

Morag smiled. 'You're all class,' she said, spraying Fiona's shoulders.

Fiona moaned, but in gratitude this time.

'Fuck, that feels better. It's so lovely and cool. What's in it?'

'Papaya,' Morag replied, working her way down Fiona's torso. Just below her burn line, at the top of her right buttock, was a small faded tattoo. She bent down to inspect it.

'You never told us about this,' she said.

Fiona peered over her shoulder to see what she was talking about, then slumped back onto the bed.

'You never asked,' she said, then sighed. 'God, it's ancient. I had it done when I was still in my twenties, before I was married. I'd almost forgotten about it.' She paused. 'Don't laugh, but Todd has one too, just the same. It's our initials. It was his idea. I went along with it because I was drunk.' Another pause. 'Among other reasons.'

Morag studied the blurry lines, trying to make sense of them. Eventually it came to her.

'Oh, I can see it now . . . There's the T, and the F.' She traced the blue swirls lightly with her finger. They were like runes, she thought, all that was left of another time, another language. 'They make something, don't they? Is it a flower?'

'A rose,' Fiona confirmed. 'Last of the original thinkers, weren't we?' She moved her arms up beneath her head and turned her face so that she was staring at the wall. 'I haven't looked at it in years. They're supposed to be capitals, but I bet they're lower case now. Everything drops. I hate this ageing shit.'

Morag straightened up.

'You're doing OK. Your arse hasn't sent me screaming from the room yet.'

'Huh,' Fiona grunted. 'It's not what it was though. Neither's my stomach, or my legs, or even my brain. At work, when a patient comes in I used to be able to say "Hello, Mrs Kerfoops" straight away. Now I need a good few minutes to dredge up their name, or I have to go and look at the appointment schedule.'

'Yeah, but you deal with a lot of patients. Yours has to be the busiest practice for miles around. They're lucky you remember them at all.'

Fiona closed her eyes as Morag sprayed more of the liquid along the length of her spine.

'So what about you, then? Doesn't it bother you, getting older?'

'I'd massage this in, but you're so burnt I might hurt you. Just lie still while it dries.' Some of the spray had ended up on her own hands. Morag crossed back to the basin and washed them before answering. She glanced in the mirror, at the fine lines around her eyes and mouth. Were they deepening? But she was fair, she chided herself. Of course there were lines. 'Yes, it bothers me,' she replied eventually. 'I work in aged care. I know what's coming. We have a joke in our department, that if any of us sees one of our colleagues collecting plastic bags or hoarding empty cans, they are to apply the Tontine treatment immediately.'

'Tontine treatment?' asked Fiona.

'Put a pillow over their face. End it all.' Morag smiled ruefully. 'It's a bit grim, but that's how you manage it, the things you see every day.' She picked her towel up off the floor and slowly dried her hands, thinking. 'I'm not all that fussed about my appearance, you know that. That part of ageing doesn't bother me—when my bum goes, it goes. What I do worry about is ending up like some of my patients. I never want to get to the stage where the most meaningful thing I can do with my days is to organise all my bits of string by length.'

She opened the fridge to put away the spray and brightened. 'Hey, this will cheer you up. Look what I got. Want some?' She held out a chilled bottle of vodka.

Fiona groaned. 'Urgh. Not now.' She frowned. 'But you don't even like vodka.'

'I know,' Morag said, putting it back in the fridge. 'I got it for you when we stopped at the supermarket. I knew you'd regret not having something later.'

'Thank you,' said Fiona, surprised. She sat up, pulling the towel around her. 'What do I owe you?'

'Oh, it's on the house. Come and grab it when you feel up to it. Now let's get dressed. Amira said to come over about seven, and it's almost that.' Morag took a sarong out of her beach bag and tied it around her waist. 'And don't worry about your arse,' she added 'Your boobs are still bigger.'

Fiona laughed. 'Thanks again,' she said. 'Maybe I *could* manage a drink.'

———

'Don't tell anyone,' Janey said, 'but I'm thinking of going on the pill.'

The bedroom was dark, so she couldn't see Tess's or Bronte's face, but she listened to their gasps with satisfaction.

'Wow, Janey. Really? That's amazing. How?'

God, had Tess become that much of a hick? 'Easy, you idiot. You just go to the doctors and ask for it.' Janey lay back, hands behind her head. The mattress was a bit lumpy, she thought. Tomorrow night she was going to sleep in her own room in a proper bed, or maybe she'd talk Tess into giving her hers and Tess could sleep on the floor. That was only fair, after all. Janey was the guest.

'But don't you need your parents' permission if you're under sixteen?'

Janey sighed. 'Mum'll give it to me,' she said, speaking with far more confidence than she felt. 'Anyway, I can easily pass for sixteen. You know Ro, from the year above us? She got into Chasers on the Saturday night before we left. I heard her group talking about it in the dunnies at school. She used her sister's ID, but still—I look heaps older than she does, especially if I wear make-up.'

'Who's the lucky guy?' Tess asked. 'Anyone I know? Someone in year eight?'

Janey sniffed. 'As if—those babies. All they know how to do with their dicks is tug them.' She paused, letting the suspense build, then admitted, 'No one in particular. I just want to be prepared. I'll be fifteen next year.'

'Not until July,' Tess said, then quickly added, 'But that's still incredible. Mum's pretty cool, but I don't think she'd let me do it.'

Bronte spoke up out of the darkness, surprising them. It was so easy to forget she was there. 'I've heard that some girls get the pill by saying that they need it for their skin, or to control their periods.'

'Yeah, well, clearly I don't need it for my skin, do I? And my periods have been fine ever since I got them, apart from

the first few months. Still, I was only eleven then, remember?'
Janey smirked at the memory. Eleven, and the first in grade
six. She'd acted horrified, but secretly she'd been thrilled.
Beat you all.

'You could say you needed it for swimming. The pill,
I mean. To skip your period when you have a big meet. You
can do that, you know.'

'Duh, Bronte,' Janey said, rolling her eyes even though no
one could see her. But she hadn't known. Could you really? she
wondered. That would be so convenient. She hated racing at
that time of the month. She felt so crampy, and she was always
worried that the string would slip out of her bathers and hang
down her leg like it had that time for one of the older girls, Jo.
She'd been bent over on the blocks for the start of a practice
relay and half the team were pointing at it and laughing, or
at least that's what it felt like. Janey shuddered.

'Bloody hell, Bronte,' Tess said, sounding impressed. 'How
do you know so much? Anything you'd like to share with us?'

'We learned it in sex ed. It's part of biology. We just did
it this year.' Bronte's voice was low and Janey knew she was
blushing. She was so uptight. Sex ed at year eight, though.
That was impressive. At Janey's school they didn't get it till
year ten. Too late for some by then.

'So is it your stroke coach?' Tess went on, unwilling to let
the subject drop. 'The one you told me about last year. What
was his name—Alan?'

'Adam,' Janey replied automatically. She rolled over onto
her stomach. 'I can't believe you remember that.'

'I can't believe you think I'd forget.' Tess giggled. 'Janey had this coach,' she explained to Bronte, 'not her main one, a younger guy who helped out, and one day when he was teaching her butterfly he made her get out of the pool and he put his arms around her to show her what to do.'

'Breaststroke,' Janey corrected. 'And he wasn't *teaching* me, he was helping to refine my technique.'

Tess continued unfazed, her voice rising with excitement. 'Anyway, to get his arms all the way around he had to press right up against her, and Janey could feel his . . . his . . . you know, his erection!' she exploded, delighted at her own daring in using the term.

'Shh!' said Bronte. 'You'll wake Amira.'

'Fat chance of that,' said Tess, falling back on her pillow, breathless with laughter. The mothers had all gone to bed early, worn out by the sun or the drive or because they were getting old.

Had it been his erection? Janey wondered. Maybe it was his belt, or his notebook. It could have been, though. Adam had certainly looked at her often enough, was always pulling her aside to impart this or that piece of wisdom, staring earnestly into her eyes until he thought she understood. Then again, maybe it was just because she was good. He wasn't the first coach to single her out. Whatever the case, she remembered now that she'd told Tess she'd given Adam a blowjob one night after training. She hadn't, duh, but it made Tess squeal and gasp and ask for all the details. That had been a bit trickier, but Janey had read *Cleo* for years so it was easy enough to make something up. There wasn't much to it, surely. How hard could it be?

'He left the club earlier this year,' Janey said. 'Went to AquaPower. Traitor.'

'What's his replacement like?' asked Tess.

'God, you're a pervert. His replacement's a woman. She's nice, but no way I'm turning lez.'

Tess laughed. Janey shifted onto her side, trying to get comfortable. As if she'd have gone on the pill for Adam, with his skinny legs and his try-hard goatee. She'd liked the extra attention he'd given her, liked that the other squad swimmers had noticed it too, but the idea of fucking him? Eww. Plus he'd probably want to time her. Janey pictured it, her lying on her back with her legs apart, and Adam standing there naked, clicking his stopwatch before he dived between them. Yuck. She *was* ready to fuck someone though, she was sure of it. Boys were all she could think about . . . the gaggle at the bus stop who whistled when she walked past on her way home; the older guys on the swim team, the way that line of hair curled from their navel to their Speedos; Bryce Jennings in year eleven who had invited her to the school formal—a rare honour for a year eight girl—and pushed his hands beneath her taffeta bodice when they were kissing at the after party. She'd liked it and pushed back, but the host's mum had walked in on them and made them go back to the others. Janey sighed. Adults were always interfering. If her mum had had her way, Janey would be going to that stupid school that Bronte went to, where boys weren't allowed. No boys! The idea made her shudder.

'Bronte's gone to sleep,' Tess whispered.

'Figures,' Janey said, not bothering to lower her voice. 'So what about you? Any talent up here?'

'Nah, not really. There's a few guys, and they're nice, but they're more like friends, you know?' Tess was quiet for a while, and Janey couldn't tell if she was thinking or drifting off too. 'I got . . .' Tess said at last, then seemed to change her mind. 'My friend Tia has a boyfriend,' she murmured instead. 'He has a car. Last week he took a day off work and drove us down to Middle Lagoon. You'd love it there.'

That boy in the pool last night, Janey thought. Was he a local? Did Tess know him? But that was ridiculous. Broome wasn't *that* small. She pressed her thighs together underneath the cotton sheet, enjoying the warmth that spread through her. He'd been nice—handsome, funny . . . He'd called her a mermaid, she thought, squeezing harder. The idea aroused her. She hoped Tess had fallen asleep too.

Tuesday

Five thirty. Surely that couldn't be right? It was already so light, the sun well up in the sky. Morag checked her watch again. Maybe she hadn't adjusted it correctly when they'd arrived in Broome, but wouldn't she have noticed that before now? She finished her stretches and pushed off along the track leading into the bush, still confused but determined to put it out of her mind. She was awake now. She might as well run.

For the first fifteen minutes the track was narrow and winding and Morag had to concentrate so that she didn't roll an ankle. Just as she was getting fed up, the path suddenly opened onto a wide sandy beach, empty apart from a lone dark figure casting a net at the shoreline. She slowed to a walk, then impulsively dropped to one knee and pulled off her shoes. Running barefoot was best for your body, but there were so few opportunities for it in the city. Morag took one step and then another, testing the grip of her feet on the powdery grains, gradually gaining pace, accelerating away from the fisherman and her own relentless thoughts.

Within a kilometre she'd found her zone. Her legs sailed across the sand, strong and flexible; her shoulders dropped and relaxed; her mind shut down. This was why she ran: not because she was some sort of fitness fanatic, as Fiona seemed to assume, nor because she was worried about her weight. She ran for her health, yes, but her mental health. She ran to clear a space in her day. She ran so that for an hour every morning she ceased being a wife and a mother and an OT, and became simply bone and sinew and cool, clear air.

Only the air wasn't so cool, Morag thought, slowing to a trot. Each breath she drew felt as if it was expanding inside her lungs, singeing her windpipe. The sun bit at her calves and the back of her neck; the glare from the white sand and the sparkling sea made her squint. She should have worn a hat and sunglasses, but who'd have dreamed she'd need either at six am? Morag peered along the coast. By her calculations she was west of the cove where they'd swum yesterday. She'd been gone about half an hour ... if she turned around and ran to the cove she'd probably get back to her room quicker than if she returned the same way she'd come, but then she'd be under the full blaze of the sun the whole way, not sheltered by the bush.

Damn, she thought. *Damn damn damn.* She was always so careful with her skin, yet here she was getting sunburnt before breakfast. When would she ever understand Australia? Ten years she'd lived here now, and it still had the power to fool her. It was the size of the country, she supposed. It was too damn big. She had a handle on Melbourne, but Melbourne was nothing like Broome, and they were both light years away from Edinburgh. Edinburgh. Feeling her eyes grow moist, she swiped at them angrily. It was just the glare, she told herself. She really did need her sunglasses.

Morag gave up trying to run and moved down the beach to trudge along the waterline towards the cove, ankles sinking into the wet sand. It was the softness she missed. The Edinburgh light had a hazy quality, as if filtered through stained glass . . . it took the edge off the city somehow, made it glow and shimmer. It blunted the corners and lit the sandstone of the New Town, it made the castle appear to hover in the misty air above the Princes Street Gardens. Fiona would say it only looked like that because it was always raining, but Morag knew that wasn't the real reason. It was the age of the place, the patina of history. It was the high grey skies and the blanketing haar, a sea fog that rolled in now and then from the Firth of Forth. Australia, in contrast, was too new, too bright. The colours were still fresh, and they hurt her eyes.

Morag smiled to herself. There'd been a haar on the day she'd first met Andrew. It was May, almost summer, and late in the season for such an event, but as her mother always said, *The weather doesn't check the calendar.* Morag had been working behind the bar at the Cafe Royal, a pub just off Princes Street, and he'd come in and ordered a pint, a guidebook clutched in one hand and drops of condensed fog still caught in his hair. They'd looked beautiful, like jewels or beads of mercury, and it had been all she could do not to reach out and touch them. Later, when she cleared the empty glass from the booth where he was sitting, she noticed him frowning over a map and on a whim had sat down beside him and asked if she could help.

He spent the night in her bed at the share house, then the next day too. The first time he had cupped her breasts she had involuntarily flinched at the roughness of his touch, and in the milky morning light the reason was clear. His hands were calloused and scarred, thick ridges of skin built up across his fingertips. She turned them over between her own smooth palms; she held one to her face to feel its rasp, its chafe. He was a furniture maker, he explained, or at least that was what he was becoming. He was two years into an apprenticeship in Australia, but he'd taken six months off to see some of the world before he returned, finished his apprenticeship and found himself a job. Not the sights, he added, lying back against her pillow as the rest of the household stirred and showered. He hadn't come to see those. What really interested him was design, ceilings especially, and he'd heard Edinburgh had some beautiful ones. He glanced across at her, as if wondering if she was going to laugh at him, then rushed on. Rosslyn Chapel, the carved wooden bosses of St Giles Cathedral, the National Portrait Gallery, the dome at the Central Library . . . they'd all been magnificent. Did she know of any more? She'd laughed, because it was such a delicious and unexpected question, because she was suddenly intrigued by this man she'd only spoken to because of the dew in his hair, and pulled him on top of her. Her own ceiling, she noticed briefly, was grey and flaking, yet it had never seemed more exquisite.

Andrew stayed for the summer. It hadn't been his plan, but that was what happened. When they'd finally got out of bed,

Morag had taken him to see the Royal Bank of Scotland at St Andrew Square, its high blue vault twinkling as if set with stars, then the City Chambers on the Royal Mile, the arcade between Cockburn Street and the Bridges, the ticket hall at Waverley Station. By then they were both a little in love, with the city as much as each other. Over drinks at Dean Brodie's tavern she filled him in on her own history—that the bar work was to pay her rent while she got through university; that she was originally from the Highlands, where her recently widowed mother still lived; that she was heading up there to visit her soon. Then she took a deep breath and added that while there weren't many ceilings of note in Fort William, she was sure there were some other attractions to recommend it. When university finished for the term, she took leave from the bar and they made the trip in a pale blue Combi that Andrew had rented, heading out across the Forth Road Bridge and up through Stirling and Glencoe. During their week in Fort William, Andrew charmed her mother every night over dinner, then waited until he was sure she would be asleep before tiptoeing across the landing to Morag's room, its walls still hung with the pony posters of her childhood. After that they pushed further north: Inverness, Ullapool, then across in the belly of a ferry to the islands—Skye, Raasay, the Outer Hebrides. The sun went down after midnight and rose again by four am; the days lingered for hours in a gilded twilight, had a short nap, then started afresh. Morag had never spent so much time in bed, and so little of it asleep.

And then he'd gone. Left one autumn afternoon for Spain, where there were more ceilings to see. 'They're a bit Gaudi,' she'd joked miserably as they said goodbye at Waverley, the filigreed dome of the ticket hall blurring above as she blinked back tears. This was planned, she'd reminded herself, this was always on the agenda, but still it stung.

Morag sighed, and wiped the sweat out of her eyes. Tiny shells crunched beneath her feet, nicking her heels. She should put her shoes back on, but she couldn't be bothered.

Spain. They'd kept in touch for a while, but that was before email, and after a month the letters had dwindled, then dried up altogether.

It should have ended there. Over the years, Morag had occasionally wondered what would have happened if it had. Would she still be in Edinburgh? Would she have a daughter? Maybe, but maybe she wouldn't have had children at all—no Torran, Callum and Finn to exhaust and delight her. She shivered despite the bite of the sun on her shoulders. But it hadn't ended. Andrew had returned eight years later, fleeing the still-smouldering wreckage of his first marriage, and by that time she was Google-able. He'd tracked her down through her job, then gone to the Royal Infirmary and sat in its cafeteria until she came in for lunch. 'Why are you here?' she'd asked him later, after her heartbeat had returned to normal. They were seated in the corner with two cups of coffee steaming between them, throwing up their own mini-haar. 'I wanted to see you,' he'd said. 'For old times' sake.' For an old time's shag, more likely, she'd thought, cautious and uncertain, but she'd smiled nonetheless. His hands were still roughened. They caught on her skin when he reached across to touch her face. Caught, and didn't let go.

Morag shook her head. The next part was fuzzy. How was it that she could recall some things so clearly—the gleam of the taps at the Cafe Royal, Andrew's calluses against her cheek—but not what came next, the rest of her life? She'd discovered she was pregnant a month after the afternoon in the hospital cafeteria. By that stage, Andrew had told her that he had a daughter, Macy, back in Melbourne; that his wife Janice had left him for the colleague she'd been sleeping with since Macy started childcare. Andrew had started a business making bespoke furniture for cashed-up yuppies, but Janice owned half of it and they still needed to sort that out. The double blue lines caught them both by surprise. Andrew laughed nervously and rued the absent condom; Morag put her hands to her stomach and mentally prepared herself for him leaving again.

To his credit, he hadn't. He'd stuck around and convinced her to go through with it, to move to Melbourne with him. She'd agreed, relieved, and had gone so far as to book their tickets when the twelve-week scan revealed twins. Immediately she'd known she couldn't do it. One unexpected baby had been almost too much to get her head around; for two she needed her mother. Margaret sold the Fort William home and moved to a small flat in Trinity, only a few minutes from where Morag and Andrew were living; the Qantas tickets were exchanged for single fares six months apart so Andrew could visit Macy. The business was sold and Andrew started a new one in Edinburgh, but five years later, when it failed, Morag knew she couldn't put off the move any longer. Andrew's designs were too muscular, too modern for a Scottish clientele, and then there was Macy, only two and a half years older than the twins, and who Andrew feared was growing up without him . . .

Morag had arrived at Tullamarine tired and nauseous and all too certain she was pregnant once more. It was a daunting trifecta: new land, new baby and a suspicious new stepdaughter. Margaret had declined their invitation to emigrate with them, that they'd pay her fare, declaring she was too old to settle somewhere else, that she'd miss her oatcakes and the heather and Jenners in the high street. Morag missed it all too, struggled daily with homesickness and morning sickness and heartsickness, sure she'd made a terrible mistake . . . until Finn and Callum started school and she met Amira, Caro and Fiona. They had got her through, she thought, recognising yesterday's beach just ahead and breaking into a jog. They had provided meals and babysitting and moral support and laughs. Things had shifted a little now that the children were older, but the connection remained important to her—two years ago she had started coaching their daughters' netball team so there'd still be somewhere they all met.

A gentle breeze drifted across her skin, cooling her. Morag felt her spirits lift as she thought of the day to come, the days still left of the holiday, time all of her own to spend with these women who meant so much to her. Her gait lengthened, her feet kicking up dust. She missed Scotland, she missed her mother, but there were compensations. And realistically, there was always a price to be paid, wasn't there? Nothing came for free, least of all love.

'Quick, Bronte,' hissed Janey, 'give me some of your Coke while my mum's not watching.'

Though she'd only just bought it, Bronte handed the can over obediently, then watched while Janey tipped half of it down her throat, swallowed hastily and wiped her mouth on the back of her hand.

'You might as well keep it now,' she said as Janey passed it back. 'I'll get another one.'

'No way,' replied Janey, turning and opening the fridge door behind them. A puff of cold air hit the back of Bronte's shoulders and she shivered appreciatively. How on earth had the nuns who founded the mission ever survived up here without air-conditioning, without refrigeration? Janey pushed the door shut and plonked a bottle of water onto the counter. 'Mum'll have a fit if she sees me drinking it. Empty calories, yadda yadda.' She passed her money across, fingers tapping impatiently as she waited for the young Aboriginal girl to work out her change. 'She's a pain in the arse about stuff like that,' she added when they were heading back outside. 'These are supposed to be the best years of my life, and I can't even have a Coke.'

Bronte followed her from the small community shop onto the grassed area just in front of it, where the others were sprawled in the shade of an enormous gum tree. She sank down next to them, glad to be out of the sun and to be sitting again after a morning on her feet. Her mother, she noticed, had her shoes off and was examining a blister on her heel;

dark semicircles stained her shirt beneath each arm. Bronte thought again of the long-ago nuns. Had they worn habits? You couldn't, surely, not in this climate. You'd suffocate under the weight of all that wool; you'd sweat yourself to death. But maybe that was just part of the deal, along with leaving their country, their family, everything they knew. They must have really believed, Bronte thought. They must have been so very sure of their faith.

'Shit,' said her mother, tossing away her sandal. 'I won't be able to wear those again. I'll have to go barefoot, like the boongs.' She glanced around, oblivious to the rest of them flinching, and her eyes fastened on Bronte. 'Sit up straight,' she said. 'Stop bloody slouching all the time. It doesn't fool anyone. And give me a sip of your drink.'

'It's empty,' Bronte said, though it wasn't, not quite. She lay down on her back. Her mum couldn't criticise her for slouching if she was lying down, couldn't remark, as she had once before, that she should be grateful for her height, that it was the only reason she kept her spot on the netball team. Personally, Bronte believed that the real reason was that they were too polite to dump her, though she sometimes wished they would. She wasn't very athletic. Bronte closed her eyes, the sun making patterns on the back of her lids, swirls of purple, blue, bright sparks of red. Ochre, she corrected herself, the colour of the land. The community gallery, where they'd spent the last few hours examining paintings, weaving and craft from the area, had been fascinating, inspirational. She wished she'd had her sketchbook with her. Maybe she could go back with it later, while the others were at the beach . . .

she'd like to show some of those designs to Ms Drummond, discuss with her how they could be transferred onto fabric. Could you do that, she wondered, or would you be breaching some sort of cultural copyright? But that painting with the russet, tan, the clusters of yellow dots—it had shimmered, it had moved. If the pattern could do that on a canvas, imagine the effect on a skirt, a dress, a sarong tied around the hips . . .

'What'd you think of the gallery?' asked a deep male voice.

Bronte opened her eyes, shading them as she sat up. It was that man Tess had pointed out to them yesterday at the beach, the father of her friend Tia, the one who killed turtles. He looked harmless enough now though, standing there smiling with a baby on his hip, white teeth flashing against his dark, dark skin.

'Oh, we *loved* it!' cooed Caro. Her own mother, Bronte noticed, had gone back to picking at her foot. She'd only lasted half an hour at the gallery before complaining that it was all just finger painting really, and that Dom could have done it when he was three. Bronte would never dare tell her, but her mother's attitude mortified her. Those words she used—*boong, abo*—they were just so awful. They made Bronte wince. They were little hand grenades that Fiona tossed into conversation. Did she intend the damage they did, or was it just the way she'd been brought up? It was true that her grandmother—Fiona's mother—was one of the sharpest-tongued people Bronte had ever met.

'This is Mason,' Amira said, hauling herself to her feet. 'He's one of the elders at Kalangalla. Mason, this is Morag, Fiona, Janey, Bronte and Caro.'

'We've already met,' said Caro, smiling back at him, her left hand going straight to her hair.

'It was amazing. All of it.' Bronte blushed as the others turned to stare at her, heads swivelling on sunburnt necks. 'I've never seen anything like it. The colours, the composition.' She hesitated. 'We haven't studied anything like it at school. I'd like to show my art teacher. I saw the sign in there about not taking photos, but would it be OK to sketch some, so I can describe them to her?'

The baby fidgeted and Mason jogged him a little, rubbing his back. 'That's there to stop the dealers. Some of them are good people, but not all. Few years back, we had one in there, snappin' away . . . found out later that he showed the pictures to some blackfellas in another community, got them to copy the painting, then bought it for less. The sign went up after that.' The baby chortled and made a grab for Mason's nose. The man's face softened. 'You wouldn't be doin' that though, so take as many photos as you like. Just make sure you write down somewhere where they came from, so you don't forget.'

'I wouldn't forget,' said Bronte. 'Thank you. And the boab nuts—those too? I love how they're carved. They're so big. It must take ages.'

'Which one was your favourite?' Mason asked.

'The one with the stingray,' Bronte said promptly. 'The cross-hatching made it look as if it was really swimming.'

Mason smiled. 'Aki did that. My wife. I'll get her to make one for you, if you like.'

'Would you really?' Bronte asked. 'That would be fabulous. I'll pay her for it—I mean, if it's not too much . . .'

Mason held up his hand. 'No money. She'll be happy to. I think she'd like the idea of somethin' of hers going all the way across the other side of the land.'

'We eat stingray sometimes,' Amira said. 'Jinup, it's called. Is that right, Mason? It's a delicacy here. You should try some before you leave.'

Bronte grimaced.

'Perhaps I should make that the price,' grinned Mason. 'Jinup stew. You eat some, you get the boab nut.'

'How did your wife learn to carve the nuts?' asked Bronte, keen to change the topic. 'Was it passed on from her ancestors?'

Mason's smile dwindled. 'Not Aki. She never knew her people. Hasn't even seen her own mum for over ten years.' He sat down on the grass next to her, setting down the child. The boy crawled straight to Fiona, who looked as if she wanted to shoo him away.

'What happened?' Bronte asked. Was that rude? Maybe, but she had the feeling that Mason wouldn't tell her unless he wanted to, and that the others were interested too. They sat or sprawled in a half-circle around him: Morag with her back pressed against the tree; Caro, still fiddling with her hair; Tess, who'd pulled Amira to her and lay with her head in her mother's lap; and Fiona, trying to stop the baby from crawling across her legs. Only Janey had separated herself from the group; she lay on her stomach with her earbuds in, rolling her bottle of water back and forth in front of her.

'Aki's mother was taken when she was just a nipper,' Mason said. 'Five or so. No one knows for sure; that was the age they guessed at the orphanage, though she wasn't no orphan. She and her mob lived somewhere east of here, in the Kimberley, when the welfare department got her and that was the last she saw of them. She already had a name, Yara, but they gave her a new one. Sally, they called her. A whitefella name.'

'What do you mean, "got her"?' Bronte asked.

'The stolen generation,' Caro said, and looked across to Mason for confirmation. 'Am I right?'

'Yeah, you're right,' he replied.

'They taught us about that in year seven,' Tess said. 'Back in Melbourne. Australian studies. Do you remember, Janey?' She went on without waiting for an answer. 'We had a test on it, like all the other topics—gold or the explorers or whatever. And then I got up here, and I met Tia, and one day she told me about her grandma, and it made me feel weird. Suddenly it wasn't just history anymore, like Burke and Wills. It was real, you know?'

Amira nodded, and so did Caro.

'I know about that,' said Morag. 'Sorry Day. We watched it on TV, with the boys, after Rudd got in. But didn't it all happen ages ago?'

Mason shook his head. 'Went on up to the sixties. Sal was taken in 1957 or '58, as far as Aki can tell. She tried to look into it but didn't find much. The records weren't good. Lots of kids were sent to Beagle Bay mission, like Sal was, just down the coast. They didn't bother with their names. Just wrote: "Girl, aged five".'

Bronte felt tears spring to her eyes. 'That's horrible!' she said. 'They just took her? Marched into her home and hauled her off?'

'Sal says she was out in the bush. Playin', lookin' for possums, and there were two white men who told her to come and get in their car. She'd never been in a car, so she did.' Mason shrugged. 'That was all she ever said about it—and that she missed her mother. We don't think she ever saw her again.'

'Never?' asked Morag. 'Did she try?'

Mason laughed, slapping one hand down on his blue jeans and raising a small puff of dust.

'Oh, I've got no doubt she tried. Tried to escape, and was probably beaten for her trouble. The officials and the nuns thought they were savin' them, you know. Uncivilised darkies, runnin' round naked . . . savin' them from the bush and themselves by takin' them away from their families and bringin' them up white.'

Bronte couldn't help herself. The sobs crowded in her throat, pushed out of her mouth like vomit. Without thinking about what she was doing, she sprang up and grabbed the baby, who had crawled over to Fiona's sandals and was sucking on a buckle, then sat back down with the startled child held tightly against her shoulder.

———

Fiona sighed. God, Bronte could be so embarrassing. First the earnest questions about the artwork, as if she hadn't asked enough in the gallery, then this—seizing that boy as if at any moment men in suits carrying clipboards were going to leap out of the bushes and snatch him away. Caro had half-risen to her feet as if to go to her, but Fiona shook her head. No one needed to make a fuss. It was just Bronte, overreacting as she always did—if Dom teased her at dinner, or someone made any sort of comment about her appearance. She was so bloody sensitive. Fiona exhaled through her teeth, cringing internally as she watched Bronte croon to the baby, who simply looked confused. How the hell had she, Fiona, raised such a thin-skinned child?

'It is sad, isn't it?' Mason said. Oh God, he was going to humour her.

Fiona shifted slightly and felt something seep between her legs. Her fucking period, which had started that morning. She needed to change her tampon, but she could hardly stand up now, with Mason giving them the whole *Roots* treatment, and just walk off. Amira would think she was rude, and besides, she didn't want them all watching her as she went. For almost a year now her periods had been getting heavier, thick and clotted, and it would be just her luck if she'd bled onto her pants. Caro would have heart failure. The thought made her smile. It would almost be worth such an undignified exit to see the look on Caro's face.

'But Sal—Yara—had her own children, at least I presume?' said Morag. 'She made a new family.'

'She had Aki when she was sixteen,' said Mason. 'Got pregnant to a cook at the mission. She was still goin' to school, but the nuns gave them all chores, and Sal's was to help in the kitchen.' He shrugged. 'The fella denied it was his, but it was pretty plain when Aki was born.'

'What do you mean?' asked Morag.

'He was Japanese,' said Amira, glancing over to see if Mason minded her taking up the story. He waved her on. 'The only one on the mission, descended from a family of pearl divers. And, well, Aki had his eyes.'

'Did he have to marry her?' Caro asked.

'I don't think they ever spoke again,' Mason said. Beagle Bay couldn't afford to fire their cook, so Sal was shipped down to the St John mission in Broome to have the baby. Then that closed, so they were moved to La Grange . . . and then Sal turned eighteen, so she left.'

'Left?' sniffed Bronte. 'But with Aki?' The child on her lap wriggled away.

Amira shook her head. 'She must have been desperate to find her people, her country. She knew Aki would be cared for. I'm sure she thought she'd come back . . .'

'You never told me that,' said Tess to Amira. 'So Aki was orphaned too, really?'

Mason lifted his hat to wipe his brow, the black curls underneath springing straight up. 'That's the thing. All those government types with their talk, your lessons at school . . . it wasn't just one generation that was stolen, it was the children that came after them too. Aki never had a mother. Sal didn't know how to *be* a mother. How could she? She grew up in an orphanage, not a family.'

Fiona fought the urge to stand up, to walk away, to head straight to Morag's room and that cold bottle of vodka, to switch on the air-conditioner and lie down with the bottle and not come out again until it was empty. OK, the whole Sal/Aki thing was pretty awful if it was true, but Mason was laying it on a bit thick, wasn't he? Maybe Aki had been better off without a mother anyway. Lord knows, some women simply weren't up to the task. Fiona had met Aki yesterday, just before dinner, when she'd come to ask Amira if she knew where Tia was, and the woman looked fine. Tall, healthy, a child on her hip, though not the one with Mason today ... she seemed to have any number of them, small brown boys with round bellies and cheeky dark eyes, and they were fine too, they were all just fine.

Fiona felt hungry and damp and annoyed. This entire thing, the conversation that had turned into a lecture—had Amira set it up? She wouldn't put it past her. It all seemed too smooth, the way Mason had just materialised like that and Amira had chimed in, some sort of consciousness-raising double act. Fiona picked up a twig off the ground and snapped it in two. She loved Amira, but jeez, give us a break. The fuss over Sorry Day—it had always annoyed her. She wasn't responsible. Why should she be sorry? And what did it mean, anyway? It was just a gesture, a front, so the pollies could pat each other on the back and people like her—people who had nothing to do with the whole wretched mess, who'd barely ever met an Aborigine, never mind stolen one—could feel good about themselves, could congratulate themselves on doing the right thing. Fuck, it was all so meaningless. She'd had a shit upbringing too—her dad had shot through, her mother may as well have for all the care she took after that—but no one had ever said sorry to her. That was life, wasn't it? It was just the luck of the draw. And *Mabo*, she thought, her anger rising; yeah, the abos should have some land if it was that precious to them, but how much did they need? It wasn't as if they were actually doing anything with it. They were freeloaders, as her mother had always said. God knows, her mum wasn't right about much, but she'd nailed that one. The handouts, the land, the special programs—that was what really upset her, made the gall rise in her throat. Everything was just given to them on a plate, while she, Fiona, had to work like a dog just to keep a roof over her head, worked harder than anyone she knew, black or white. It made her blood boil.

A hush had fallen over the group and Fiona prayed that they were done, that she could finally get to the loo and then have something to eat, but Bronte couldn't let it go.

'So Aki grew up in an orphanage too, just like Sal? Is that where you met her?'

Mason chuckled.

'Nah. Aki stayed at La Grange, but she was OK. That was one of the good ones, where they didn't try to turn the blackfellas white, just let them be who they were. There was a priest there who learned the local language, and set up a footy team just for the black boys. They sent Aki down to Perth to finish high school, because she couldn't do it there. She stayed, got a job . . .' He dropped his gaze, plucked at a tuft of grass near his boot. 'We met when she was working in a bottle shop. I was a pretty regular customer. Bit too regular.'

'Were you an alkie?' needled Fiona. Bronte shot her a look, but stuff her. It wouldn't hurt her to see that it wasn't only the whites that mucked up.

'Near enough,' said Mason. 'Then Tia was born and I knew I had to get my shit together. My act, I mean.' He grinned around the circle. 'Sorry, ladies. That was when we moved here, to get away from temptation.'

'And now you work in the garage, and Aki runs the gallery and helps out at Wajarrgi,' said Amira proudly, as if she was personally responsible for the turnaround.

'What about Sal?' asked Morag. 'Did you ever see her again?'

'Just once. Tia must have been about three—it was before we had any of the boys. Aki got a call from a historian who was doin' some research into the mission kids, what happened to them, and he'd tracked Aki down through La Grange. Told us that Sal was back in the Kimberley, a place called Durack, about a day and a half from here. We met the guy and he drove us over. I think he was hopin' for a big reunion scene.' Mason stretched his arms out in front of him, cracking his knuckles. 'Didn't get it. Sal was three sheets to the wind. He was the one who ended up fillin' us in on her history—the little she knew, anyway. She was too drunk to even know we were there.'

'What did you do?' whispered Caro.

'Came home again. Went fishin'.' He smiled at Caro's stricken expression and stood up. 'I just came out to get lunch—I better get back to work. Good talkin' with you. Might see you down the beach this afternoon.'

He scooped up the child, who had crawled back to him, and strode off, pushing his hat down onto his head.

'That was so sad . . .' Bronte began, but she was interrupted by a loud snore from Janey, who had fallen asleep.

Lucky bitch, thought Fiona.

Janey squirted some sunscreen into her palm and smeared it haphazardly across one shoulder. She'd used too much, and thick white droplets spattered onto the floor behind her, befouling the carpet like bird droppings. She paused to rub them in with one toe, then wiped her hands across her stomach, careful not to get any on her bikini. From the bathroom came the sound of humming—her mother, faffing around with her hair or her face. Cow. As if it would make any difference.

Janey picked up the sunscreen again, then changed her mind and snapped the lid shut. She hadn't done her back, but there was no way she was going to ask Caro, not after the scene she'd made that morning in front of all the others, shrieking so loudly that the girl behind the counter in the shop had come out to see what all the fuss was about. For God's sake, she'd only been having a nap! It wasn't a crime. So she hadn't listened to some story—big deal. She was tired. Her mother would be too if she'd had to spend the night on Tess's bedroom floor, and anyway, she'd done well not to nod off before that, in that boring gallery. Fiona was right. All the pictures *had* looked the same.

Janey wriggled into her shorts and held her breath as she did up the zip. Were they tighter than the last time she'd worn them? Her coach had told her that for every week missed in training it would take another week to get back to the same fitness level, so that essentially this holiday was putting her a fortnight behind—time, he'd remarked, that she couldn't afford with the state championships coming up in December. Fuck it, Janey thought, looking around for her sunglasses. Some bloody holiday. When her mum had told her they were going to Broome she'd imagined a resort, a pool, with waiters and big shady day beds and her sheets turned back every night with a chocolate left on the pillow. Not this, not some godforsaken hole where the lights went out after ten and there wasn't even a restaurant. And yes, the beach was beautiful, but you had to hike for twenty minutes in the boiling sun to get there, and it only had two tiny shelters that they couldn't all fit under . . . Janey located her glasses and jammed them on top of her head. She wished she was in Italy, like her father. She'd sightsee and order room service and smile coyly at all the men who whistled at her in the street. She'd drink wine and buy shoes, and there was no way she'd keep a travel diary, as her mother always insisted. She'd do what she liked, just as her dad did.

Janey sat down on the bed. It wasn't fair, him always jetting off like he did, leaving them behind, leaving *her* behind. She couldn't wait to finish school and be free, like him. Her father, she thought, saw the big picture, was involved with big things—not like her mother, who was always fussing over details, hyperventilating if the towels in the bathroom weren't straight, or Janey's homework was a day overdue. April was going to be just the same, she could see it already. Little Miss Perfect, with her symmetrical plaits and her pre-ruled margins in her exercise books. She'd never be much of a swimmer though, surely? Oh, they'd moved her into the intermediate squad, which was higher than Janey had been at the same age, but that was just a fluke. She'd get found out. She had to.

Caro emerged from the bathroom wearing eyeliner and lipstick. Lipstick. They were going to the beach, not a nightclub; another fabulous afternoon picking sand out of Amira's salad rolls and trying not to get fried and listening to Tess going into raptures about shells. It was good to see her again, but honestly, she'd turned into such a yokel—she hadn't even heard of *The Voice*, and her hair was mostly split ends. It was tragic. That was what happened to you when you didn't have the internet.

'Janey, can you run next door to Fiona's room? I think I must have left my sarong in her bag yesterday. I can't find it anywhere.'

Caro was bent over in her underwear, hunting through the chest of drawers, bottom in the air. Her Pilates wasn't going to hold things for much longer, Janey thought. Her mum would have to do something that actually involved a bit of sweat.

'Can't you?' she complained.

'Oh, for God's sake, Janey, can you think of someone other than yourself for one minute?' asked Caro, straightening up.

'Fine,' Janey said, stung. It wasn't like her mother to criticise her. She must still be pissed off about that nap. 'Perhaps you might like to put some clothes on while I'm gone, so I don't have to look at your fat arse.' She stormed out before Caro had a chance to respond.

There was no answer when Janey knocked on the door to Fiona and Bronte's room, so she pushed it open and went in. 'Fiona?' she called out. Nothing, though she could hear the shower running in the bathroom. 'Fiona, it's Janey,' she said more loudly, so she could be heard over the water. 'Mum thinks she left her sarong in your bag. I just need to grab it.'

'It's Bronte,' came the reply. 'Mum's at the shop. That's fine.'

Janey was turning away when she had a sudden impulse. Before she could think better of it, she'd pulled her phone from her shorts, set it to camera, and gently pushed the bathroom door ajar. The shower curtain gaped wetly, and through the gap Janey could see Bronte washing her hair, eyes closed. Janey smirked—Bronte must have worked up quite a sweat in all her excitement over the pictures in the gallery. She raised her phone and silently snapped once, twice. The resulting images on her screen were a bit blurred, but you could see Bronte's breasts, what there were of them.

Janey backed away from the bathroom door and peered around the room again. There was crap everywhere—at least her own mother was anal about putting stuff away—but eventually she located Fiona's beach bag hanging from a hook on the back of the door. She reached inside and grabbed the sarong. Nestled underneath was a book, *To Kill a Mockingbird.* Bronte's school novel, the one she'd been underlining on the beach yesterday. Janey felt a flash of irritation at her for being such a swot, for bringing homework on holiday. It served Bronte right that she'd taken her photo. She wasn't sure how, but it did.

'Thanks,' she sung out and left, the phone wedged back in her pocket.

'Caro, what about you? In or out?'

Caro swung her head around to find Amira looking at her expectantly.

'Pardon? Sorry, what did you say?' She had been gazing out to sea, watching a tiny fishing boat in the distance, lulled by the way it rose and fell on the waves. A dark figure stood at its bow, fiddling with a net or a rope. She wondered if it was Mason. Or would he be at work now? But when she'd run into him around this time yesterday he had just been returning from fishing, so maybe he finished early every day . . .

'Wajarrgi, tomorrow,' Amira went on. 'The resort, remember? I've booked us in for lunch there. I was asking if anyone wanted to do one of their tours as well.'

Caro glanced across to the others to see what they thought, but Morag was reading a brochure and Fiona was lying on her stomach with her eyes closed.

'I guess so,' she said. 'What does it involve?'

'"Cultural tagalong tour,"' Morag read aloud. '"Your local guide from the Djar . . . Djarindjin community will show you ancient sites and tell you tales from the capital-D Dreaming. Visit an Aboriginal community and experience their traditional way of life. Witness cultural rituals and make and decorate your own ceremonial spear."' Morag looked up. 'Open brackets, "spear optional", close brackets.'

'Good luck getting that home again,' said Janey, who'd been listening from where she lay on her towel just outside the beach shelter.

'Cultural rituals? What, do we get to watch them sit around and drink?' said Fiona. 'We could do that back in Broome. Besides,' she added, rolling over, 'aren't we already visiting an Aboriginal community?'

'Wajarrgi's different,' Amira replied earnestly. 'It's set up like it was before white people came, with humpies and a campfire and everyone just wearing pelts or loincloths. They perform a corroboree, and afterwards they'll take you down to the lagoon and show you how to use the spear.'

'On the fish or each other?' asked Fiona.

Morag closed the brochure, folding it carefully along its creases.

'I'll go,' she said. 'I don't know enough about that sort of thing. It sounds interesting.'

'Me too,' said Bronte. She was hunched in a corner of the crowded shelter, legs pulled to her chest, clearly anxious to keep herself out of the sun. Caro moved over to give her more room and was rewarded with a grateful smile. It was a shame Bronte didn't smile more often, Caro thought. She was surprisingly pretty when she did.

'What does it mean, tagalong?' Morag asked.

'That we follow them, in our own vehicle—the transport isn't supplied,' said Amira. 'All the roads are dirt or sand. You have to have a four-wheel drive. If you want to do it I can take you in the troop carrier.'

'Is that OK?' asked Morag.

'It's fine. I enjoy it. Tess'll come too, won't you? She caught a big fish last time we went. We brought it home for dinner.'

Tess nodded and Janey rolled her eyes. 'God, Tess, you're practically native. You're going to be the Bear Grylls of Salisbury High when you come back.'

'*If* we come back,' Amira interjected playfully.

'What do you mean?' Caro asked, finally paying her her full attention.

'Oh, I'm joking. Melbourne just seems a continent away sometimes.' Amira frowned. 'I suppose it is. A hemisphere, then. A planet. A whole other solar system. Now, what about you?' she prompted, changing the subject. 'Are you coming? No pressure, but there'll still be plenty of time for lunch and snorkelling if we stay the whole day. Wajarrgi's only fifteen minutes from here.'

'I suppose so,' Caro replied. 'Janey too, if Tess and Bronte are going.' Janey was rhythmically flicking through a glossy magazine, turning each page almost before she'd had a chance to scan it. She pulled a face but didn't look up.

'So it's just you left, Fiona,' Morag said. 'You have to join us. You can't sit in the restaurant drinking all day.'

'I don't see why not,' said Fiona, pulling her hat down over her eyes. She was silent for a moment, then sighed. 'Oh, God, OK then, if you're going to guilt me into it. Put me down for a bit of black magic—but I hope you're right about the loincloths.' She licked her lips suggestively. 'The smaller the better. I wouldn't mind getting a glimpse of those ceremonial spears.'

Morag threw the brochure at Fiona and it stuck to her chest, which was glistening with sweat. Fiona peeled it off, laughing, and dropped it at her side, where it joined a couple of apple cores, an empty chip packet and some chewing gum wrappers.

Caro turned away and stared back out to sea. The boat was still there, rocking gently in the swell. She could see a second, smaller figure now, a child. Had they caught anything? She imagined the tension on the line and Mason bending over to inspect his catch, to haul it in, those broad shoulders taut, the powerful muscles straining beneath his ebony skin. He'd be in shorts again, like yesterday, and nothing else. It wasn't a loincloth, but it was close . . . She had a sudden recollection of the way the drop of water had inched down his torso while they'd talked on the path the previous afternoon, how she'd watched it as he gave her directions—slipping from his chest to his stomach, sliding into his navel, re-emerging to run alongside the line of black hair disappearing into his waistband . . .

Caro hurriedly stood up, wrapping her towel around her waist. This was ridiculous. She needed a swim. Why was she even thinking about Mason like that? He seemed nice enough, and Amira clearly doted on him and his family, but he was hardly Caro's type—barely educated, barely groomed . . . she hadn't yet seen him wearing shoes. She was being silly. She loved Alex, and Mason was clearly committed to Aki if all those kids were anything to go by—five, she'd counted, Tia and then the four small boys. It must be the sun, or being on holiday, or . . . she stopped. What was that expression Fiona had used? Black magic. She turned it over in her mind, then dropped the towel, strode towards the sea and plunged into the water, diving head first rather than letting herself gradually adjust to the temperature as she normally did. When she came up she was blushing. Black magic. It was one of the oldest clichés in the book, and she'd fallen for it. How Fiona would laugh. She could almost hear her cackling, *You just want to know if he's got a big dick.*

—

'Well, what about this one?' Janey asked. 'Have you heard it?' She held her iPhone up to Tess's ear, watching her critically. A jangle of bass and synthesiser escaped the tiny speaker, shrill and metallic, without any discernible beat. Tess shook her head. Thin-lipped, Janey clicked forward to the next song, almost pushing it into Tess's face.

'Oh yeah, I know that one,' Tess lied. 'Jago—Tia's boyfriend— was playing it in his car.'

'Bullshit,' said Janey, tucking her phone back inside her bikini top, being careful not to drop it in the shallow waters where they were sitting. 'You don't have a clue. Honestly, Tess, you've lost touch with everything since you moved up here. Everything! You don't even have any new clothes.'

Tess lay back, propping herself up on her elbows. The sky above her was blue; always blue. She loved that. She hadn't missed Melbourne's winter at all. Her hair fanned out behind her in the sea, and she shook her head slightly, enjoying the drag and the flow of it. The water embraced her, caressed her. Was this how Janey felt when she swam? Somehow she doubted it.

'Nowhere to go shopping up here.' She shrugged, closing her eyes. Even wearing sunglasses the light hurt her eyes. No wonder Bronte had retreated back up the beach to the safety of the shelter. That, and she probably didn't know any of Janey's top forty either.

'What about Broome?' Janey persisted. 'You have to go there for groceries, don't you? Surely they've got some decent shops?'

'The elders don't let us kids go,' Tess said. 'They need the room in the car for the food.' It was another lie. She could accompany whoever's turn it was to do the shopping if she wanted to, but the fact was that she didn't. The trip was too long and hot and jarring. Even if it had been easier she didn't really want to leave Kalangalla. Why be dragging around Coles or getting shooed out of the upmarket pearl stores on Dampier Terrace when she could be exploring the mangroves with Tia, or spearfishing off the rocks, or simply lying in a hammock reading?

Books had been an unexpected source of company when she had first arrived in the north. Before then she'd never read much more than the novels they were set at school, but in those first few weeks at Kalangalla, feeling isolated and overwhelmed by the heat, she had wandered into her mother's room one day and arbitrarily picked something out of her bookcase. Her mother loved to read; had named her, as she was always being told, after the heroine of her favourite novel by some English guy a century or more back. She must get to that someday, she thought, but there was no hurry. First she had read *Rebecca*, the paperback she had selected at random, her heart thumping in her chest as she suddenly understood what had happened to the first Mrs de Winter. Next her mother had suggested *My Cousin Rachel*, and when she finished that, *Jane Eyre*, amazed and delighted at Tess's suddenly voracious appetite for text. Then *Penmarric* and *Gone with the Wind* and *The Thorn Birds*, for something more local . . . *Wuthering Heights* was on the agenda, but her mum had told her to save that until everyone had gone home and the wet had begun, when they'd read it together. To her own great surprise, Tess found herself looking forward to the prospect.

She felt something skim across her hand, and opened her eyes to see a small silver fish. A dart, she thought, identifying it by the central black spot on its body, pleased she could do it so easily. That feeling of isolation hadn't lasted long. She had the books, and then Tia, lovely Tia. Meeting her had easily been one of the best things about Kalangalla; she was funny and friendly and she knew so much about the area—*country*, as she called it—like where to find turtle nests, or how to get the biggest mud crabs out of their holes. Tess frowned. She'd asked Tia to join them on the beach today, but the girl had been uncharacteristically reticent, and wouldn't look Tess in the eye. Was she jealous? Tess wondered. Was she intimidated by Janey, or just bored by her conversation? Janey and Tia didn't have much in common. Come to think of it, Tess and Janey didn't have much in common anymore either.

'Tess . . . Tess. I'm just going up to the office, OK? I need to book the tour for tomorrow.'

Amira was shouting to her from in front of the beach shelter. Tess raised her arm in acknowledgement and her mother ambled off across the sand before disappearing into the bush.

'Your mum's put on weight. She needs to watch it,' observed Janey, pulling out her phone again. There was no connection, of course, but that hadn't stopped her from fiddling with it incessantly, listening to snatches of songs and scrolling through old messages, occasionally holding one out for Tess to read.

'She hasn't really,' Tess said, taken aback. 'You're just not used to seeing her in bathers.'

Janey tossed her hair back over one shoulder, continuing to stare at her screen.

'God, Tess, you've got no idea. She looks like she's smuggling rockmelons in her shorts.' She brought up a photo of the four mothers taken outside the gallery that morning, scrutinised it for a moment, then pressed delete. Caro, Morag, Fiona and Amira vanished instantaneously, as if vaporised.

Janey turned to look at Tess, blue eyes cool. 'It's because *you're* not used to seeing her in jeans anymore. You've totally lost touch out here in Hicksville. Do you even remember the real world?'

'I'm still in the real world!' Tess exclaimed, stung. 'Anyway, I had a letter from Callum the other day. He definitely hasn't forgotten me.' Damn, why on earth had she told Janey that? She made you talk, Janey. She pushed and prodded at you until you couldn't be held responsible for what came out of your mouth.

'Callum?' Janey sat up, her interest piqued. 'Since when do you care about Callum?'

'I don't,' Tess mumbled. 'I mean, he's just a friend, and it was good of him to write . . .'

'Can I see it?'

Tess shook her head. 'It's in my room, hidden, so Mum doesn't find it.'

'Must be a pretty interesting letter if you have to hide it,' Janey remarked. 'I always thought you two were a bit keen on each other. Wonder what Morag would make of that?'

'Don't tell her,' begged Tess. She wouldn't put anything past Janey.

'Oh, your secret's safe with me,' said Janey. She tapped once more at her phone, then passed it to Tess. 'Have a look at this.'

For a second Tess had no idea what she was looking at, the display just a blur of dark and light. Then all of a sudden it came into focus: Bronte, head back, eyes closed, her hands in her hair, naked from where the photo began at the base of her stomach. She looked wet—was she in the shower? She must be. Tess peered closer, trying to conceal her interest. Bronte's nipples were dark and erect, her breasts small but pretty. Tess hadn't even realised before that Bronte *had* breasts; she was always wearing those shapeless tops and baggy windcheaters. When had they stopped showing each other their bodies? she wondered. In grade six all they could do was stare and point and giggle every time they changed for sport, loving the thrill and the trespass of it, but something had happened when they hit their teens. They'd retreated, Tess thought. Everyone was too afraid of being laughed at.

'What do you reckon?' Janey said. 'Pretty funny, huh? I'm thinking of emailing it back to a few people at school.'

Tess gaped at her, horrified.

'You can't do that! Does she even know you took it?'

Janey switched off her phone and stood up out of the water.

'I'm just joking,' she said. 'Have you lost your sense of humour as well as everything else? I can't even get reception here, remember?'

Tess watched her as she walked away up the beach, a fine silver chain flashing on her ankle. She was glad she wasn't Bronte.

———

Amira hurried through the scrub, the note clutched in her hand. *URGENT*, Jen at the office had written across it in red, underlining the word twice for good measure. All the same, she hadn't remembered to give it to Amira until Amira had made the tour bookings and was almost out the door again, when Jen called her back, looking a little sheepish. Amira had asked Jen if she had any idea what it was about, but Jen had shook her head. 'Nup,' she'd said, 'just that your friend has to ring her husband immediately.'

Amira stopped to catch her breath and unfolded the piece of paper to see when he'd called: 2.06 pm. Immediately. Huh. That was over three hours ago now. Would it have killed Jen to try to find them, rather than let it wait until Amira had wandered into the office? She sighed and smoothed out the scrap of paper, now damp from her sweaty hand. She loved the north, loved the way of life and how laidback everyone was, but sometimes they were all just a little too relaxed. Up here, *urgent* seemed to mean anytime within the next week; *when you can* was an invitation to stretch things out indefinitely. Amira fanned herself with the note, then broke back into a trot.

Her friends were arrayed much as she'd left them thirty minutes ago: Fiona lying on her stomach under the beach shelter, her back still bright red; Morag next to her, reading a guidebook; Caro a little distance from the others, sitting right at the edge of the shelter with her pale legs manoeuvred into the sun, no doubt trying to get a tan. The three girls were dotted separately around the beach, each seemingly lost in her own world. No one spoke.

'Morag!' Amira cried as she hurried towards them. 'There was a message for you at the office. You have to ring Andrew as soon as you can.' She pulled up next to her, panting, and thrust the note into her face.

Morag dropped her book in the sand without marking her place.

'Andrew? But he's in Tasmania with the boys.' She reached for her beach bag and started to go through it, then remembered. 'My phone doesn't work here.'

'I'll take you up to the office,' said Amira. 'Do you recognise the number?'

Morag reached for the piece of paper, hand trembling slightly. 'It's his mobile,' she said. 'He must have tried mine and got no answer, then looked up Kalangalla. He wouldn't have done that if it wasn't important.' She turned to Amira, freckles prominent in her white face. 'What do you think's the matter?'

Caro had moved across to listen to the conversation. 'It's probably nothing,' she soothed. 'Maybe he's lost something, or one of the boys has twisted his ankle.' Fiona had looked up but for once was mercifully silent.

'He wouldn't call for that,' Morag said, scrambling to her feet. 'He never calls. He goes hiking to get away from it all, that's what he always tells me.'

'It'll be fine,' Amira said, though she didn't feel as confident as she sounded. Andrew was the sort who took charge, be it MCing the school fete or allocating tasks at a working bee.

He wouldn't be calling about a sprained ankle. 'Come on, let's go and find out.'

To give her friend some privacy, Amira waited on the verandah while Morag went into the office to phone Andrew. 'I'm here if you need me,' she called after her, and Morag nodded but didn't turn around.

Amira sank down onto an old timber bench. Night came early up here. It was still hot, but the orange sun had already begun to slide down the sky, casting long shadows across the dirt roads and coarse lawns of the community. A sprinkler spurted to life nearby, startling her; a banded gecko appeared at the end of the bench, regarded her with tiny jet-black eyes, then scurried up the office wall. If Andrew was calling he must be OK, so that was something—she just hoped it wasn't one of the boys. When Tess and the others were in grade three, a child in a lower class at their school had wandered away from her parents at a barbecue and been discovered fifteen minutes later face down in the family pool. Quarter of an hour, that was all it took; possibly less. Children were so impossibly fragile. How did any of them make it to adulthood?

Tess, too. Amira shivered, though perspiration gathered at the nape of her neck and trickled beneath her knees. That day when she was barely nine months old ... Davis was unemployed (and unemployable), so Amira had returned to teaching, leaving him home with the baby. It had been her first week back in the classroom, and she'd phoned every chance she got: lunchtime, little lunch, when her grade had gone to PE and she should've been working on her lesson plans. 'She's fine,' Davis had repeatedly told her. 'Stop worrying. Concentrate on your work.' Only Tess wasn't fine. When Amira arrived home after her third day, Tess was pallid and fretful in her cot, floppy with fever, though her hands and feet were cold. 'I didn't want to bother you at work,' Davis said. 'It's just a bug. Kids get them all the time.' She had wanted to believe him, though he had no more experience of infants than she did; she might have believed him had she not removed Tess's jumpsuit to sponge her down and seen the rash.

Meningitis, they'd told her at the hospital. It was lucky Amira had brought her in so quickly, but even so there could still be brain damage. It was touch and go. She'd turned on Davis then, screaming and clawing at him in front of the entire emergency department, the adrenalin of panic coursing through her veins. 'You told me she was fine!' she'd shrieked. 'You didn't even check on her, you lazy shit.' Tess, thank God, had recovered, but their marriage didn't. She couldn't trust Davis after that, couldn't look at him without her lips curling into a sneer. When he'd left them both barely two months later her main emotion had been one of relief. 'And don't come back!' she'd shouted childishly as he reversed out of the driveway, his old car blowing blue smoke into the morning.

Thankfully, he hadn't. She'd held her breath for the first week, willing him to stay away, tensing every time the phone rang or she heard a car door slam outside the flat. Surely he'd want to see Tess, claim her, if nothing else? Yet when Davis finally did return a month or so later it was only to collect his few possessions: a box of CDs with cracked plastic covers, the bread-making machine, his loom. Tess was asleep in her cot and he didn't ask to see her. He told Amira that he had moved to a commune in the hills established by a potter he had met at a local arts festival. He felt at home there, with the other craftists, he went on; they inspired and supported each other, bartering their work and skills for whatever they needed. As a weaver, he was particularly important because he could make clothes and blankets for the community, though he hadn't actually done so yet. Amira nodded respectfully, restraining her giggles until she had shut the door behind him; then she raced to smother Tess with relieved kisses, waking her up.

The marriage had been a mistake from the start. She knew that now, but she wasn't ashamed of it. They'd met in teachers college, before Davis had dropped out at the end of the first year. Amira had been desperate to free herself from her overprotective parents, who expected her home by seven every evening and were forever introducing her to the dark-eyed sons of friends and exclaiming at what a lovely couple they made. Matrimony outside of their Lebanese circle was the easiest exit, the perfect method—she'd thought—of casting off the familial devotion that stifled her. Of course, once Davis left it was her parents she turned to, and they'd been magnificent. Her mother had cared for Tess while Amira was working; her father had fixed the spouting of her tiny unit, then painted it inside and out. It was a shame, Amira sometimes reflected, that she'd had to escape her parents to appreciate them.

Even with her parents' help, it hadn't been easy. Early on, Amira had made the decision not to seek any maintenance payments from Davis—he had no money, for a start, but more importantly this way he had no hold over her, no claim on Tess. He drifted in and out of their lives, sending a postcard every once in a while, usually remembering to call about five days after Tess's birthday. Amira hadn't minded. There were lots of things they'd gone without—dancing or music lessons for Tess, holidays anywhere more exotic than a rental by the beach with her mother and father—but she had never had to pack her daughter's bag and hand her over for a week, had never had to listen to Tess chatter about her other home, her other life. Next to that, being poor was nothing. Besides, she thought, in Kalangalla not having much made them normal, made them average. It was liberating not always comparing herself with everyone else, not being compared in return. Money was overrated. Perhaps she was more like Davis than she had realised.

'That *bastard*!' Morag stormed out of the office, banging the door behind her.

Amira sprang to her feet. 'Is everything OK? Are the boys alright?'

'They're fine,' Morag spat out. 'Which is more than I can say for Andrew once I get my hands on him.' She went down the verandah steps in a single stride, thundering towards the beach. Amira had to jog to keep up.

'What happened?' she asked. 'Why did he call?'

'To dump Macy on me, that's why.' Morag stopped abruptly and spun around to face Amira, eyes blazing. 'She got into trouble at school, just for a change. She's a soloist with the choir, and they're rehearsing over the holidays for some eisteddfod. She wasn't on stage when she was meant to be, and when the music teacher went looking for her she found her in the boys' dressing room with the lead guitarist.'

'That's not so bad—' Amira began.

'I haven't finished,' Morag said, holding up her hand. 'She was already on a warning. Apparently it's not the first time this has happened, plus she failed most of her mid-year exams—she *never* studies—and the school had already told her that if she made one false step she was out. Knowing Macy she wouldn't have believed them, but they stuck to their word and threw her out of the production. So she fumes off home to see if Janice—who's on the board there—can wangle her back her spot, but Janice has had it with her and all her carry-on, and tells her she deserves it. Macy isn't used to Janice not taking her side, so she screams at her mother and tells her she hates her and that she's going to stay with Andrew instead—only of course when she gets to our house, no one's there.'

'So?' Amira asked. She was barely keeping up. 'She'll just have to go back to Janice's, won't she?'

'That's what I'd have thought,' Morag said grimly. 'But you don't know the hold she has on Andrew. She rings him in tears, tells him everyone is against her and they've all jumped to conclusions, that she hasn't done anything wrong. He felt so guilty that he wasn't there for her that he booked her a flight.'

'To Tasmania, to join him and the boys?' Amira said, confused.

'I wish,' seethed Morag. 'No, they're too far into the hike and she couldn't catch up to them. Instead my beloved husband had the great idea, without consulting me, of sending her here, on the only break I've had by myself in fourteen years.'

'Here?' echoed Amira.

'Macy's joining us,' Morag said. 'She flies into Broome tomorrow.'

Wednesday

The lagoon shimmered in the morning haze, blue and white and beautifully, perfectly deserted. Tess paused at the end of the track leading out of the scrub, drinking it in. It was like a child's picture of what a beach should be, all broad lines and crayon-bright colours: the crescent of sand, the azure water, a yellow sun unobscured by clouds. She wasn't religious—her mother hadn't raised her to believe in anything other than herself—but there was something about this place, about the combination of land, sea and sky that made her want to drop to her knees, to bow her head. She closed her eyes in a moment of pure gratitude, then sprinted towards the shallows, small puffs of silica rising in her wake.

After her swim she headed for the rocks at the northern end of the beach and positioned herself on a large, smooth slab where she could lie down and dry off. Though it was still early, the stone had already been warmed by the sun, and

Tess stretched out her limbs, soaking up the heat. This was what it must feel like to be a lizard, she thought, flicking out her tongue as if to catch a fly, imagining the march of scales down her spine and across her back.

'I'm glad you moved. I was just beginning to wonder if you were dead.'

Tess sat up, shading her eyes. It was Tia. She'd snuck up without Tess hearing her.

'I was hoping you'd come,' Tess said. 'Did you bring the gear?'

Tia held up two handlines in response, already baited. She passed one to Tess and sat down beside her.

'Quiet here,' she said. 'Where are all your mates?' Her sinker slipped into the water without making a splash.

'Still asleep, I guess,' Tess replied. Janey and Bronte had slept in their own rooms last night, with their mothers. Bronte had told her she was jetlagged and needed to go to bed straight after dinner; Janey had simply said that there was no way she was spending another night on somebody's floor. Tess hadn't minded. She'd be spending all day with them, and their absence had given her the chance to come to the beach and meet Tia, as she did almost every morning before breakfast. She'd hardly seen her since the others arrived. 'We're going to Wajarrgi round eleven for lunch and a tour. Why don't you join us?'

Tia shook her head, peering over into the water to check her line for snags. 'Nah. Got other things to do.'

'What other things?' Tess grumbled, slightly stung by the rejection. 'Changing your brothers' nappies? Sitting under the tree outside the store?'

Tia's nostrils flared slightly, but her face remained as flat and impassive as the line of the horizon.

'Jago said he might come up.'

Tess was silent. She wasn't sure she liked Jago. He'd been nice enough to her on the few occasions when she'd met him at Kalangalla, and he had invited her along on that trip to Middle Lagoon. But there was something about the way he put his arm around Tia, something . . . proprietorial, she thought, trying out the word, which she had recently come across in one of her books. It was a good one. She'd looked it up in the dictionary in her mother's classroom. There was something, too, about the way Tia closed herself off from Tess when she was with him, how she never told her anything about what went on between them, as if she wanted to keep it to herself. Tess gave herself a mental shake. Maybe she *did* want to keep it to herself. Not everyone was like Janey, who had absolutely no concept of privacy. A fish jumped out of the water just in front of where their lines bobbed, then disappeared with a splash.

'Hey!' shouted Tia. 'Don't tease us! Get on my hook or go away!'

Tess giggled. It was easy to be with Tia; easier than with Janey. They could just sit, they didn't have to endlessly analyse or bitch or compare. Tia was probably smart not to tell her about Jago.

'Do you think fish know what's happening when they do that?' Tia asked. 'It can't be as if they plan it. One minute they're just swimming along, the next it's all "Whoa, where did the water go? And what's this dry stuff in my gills?"' She paused. 'It must be pretty freaky.'

'Maybe they think it's a dream,' Tess said. 'Maybe that's what we do when we dream, we jump out of our habitat.' Another good word. She wished Amira had heard her use it, so she could see that Tess had actually learned something since they'd been up here.

'Yeah, maybe,' said Tia thoughtfully, leaning back with her toes trailing in the sea. 'Or when we're imagining something—what do they say? A leap of the imagination. Is that what the fish did, imagined itself into the air?'

'I just wish it would imagine itself straight onto my line,' said Tess. As the words left her mouth she felt a sudden downwards tug, saw her red and orange float go under. 'Tia, I've got something!' she called, but Tia was already leaning forward, holding the bucket out. The nylon between Tess's fingers went taut, bit into her skin, and for a moment she thought she'd lose whatever was on the other end.

'Come on, girl,' Tia said, willing it up. Tess pulled hard, locking hand over hand, and something flashed in the depths, fighting her. She yanked again, and this time Tia got the bucket underneath it.

'Golden trevally,' she said, peering in. 'Nice work!'

Tess relaxed her grip on the line, then shook her hands to get the blood flowing through them again. She put down the reel and reached into the bucket to remove the hook from the fish's lower jaw, its bottomless eye regarding her mournfully as she did so.

'Nice,' Tia said again, watching her technique. 'God, to think you could barely bait up without fainting when you first arrived. We've made progress, huh?'

Tess laughed, thrilled at herself. She couldn't wait to show her mother. Maybe they could have it for dinner.

They fished for another forty minutes, the trevally occasionally jerking between them in the bucket. Tia caught two undersized bluebone, but let them go; Tess's line remained motionless, drifting in the current. She didn't mind. She'd had her luck; it would be greedy to expect any more. As the sun climbed higher they started to sweat, and without a word both laid down their reels, peeled off their t-shirts and dived into the water. Tess had her bikini on, but Tia, she noticed, was wearing a tight singlet underneath her top, and shorts that she didn't remove. Normally she swam in her bra and undies, or less. Maybe she had her period.

'When's Jago arriving?' Tess asked, treading water.

Tia pulled herself back onto the rock where they'd been fishing, and sat there, arms wrapped around her stomach, staring out to sea.

'When he gets here, I s'pose,' she said.

'Are you excited?' Tess asked. The turquoise water beneath her was deep but clear. She could see all the way to the bottom, almost twenty feet down. 'It's been a few weeks since he visited, hasn't it? Bet you're glad I'm not going to be here to cramp your style.'

The last line had been meant as a tease, a joke, but to her surprise Tia stood up, wrung out one side of her dripping shorts and said, 'I wish you were.'

Tess opened her mouth to ask what she meant but was interrupted by a shout from the beach. Someone was calling their names.

'That's Dad,' Tia said, grabbing the bucket. 'Let's show him your fish.' She darted off across the rocks towards the shore, bare black feet skimming over mussels, crabs and sharp stones, always instinctively knowing where to land. Tess hauled herself out of the water, the salt drying almost instantly on her skin. She glanced at the sky. It was time she got back, before her mum sent out a search party.

When she caught up to Tia, her friend was bent over the bucket with Mason, who was exclaiming over her fish.

'It's a big one!' he said, running one hand admiringly over the burnished tail. 'Plenty of good eating in him. Your mob don't need to go out to lunch now!'

Tess laughed. 'You try telling Fiona that. I think she's hoping for something deep-fried.'

'Ah, he's beautiful,' Mason said, then straightened up. 'He's a Bardi fish, you know. Raari, in our tongue. You're one of us if he let you catch him.' A smile broke across his face. 'You're starting to look like one of us, anyway. You and Tia could be sisters.'

Tess glanced down at her toes, brown against the sand, her deeply tanned arms cradling their lines. It was true. She'd always been olive-skinned, courtesy of her mother's Lebanese heritage, but after nine months in the north she was darker than she'd ever been.

'Thank you,' she said, smiling back at him, knowing the words were a compliment, an inclusion. 'I love it here. I'm not sure I ever want to go home to Melbourne. There's nothing there I really miss.' A face flashed into her mind: Callum, at the bubbler, just before he kissed her. *You, I'd miss you*, she realised. Funny that she hadn't thought of Janey.

'It's pretty good, eh?' Mason said. Then his tone became serious. 'See how you feel after a wet, though. Or when you want to go to uni but you'd have to move two thousand miles away and leave everyone and everythin' you've ever known. Or when the people you've grown up with get on the grog and never come back.'

'I know,' said Tess, though she didn't, not really. She suddenly felt like the fish they'd seen earlier that morning, momentarily suspended between two worlds. Further up the beach, Morag jogged past, arms pumping, head down. Mason watched as she drove her feet over the unrelenting sand.

'She's pretty quick,' he remarked. 'What do you think's chasin' her?'

Perfume, Amira thought. She'd almost forgotten about perfume, but suddenly it was all she could smell, filling the troop carrier headed to Wajarrgi with its heady promise. She sniffed the air. Caro's Paris was the top note, of course—it was all she ever wore, her signature scent—but she could detect at least two or three others. Arpège? Did anyone still wear Arpège? There was something spicy too, and another that smelled like baby powder or bubble gum, though that might actually *be* bubble gum, she realised, catching a glimpse in the rear-view mirror of Janey chewing while she stared out the window.

Amira tried to remember the last time she'd worn perfume. Maybe on one of those miserable dates she'd allowed her friends to set up for her in the years after Davis had left? If she had worn any, it clearly hadn't worked. Of course, up here no one ever wore perfume. Far stronger chemicals were required to mask the odours of sweat and dirt, and anyway, it reacted with the sun, staining the skin. She'd been happy to give it up, along with ironing and foundation and blow-drying her hair, all of them rendered useless by the climate.

No one had told her friends though, and here they were, painted and primped as if they were about to take tea at The Windsor back home. Caro had clambered aboard wearing heels; Fiona sported a full face of make-up. Amira had complimented her, to show that she'd noticed, and Fiona had batted her curled and mascaraed eyelashes. 'I've got the works,' she'd said. 'Eyeliner, lip liner, panty liner.' Everyone had laughed—everyone except Bronte, who had sunk lower in her seat, gazing at the floor. Fiona had noticed and passed her a tube of lipstick. 'Here,' she'd said, thrusting it into her hands. 'If you can't find a smile, draw one on.'

Even Morag had made an effort—Morag, who was the most likely of them to turn up to school drop-off in her slightly damp running gear, and to still be wearing it at pick-up six hours later. Today, though, she had put on a dress. Amira hadn't known that Morag even owned a dress.

'You look nice,' she'd said as Morag climbed into the front seat beside her.

'Huh.' Morag had exhaled so heavily that her fringe rose in the updraft. 'It's my last taste of freedom. Thought I better make the most of it.' She looked at her watch. 'What time did you say the mail van gets in—around four? I've got five hours left. Step on it.'

Amira had backed carefully out of the community car park, swung the vehicle around, then turned left at the sign pointing to Cape Leveque. As soon as they hit the bitumen she called back to Fiona, 'Hey, there's an esky behind the back seat. I thought we could all do with a pre-lunch drink.'

Fiona undid her seatbelt and contorted herself to find it, bottom thrust into the air.

'Woo hoo!' she said, coming back up clutching a can of premixed spirits and a bottle of Corona. 'Gin and tonic—that's for me. Who else wants one, or a beer? They're cold too.'

'There's some cans of Coke for the girls, and a few bottles of Matso's,' Amira called over her shoulder. 'That's ginger beer from a little brewery in Broome. It tastes amazing, and it's alcoholic—it is our day out, after all.'

Fiona yanked back the ring-pull on her can of gin and tonic and took a long first swallow. 'You're alright, once we get you away from that place. God, I needed this. Cheers!'

'Are you going to have anything?' Morag asked, accepting a bottle of Matso's passed up by Caro.

'One of the Cokes, if there's any left.' Amira negotiated a cattle grid, then said, 'So you obviously didn't change your mind about going to pick Macy up yourself?'

'No fear,' replied Morag, twisting off the cap. 'I s'pose if there hadn't been any other option I could've taken one of the community cars like you suggested, but I didn't fancy doing that drive by myself.' She lifted the bottle to her mouth, took a sip and coughed. 'Wow—that's spicy. Good, though.' She swallowed again. 'But it wasn't really the drive, anyway. I mean, bugger Macy, and bugger Andrew too. Why should I waste a whole day racing off to fetch her? I've only got a few left. The mail van will be perfect—and if it arrives at Kalangalla before we get back, well, she can just sit tight and wait. It's not like I've never hung around for her before.'

Amira smiled. 'Andrew's lucky to have you.'

Morag snorted. 'Yeah, well, can you tell him that? He thinks I should try harder with her, talk to her more often. Fat chance. When she's with us she's too busy teasing Torran, or she's locked away listening to music. Besides, she doesn't want to talk to me. I'm just the housekeeper, the one who nags her to strip her bed at the end of the fortnight, or bloody well tell me when she finishes all the orange juice rather than just leave the container in the bin. She doesn't even recycle!'

Amira had to stifle a laugh. 'You're the wicked stepmother, huh?'

Morag stared out the window, the bottle nestled in her lap. 'Not wicked. Irrelevant. I'm nothing—or worse, I'm just a nag, that shrew that her father's married to. She adores Andrew and the boys, but I just serve the meals and buy the washing powder. She's never once asked me about my life, about my job or my mum or anything I'm interested in.'

'She's probably the same with Janice, you know. What you're describing sounds like pretty typical sixteen-year-old behaviour to me. It's rarely terminal. She'll grow out of it.'

'Maybe. If I don't kill her first.' Morag sighed. 'But anyway, it's different for Janice. She loves her regardless, like you love

Tess and I love Finn and Callum and Torran. It's so much harder loving somebody you didn't choose. It's not impossible—she can be fabulous—but it's love you have to work at, like practising your French, or keeping up with the weeding, or . . . or . . .' She cast around for inspiration. 'Or doing your pelvic floor exercises.'

This time Amira laughed out loud. 'Sorry,' she said, glancing across at Morag. 'So Macy inspires you to clench and release, to keep yourself toned? Andrew should be grateful for that, at least.'

'Oh, you,' Morag said, but she was smiling too.

Bronte was the first out of the car when they arrived at the resort.

'This place is amazing,' she said, looking around. 'Those cliffs—they're so red. And the beach. It's just beautiful, and there's no one on it!'

'That's the western beach,' Amira said. 'It's a bit dangerous for swimming—strong tides and deep water—but it's great for walks, and there's wonderful snorkelling just around the corner on the eastern beach.' She paused while the others climbed down from the troop carrier. 'We're on a point, the very tip of Cape Leveque. The restaurant and some of the campground is here, but the other accommodation is up the hill, below the lighthouse.'

'Wajarrgi,' said Bronte, reading the sign. 'But you just called it Cape Leveque.'

'It's the Bardi name for this area,' Amira said. 'They're the local tribe. The community at One Arm Point just up the road owns this place. A lot of them work here. The plan is that one day it will be wholly Aboriginal run.'

'It isn't now?' Bronte asked.

'Not yet. You'll see lots of Indigenous staff, but the management are still white. It all takes time.'

'Oh, thank *God*,' shrieked Janey, gazing at her phone. 'They have wifi here. It's working! I can check my emails and update Facebook.'

Immediately Caro, Fiona and Morag were fossicking in their bags, while Tess craned her neck to see what Janey was doing. Out of the corner of her eye, Amira caught a glimpse of movement, a flash of black and white. She turned her head towards it, gazing out over the ocean. There it was again . . . a whale, probably a humpback on its annual migration, breaching far out to sea. 'Hey!' she shouted, but nobody looked up. They were too busy checking their phones.

———

Caro excused herself and moved to the furthermost edge of the deck where they were sitting, checking the reception on her phone as she went. One bar, two . . . that would do. Fiona had tried to stop her, had poured a glass of wine and held it out invitingly, but Caro had pushed in her chair and walked away. The wine could wait. Speaking with April was far more important.

The line was engaged. 'Damn,' Caro muttered under her breath. Who could Maria be talking to? She never used the phone much, too conscious of her limited English, and seemed to be becoming even more afraid of it as her hearing failed. Caro made a mental note to take her to the audiologist when she was home again. Maria would probably be too vain to wear a hearing aid, but Caro still had to try, didn't she? It wasn't as if Alex would do anything about it. She selected the number again and waited, palms sweaty. Still engaged. Caro felt her chest tighten. She just wanted to talk to April. Was that too much to ask? It had been three days since she had seen her. They'd never been apart that long before. She'd checked her messages as soon as she'd arrived at the resort and there were none from Maria, but that didn't mean everything was OK. April would have to be lying unconscious in a hospital bed before Maria would think to try to contact her. The thought sent a wash of nausea through Caro's gullet, and sweat broke out on her forehead. She could see it so clearly: April pallid and unresponsive, a bandage wrapped around her scalp, dotted in places with blood, her blonde hair shorn off so that the surgeons could get to her skull fracture. *Stop it*, she told herself, pinching the inside of her wrist. It was a trick her therapist had taught her, the idea being that the pain would return her to reality, derail the escalating anxiety. Yet the image of April remained—inert, all alone in a cold white room while a heart machine beeped accusingly beside her. In desperation, Caro bit down hard on her tongue. That was her own trick, the one she kept for when the pinching didn't work. The rusty tang of blood spread through her mouth, making her gag, but she was calmer now. She was just being stupid, she told herself, dialling again. April would be fine.

This time the line was free, and after four rings Maria picked up.

'*Pronto*,' she said.

'Maria, it's me. Who were you talking to?' Caro demanded, suddenly furious at her for not answering her when she'd first called. As she spoke, a fleck of blood flew from her mouth onto her arm. Caro licked her index finger and rubbed it away. Thank goodness it hadn't landed on her white shirt. She had to be more careful.

'Ah, Caroline,' said Maria. 'I have been speaking with Alessandro. He a good boy, he ring his mumma.'

Caro did a quick calculation. It was early morning in Rome. A good boy? Huh. She wondered when he was planning to ring her. There hadn't been a message on her phone from him either.

'He had dinner with Tony last night,' Maria went on. 'He wanted to tell me about it. You remember Tony, he married to Teresa, my sister's second girl. They have three children. Alessandro said they went to a very nice place—'

'Is April there?' Caro interrupted. She wanted to scream. She didn't care about any of it, she just wanted to speak to her daughter.

'*Scusi,*' Maria said with an injured air. She let the silence between them hang for a moment, in case Caro wanted to apologise. When it became clear that this would not be forthcoming, she went on, 'April is at Natarsha's. The one from her class. They are having a play date.' She pronounced the last two words slowly and carefully, clearly pleased with herself for remembering the expression. Caro barely heard her. Hot tears sprung to her eyes. She blinked furiously, staring unseeingly at the red cliffs edging the ocean. It was silly to be so upset, but she missed April. She adored Janey every bit as much, of course, but somehow her love for her younger daughter felt easier, less fraught. Maybe it was just that April was still a child, had not yet been overthrown by adolescence; maybe, she admitted, it was because April still told her she loved her, still wanted to climb into her bed and cuddle up with her, didn't wince or pout or sigh every time Caro spoke to her.

'Oh.' Caro swallowed. 'I was hoping to talk to her. How is she? Is she OK?'

'She fine. She good girl. Good eater.' Maria paused, then added, 'It is very nice to have her. You don't bring her here enough.'

Caro's temper flared. Right, because she had so much time to be lugging April across town to visit Maria, what with her work and Janey's swimming, and running the house and Alex never home . . . Alex, she thought, Maria's precious Alessandro. Didn't he have a role to play in this? She could bet Maria hadn't spent her phone call to her son ticking *him* off. Alessandro could do no wrong.

'She should stay more often,' Maria continued. 'It is better with her here. The house is . . . happier.'

And just like that, Caro's anger evaporated. Maria was lonely, had been lonely and aimless and bereft ever since Alex's father died two and a half years earlier. Caro knew that, she just didn't like to think about it too much. She was too *busy* to think about it. If she acknowledged it she'd have to do something about it, and ignorance was easier to sustain than guilt. She should make more of an effort with Maria, she really should; the woman was old and isolated, and she wouldn't be with them forever. But Jesus, she thought, clutching the phone, Maria had two sons. Why should it fall to her, the barely tolerated daughter-in-law, to look after their mother? Why did anything involving caregiving automatically become the domain of women?

Caro promised that she would bring the girls over more often, then mumbled her goodbyes and ended the call. It had only been three or four minutes, yet she was utterly exhausted. Conversing with Maria invariably left her like this: drained, irate, found wanting. She needed to sit down; she needed that wine. Caro started back to the table. Did Maria feel the same? she wondered. Did she also hang up feeling frustrated, misunderstood, and not quite sure why? It must be tough watching your child fall in love with someone else, witnessing the transfer of their allegiance. Being a mother was hard enough; she wasn't sure she could cope with becoming a mother-in-law. Still, Caro realised as she rejoined the group, the alternative was worse. Her own mother had never had that option.

'Sorry I was so long,' she said as she sat back down at the table. 'Have you ordered? I hope you didn't wait for me.'

'Not yet,' said Amira. 'We've been a bit distracted.' She tilted her head slightly in the direction of the adjacent table. It had been empty when Caro left to call Maria, but it was now crowded with men. Young men. So was the one next to it, Caro noticed, and also the long table at the front of the deck overlooking the sea . . . In her absence, the tiny restaurant had been overrun by flashing grins and broad shoulders and large strong hands lifting glasses to mouths.

'Lordy,' she said, looking around. 'We're outnumbered.'

'Isn't it great?' said Fiona, fanning herself with her menu. 'You didn't tell me lunch was going to be a smorgasbord, Amira. I think I'll just pick the dish I want. Or dishes.'

Amira laughed. 'Believe me, I wasn't expecting it either. I didn't think there were this many men on the Dampier Peninsula.'

A waitress appeared at Morag's side and stood with her pencil poised above her notepad.

'Are you ready to order?' she asked.

'Well, where'd they all come from, then?' Fiona cried, ignoring her. 'This is like something out of my fantasies. It's Boys R Us.'

The waitress leaned into the table, dropping her voice.

'They're an AFL development squad. You know, the ones that eventually go into the draft. Kids hoping to make the big league.' She smiled conspiratorially. 'We probably should have warned you when you booked, but we didn't think you'd mind.'

'We don't mind,' said Fiona, unable to tear her eyes away from the dazzling array of young flesh.

'Stop drooling,' Morag told her. 'Or at least put your serviette over your mouth. You're putting me off my lunch.'

Fiona raised one finger in response, lasciviously licking her lips. 'Not me. I'm working up quite the appetite.'

The boys were just kids, Caro realised, at least some of them. Most didn't look as if they shaved yet, and only a handful would be old enough to drive. What were they—sixteen, seventeen? Their biceps and bravado made them appear older, but really they were teenagers. Was it necessary to be grooming them for the draft already? She picked up her glass, but quickly put it down again. The wine was lukewarm. Nothing stayed cool in this climate for long. The waitress took Morag's order and moved on to Amira. Caro bent over the menu and tried to make a decision.

A wolf whistle sliced the air. Caro's head shot back up. Three seats away, Tess giggled. Janey had risen from her chair and was sashaying towards the railing at the end of the deck, tight shorts clinging provocatively to her equally tight buttocks. She looked innocent enough, as if she was just going to take a picture of the view, but Caro sensed that her daughter knew exactly what she was doing, the reaction she could provoke. Another whistle. Caro turned, accusingly. This one came from a dark-skinned boy at the table to her left. Actually, they were all dark, or almost all of them.

'Hey, gorgeous,' he called out, holding up his phone. 'Give me a ring. It's 1800-SEXY.'

As usual, Janey's head was bent over her own mobile, but she tore herself away from it long enough to throw him a dazzling smile over one shoulder.

'I'm in love!' exclaimed the boy, thumping his hands and phone to his chest and falling back into his seat as if shot. Tess laughed again, eyes ablaze. Janey coolly returned to her texting, one hip slightly cocked, her legs honey-brown in the afternoon light.

'Boys,' Amira said. 'They never change. Remember when it was us who used to get whistled at?'

Caro nodded and picked up her glass again, swallowing a mouthful regardless of the temperature. She did. She did remember, and the fact that it was now Janey's turn made her feel both proud and piqued. Proud because her girl really *was* beautiful, really did turn heads; piqued because once upon a time that had been her. She'd never been as slim as Janey, true, but she'd had lovely curves—hips that swung, a décolletage that demanded the attention of any male within a hundred-metre radius, thighs that Alex had loved to sink into. Caro glanced around the deck. Almost every male face was turned towards her daughter, focused on those white shorts and golden legs. *Stop it!* she wanted to scream at them. *Stop looking at her!* She needed to protect Janey, she told herself. No matter what Janey thought, Caro knew she wasn't old or experienced enough to manage this sort of situation. Caro opened her mouth, but nothing came out. There was no point. No one was paying any attention to her.

———

It was him, she was sure of it. Janey had recognised him, the man-boy who had dived into the darkened pool with her on their first night in Broome, as soon as his group had arrived at the restaurant. He hadn't seen her yet; he'd been too busy talking and laughing with his mates. She'd watched them covertly from behind her sunglasses. There were twelve or so guys at the pool boy's table, all tall, all lightly muscled, all wearing matching black polo shirts with a red insignia printed on the left side of their chests. Not one of them, it seemed, could sit still. They jostled each other as they took their seats; they flicked menus and serviettes across the table; they pushed up their sleeves and fiddled with their cutlery. Energy radiated from their restless fingertips, from their taut calves jiggling as they waited to order. The atmosphere in the restaurant changed, thrummed, moved up a gear. The new arrivals were like chimpanzees in a circus, Janey thought; probably quite well trained but not entirely predictable.

She pushed her chair back. 'Where are you going?' Tess hissed.

'I need some fresh air,' Janey replied, jamming her phone into her pocket.

'But we're already in the fresh air,' Bronte said, gazing around the deck.

Janey sighed. Poor stupid Bronte. That scholarship clearly wasn't for common sense.

'I'm going to look at the view, OK?' she smirked. 'Or create one of my own.' She shook out her hair and made her way between the tables to the railing. Damn the pool boy for not noticing her. She would make sure he knew she was there.

It only took a few moments. She glanced his way when that other guy called out to her, and was gratified to see recognition spreading across his features. Then she turned back to her phone as if she couldn't care less and scrolled through some old texts, leisurely counting to one hundred in her head. When she had finished she tucked it back into her shorts, turned around without making eye contact with anyone and sauntered off in the direction of the beach. She hoped her mother wouldn't notice. The other adults were already on their second bottle of wine and could hopefully be relied on to stay where they were, getting slowly sozzled in the afternoon sun, but if her mother saw that she was missing she'd worry and come looking for her. Janey sighed. Her mother was *always* worrying, that was the problem . . . about her dad when he flew, or whether Janey had had enough sleep or had eaten her vegetables or if her top was too tight. She felt her hands clench. It drove her nuts, all that worrying, her mum barely ever looking at her without that half-frown of concern, her eyebrows drawn together. It was just so irritating, so . . . weak. It made Janey want to give her something to worry about.

Janey followed a sandy track down to the beach, the clamour of the restaurant gradually fading behind her. She positioned herself in the shade of a red cliff, taking in her surroundings for the first time. Aquamarine water lapped at the shore; a translucent ghost crab dug at her feet, diligently rolling its leavings into tiny spheres that festooned the shoreline like cachous on a cupcake. It was beautiful here. For once Amira hadn't been laying it on. Janey kicked off her sandals and stretched out her toes in the sand, admiring their fuchsia polish. Then, when the pool boy didn't materialise as she'd expected, she reached for her phone and switched it on, waiting impatiently as it came to life.

There were two messages in her inbox. Janey clicked on them greedily, impressed that even here on the beach she could get a signal. It was almost like being back in civilisation. The first was from a girlfriend in Melbourne whom she had texted as soon as they'd arrived at Wajarrgi. It didn't say much, but then neither had Janey's. They were just touching base, reasserting to each other that they still existed, were still relevant.

The second was from her father. *Hey Janey girl, hope you are having a good time up north. I went shopping today and bought you and April some DVDs. Do you still like One Direction? Kidding!! Srsly, tell me what colour (black? brown?) and I'll get a handbag for you. They're beautiful here. Be nice to your mum and have a great time. Dad xxx* Huh. Janey grunted. Be nice to her mum? He should be telling Caro to be nice to her. She began composing a reply, and opened the file containing the photos she'd taken on the trip so far to choose one to attach. Maybe one of the lagoon, or the selfie she'd taken on their first night in Broome, at the Aarli Bar. She peered critically at the shot. God, that seemed ages ago now. She looked so white. Janey scrolled through the images: Tess smiling from beneath a sunhat; Amira and Caro with their arms around each other at dinner in Kalangalla; Bronte in the shower. Janey scowled. Just seeing Bronte maddened her. *But we're already in the fresh air.* Idiot. Goody-goody. She was probably sitting hunched over her lunch right now, scared to look up in case a boy tried to talk to her.

Without pausing to think, Janey opened Facebook on her phone and uploaded the photo, then added a caption: *Shower scene, WA-style. Watch out for the psycho!* It wasn't very funny, but it didn't give anything away either. Hardly anyone would even know it was Bronte. Besides, she'd just leave it up there for a bit and delete it as soon as they got back to Broome on Saturday. Bronte was so stupid she'd never even know it had been there.

'Hello, mermaid. I thought I'd find you here, on the beach.'

Janey looked up and smiled, though more out of triumph than pleasure. The boy from The Mangrove loomed above her, his broad shoulders almost blocking out the sun.

'What took you so long?'

'I couldn't just get up and go—they watch us like hawks. Told the coach I didn't feel well and had to go to the bathroom.' He snuck a look at his watch. 'I've only got a few minutes.'

'Coach?' Janey asked.

'AFL development squad. It's our end-of-season trip—we play a few games against the local teams, pose for photos, do some "team bonding".' He made a wry face at the term. 'God knows why though; in a few months we'll all be fighting each other for the same few spots.'

He wasn't just tanned, Janey realised. His lips, that hair . . . he was Aboriginal, at least partially. A thrill went through her. This would spice up the story back at school. None of her friends had ever had an Aboriginal boyfriend. Hardly any of them had had a boyfriend at all, but that was beside the point.

'Are you enjoying it?' she asked. 'The trip, so far?'

He shrugged, then looked at his watch again. 'It's OK. Hey, I really do only have a few minutes.'

Janey eased herself back onto her elbows, the white sand soft beneath her. 'How should we spend them, then?'

'I can think of a way,' he said, dropping lithely beside her. Before she knew what was happening, his mouth was on hers, his tongue pushing its way between her teeth. She put her arms around him and let her body go limp. He tasted of beer and fried food; every boy she'd ever kissed had been the same. She should get a photo of him, Janey thought. Proof to show her friends, plus maybe he'd actually be famous one day. She could friend him and put the picture on Facebook, and then if he got drafted she could say she knew him first. She hoped he'd play for Carlton, who her father barracked for, or even

Essendon, or Richmond. Then he'd be in Melbourne and she could go and watch him and tell everyone she was going out with an AFL player, and invite him to the formal once she was in year eleven. She kissed him passionately, turned on by the thought, then froze as she felt his hand slip beneath the waistband of her shorts.

'Are you wet, mermaid?' he breathed against her lips. 'You should be.'

Janey fought the impulse to sit up, to push him away. Instead she arched her chest towards him, hoping to divert his attention to her breasts. Wasn't that the way it was usually done? Kissing first, then if she liked the boy she'd let him feel her tits through her clothes, and once, with Bryce Jennings, even under her clothes . . . No one had ever touched her below the waist before, never mind without asking. Maybe if she could undo her bra . . . She made an attempt, but the clip was at the back, and the boy's weight was pushing her down, pinning her arms. She held her breath as his fingers moved between her legs, pulling aside her undies, the first person other than herself to stroke the soft skin. Or her mother, Janey thought, mind racing, back when she was a baby and needed changing—but why the fuck was she thinking of her mother right now, as the boy's fingers slipped inside her, one then two? She opened her eyes and stared up at the sun. It didn't hurt, as she'd feared, but it didn't feel like much either—no more than inserting a tampon.

'God, you feel good, mermaid,' he sighed against her ear.

Janey forced herself to relax, to keep her legs open. He

155

probed further and she took a deep breath, up from her diaphragm, as she'd been taught in squad.

'Touch me,' he commanded, pulling her hand to his body.

She fought against flinching, against pulling away, repulsed and then intrigued by the swelling in his shorts. It was harder than she'd expected, and warmer too, almost burning through the fabric. She grasped it tentatively, frantically trying to remember everything she'd ever read in *Cosmo*. *Hold his penis like a tennis racquet, with a firm grip, but not too firm.* That was all very well, but she'd never played tennis.

There was a fumbling at her middle, and Janey gasped, realising he was trying to undo her shorts with his free hand. This was getting out of control, going too fast. She took another deep breath as she felt the first button pop, the second—and then a piercing whistle rent the air.

The boy sat straight up, pulling his fingers out of her and wiping them on his shirt.

'Shit. The coach must be looking for me.' He smiled down at her, a lazy, self-satisfied grin. 'You can let go now.'

Janey looked down and saw her hand on his erection, still determinedly aloft.

'Sorry,' she said, and removed it as if burnt.

The boy stood up, smoothed down his clothes and picked up his thongs from where he'd kicked them off. The ghost crab was gone, Janey noticed. She could hardly blame it.

'Thanks, mermaid,' he said. 'I might see you around.' Then he turned and jogged away up the beach, a surprisingly small figure against the rust-coloured cliffs. Janey lay back and watched him go. Some boyfriend. She didn't even know his name. He hadn't bothered to ask hers.

———

How did they do that? Morag wondered. The Indigenous man was positioned in a deep squat with his haunches just a couple of inches from the ground, yet he looked as comfortable as if he were sitting in an armchair. Morag was fit and flexible, but there was no way she could maintain something like that for more than a minute or so, never mind the quarter of an hour he'd already been there. Maybe Aborigines were built differently, she pondered; maybe their muscles were longer or more supple. The theory had merit. It was always black men and women winning the sprints at the Olympics, wasn't it? Caucasians were lucky to make it into the finals, and when they did there was never more than one or two of them, looking pasty and anaemic next to their glossy competition. She remembered once watching the Commonwealth Games with Andrew, and him jokingly suggesting that to make it fair there should be two divisions in the athletics events: one for the black runners, and one for the white. At least she hoped he'd been joking. If Fiona had said the same thing Morag would have called her a racist.

'We'll start today with a demonstration of the didgeridoo,' said their tour guide, a caramel-skinned girl in her twenties dressed in neatly pressed khakis bearing the Wajarrgi logo. She held up a long hollow piece of wood, then passed it to the squatting man. 'No two didgeridoos sound exactly the same. That's because no two are formed in exactly the same way—unless, that is, they're made in a factory, and those aren't didgeridoos, they're pipes.' She smiled, and her audience—their Kalangalla party, plus another five or six tourists—smiled back. 'Real didgeridoos,' she went on, 'are created when a living tree, usually a eucalypt, is partially eaten out by termites. They're not just logs picked up from off the ground—the trick is to find a branch before the termites have chewed all the way through, then to cut it off and cure it so it doesn't develop cracks. This can be done by leaving the wood in a billabong for a week or two, or up here, among us Bardi people, the ocean.' She grinned. 'This is saltwater country. We reckon our didgeridoos have the strongest sound of all, because they're formed in the sea, like we were.'

Saltwater country. Morag repeated the words to herself, liking the sound, the way they conjured up exactly what was in front and behind and all around her: sand and scrub and the constant blue glimmer. Wajarrgi, as Amira had told them, was situated on the point of a peninsula. Everywhere you looked there was ocean, flat and sparkling in the afternoon sun, spread like a carpet of sequins to the horizon. She was glad she'd come. The laughter-filled lunch with her friends, the cultural tour—all of it was calming her, renewing her, taking her mind off Andrew's appalling decision. She was grateful they weren't still at Kalangalla, where she probably would have sat and brooded all day; she was enjoying being somewhere new, learning something about this country she'd washed up in.

'Now, many people think that the didgeridoo is just like an overgrown recorder—you blow into it and the sound comes out. Well, I'm here to tell you that the didgeridoo is *nothing* like a recorder, thank goodness—and I say that with authority, because two of my kids are learning the recorder at school.'

Two of her kids? Morag started. The girl didn't look old enough to have one child, never mind more than two. And why on earth were they learning the recorder when they lived in an Indigenous community?

'For a start, the recorder is much more high-pitched—and irritating,' the girl continued. 'More importantly, the didgeridoo requires a special technique called circular breathing, where air is breathed in through the nose at the same time as it is blown out the mouth. It's quite difficult—try it yourself.' She stopped while they all attempted the method, wheezing and gasping like a conference of asthmatics.

'That's not difficult,' Fiona panted, red-faced. 'It's bloody impossible.'

'It is tough,' their guide conceded, 'but it's what gives the didgeridoo its unique sound, that drone that everything else is built upon.'

As if on cue, the Aboriginal man still squatting in the red dust positioned the didgeridoo between his thighs, raised it to his mouth and began to play. A long low note emerged, hanging in the still air like a mirage, then transformed seamlessly into another, and another. The guide was right: there were no gaps, no breaks, just one sustained tone. Morag listened, transfixed, as the music hummed between them, snaked around their ankles, crept beneath their skin. She had heard didgeridoos on the TV and in the occasional pop song, but never up close, live, like this. This was something else; it was an incantation, a spell. The sound that thrummed through the small clearing where they stood wasn't a tune as such, it had no melody or refrain, but it held something richer, more resonant, something as ancient as the land itself.

'That's so cool!' exclaimed a large auburn-haired woman standing in front of Morag. 'Can I have a go?'

The didgeridoo cut out abruptly, and its player and the guide exchanged a glance.

'Uh . . . I'm not too sure about that.' The guide shot another look at her colleague, but he stared straight ahead, still crouching on his haunches. 'Traditionally, the didgeridoo is a male instrument,' the girl stammered. 'Women are prohibited from learning it.'

'Well, that's pretty sexist,' the woman said. Was that an American accent Morag could hear, or was she just imagining it, projecting her own prejudices?

'I guess some women probably do play, but not at any of the ceremonies or corroborees . . .' The guide's voice trailed away uneasily. Dark patches had begun to appear under her arms, turning her khaki shirt olive.

'We're not at a ceremony now, are we?' the woman said pointedly.

The guide dropped her head, gazing at the ground. 'I guess not,' she conceded, then turned and held out her arms to the man. 'Leon, may I?'

For a moment Morag thought he was going to refuse, but then he passed it across without meeting the girl's eyes. In turn, she handed it to the red-haired woman. 'There you go,' she said. 'In through the nose and out through the mouth, just as I told you.'

'Film me, Alan,' the woman instructed her husband, then took an enormous breath, as if she were about to dive underwater. She lifted the didgeridoo to her lips and exhaled with a grunt into the instrument. There was no sound other than the air escaping from the bottom.

'Try it a bit more gently,' the guide suggested. 'Remember, you have to be breathing in at the same time.'

The woman inhaled and blew, inhaled and blew, but still to no effect.

'At the same time, Janet,' her husband called out, camera wedged to his eye. 'You're doing it all wrong.' She squinted at him angrily, took another lungful of air, and immediately began to cough.

'That's just stupid,' she said, pushing the didgeridoo back at the guide. 'You can't breathe in and out at the same time. It's not possible. And turn that bloody thing off, Alan,' she shouted at her husband.

'I'm told it is a difficult thing to learn,' the guide consoled.

'Or mebbe the spirits don't want you to play,' the Aboriginal man interjected, flashing the disgruntled woman a grin as if to indicate he was joking. Morag knew he wasn't. She found herself glad that the woman had failed, glad that she'd made a fool of herself. Served her right for being so pushy. The guide handed the didgeridoo back to its owner, who wrapped it carefully in an old blanket. No one else asked to have a try.

'Next we're going to witness a corroboree,' the guide went on, pushing her damp fringe away from her face. She had lost some of her poise, Morag thought, but she was still game, still determined to make the tour a success. 'A corroboree is an Aboriginal ceremony that involves singing and dancing. The correct term is actually *caribberie*, but the first European settlers misheard that, and "corroboree" has stuck.'

Fiona nudged Morag. Six Aboriginal men had materialised about thirty metres behind the guide, their bodies adorned with yellow and white markings. Two held spears, and one cradled a didgeridoo. All were naked except for a tiny red loincloth.

'Showtime,' Fiona whispered. 'Look at those chests. I'm glad you made me come.'

'Corroborees are performed for different reasons,' continued their guide, oblivious to Fiona's comments. 'Some are instructional, to pass on the stories or history of that particular group of people, their Dreaming. Others are to influence the weather, to celebrate an event, or as part of a traditional ritual, such as when boys are initiated into manhood. Corroborees also used to take place to ask the spirits to bless the land—to protect it and keep it bountiful, so the tribe would be nourished and strong. This was before supermarkets, of course.' A few dutiful titters. 'Corroborees always involve music—the didgeridoo, clapsticks and rattles, plus the voices of those who are performing and watching. Some corroborees are sacred to a particular gender, either male or female, and cannot be viewed by members of the opposite sex.' The girl glanced towards the red-headed woman as if expecting her to protest, then hurried on. 'The ceremony we're going to view today tells a story from the

Dreamtime, which is when the gods and spirits created the land and roamed upon it, sometimes getting up to all sorts of mischief, as you'll see here.'

She stepped back and the dancers glided forward, flowing over the baked earth like lava. They moved lightly, barely appearing to make contact with the ground, the designs on their bodies writhing as their muscles flexed and leapt. As they approached, they held their hands up in front of their face as if shielding themselves from an enemy, and Morag was struck by how pink their palms were compared to the darkness of the rest of their skin. Pink, and somehow vulnerable, flesh that could be easily broached.

Next to her, Alan picked up his camera and began to film. Morag felt a second, renewed flash of irritation. Weren't you supposed to ask permission before you took any images—a photo or video—of Aborigines? She thought she had read something like that once, that they thought it was akin to stealing their souls—or was that the American Indians? Anger surged inside her—at herself for not knowing, at Alan for filming on regardless, at his stupid wife, whom she still couldn't forgive for insisting on her right to play the didgeridoo. The whole thing was a farce, she thought suddenly. Who knew if this actually was a traditional corroboree, or just something knocked up to appease the whitefellas, to make some money out of them? And who could blame the dancers if it was? The guide had been careful to use the word 'settlers', but really the Europeans were invaders, weren't they? Trespassers, destroyers. Morag's friends didn't see it like that, but then they had been born here, they had no perspective. Her mind raced. Their white ancestors had stolen the land, had corrupted the language, and here they were, still invading—filming a ceremony they probably had no call to even be witnessing; trying to peer beneath the men's loincloths as they jumped and spun.

You could argue, Morag thought, that all of this—the corroboree, the tour, Wajarrgi itself—played an important role in education, in reconciliation, in the two cultures understanding and living alongside each other. But did it really? Or was it just entertainment—worse, exploitation? Complicit, maybe, the blacks wanting in on the tourist dollar every bit as much as the whites did, but exploitation nonetheless. Had the guide passed the didgeridoo to the red-haired woman because she didn't want to offend or because she knew she had to do everything in her power to keep the tourists happy, keep the cash flowing in? The ululations of the didgeridoo throbbed in Morag's skull, the clapsticks beat faster and faster, working themselves into a frenzy. Someone was making money out of these people. She'd bought into it because she'd wanted to learn something about Aboriginal Australia, but when it was all over would she know any more, grasp the issues any better, or was it just so that she could say she'd tried, shown an interest? You did the eco-tour, bought a dot painting, and then you could tick Indigenous culture off the list and go back to your sunbathing.

A dancer gyrated inches from her face and Fiona whooped. He looked like one of the young men who had been sitting in the restaurant at lunch—such graceful bodies, agile and powerful. And that was another thing, Morag thought. Aborigines were an accepted—indeed, admired—part of football, but did you ever see them anywhere else? Andrew had dragged her along to a few AFL games, and black faces were everywhere—taking marks, evading opponents, streaming down the wing with the ball moving like a yo-yo in their hands. Yet she'd never met an Aboriginal doctor in all her years in the health system, nor a solicitor, electrician or accountant. It was that tokenistic thing again: the souvenir boomerang, the black half-forward. Take the bits of the culture you like or can use, and ignore the rest. Wajarrgi was a prime example. If the Bardi people owned it, as Amira had said, how come none of them actually ran it?

The corroboree ended, the men whirling to a stop in a cloud of dust. Caro and Amira clapped, Alan kept filming, Fiona put two fingers in her mouth and gave a loud wolf whistle. Morag sighed. She was probably just still grumpy about Macy. Did any of her qualms matter? Working here was better than them living in poverty, or being completely dispossessed of their land and culture. And was it any of her business? Australia was where she lived, but it still wasn't her home. The realisation chilled her, brought out goosebumps on her sunburnt arms. Torran had been born here, and so too Andrew. Finn and Callum had been naturalised, but she herself had never gone through with it. She didn't have time for all the paperwork, she said whenever someone asked, but was it more than that? She'd lived here for almost a decade. Surely she belonged by now?

'I hope you all enjoyed that,' the guide chirped, smile firmly back in place. 'Now we're going to head to the village, where you can try your hand at some traditional weaving.'

'You sure you don't want to join in, Bronte?' asked Amira. 'You can share my spear if you like.' She waved the spear resting on her shoulder.

Bronte shook her head. 'No, thanks. I'm happy just to watch and finish my weaving.' She snuck another look at the small piece of matting in her lap, an umber-coloured circle emerging from its fibres. A thrill went through her, racing along her limbs and down her spine, like that time she'd stuck a knife in the toaster trying to free a jammed crumpet, only far more pleasant. She was doing it. It was working! Her fingers moved to select the next piece of dyed pandanus, and she paused, contemplating how it could be integrated into the design. She didn't look up as Amira turned away and splashed into the shallows of the village lagoon. *Across . . . under . . . across . . . under . . . rotate and tie off.* Bronte mouthed the instructions to herself, concentrating fiercely. She was on her own. The old woman who had demonstrated the weaving was no longer with the group, dismissed as soon as they had moved on to making spears. Bronte had wanted to ask if the woman could stay with her and she could give the whole fishing thing a miss, but she'd been too shy, afraid that the woman might say no or her mother would roll her eyes. Still, this was the next best thing, sitting under a tree while the others stalked their prey, the handful of pandanus in her lap, her fingers finding their own rhythm, the fibres aligning, shifting, becoming something else.

No one else had enjoyed the weaving, she knew. Caro had glanced at her watch while the old woman showed them the items she had made: a mat, a basket, something she called a dilly bag; Tess had yawned, then smiled apologetically when Bronte caught her eye. 'Got up early to go to the beach,' she'd whispered in explanation, and Bronte had nodded, returning her attention to the demonstration. The woman's hands were knotted with arthritis, yet they moved so deftly over her work it was almost as if they were dancing. Bronte had watched, spellbound; she'd wanted to stand up and move closer. It was the colours, she thought, so vibrant, so alive. She'd had the same sensation on her first day of primary school when all the students had received their own box of crayons. Up until then she'd made do with Dom's hand-me-downs, jumbled and broken in a grubby plastic lunchbox, tips blunted, labels shredded. As the teacher continued on past her desk, distributing the bright yellow packets, Bronte had glanced around, wondering if she was allowed to open them or if they were to be kept for special like the 'good' scissors her mother wouldn't let her touch. Other children were ripping at their boxes, tearing the cardboard, but Bronte sat patiently, waiting to be told what to do. When Miss Kirkland had finally nodded at her, she eased back the lid and carefully shook the crayons out onto her exercise book, holding her breath. Jewels emerged, perfect and whole, rubies and sapphires and emeralds, their glorious hues tumbling across her blue-lined page. They were so beautiful she'd gasped, and the boy sitting next to her laughed and said, 'They're just dumb crayons, stupid.'

But Bronte had never forgotten those crayons. Unable to bear being parted from them at home time that afternoon, she'd smuggled them into her bag. After dinner, Fiona had discovered her drawing furiously in her room when she should have been getting ready for bed; rather than being angry with her as Bronte had feared, she had sat down next to her, picked up the purple crayon and drawn a dragon. Bronte hadn't known her mother could draw dragons. Together they covered it in scales, then coloured them in, orange and pink and cyan and crimson; a harlequin dragon, a kaleidoscopic creature. The drawing had hung on the fridge for at least a year afterwards.

Even Janey had understood how Bronte felt about those crayons. When Patrick, the boy who had laughed at her, had accidentally snapped her favourite crayon, the cobalt one, Janey had noticed her quivering lip and passed Bronte her own box.

'Take the one he broke,' she said. 'I don't care. They're only baby crayons.'

It was a typical backhanded Janey comment, Bronte realised many years later, but kind nonetheless. Janey could still do that occasionally, reveal a hint of humanity beneath her shellacked exterior, but the glimpses were getting further and further apart.

Bronte shifted in the sand. Truth be told, she was scared of Janey, of her razor-sharp tongue, her blonde indifference. For a while at primary school she had considered her a friend—mainly, she supposed now, because their mothers were close, so they were always at each other's houses—but Janey, no doubt, had never shared the delusion. Even as a six year old she'd had the same cool blue gaze, had been able to sum up any situation in an instant and know how to work it to her advantage.

Bronte looked up from her weaving, suddenly curious as to how the ice queen was handling the *Survivor*-esque antics going on in the lagoon. When Tess had proudly shown them her just-caught fish that morning they had both recoiled—Bronte because she hated to see any animal suffering, Janey because she was terrified of getting blood or slime on her fresh white singlet. This catch-and-kill thing was never going to be Janey's style. Sure enough, there she was, lying face down on her towel further along the beach, earbuds in, her bikini top fluttering like a red flag from the spear rammed into the sand next to her. The side of her breast was clearly visible. Bronte flushed. Just say someone saw? But that was the point with Janey, she supposed. Being seen was always the point.

Bronte leaned back against the tree, letting her weaving fall into her lap, and took in the scene in front of her. The tourist who had made such a fuss about the didgeridoo was posing on the beach with her newly minted weapon, her husband obediently filming her every move. Caro fluffed around in the shallows, clearly nervous about getting her silk sarong wet, while the guide hovered on the sand making sure that everybody was safe and enjoying themselves. Tess and Amira laughed together as they stood, spears poised, in water over their waists. They could be natives themselves, Bronte thought. Their dark skin, yes, but also how at ease they looked in that setting, as if they spent every day up to their bras in a lagoon. Maybe they did. A pang went through her—not for the fishing, which she was happy to avoid, but for their tranquil companionship, that they could spend time together without harsh words being spoken or feelings getting hurt, without either one of them turning around and stalking off.

She sighed. Tess and Amira were a team, were equals. Tess spoke, Amira listened; Amira suggested and Tess complied. There was none of the struggle she felt between herself and her own mother, or indeed between Janey and Caro. Why was that? Was it because Tess's father was out of the picture, and Tess and Amira had had to rely on each other instead? Was it the time spent up here, thrown together in a new land, a new culture, with none of the distractions of home? Or was it simply dumb luck? Amira was a good mother, Bronte thought, then immediately felt guilty. Her own mother was a good mother. They were just going through a bad patch. Her mum worked too much, she was always tired and it made her short-tempered, plus she worried about Dom . . . And what about Morag? Bronte wondered, catching sight of her moving towards Caro, eyes focused on the blue-green depths in front of her. How did she feel about Macy? Did it bother her that her stepdaughter had been thrown out of school? Or was it only blood that made you care about such things, brought the two of you to loggerheads about the length of your skirt or the curve of your shoulders?

Bronte picked up her weaving again. Macy. Ugh. She'd only met her a few times, but she was afraid of her too. Bronte, Tess and Janey had their moments, but at least they were used to each other, they could muddle along for the few days they had left. Macy would change all that, and Bronte hated change. Change was overrated. Far better to know where you were and what to expect . . . Still, though, imagine being banished by your father to the other side of the country, being delivered by the post van like a dog-eared parcel. Bronte shuddered. She didn't know how Macy could stand it.

A cry went up from the water and Bronte craned her neck to see what was going on. Her mother was standing about ten metres from the shore, holding out her spear, a grey-green fish flapping from its point. 'I got one,' she cried, sounding surprised, then raised the shaft higher in triumph. 'I got one, did you hear that? I won! I won!'

Pride flushed through Bronte. If anyone was going to catch a fish she would have expected it to be Tess, who'd done it before, or the precise, methodical Morag. 'Good on you, Mum!' she shouted, jumping to her feet, then sprinted down the beach to congratulate her. She must get a picture, she thought, something to show Dad. He'd never believe them otherwise.

—⁓—

'I'm going to the bar,' said Amira. 'Do you want a drink?'

She and Fiona were back on the deck of the restaurant at Wajarrgi, the footballers they'd seen at lunch playing kick-to-kick on the grass nearby.

'Stupid question,' replied Fiona. 'Get me a glass of sauv blanc. Actually, make it a bottle. You'll share it with me, won't you?'

Amira pulled a face. 'Not a whole bottle. I've got to drive back in an hour or so, when the others have finished snorkelling.'

'God, Amira, it's only ten minutes away.' Fiona sighed. 'Have you ever even had a booze bus anywhere near Kalangalla? It wouldn't make it up that bloody road.'

Amira smoothed her hair back from her face and knotted it at the base of her neck. 'It's still not a good look.' She shrugged. 'Being an exchange teacher and all.'

'You're such a good role model.' Fiona opened her purse and pulled out a fifty-dollar note. 'Get a bottle anyway. You can have a glass. Actually, get two—one to take back for dinner tonight.'

Amira leaned across the table for the money. 'It's going to be quite the feast, what with your catch of the day and Tess's fish from this morning.'

'Yeah,' said Fiona. 'Now all we need is for someone to spear some hot chips.'

She watched as Amira ambled into the restaurant. Was it her imagination or was she broader across the beam than Fiona remembered her being in Melbourne? You wouldn't think you'd put on weight up here, what with all that bloody healthy living and no grog. Amira was that type though, she mused. She only had to look at food to add an inch to her arse. Tess was gorgeous now, but she was going to be the same once she finished growing. You could see it coming. Fiona sat back in her seat and peered out along the beach below the cliffs. Not that she could talk. Had there ever been a time when she hadn't felt self-conscious about her stomach? And now her hips had joined in, moving past *childbearing* and into a territory where they'd soon need their own postcode. But it was the soul that mattered, not the body—wasn't that what all the womens' magazines were always spouting? She should embrace getting older; it was empowering. The lines deepening around her eyes were a sign of wisdom, of a life spent laughing and loving. Fiona shook her head. If Todd overheard her he'd be only too quick to point out that actually they were from not using sunscreen until her thirties and not giving up smoking for another decade after that. Worse, he'd be right. God, women told each other a heap of crap.

There they were. Fiona could just make out Morag, Caro and the three girls at the edge of the ocean, pulling on flippers and rash tops, Janey's bright hair glinting in the sun. They were welcome to it. There was no way she was going snorkelling, not while she had her period. Every shark in the area would be onto her within minutes. Shit, she was probably meant to embrace that too, wasn't she? The beauty and wonder of her monthly cycle, the miracle of bleeding like a stuck pig, of cramps that knocked the wind out of her and undies that had to be left to soak for days. Beneath the table, the fish that she'd caught twitched in its polystyrene esky. Fiona kicked the box. Wasn't it dead *yet*? She hadn't even gone into the lagoon past her knees, though that black girl had told her it was perfectly safe. Fiona scoffed. She was young but she'd learn. Nothing was safe, never mind perfect.

Amira placed two glasses and a dark green bottle, already sweating, in the centre of the table, then pulled out the seat opposite Fiona.

'I got some more ice for your fish,' she said, tipping it into the esky.

'Good. Hopefully it will freeze to death. I think it thinks it's coming back with us as a pet.'

Amira sat down and reached for the wine Fiona had poured. 'Cheers,' she said, lifting her glass.

'Cheers,' Fiona replied. 'Thanks for staying with me. I'd've hated to have to drink alone.'

'Like that's ever stopped you before.' Amira smiled. 'Did you ring Todd? What's news from home?'

'Nah, couldn't be bothered. I've been gone four days and he hasn't even left a message.'

'He might be busy,' Amira said.

Fiona took a slurp of wine and held it in her mouth, cold and crisp, until it made her teeth ache. Who'd choose snorkelling when they could be doing this? She swallowed, the familiar warmth blooming down her throat and into her stomach. 'Yeah, I bet he's busy . . . busy lying on the couch, busy at the TAB, busy drinking beer with Dom.'

'I'm sure he's missing you anyway,' Amira said.

'It's alright, Amira.' Fiona held her gaze across the table, then reached for the bottle to top up her glass. 'You don't have to pretend. We both know he isn't. Just like I'm not missing him. I'm glad to have a break from all his shit for a while, if you must know.'

Amira opened her mouth to reply, but just then a football came sailing across their table, narrowly missing the wine. Without thinking, Fiona put up her arms and caught it, the warm leather stinging her palms.

'Nice one!' cried the young man bounding to their table to retrieve it. 'Sorry about that, but it was a good mark.' Fiona tossed him the ball and he grabbed it, then peered more closely at her. 'Hey, you ladies were with that blonde girl earlier today, weren't you? Is she still here?'

Fiona winced. *Ladies*. She hated that word.

'She's gone,' she said. 'She was taken by a crocodile just after lunch. Tragic. So young.'

The boy stared at her, then laughed.

'I thought you were serious for a second.'

He was like a labrador puppy, Fiona thought, bouncy and cute and none too bright. A chocolate lab. She stood up from the table. 'I want to play too.'

The boy had started back towards his mates, but turned around at her words. 'What?'

'Kick-to-kick,' Fiona said. 'I want to join in. I used to play it with my husband . . . I'm pretty good. You saw my mark.'

'I don't know . . .' The boy hesitated, trying to work out if she was pulling his leg.

'You would have let the blonde girl play though, wouldn't you?' Fiona said. The sea and the cliffs were spinning slightly, sliding into each other in a blur of red and blue. She must have got up too quickly.

'Probably,' the boy conceded. 'If she was still alive.'

'Hah!' Fiona barked. 'I'm in. Just don't expect me to go easy on you.' She pulled off her shoes and jogged towards the group of youths on the grass, still waiting for their ball. Lady, huh? She'd show him. And it was true, she had played with Todd, years ago when they were first dating. They'd been on a picnic down by the Yarra with some other builders he'd gone to TAFE with. While Todd manned the barbecue, one of them had pulled out a Sherrin, handballing it to her while she stood watching. Fiona had three older brothers and she'd kicked it back without thinking, a long low drop punt that streaked through the air like a missile. Todd had put down his tongs and whistled appreciatively. It was one of the last times she could remember impressing him.

'You go up that end,' the young man said as they reached his teammates. 'Guys,' he called out, 'we have a guest. This is . . .' He looked at her.

'Fiona,' she said, panting slightly. She really had to get back to the gym.

'Fiona,' he repeated, 'and she's got good hands, so watch out.' He tossed her the ball and she grasped it deftly, conscious of the twenty or so pairs of eyes on her. Fuck, she hoped she could remember how to do that drop punt. She walked back to the edge of the grassed area, trying to recall what her brother Stevo had taught her. *Take a few small steps, arm raised for balance . . . drop the ball straight down and meet it with your foot . . . follow all the way through.* As soon as her foot made contact with the leather she knew it was good. The kick was hard and straight, made the distance and then some. A spindly boy at the other end rose up from the pack as if on strings and plucked it out of the air.

'Alright,' grunted the player next to her, then moved to take the mark as the footy flew back. He passed it to her and she kicked again, bare skin stinging as it smacked the red leather. It hurt, but Fiona didn't care. Alright? She was bloody fantastic. If only Todd could see her. She still had it; she'd show them all a thing or two.

The next thing she knew she was flat on her back, staring up at the sky, her mouth filling with blood. The good-looking boy who'd come to their table was bending over her, face anxious.

'Are you OK?' he asked. 'I'm sorry. I shouldn't have kicked it so hard. I thought you'd mark it again, like you did last time.'

Mark it? Fiona closed her eyes. She hadn't even seen it. Her tongue probed for the source of the wound and came up against something gritty. Oh, fuck. Please God, not her teeth.

Someone thumped down beside her. 'Fiona!' Amira shrieked in her ear. 'Are you alright? Do you need a doctor? Can you sit up?' She started tugging at Fiona's blouse and Fiona pushed her away, scared she was going to tear it.

'I'm fine,' she said, struggling to rise. A trickle of blood seeped down her chin and she swiped at it with the back of her hand, embarrassed.

'We need to get you back to the table so I can have a look at you,' Amira said, hauling her to her feet. 'Do you want me to fetch Bronte?'

'What use would she be?' Fiona snapped. She allowed herself to be led away, careful not to meet the gaze of any of the development squad.

Amira eased Fiona into her chair, then dabbed at her mouth with a serviette. 'I think it's OK,' she pronounced. 'You've cut your top lip, but everything else seems intact. Have a rinse with this so I can be sure.' She handed Fiona a glass of water, and Fiona took it obediently, swishing the tepid liquid around her mouth, then spitting it onto the ground.

'Are my teeth all there?' she asked, leaning across the table and opening her mouth as wide as she could.

'They're fine,' said Amira.

A surge of relief washed through Fiona. It must have been dirt she had felt, or sand or grit, something off the football.

'God, I'm an idiot,' she said. The relief was quickly ebbing, replaced by shame. 'Fuck, I thought I was so good, mixing it with the big boys.'

Amira allowed herself to smile. 'You *were* good. Right up until the moment you got one in the gob.' She reached for Fiona's hand. 'It must have hurt. Are you sure you don't want me to find Bronte? We can get going if you like.'

Fiona shook her head. 'I told you, she's no help. She'd only get all upset and go to pieces.'

Amira sighed. 'You're too hard on her, you know. She's a lovely girl—clever, attractive, caring.'

Fiona laughed, then winced. Her lip was throbbing. 'She cares too much, that's her problem. She's always mooning over books or pictures, or fretting about something someone said to her. She couldn't sleep last night, and when I told her to stop tossing and turning she said she kept thinking about what your friend Mason said yesterday, about what happened to his wife's mother.' Fiona peered around the table. Bloody hell, had the waiter cleared the wine while she was off being Jesaulenko? 'If I'm hard on her, as you say, it's because she needs to toughen up. Otherwise the world's going to eat her alive.'

With her free hand, Amira rolled the bloodstained serviette into a ball and dropped it on the table. 'Maybe she needs to find that out herself. Maybe she'll surprise you. And maybe, too, the world would be better off with more people like Bronte in it, people who give a damn.'

'I'm just thinking of her,' Fiona said stubbornly. 'She's smart—she's really smart, you know that. She got that scholarship without even being coached for it, without me lugging her off to Kumon every week like the Asians do with their kids. I just don't want her to waste her opportunities, to end up spending her days caring for sick kittens or homeless people or something, or with a huge mortgage around her neck like us. She's better than that. I want her to have it all.'

'Yeah, but what does *she* want?' Amira asked. 'If it is to look after sick kittens, what are you going to do? You can't change that. Kids are who they are. We all are.'

Fiona risked a glance at the footballers. They'd gone back to their game, leaping and spinning as gracefully as if they were in a ballet. 'I wanted to study volcanoes when I was fourteen,' she said eventually. 'I thought they were fascinating. Still do. The way they just erupt like that and no one can predict it. I told my mum when we had to choose my subjects for year ten, and she laughed at me. Said only really smart people got to do stuff like that, and that I should learn typing instead because it would always come in handy.' She picked up a wine glass although it was empty. Her mouth stung. God, she needed a drink. 'I didn't get a choice, and sometimes I still wonder what would have happened if I had. I'm not going to let Bronte waste hers if it kills me.'

'Oh, Fiona,' Amira said, still holding her hand. 'What are we going to do about you?'

'I'm not sure,' Fiona said. She felt stupidly as if she might cry. It must be the sun, or the knock to her mouth. 'Maybe open that bottle in the esky for a start.'

Thursday

Thump.

Macy's eyes flew open. Something had knocked into her bed. She lay in the half-dark, ears pricked, trying to work out where she was and what was going on. Was it her dad's place this week? In that case it was probably only Torran trying to climb in beside her to snuggle up. Callum and Finn had long since grown too old for that, but while she sometimes pretended to complain whenever Torran came creeping under her doona to wake her up, she was secretly glad he still did it. It felt good to be loved like that, so simply, without strings, to lie in the warmth of two bodies, an arm flung around you, without having to think about how you were going to get home afterwards and if this really was such a great idea.

The room was still. Perhaps she'd dreamed it. Macy closed her eyes. She was just drifting off when it came to her—she wasn't at her dad's or her mum's, she was in Broome. Some place near it, anyway, though 'near' was a relative concept given that interminable red road she'd endured yesterday.

There was another thump, this one heavier.

'Ow!' hissed Morag, then added 'Sorry.'

Macy lay perfectly still, pretending to be asleep, in case Morag thought she'd woken her and took the opportunity to talk. She heard Morag breathing softly, in, out, as she hovered above her in the shadows, then she quietly left the room, latching the screen door behind her.

When she'd gone, Macy turned over, trying to get comfortable. Did the woman ever relax? She'd probably gone for a run, even though she was on holidays. In all the years she'd been spending alternate weeks at her father's house, Macy had never once got up before her stepmother, had invariably sloped into the kitchen with sleep in her eyes to find Morag showered and dressed and just about to put out the second load of washing for the day in between making the boys pancakes. Pancakes! What was wrong with toast or Weetbix? Why did Morag always have to go the extra mile? Once when Macy had returned from her allotted seven-day stay still smarting at some now-long-forgotten rebuke from Morag, she had told her mother about the pancakes. Her mother had sneered, as Macy had known she would, but then added, 'She's probably only doing it to impress you, you know.' The idea had stunned her. Why on earth would Morag be trying to impress *her*? Macy wasn't anyone Morag needed to impress. She was just the stepdaughter, an irrefutable reminder that Morag's husband had once loved—and slept with—someone else. Macy should probably be grateful Morag wasn't chopping her up and mixing her into the batter.

Still, Morag was alright, she thought, pulling the sheet around her body, twisting it tight across her breasts and about her shoulders. She liked it like that, liked the sensation of being swaddled, constrained, gently held in place. Morag was driven and way too neat and got her knickers in a twist about them all having dinner together every night, but otherwise she was OK. She gave Macy her space; she didn't arc up at the smallest thing. Not like her mother . . . Macy clenched her teeth as she remembered the scene of two days previously. So she'd missed her cue. It happened—and it was only a rehearsal, anyway, not the real thing. She'd been getting ready to go on when she'd suddenly had a fab idea about how to end the number. She knew she had to tell someone right that minute or she'd forget, so she'd started looking for the music director. He was usually backstage, watching in the wings like she was, but for once he wasn't there, so instead she'd gone to find Micah, who she knew was rehearsing in the boys' dressing room, awaiting his own call. Micah was cool. He got her, and he loved her idea. She knew he would. They got so involved in talking about it, trying out different harmonies, that she forgot to go back in time. The look on Miss Bateman's face when she found them together . . . silly old cow. It wasn't as if she and Micah had been doing anything other than singing. Everyone knew Micah was gay. Alright, she'd been caught hanging out in the boys' dressing room once before, and yes, that time she was smoking, but chillax! It could have been worse. At least she wasn't going down on them one by one, as she'd once seen Leisa do.

Macy tried to roll over again but the sheet rode up and stopped her, tangling around her neck. She lay there, tethered, staring at the wall, tears welling in her eyes. It was so unfair! She couldn't believe they'd thrown her out of the eisteddfod for that—she was the lead vocalist. And her mother hadn't even taken her side! Janice was probably just worried about how it reflected on her, thinking that everyone would be whispering about how the president of the Parents Association couldn't even control her own daughter. *The goth one, that's right. Sweet voice, but have you seen what she looks like?* Her mother should have just made her apologise and promise never to do it again, should have cut her some slack. That's what parents were for, weren't they? She hadn't asked to be born, and her mother was meant to support her. She was doing year eleven. She was under pressure.

And as for her father . . . normally her dad was pretty relaxed, but this time he'd freaked out too. Sending her all this way for four days was ridiculous, as if she'd self-destruct if she wasn't supervised. Macy groaned. She was sixteen! She could have just stayed at his place—she had the keys, she'd done it before. 'Yeah, and that worked out well, didn't it?' he'd sighed down the phone. Macy knew what he was referring to. A few months earlier when she was arguing with Janice about something or other, Macy had begged to be allowed to stay at Andrew and Morag's house by herself for the weekend while they were away with the boys on one of her dad's beloved camping trips. Morag had been the one who'd talked him in to it, but she was also the one who found the condom wrapper in the bin on Sunday night. Macy had tried to deny any knowledge of it, telling her father that it could have been one of his, but it hadn't worked. 'I haven't used condoms since I was twenty-five,' he'd shouted, then looked at her in disbelief and said, 'I can't believe we're even discussing this.' Morag had just muttered that she hoped Macy had washed her sheets, though of course she had. Duh.

So because of that one stupid little incident she'd had to come here, to the other end of Australia, packed off like a naughty child to boarding school. To kindergarten. How old were those other girls, anyway—twelve, thirteen? She hadn't seen them for a few years, not since Morag had dragged her and the boys along to some ballet recital in a dusty church hall. It was hell in tutus, from what Macy could remember. She'd tried to beg off, but her stepmother was adamant. She intended to support her friends by watching their daughters perform, she'd said. Andrew was away on business, so the four of them—Macy, Callum, Finn and Torran—were coming with her. It had been a disaster. First Torran had dropped the Nintendo he'd smuggled in, which started beeping incessantly, then one of the junior ballerinas, an awkward, gangly one, had leapt in the air and fallen flat on her face, and Macy couldn't stop laughing. Morag, at her wits' end, had shot her a warning glance; when that didn't work she'd reached across and pinched Macy hard on the thigh to still her giggles. The shock was far worse than the pain. Morag had never hurt her before. She was determinedly anti-smacking, and had put Torran through more time-outs than he'd had hot dinners. For the rest of the

184

performance, Macy stared at her lap, flagrantly refusing to watch one more spin or leap. She couldn't be sure, but she'd bet it was the tall one that she'd been introduced to last night who had embarrassed herself at the recital. She still had that look, as if she wasn't quite in control of her arms and legs. Macy's hand went to the slender metal ring in her navel and rotated it gently, feeling it slide through her skin. What was her name—Belinda? No, Bronte. Then there was a dark girl who'd smiled and held out her hand, and the blonde who kept flicking her hair. Macy had seen her type before. They came to auditions expecting to be given the lead role, and ended up in the chorus instead—or dropped out when they realised that the spotlight wasn't going to be on them. Thank God it was only four days.

With an effort, Macy tugged at the sheet caught around her throat and yanked it to her waist. She lay there panting for a moment—the room was already uncomfortably warm—then rolled over and groped for her handbag on the floor. There was no way she'd be able to go back to sleep now, but she didn't want to have to get up and face the playgroup either. She pulled out her iPod, jammed the buds in her ears, lay back and hit shuffle. At first there was only silence. Her skin prickled. She loved this moment, loved the suspense of waiting, the thrill of anticipation, loved the way the music suddenly flooded her mind as if a tap had been turned on. Macy closed her eyes. Drumsticks tapping, then a gentle electric guitar . . . 'One' by U2. She knew it immediately, but then she knew all the thousand or so songs on her iPod, could identify them before the first few notes had faded away. And this was a good one, soothing, hypnotic, perfect for her state of mind. Funny how it was her mother's music really, how she'd only come to love it because Janice had played the album over and over all through Macy's childhood. Strange to connect Janice with such a yearning, passionate song. All her mother ever seemed passionate about now was the Parents Association.

The song finished, and without opening her eyes Macy scrolled back with her thumb, starting it anew. She didn't want to go on to something else; this was the right song for her now. Sometimes she would listen to the same tune eight, nine times in a row if it was speaking to her, and this one, with its themes of hurt and longing, perfectly captured how she felt right now. Music had always done that for her, taken her out of herself, transformed whatever she was feeling into something rich and pure and true. It had consoled her through those years of primary school before her dyslexia was picked up; it had been the backdrop to everything important that had ever happened to her. First kiss, first job; the first time she got drunk, got laid; the first time someone looked at her in astonishment and told her that she could sing, really sing. And it was true. When she sang she wasn't herself anymore, Macy Whittaker. When she sang she was the song.

Except she wasn't going to sing, was she? Macy's mood plummeted again as she remembered the rehearsal and why she was here. 'One' finished for a second time and she lay still in the hush left behind, her stomach churning, sweat breaking out under her arms and between her breasts. It was *so* unfair! It was all wrong. Her mind raced. There were still three weeks until the eisteddfod after she returned from this hell-hole and term four started. She'd work it out somehow; she'd *make* them take her back. Surely by then they'd have realised their mistake? Her understudy was crap.

———

On the wekend we went to one arm poynt to see my auntie and cosins. My mum took me and my sister and my brother. My dad didnt come because he wanted to watch the footy. My cosins are jack and sam and ruby. There house is right near the beach. we went fishing. Jack caught a baramundie and my auntie bort us coke and we had them for tea.

Amira sighed and reached for her pen. She read to the end of the page, then went back and circled the spelling and grammatical errors. By the time she had finished, the essay appeared to have developed chicken pox, every line disfigured by bright red circles. Twelve, she thought in frustration. The student who had written this was twelve years old. He was due to start secondary school next year, yet he didn't seem to know that proper nouns needed a capital letter, or the distinction between *there* and *their*. Her grade three class last year could have done a better job.

She went to the fridge and poured herself a glass of orange juice. The sugar would help, she told herself. She shouldn't be marking with a hangover, but she needed to finish it before the new term started next week, and with the house so quiet it was too good an opportunity to waste. She'd try to get it done before Tess got up, she thought, then she suddenly wondered if Tess was even there. The other girls were bound to be in their beds—on their first day at Kalangalla, Janey hadn't emerged until almost eleven. 'That's the trouble with kids,' Caro had said. 'You can never get babies to sleep, and never get teenagers to wake up.' Amira had laughed—Tess had certainly liked her lie-ins back in Melbourne—but up here she'd changed. Now, some mornings when Amira rose it was to a kitchen with the blinds pulled up and a note on the table that Tess was out swimming or crabbing or simply with Tia and would be back before school or lunch, depending on whether it was a weekday or the weekend. She glanced around to make sure Tess hadn't left her anything, then sat back down to the marking.

The next essay was even worse. Again there were no capital letters, but there were also no commas or full stops. Amira's eyes darted to the smudged name at the top of the page: Jamaya, a skinny girl of nine or ten who was always barefoot. From memory she was in grade four, though it had become apparent to Amira that grades were a fairly arbitrary concept here. They rarely correlated with the same level in the east, and not at all with the new national curriculum that was being so optimistically pushed down everyone's throats. Still, though, grade four. That gave Amira a bit of time to improve Jamaya's reading and writing; there were a couple of years left before she'd need to be ready for high school.

Amira put down her pen. What was she thinking? Time— she didn't have any time. She was going home in January, just three short months away. Going back to a classroom where daily attendance was a given and not a goal, where the kids wore uniforms and shoes and knew to put their hands up to ask a question, where show and tell had never once involved a very angry goanna with a piece of string around its neck as a leash, as it had in her first week here. The thought worried her. In some ways she was looking forward to returning to Melbourne, but she was needed here. She was needed *more* here. If her upper primary students could barely put together a few coherent paragraphs about their weekend, how on earth were they ever going to analyse texts in secondary school, or write the essays they'd need to get through year twelve, or even fill out a job application? She'd known that literacy and numeracy levels would be lower here than in Melbourne, of course she had, but what she hadn't been prepared for was how great the gulf between the two actually was. Some of the older children were still struggling to spell words like *house* and *should* . . . At fourteen, Tess had already had far more education than most of Amira's current class would ever receive. And this was Kalangalla, a relatively stable and solvent community, where by and large her students' parents were still together and might even try to help the kids with their homework, or at least see if they'd done it. She couldn't imagine how bad things must be in some of the really remote areas. It was terrible, it was scandalous even, but it was also somehow oddly inspiring. She had always wanted not just to teach but to make a difference. She could make a difference here.

Tess's bedroom door swung open and her daughter emerged, rubbing her eyes.

'Good morning,' Amira said. 'I wasn't sure if you were even here. No early swim today?'

Tess shook her head, her curly hair fanned out like a halo around her face.

'I thought about it, but I felt too sleepy. It was pretty late last night, wasn't it? And then I started reading instead.'

'Oh? What book?' Amira asked casually. Tess's interest in the written word was still so new, so surprising and gratifying, that she was almost afraid to draw attention to it in case she scared it away.

Tess returned to her bedroom and came out clutching a novel with a purple cover.

'This,' she said, handing it to Amira. 'I got it from your bookcase. I hope you don't mind.'

Amira turned it over to see the title. *The Bell Jar*. Madness, suicide attempts, electroconvulsive therapy . . . did she really want Tess devouring this? Then again, it was preferable to *Twilight*.

'Are you enjoying it? It might still be a bit old for you.'

Tess shrugged, taking back the book. 'There's bits of it I don't get, and it's pretty old-fashioned, but I like Esther, the girl in it. She's not all perfect like the characters in some other books. She doesn't know what she's doing half the time.'

Amira laughed.

'You're right. The author based it on her own life, did you know that? She was a famous poet. I'll show you some of her poems one day.'

Tess didn't reply. She had already sat down at the table and started to read. Amira collected her marking together and went to turn on the kettle, dropping a kiss on Tess's head as she passed.

'Yesterday went well,' she said five minutes later, placing two steaming cups of coffee on the table.

'Thanks,' said Tess, pulling the sugar bowl towards her. 'Wajarrgi, you mean? Yeah, I think everybody liked it.' She looked up and grinned. 'Having all those hot boys there helped. Janey said it was the best day so far.'

Amira shook her head in resignation. 'Janey would.'

'Did you notice she was drinking last night?' Tess asked. 'Her mum let her have a glass of wine at dinner, but she kept refilling it when no one was looking.'

'That's the Italian way, I guess, to have some wine at meals. They probably do it at home, too.'

'Well, I don't think it's the Italian way to end up spewing in the bushes, like Janey did before she went to bed. Didn't you see? Over by the laundry for the campers. It was disgusting.'

Amira paused as she was lifting her cup to her mouth. She hadn't seen. She'd had no idea, probably because she'd had more than a few glasses of wine herself.

'Does Caro know?'

'I doubt it. You lot were carrying on so much you wouldn't have looked up if George Clooney had strolled in naked.' Tess wiped her mouth. 'Mind you, all that shrieking would have driven him away before then.'

'Oh dear.' Amira flushed. 'Were we really that bad?'

'Pretty much,' Tess said, then smiled. 'It's OK. You were funny. You've missed them, haven't you? There's no one here you laugh with like that.'

Amira nodded. It was true.

'Was Janey OK?' she asked. She felt guilty that she hadn't noticed what was going on, but really, she told herself, it was Caro's problem.

'I think so. Macy was with her when she was sick. She held her hair up.'

'That was nice of her,' Amira mumbled. More guilt. She'd barely said anything more than hello to Macy herself. Probably too busy shrieking, if you asked Tess.

'Not really,' Tess went on. 'Janey was only drinking that much because Macy was there. She never does it around us.' She opened her book again, cracking the spine to lay it flat on the table.

Amira winced.

'What's she like, Macy? Do you all get on OK?'

Tess grunted. 'Too soon to tell. She doesn't want to be here, that's for sure. She spent most of the night going on about how she should be at rehearsals. To be honest, it was a relief when Janey started chucking. Far more entertaining.'

Amira laughed, then put her hand to her head. The coffee hadn't helped her hangover.

'Hey,' Tess said a minute later, still reading *The Bell Jar*. 'Esther says there's nothing like puking with someone to make you old friends.' She looked up, eyes merry. 'Janey and Macy will be set, then.'

Janey wandered aimlessly back towards the room she shared with her mother. She didn't really want to go there, but what other choice did she have? She couldn't hang around out here by herself. Everyone would think she had no mates. She sighed and pushed her sunglasses back up her nose. Ten minutes outdoors and she was already sweating. This climate was a joke. She went over in her mind all the places she'd tried, making sure she hadn't missed any. First the big outdoor eating area by the barbecues where they'd had dinner last night—no one there. Next she'd gone to the shop, half expecting to find Tess and Bronte lolling on the grass under the trees outside it, but the shady green expanse was empty save for two lorikeets squabbling near the rubbish bin. She'd bought a can of Coke because her mother wasn't there to tell her not to, drank half, then threw it away as soon as it started to get warm. The church and art gallery were similarly deserted. Where *was* everyone? It had been a late night but surely they were up by now. It was almost lunchtime.

Janey let the screen door bang behind her, and for want of anything else to do, lay down on her bed with a magazine. It was one of Fiona's that she hadn't yet read, but every story felt familiar and formulaic. *Celebrity post-baby bodies. Easy ways to spice up your marriage. Forty magical ways with mince.* God, why would you even bother with *one*? She tossed it aside and stared at the ceiling. Maybe she should have gone with her mother after all. Then again, three hours in a boat, under that sun, just bobbing up and down . . . She'd bet that Caro wasn't feeling quite as enthusiastic about it right now as she had been when she'd announced her plans at dinner the previous evening.

'Fishing?' Janey had asked her. 'You don't even like fishing.'

'You don't know that,' her mother had replied. 'I've never tried it.'

'Fishing gets you dirty,' Janey muttered. 'It's not your scene.'

Amira leaned over and topped up Caro's glass. 'That's great, Caro. Who are you going with?'

'Mason invited me,' Caro said, flushed from the heat and the alcohol. 'I ran into him just after we got back from Wajarrgi.'

'No wonder you're going.' Fiona cackled. 'Bet you can't wait to jump into *his* boat.' She paused for effect. 'I'm sure he has a sturdy vessel.'

Morag almost choked at that, spraying a mouthful of wine across the table.

'The invitation's open to everyone!' Caro protested. 'You should come.'

'Nah,' Fiona said. 'I think this is a pleasure cruise just for two. I wouldn't want to rock the . . . vessel.'

All the mothers had just about asphyxiated, they were laughing so much, Janey recalled. What had Fiona meant, though? *Vessel. Pleasure cruise.* Surely she didn't think that Janey's mother was interested in that man who'd spent so long haranguing them about what had happened to his wife, or whatever it was. God. Imagining her mother attracted to anyone was bad enough, but a black man? Surely not. Her mother was too . . . neat for that. Caro liked her things coordinated, all matchy-matchy. She was nutty about it, and there was no way a black man would fit into any of her colour schemes. Janey giggled and rolled onto her side.

God, she was bored. She almost wished she had a training session to go to, though she'd never really swum for the love of it but rather because it was something she could *do*, something she excelled at. Probably the only thing, she thought, then immediately pushed the notion from her mind. That first race, at a school carnival, when she was, what—seven, eight? Churning through the water, touching the wall, then looking around to find to her astonishment that not only had she won but that the others were still going some metres back. The look on her mother's face, the fuss everyone had made of her ... It still felt wonderful, touching first; it was what drove her through the water and the endless squad sessions, only now the stakes were higher, the margins smaller. State championships were only eight weeks away. She pictured it in her mind, the way her coach had taught her to: standing behind the blocks, swinging her arms to keep the blood flowing through them from her warm-up. Pulling down her goggles onto her face, pushing against them with the flat of her palm to force the air out and make them watertight. The whistle blowing ... stepping up onto the block, staring down at the water. *Take your marks.* Her fingers curling around the lip of the block, pulling back, hard, so as to maximise her propulsion into the pool. The sharp retort of the gun, the sweet relief to finally be in the water, racing, rather than forever thinking about it, preparing for it. Streamline, pull, one kick, surface ... Then the race, one long red ache, her muscles alight with pain, every breath torn out of her lungs ... turn, streamline, resist the temptation to glance around, see how she was doing. *Swim your own race*, her coach was always telling her, and so she would, she did, she swam and swam and swam until she hit the touchpad and her name flashed up first on the giant scoreboard.

Only, just say it didn't? Just say it was second, or third, or not even in the medals at all? Janey felt a chill go over her,

her skin erupting into goosebumps despite the heat. The other swimmers would give her a hug and say, 'Bad luck,' though they would be secretly pleased; her coach would smile at her but somehow shake his head at the same time. And her mother . . . her mother would put on a brave face and say it didn't matter, but what the fuck would she know?

Janey jumped up from the bed. She needed to do something, she needed to sweat and pant, she shouldn't just be lying around. The beach, she thought, rummaging through her chest of drawers for the only one-piece swimsuit she'd brought. The lagoon was pretty sheltered—she could get in some training there, or at least do some strength work on the sand. She might even run into the others, though suddenly that didn't seem so urgent anymore.

Janey noticed them halfway through her swim. It was the smoke that gave them away, the scent drifting across the mirror-flat lagoon, taken in at a gulp as she breaststroked across it. She stopped and trod water, sniffing the air, fearful of a bushfire, but when she traced the fine haze back to its source she saw it was just two people sitting cross-legged about twenty metres away on the rocks that jutted out into the sea, each with a cigarette in their hands. She shaded her eyes, making sure they weren't going to spear her or something, then resumed her drill. One of them was Tia, she thought, concentrating on her stroke, on snapping her ankles together midway through each kick. Tess had introduced them on the first day at Kalangalla. Janey had wondered if she was meant to shake her hand, but she hadn't, making do with a little half-wave instead. Tia had looked grubby, dressed in a faded yellow t-shirt and an old pair of men's jeans cut off at the knees. Janey didn't understand people who didn't make an effort. Four days later, as far as she could tell from this distance, it appeared that Tia was still wearing the same top.

They were probably watching her, Janey reflected, flipping over into backstroke. People did. She was always being told what a lovely style she had, how natural she looked in the water. Could Aborigines swim? She didn't think so. They were good runners—Cathy Freeman was still doing Coles ads on TV on the back of her solitary gold medal—and she thought she could recall hearing about one winning Wimbledon once. But swimming? Nah. They must be admiring her, watching her streak through the water and wishing they could do it too. She changed to freestyle, putting her head down and sprinting as fast as she could, until the sky blurred into the sea and everything spun.

When she'd finished her program she made her way towards the rocks. It would be rude not to say hello, after all. They might even have some questions for her.

'Hi,' she said, floating on her stomach just beneath them. The second person, she could now see, was a dark man in his late teens or early twenties. He was lighting another cigarette; judging from the number of butts scattered around him on the rocks, he'd been smoking the whole time he was there. 'It's Tia, isn't it? I'm Janey. Tess introduced us.'

'I remember,' Tia mumbled. Her eyes were red, Janey noticed. It must be the smoke. 'This is Jago,' she added, thumbing in the direction of her companion. Janey could feel him watching her, checking out her arse through the crystal-clear sea. She felt a flush of pleasure. It was a good arse, firm and high from all those laps. Her mother had told her once when she'd had a few wines that one day Janey would have to choose, that as women aged it was either the face or the arse that went, and you couldn't keep both. What bullshit, Janey thought, enjoying Jago's gaze on her, his eyes on her breasts, her legs. She was going to keep both. She intended to have it all.

'You've been goin' pretty hard,' he drawled, exhaling.

'Thanks. I'm in training. Got states coming up soon.'

'States?' Jago narrowed his eyes, peering down at her as if she were something he'd just caught and wasn't sure what to do with.

'State championships. Swimming. I'm the current record holder in the hundred-metre breaststroke for girls fourteen and under. Might go to nationals if I win again this time.'

'Nationals, eh?' Jago whistled. 'Fuck me.' Janey grinned, warmed by his approbation, but he hadn't finished. 'You whiteys are a joke. You're at one of the most beautiful beaches in the world'—he removed his cigarette from his mouth and gestured across the sweep of turquoise and white—'and you're fuckin' trainin'.' He laughed, a hard, closed-up sound. 'That's fucked. No wonder you lot never look happy.'

Janey flinched. *Whitey*. Had she just been racially abused?

'Yeah, well, it's better than sitting around getting pissed all day,' she snapped, then turned and swam for shore before he could respond. Whitey. How dare he? And she'd been thinking too that he was really quite handsome. For an abo, anyway.

———

'You feelin' OK?' Mason asked. 'Not seasick or anything?'

Caro shook her head. They were a long way out, the Kalangalla beach now just a smudge behind them, but still the ocean was serene and unruffled, no more frightening than a paddling pool.

'I feel great,' she said. '*This* is great. Thanks so much for inviting me.'

'No problem.' He grinned, cutting the small motor on the dinghy. 'You come all this way, you might as well see as much as you can . . . the real stuff, not all that hokum they would have fed you yesterday. It's a shame none of your mates wanted to join us.'

Caro didn't think so. 'Morag can't be in the sun for too long, and Fiona's probably still asleep. Besides,' she added, looking around, 'it would have been a bit crowded, wouldn't it?' The tiny boat was laden with lobster pots, an array of tackle, assorted strands of rope and a few fraying lifejackets. She reached for one, pulling it closer to her just in case. For a second she wished Janey was with them. If anyone had to swim for help, she'd be the best bet.

'What's that girl of yours doin'?' Mason asked, as if he knew what she was thinking about.

'Oh, I think she wanted a quiet morning,' Caro said vaguely. 'It was a big day at Wajarrgi, then we had a late night.' The truth was that she hadn't actually invited Janey. Janey hated fishing, she told herself, and it was good for the two of them to have a bit of a break from each other. There was no need to feel guilty.

Mason nodded. 'They've got their own agendas, haven't they? My Tia's the same.' He turned away from her, scanning the limpid sea. 'Got a good haul of trevally round here the day before last, just drift fishin' with the net. Might have another go at it.'

Caro couldn't for the life of her see how this patch of blue could be distinguished from any other, but nodded politely. She watched as Mason stood up and removed his shirt, tucking it into the bow of their craft.

'The net's pretty mucky,' he said in explanation. 'Full of fish guts and seaweed. Aki'll go off at me if I ruin another top.' He gathered the net to his chest from a puddle in the floor of the boat, then straightened up, made some adjustment with his wrists, and flung it effortlessly, a sheet of mesh, across the glittering sea. The muscles in his back flexed and stretched; his strong arms cast off the heavy net as if it was a cobweb.

'Now we wait,' he said, sitting back down. 'Do you want to throw a handline in too?'

'That's OK,' Caro replied, distracted. She couldn't care less about a handline. She just wanted to watch him do that again.

'You know, they used to round up the blackfellas and make them dive out here, all along the coast.' Mason pulled down his hat to shade his face.

'Dive?' said Caro. 'What, from the cliffs?'

'Nah, from the luggers. Pearling. The blokes in charge would go into the bush, round up as many darkies as they could find, put them on a boat and keep them goin' up and down, bringin' up oysters, from sunrise to sunset.'

Caro was shocked. 'That's awful!' she said.

Mason gave a dry little chuckle. 'Yeah. The romance of the pearl, eh? Blackbirding, they called it. It wasn't just the menfolk, either. Gins and kids got roped in too. They say they used to send them down thirty, forty foot; the captains had big sticks they'd use to stop them climbin' back on deck till they'd got a bagful.' He observed her silence. 'They didn't tell you that at Wajarrgi, hey?'

'No,' Caro mumbled.

Mason looked out to sea. 'It's no secret. It's in the museum at Broome, if you get a chance to have a look when you're back there. Wajarrgi just want everything pretty, just want to tell you about the Dreamtime and corroborees. They don't want to make you feel guilty when you're payin' for stuff. Bad for business.'

'God,' said Caro. 'Children too. You must all hate us.'

'Nah.' Mason laughed. 'I mean, some do, but not everyone. There's always a few, aren't there? On both sides. And your boss man apologised.'

Caro couldn't read the tone of his voice, couldn't tell if he appreciated the intention behind Sorry Day or was mocking it. Before she could ask him, Mason sprang to his feet.

'We've got ourselves dinner. There's somethin' in the net.'

He leaned over the side of the boat, making it lurch alarmingly, tugging the catch towards him. As it came closer, Caro saw that they'd snagged a turtle, its flippers waving helplessly in the weave.

'Oh, how gorgeous!' she exclaimed. 'Can I pat him?' The creature was every bit as large as the one Bronte had ridden behind on their first afternoon at the beach, its ancient shell encrusted with barnacles. It reminded her of the friendly sea turtle Crush from *Finding Nemo*. Janey had loved that DVD, had gone through a stage as a toddler of demanding to view it the moment she woke up.

'What?' said Mason, busy wrestling the enormous animal into the dinghy. 'Hey, can you give me a hand? We'll get some nice steaks out of this one.'

Caro froze. He wasn't going to kill it, was he? Not Crush. You couldn't eat Crush. God, the thought was dreadful. She started to protest, then shut her mouth. It was just a turtle, she told herself. It was probably like a cow to them, as natural as eating beef. Hadn't she been celebrating Aboriginal culture yesterday, at Wajarrgi? Hadn't she said something to Morag about how important it was to try to bridge the gap, to understand each other as races? Yet today, the moment she was confronted with something personally unpalatable from that very same culture she was ready to condemn it. Worse, to tell Mason to stop—Mason, whose ancestors had been forced by hers to dive until their ears must have bled, until their joints bubbled with nitrogen and their lungs screamed for air.

The turtle gave a powerful heave, fighting to return itself to the ocean.

'Grab it!' Mason yelled.

Caro lunged from her seat but then hesitated, unsure what to do. The creature had extricated itself from the net and was frantically trying to clamber over the bow. Gingerly, she reached for its shell, but her hands slid off the slimy surface. Mason thumped to his knees beside her, rocking the boat. He grabbed the animal by its back flippers, but was similarly unable to maintain his grip. With a mighty push, the turtle slipped from his grasp and into the water.

'Damn,' muttered Mason, wiping his palms on his shorts. 'We'll need the net again. The old fella's not gettin' away that easily.' He hastily gathered the net in his arms and heaved it in the direction that the turtle had escaped, but the throw was jerky, and one edge of the webbing snagged on a rowlock.

'I'll fix it,' Caro sang out. Here at last was something she could manage. She hurried to the side of the dinghy and reached down into the water to lift the net away from the boat. It was surprisingly bulky and she was struggling with it when a sharp pain burst along the underside of one wrist and up to her elbow. 'Shit!' she cried, dropping on to the floor of the boat and clutching her arm. For a second she thought the turtle had either bit or scratched her, but then she saw it was gone, just a dark shape gliding out to sea.

'What've ya done?' Mason was suddenly beside her, his dark eyes worried.

'I don't know,' whimpered Caro. The pain was deepening, spreading, moving out into her fingertips and up towards her shoulder.

'Show me,' he said, slowly peeling her arm away from where she'd cradled it against her chest.

'Fuck!' she screamed, the movement unleashing a further, denser level of torment. Bile rose in her throat and for a moment she was terrified she would vomit onto Mason's feet.

He bent over her arm and whistled.

'Somethin's got you good,' he said, his tone sympathetic. 'That hurts, doesn't it?'

Caro glanced down. The skin along her forearm was covered with a thick mat of raised welts, red-white and pulsing. Tears rolled down her cheeks. Yes, it fucking well hurt.

'Is it Irukandji?' she asked fearfully, remembering something Morag had read out from her guidebook on the plane. *Highly toxic*, she recalled, then something else: *Can be fatal*. 'Oh God,' she moaned, 'am I going to die?'

Mason carefully placed her arm in her lap, then went to scrabble through the gear at the back of the boat. He returned bearing an old plastic milk container filled with clear liquid, which he poured without ceremony over her welts. Caro screamed again, sunbursts of fresh pain exploding behind her eyes, her uninjured hand shooting out to support herself as she thought she might faint.

'Sorry,' Mason said. He softly placed his large hand over her own. 'Are you OK? It's vinegar. It'll help. I know it doesn't feel like it, but it will.'

Caro's teeth chattered. A seagull squawked overhead, and she felt the noise go through her, travel along each and every nerve.

Mason bent over her arm again, inspecting her wounds.

'It's not Irukandji,' he reassured her. 'You don't get anythin' like this with those—often people can't even see where they've been stung. It's not box jellyfish, either.'

'Are you sure?' asked Caro. The throbbing was receding

slightly, enough so that she could open her eyes. 'How can you tell?'

'You'd be dead by now,' Mason replied. He took a final look, then straightened up. 'I'm guessin' it was a hair jelly. A snottie, we call it. It's harmless, apart from the pain, but we'll get you back to shore so they can have a look at it at the clinic. I've got some Panadeine Forte in my kit, then I'll get you lying down. You'll feel better that way.' He squeezed her good hand. 'It was pretty bad, eh? A shame when we were havin' such a good day.' Mason leaned towards her. For a second Caro thought he was going to kiss her, felt her own body instinctively lean in—and then he gently picked up her arm and positioned it once more against her body.

The clouds moved so fast, she thought, watching them race overhead from her position in the bottom of the dinghy. It was surprisingly comfortable, her head and shoulders cushioned by a nest of lifejackets, her feet resting on her beach bag. Or maybe it was the boat that was travelling quickly . . . Mason had been right to have her lie down; she never could have clung on sitting up with her injured arm. And the sky was such a rich blue, too. She hadn't noticed before. Azure, you'd call it, or maybe lapis. Cerulean? Was that even a word? She'd have to ask Bronte. Bronte would know.

Caro felt herself drifting off. The Panadeine had kicked in and left her light-headed and slightly high; the release from pain was such a relief as to almost be an opiate itself. It was lucky Mason had the tablets and the vinegar, otherwise he would have had to pee on her welts. Isn't that what people did? She'd seen it on an episode of *Friends* once, when Monica got stung by a bluebottle. Caro giggled. Imagine that, imagine Mason having to tug down his shorts and urinate all over her. Instead he was prepared. *Be prepared.* He was a good little Scout. She twisted her head around to tell him, but as she did so she heard something—fainter at first, then more distinct. A humming, a low drone rising and building as if a light plane was flying towards them, or a swarm of bees. Yet apart from the clouds the sky was clear. Blue and clear. She shook her head, noticed Mason cock his. Still the noise. 'What's that?' she asked.

'Nothing,' he replied. 'Forget about it. Lie back down. If you move too much your arm will start hurtin' again.'

She must have fallen asleep. There was the crunch of sand beneath the hull; there was Mason bending over her and lifting her to his chest. His heartbeat thudded against her ear as he carried her across the beach and then along the path beneath the trees, the long boab branches above drowsily waving at her through the warm air. She started to wave back, then winced as she lifted her arm.

'You're awake now, huh?' Mason said. 'I'm going to take you to your room, then get some ice and the nurse, if I can find her.'

'Thank you,' Caro murmured. She could smell him, his still-bare chest, a delicious mixture of sun and saltwater. Had Alex ever carried her like this? She didn't think so. She'd be scared he'd hurt his back if he tried.

Mason reached their collection of rooms and went to hers without needing to be directed. He opened the screen door with his elbow and then lowered her onto the bed. The room was dark and cool; Caro's head fell back gratefully against the pillow. Here, she thought. Here was her chance to seduce him, to entice him to lie down with her. All she had to do was loosen her sarong, get her t-shirt over her head . . . Her fingers went to her waist, but it was all too much. She had fallen asleep before Mason even left the room.

———

Twisties, Cheezels, Cheetos . . . packets and packets of them, their bright yellow graphics clamouring for her attention. Bronte dropped her gaze to the next shelf. Corn chips, crinkle-cut chips, thinly cut chips, Noodle Snax . . . what the hell were Noodle Snax? Below those were at least eight varieties of Kettle chips, tubes of Pringles and bags of Burger Rings. There were only two aisles in the tiny Kalangalla shop, and most of one was filled to overflowing with chips.

'It's pretty bad, isn't it?' said a voice behind her. Bronte turned to find Amira peering at the same display, a plastic basket over one arm. 'I came in to get some stuff for a salad for tonight, but all they've got is some spinach and a few old pineapples. Looks like we'll be eating Cheetos instead.'

'It does seem a bit . . . excessive,' Bronte replied. It was no wonder so many of the kids in the community were fat. She'd noticed it in her first couple of days here, how they'd saunter around with a Coke in one hand, a packet of chips in the other—and not just a can of Coke but a two-litre bottle, and the family-size bag of chips. It made her feel a bit sick, to be honest, but she could hardly say that to Amira without sounding judgemental. And at least there wasn't any alcohol here, as Amira kept pointing out, but Bronte wondered if replacing it with junk food was much of a step forward.

She moved down the aisle, Amira following behind her. 'What were you after?' Amira asked.

'A new sketchbook,' Bronte said. 'I've filled up the one I brought with me. I didn't expect to—there were heaps of pages left—but there's been so much that I wanted to get down, to show my teacher back home.'

Amira smiled. 'That's fantastic. I'd love to see your drawings. Have you shown them to your mum?'

Bronte hesitated. Show them to her mother? What, and have her laugh like she did when Bronte had shown her the card from the modelling agency? Not a chance. Bronte would rather go naked to the beach than show her mother her sketchbook. 'Not really,' she eventually answered.

Amira regarded her for a moment, basket propped on one ample hip.

'You should,' she said. 'And Fiona should look. I'll make her, if you like. I'll withhold all wine until she does.'

Bronte laughed to cover the stab of jealousy she felt. Did Tess know how lucky she was? 'It's OK,' she said. 'Mum and I are into different things. I get that.'

'Yes, but—' Amira broke off as Macy came around the end of the aisle, a scowl on her face.

'This place sucks,' she said. 'I had to get packed so quickly I forgot to bring any toiletries. I realised on the plane, but then I thought I'd be able to buy them up here, you know, like in any decent civilisation, but all this dump has is two bars of soap and a packet of dental floss.'

'I'm surprised by the dental floss,' Amira said. 'I'll buy it if you're not going to.'

Macy had the grace to smile. She was pretty when she did that, Bronte thought, despite the ring in one nostril and the studs through her eyebrow, despite her white-painted face and black-rimmed eyes. She might have forgotten her toothpaste, but she'd clearly remembered her make-up.

'Knock yourself out,' Macy said, then added, 'How do you survive up here?'

'I drive to Broome once a month and do a big shop at Coles. That tides us over. I usually only come in here for bread, which they bake next door, or fruit and veg. Not that there's much of that today.' Amira paused. 'There is something like a supermarket up the road at One Arm Point, though. Why don't we go there? It's expensive, but I need to get the salad for tonight, and I know they've got plenty of other stuff. You could probably get that sketchbook, Bronte, and there's sure to be shampoo and what have you.'

'Is that a black "up the road" or a white "up the road"?' Macy asked suspiciously. 'I don't want to spend two days travelling through the Kimberley just so I can brush my teeth.'

Amira laughed. 'You're a quick learner. White. It won't take long—ten minutes or so each way. If we go now we'll be back in an hour. Tess has gone to see Tia, so I don't have to worry about her—do you two need to check with your mothers?'

'Mum went off for a nap after lunch,' said Bronte. 'She's

been doing it every day. Says it's too hot to go to the beach before four, so I told her I'd see her then.'

'I don't need to check,' said Macy. 'My mother's four thousand kilometres away.'

One Arm Point was a bit of a ghost town, Bronte thought as she sat on a graffiti-scarred bench outside the supermarket waiting for Macy and Amira. It was much bigger than Kalangalla, but there didn't seem to be anyone around, only an old Aboriginal woman shuffling away from the store with a packet of cornflakes tucked under her arm. Maybe they were at work, but what was there to do here? The community appeared devoid of any industry whatsoever, lay stunned before her, its dusty streets shimmering in the oppressive afternoon air.

Bronte flicked through the blank pages of her new sketchbook, mesmerised as always by their creamy possibility, then pulled from her backpack the one she'd already filled. A surge of pride ran through her as she studied her work. The first few drawings weren't great, she knew that—too stilted, self-conscious, her hand stiff around her pencil—but oh, the rest . . . Ms Drummond was always telling her to relax, to let the lines emerge rather than trying to force them onto the paper, and Bronte had nodded, but she'd never really understood what she meant until now. This sketch of a dog, for example, that she'd done in charcoal—it was just a dog, fast asleep in someone's front yard, but it looked as if it might yawn and stretch at any minute, might cock one eye at you while scratching behind a mangy ear . . .

'Did you do that?' asked Macy, peering over her shoulder. 'It's fantastic. Show me the rest.'

They were still looking at the sketchbook when Amira joined them ten minutes later. Macy wasn't so scary when she was like this, Bronte thought. At first she'd assumed the older girl was just being polite, but then she could have stopped after a page or two. Instead she'd taken the book onto her lap and gone through it, drawing by drawing, right from the start, examining every detail. She was so relaxed, Bronte thought. There had only been four or five other customers in the shop, but each had stopped in their tracks and stared as Macy went by. Bronte could hardly blame them—Macy certainly stood out, dressed as she was all in black and with her piercings and heavy make-up—but didn't Macy *mind*? She certainly didn't seem to. It was bizarre. Most of the time Bronte wished she was invisible. It was bad enough having people gawk at you because of something you couldn't help, like your stupid height, but why invite that sort of attention?

'We've been pretty quick,' said Amira, checking her watch. 'Do you want to call into the hatchery on the way back? It's fascinating—they've got about twenty small pools, filled with local tropical fish and turtles, and you can handfeed them all. I was actually thinking of suggesting we all came up and visited tomorrow morning.'

'I don't think Caro will want to go near any more turtles for a while,' said Macy.

'Oh God, no,' said Amira, clapping a hand to her mouth. 'Oh, that was awful, the poor girl. She showed me her arm when I took her in some lunch. It was like someone had whipped her, all bright red and—'

'Shhh,' Bronte said. She didn't mean to be rude, but she wanted to listen. Ever since she'd come out of the supermarket she'd noticed a faint hum in the air, a murmuring. At first she'd assumed it was some kind of insect, but it was gradually getting louder, building into a buzz, a throb . . . a voice. Voices, more than one, raised together, growing, soaring, pulsing towards her across the red earth.

The others heard it too. For a moment they all stayed perfectly still, not looking at each other, absorbing the sound. Macy broke the spell. 'What is it?' she asked.

'Someone's died,' Amira said. 'Probably an elder, someone important in the community. The dead person's family and some of the other adults are singing the spirit home, so it leaves the area and returns to its birthplace, where it can be reborn.'

'Wow,' Bronte said. 'Have you heard it before?'

'Just once, though it would have been different. Every funeral song is. The Aborigines sing the sacred names of the dead person's waterhole and country, so their spirit will be enticed there.' Amira hugged herself as if she was cold. 'I did some reading about it after I heard it the first time. It scared me a bit, I have to say. It sounded so eerie. The song gets right inside you, like the wind. But it's beautiful too, isn't it?'

'It's amazing,' Macy said. 'I'd love my friend Micah to hear it. I wonder if we could do something like that together?'

Amira shook her head. 'You can't. It's not yours; it belongs to them. Anyone who hears it today and knows the person who has died will join in. It might go for hours—for days, sometimes.'

The song wound between them, a wail, a chant, insinuating itself under their skin. Bronte closed her eyes and gave herself up to it, felt it vibrate in her bones. She wondered if they could hear it back at Kalangalla. Her mum was *really* going to hate that.

———

'Right, who's next?' Janey's eyes narrowed, peering around for her next target. 'Macy,' she pronounced. 'You haven't had a go yet. Truth or dare?'

Macy had her earbuds in and lay, oblivious, on her towel with her eyes closed behind her sunglasses. Tess had been surprised when she'd joined them for their late afternoon swim—you never usually saw goths at the beach—but Macy had pulled off her long, shapeless dress to reveal a tiny bikini, and gone straight in. It was black, of course. Black hair, black nails, black bathers. You had to admire that degree of dedication.

'I don't think she can hear you,' Bronte said unnecessarily, her own skin covered by a sarong and a cotton shirt with the collar up and sleeves buttoned to her wrists.

'Duh,' Janey replied, then leaned across the sand and pulled out the nearest earbud.

The older girl's eyes shot open.

'Fuck, Janey, I was listening to that.'

'Truth or dare?' Janey repeated, then, as Macy snatched

the earbud back, quickly said, 'Truth, then. How old were you when you first had sex?'

'Janey!' Bronte exclaimed.

Macy rolled onto her stomach, turning her head away from them. 'As if I'm going to tell you. It's none of your business.'

'It's a game.' Janey pouted. 'I'd tell you.'

You mean you'd make it up, Tess thought, but didn't have the guts to say the words out loud. Instead she caught Bronte's eye and raised one eyebrow.

'Hah.' Macy jeered. 'Because you're soooo experienced, right? Like with the wine last night at dinner.'

Janey coloured. 'I've had boyfriends. Plenty of them.'

'Macy, do you want me to put some sunscreen on your back?' Bronte interjected. 'You can still get burnt, even at this time of day.'

'Nah. I'll put my clothes on in a minute,' Macy said. 'I'm just enjoying the warmth. It still felt like winter in Melbourne when I left. God, it's amazing here.'

Tess smiled to herself and picked up *The Bell Jar*. It was. She loved this time of day almost as much as she loved the clear, still mornings; loved how the sun turned the water golden as it sank in the sky, loved the cicadas warming up and the cool caress of the first evening breezes.

'You lot are so *boring*,' Janey complained. 'Worrying about sunscreen. Reading books.' She glared at Tess. 'I'm surprised you didn't bring your knitting with you—or maybe we should have a nice game of bingo. It's all so lame. What happened to Truth or Dare?'

'Fine,' Macy said, raising her head. 'I've got a dare for you, Janey: a skinny dip. In the lagoon.'

'Now?' asked Janey. 'It's broad daylight.'

'Hey, you wanted to play,' Macy said. 'Are you chicken?' She started making clucking noises at the back of her throat. '*Burk, burk, burk burk.*'

Tess couldn't help herself. She giggled.

'I'm not chicken!' Janey protested. 'But I'm not doing it by myself. You'd probably all run off with my clothes or something. I'm only doing it if everyone does . . . but I bet you're all too gutless.'

Tess swallowed. She'd swum once or twice at night without her clothes, but only when there was no moon and she was certain she wouldn't get caught.

'No way,' said Bronte. 'I can't even bear to look at myself naked. You'd all just laugh.'

Macy stood up. '*I* will,' she said, hooking her thumbs through the sides of her bikini bottoms and pulling them down, then undoing the top. Both pieces fell to the sand, and she casually stepped out of them, completely unselfconscious. 'Bronte, you're mad,' she said, but not unkindly. 'You've got a fabulous body. The best of all of us.' Then she turned and started walking towards the sea, her petite pale buttocks rising and falling with each step.

'Wow,' breathed Bronte. 'Did you *see*?'

Tess nodded. Not only was Macy's navel pierced, as they'd already noticed, but both her nipples were too—a small silver ring through one, two diamante studs adorning the other.

'That's gotta hurt,' she said. 'I wonder if her mum knows? Or Morag?'

'As if,' Janey snapped. 'God, what a show-off. She only suggested that dare so we'd have to look at her. She's such a fake.'

'The dare was for you,' Tess said. 'You were the one that said we all had to do it—and I notice you've still got your bathers on. If anyone's a fake it's you.' The words were out of her mouth before she could stop them; grew wings and flew away across the turquoise lagoon, where Macy was paddling in the shallows.

Janey swung around, face red. 'You bitch! You total bitch. It's not like you were ever going to get your gear off either, you're so bloody uptight. And you.' She turned to Bronte. 'Macy needs a guide dog. Fabulous body, my arse. You should be in a fucking circus.' She jumped up and started sprinting up the beach, towards the community, then spun around and yelled, 'Don't you go anywhere! We haven't finished this game yet. I'm coming back.'

Bronte made a small strangled sound. Tess put a hand on her arm. 'Are you OK?' she asked, then realised that Bronte was laughing, not crying.

'Oh, the look on her face when you said she was a fake. I thought she was going to explode!' Bronte giggled. 'And when Macy took off her bathers! Janey knew she'd been outplayed. It was beautiful. It was worth coming on this trip just for that.'

Tess grinned. It had been funny, though she couldn't say why. She'd just insulted her best friend—she should be feeling remorse, not this soaring elation, this adrenalin. 'I think I need a swim after that,' she said. 'Shall we join Macy?'

'That was sick,' Macy said as the three of them walked back to their towels. 'The water's so warm it's almost like having a bath. I could stay in there all day. I might tomorrow.' She paused to squeeze the moisture from her hair, silver droplets running down her wrists. 'Though maybe I'll wear bathers. Don't want to give Morag a heart attack—or have her telling Dad on me.'

'Do you think she would?' Tess asked, glancing again at Macy's nipples. It was hard not to look at them, the two diamantes flashing in the sun.

Macy shrugged. 'Maybe. Maybe not. It would depend on how much I'd pissed her off at the time.' She retrieved her dress and pulled it over her head, extinguishing the tiny lights on her chest.

Tess lay down on her towel without drying herself. There was no point. It was almost five, but the air was still balmy; would be for another few hours.

Bronte reached for her shirt. 'Where do you think Janey went? To check on her mum?'

'I doubt it,' Tess said. 'That would involve having to think about someone other than herself.' It was addictive, this criticism, these gloriously subversive thoughts. Now that she'd started she couldn't seem to stop.

'You can ask her,' Macy said. She settled herself on her towel. 'Here she comes now.'

Tess looked up. Sure enough, there was Janey flying towards them, her feet skimming the sand, a piece of paper clutched in one fist. She pulled up, panting, in front of them, tiny beads of sweat on her upper lip, blue eyes malicious as she looked at Tess.

'Right, Tess, your turn,' she said. 'Truth or dare? Actually, I think we'll go with truth. Who's your secret love in Melbourne?'

'I-I don't have one,' Tess stammered. She didn't feel so brave all of a sudden.

Janey tutted. 'You're not telling the truth, Tess, and so you'll have to be punished.' She unfolded the sheet of paper and in a loud voice began to read. *'That's pretty much all the news. Nothing has really changed here, I just wanted to see how you are and to say that I still think about the year seven—'*

'Janey!' Tess yelped. It had taken her a moment to work out what was going on, but now she lunged for Callum's letter, trying to yank it from Janey's grasp. Janey held on tightly though, and the letter tore apart, leaving the bottom third of the page still in her hands. 'Janey,' Tess cried again. 'How could you? Where did you find it?'

'Under your mattress, Einstein,' Janey said coolly. 'Dumb choice. It's the first place anyone ever looks.'

Tess gazed down at the letter, its serrated edges fluttering in the evening air. Ruined. It was ruined, and she could never get it back. A sob rose in her throat. She wanted to kill Janey. She wanted her mother. As the tears began to fall she got up and ran for home.

Dinner had been finished for half an hour, but still their plates sat in front of them, fish bones gleaming with grease, scraps of salad wilting in puddles of oil. No one could be bothered clearing the table. Usually darkness brought a release from the heat, but tonight it only seemed to have increased, the humid air cloaking them in a stifling embrace. Morag wiped a bead of sweat from her temple. They had eaten outside, and the evening sky seemed lower somehow, closer to them. Something was brewing.

'The girls were quiet,' Caro ventured.

Fiona reached for the bottle of wine. 'Quiet? They didn't say boo—just ate and then pissed off again.' She filled her glass. 'At least it was a nice change from having them chucking up in the bushes.'

Caro flushed. 'I think Janey had sunstroke last night. She never wears a hat. Wants her hair to go blonder.'

'How's your arm?' Morag asked before Fiona could respond.

Caro held it up. The welts had gone down somewhat but were still visible in the light from the candles placed along the table.

'It's not throbbing anymore,' she said. 'Still hurts if I brush it against anything though. I'm not sure how I'm going to sleep tonight.'

'Alcohol,' Fiona said. She lifted the bottle again and proffered it to Caro. 'Best painkiller I know.'

Morag expected her friend to decline—she'd already had a few over dinner—but Caro pushed her glass towards Fiona.

'Go on, then,' she said. 'God, what a day. The sting, that

weird humming, the girls . . . What should we do about them? Should I go and talk to Janey? I hope nothing's wrong.'

'Too bad if it is,' said Fiona. 'Bugger them! They're not babies anymore. They can work it out themselves.'

'They're probably just tired,' Amira said. 'It takes a while to get used to the heat, and they had a long day yesterday. I'm sure they'll be fine in the morning.'

'But Tess is used to the heat,' Caro persisted, 'and she was the quietest of them all. I don't think she said a single word.'

Morag felt her shoulders tighten. 'I bet it's because of Macy,' she said. Two ants were scurrying across the tablecloth in front of her, carrying crumbs of bread. She flicked one off, then pressed her index finger down on the second. 'Having her here has probably altered things between the others. I could kill Andrew. I'm never going to sleep with him again after this stunt.'

'What? You still do?' asked Fiona.

Amira giggled, then glanced guiltily at Morag. 'Don't judge everyone by your standards, Fiona.'

Fiona sat back in her seat and fanned herself with a serviette. 'I just think sex should be optional after five years of marriage. You've done it all by then, anyway. It's just another chore, like emptying the dishwasher.'

Caro lifted her glass to her mouth. 'What about if you're trying to conceive?'

'Pffft,' Fiona said, waving her hand. 'Fine. Go for it. But you should probably try and have kids in the first five years too, while you still like each other. Better chance your partner will actually change a nappy if he's trying to score points with you.' She paused, drank, swallowed. 'Not that it actually worked like that with Todd, but still. He's different.'

Morag regarded her across the table. Fiona was still pink from her first day's sunburn, and there were deep lines etched in her cleavage. 'So no sex then, right? And Todd's OK about that?'

'Oh, he gets his leg over occasionally, when I can't bear the nagging anymore or I don't have the energy to keep avoiding it.' Fiona spoke breezily, but her face had hardened. 'That's what frustrates me. When he doesn't get any, it's my fault. It's because I'm frigid, or a bitch, or he thinks I'm punishing him for something, for not washing up or for forgetting my birthday or whatever. He doesn't think for a moment that maybe it's because of him . . . that I'm not interested not because I'm sulking or trying to teach him a lesson, train him to do better, like a performing seal, but because there's nothing there that would make me *want* to sleep with him—no warmth, no consideration, just his fucking boner prodding me in the thigh.' She stopped and peered around at them. 'Shit, that's a bit deep for me, isn't it? He does have a nice cock though, I'll give him that. It's a bit of a waste, really. A nice cock, attached to a great big dick.'

Morag sputtered with laughter. She couldn't help it. She had been thinking she should clear the table, but now she settled back in her seat, her own anger towards Andrew fading.

'I know what you mean,' Amira said. 'About it being your fault, that is, not the part about the dick. It's been ages since I've seen one of those. Here, give me some of that wine.'

'None left,' Fiona said. 'Please tell me someone has some more in their room.'

'I do,' said Caro, rising from her seat. 'I'll get it. It will give me a chance to check on Janey.'

'You shouldn't have let her go,' Fiona hissed at Amira as soon as Caro had left. 'She'll just meddle, make things worse.'

'*I* shouldn't have let her go? What about you? And as if anyone can stop Caro when her mind's made up. She's as difficult to control as you.'

Morag thought Fiona might argue, but she just stuck out her tongue. 'You've missed us,' she said.

'I have,' Amira admitted.

Caro soon returned, triumphantly brandishing a green bottle with an orange label. 'No wine, but I've got this. Champagne!'

'Veuve,' observed Morag. 'Fantastic—but are you sure? That stuff's not cheap.'

'Of course I'm sure,' said Caro, peeling back the foil. 'I brought it to share.'

'Now I feel dreadful about all the terrible things we were saying about you while you were gone,' Fiona said, pushing her glass towards Caro. 'How's Janey?'

'Fast asleep. Or pretending to be. I turned on the light and rattled around but she didn't stir.' Caro carefully unscrewed the wire over the cork. 'It doesn't matter, I'll find out tomorrow. Oh God, this feels lovely and cold. I bought it for our final night here together, but this is close enough. I know how you love it, Amira, and you probably haven't had much lately.'

'Are we still talking about champagne?' asked Fiona.

'Thanks, Caro,' said Amira. She sounded touched. 'That was really sweet of you—to remember, and to think of it.'

Caro angled the bottle away from her and closed her eyes. There was a loud pop and the cork flew off into the night, startling a bat that swooped briefly over their table.

Amira cheered, then held up her glass for Caro to fill.

'To us,' she toasted.

'To us,' Morag echoed.

'To great big dicks!' proclaimed Fiona.

'So what were you going to say, Amira?' Caro asked. 'Earlier, when Fiona was talking about Todd.' She hesitated, cheeks dusky. 'It's none of my business, I know, but it sounded interesting, and we're all friends here . . .'

Her voice trailed off.

Morag took a sip of her champagne and felt herself unwind. Bubbles danced along her tongue; the liquid was tart and cool in her throat. She exhaled. Maybe Macy *was* causing waves—but Macy wasn't there right now. She didn't have to think about her. She could just enjoy the night.

Amira set her own glass down.

'I just wanted to say that I agreed with Fiona—that it happened to me too, with Davis. The first year we were together I'd sometimes make the big effort: stockings, suspenders, push-up bra, you name it, then I'd surprise him at the door.' She threw back her head and laughed. 'Suspenders! I *hate* those things. They're so difficult to do up at the back, and a tight band of elastic around thighs like mine isn't the greatest look anyway . . . but I thought it was what you did. I thought it was what I should do, that it would keep the marriage ticking over, that it made me a good wife. But I was so busy being a good wife and manoeuvring myself into suspenders that it took me a while to realise that he wasn't making any sort of equivalent effort himself, that he wasn't being a good husband. Then when I stopped bothering with all that stuff he accused me of losing interest—he never seemed to realise that it was a two-way street, that you both do the work.' Her eyes sparkled in the candlelight. 'I think in the end I used the suspenders to stake the roses along the front fence. Possibly the stockings too. At least they achieved something there.'

A drop of condensation ran down the neck of the champagne bottle. Caro leaned across and wiped it away with one finger, her nail polish, Morag noticed, still intact. 'I know you don't miss Davis, but do you miss sex?' Morag asked.

Amira pushed her fingers through her hair, holding it away from the nape of her neck. 'It's funny,' she said, 'I thought I would, but I don't, not really. It's easy enough to have an orgasm—you don't need anyone else for that.' She dropped her hands and let her thick curls settle back onto her shoulders. 'What I do miss is the intimacy, the being held. And not just that, not just the physical stuff—it's those times when somebody at a party says something, or there's a scene on the TV, and you look over at your partner and he looks at you, and you both know what the other is thinking. It's the knowing I miss.' She paused. 'It's better up here though. I haven't felt as lonely here as I sometimes did in Melbourne. There everybody stays shut away inside their own four walls, and if you talk to someone you don't know they won't look at you, as if you might be mad. Here it really is a community. I can always wander out to the beach or the shop or even just stand in the street if I need a bit of company—but I can get away from it too, if I don't. You've got the best of both worlds. It's a good way to be if you're single.'

'It's probably a good way to be, regardless,' murmured Fiona. 'You can get lonely in a marriage too.'

Caro poured them all another glass of champagne. The clouds overhead parted for a moment and Morag glimpsed the stars behind them. There were so many stars in this part of the world, away from the cities, from civilisation—almost more stars than sky. Despite the wine with dinner and now the Veuve she felt curiously clear-headed, alert, each of her senses alive. In all their years as friends they'd never talked like this before. They'd discussed toilet training their children, and their own incontinence suffered after childbirth; they'd confided in each other about abortion (Fiona) and the odd one-night stand (Amira); they'd argued about politics and climate change. But this was new, this was something apart. She felt closer to them than she ever had.

———

Fiona picked up her glass and drained it in one gulp. She could kick herself. What on earth had she said *that* for, about being lonely in her marriage? Now they'd all laugh at her. Worse, they'd look at her with big sympathetic eyes, pat her arm and nod consolingly. They'd pity her, for God's sake, and pity was the one thing she couldn't bear. She didn't want it, and she certainly didn't need it.

Only no one turned to her at all. They were listening to

Caro, who was mumbling something with her eyes firmly fixed on the table. Fiona leaned in, straining to hear.

'I don't get lonely, but I do get jealous,' Caro said. Her hand went to her throat, toyed with her pearls. 'Not that I think Alex is going to run off with someone, or have an affair . . . he travels so much by himself that I'd go mad if I let myself worry about that. It's not that there's another woman.' She hesitated, the lustrous beads around her neck now clenched between her fingers. 'Or rather, there is. There's two women. The girls.'

Fiona's mind raced. Secretaries at his office, maybe—or was Caro talking about some of his contacts in Italy?

'You mean Janey and April?' Amira asked softly.

Caro nodded, still staring at the ground. 'It's stupid, isn't it?' she said, voice wavering. 'He's a great father, and of course I know he loves them—I want him to! But he's so fascinated by them as well. Whenever he's away and he rings it's them he wants to speak to; his eyes light up when he returns home and sees them again. Even if we're just having dinner, all he wants to talk about is how their day was, how squad went for Janey or what April learned at school . . . I watched him put April to bed the other night. We'd been out with clients, and the babysitter had let her fall asleep in front of the TV, so Alex carried her to her room. He tucked her in, but then he bent down, kissed her forehead and started stroking her hair. April didn't wake up, but he just sat there like that for another five minutes, gazing at her with such devotion that I wanted to cry—and not because I was touched.' Caro finally looked up, her eyes darting around the table. 'I was *jealous*. Is that mad? I can't believe I'm telling you this.'

Amira shook her head. 'It's not mad. You wanted him to look at you like that too, didn't you?'

'Yes!' Caro cried. 'It's nuts. He remembers our anniversary, he cooks if I'm stuck at work, we have regular sex—he's Italian, of course we do . . . I know he still loves me. But he's not fascinated by me anymore, the way he is with the girls; he knows too much about me. I'm familiar, I'm all about what has to be done in the garden and did the rates get paid, and they're fresh and new and changing all the time.' She stopped. A puff of wind stirred the air, made the candles flicker. 'But I get that too. I look at them some days and can't believe that I had any part in making something so beautiful.'

Morag shifted in her seat. 'They didn't put any of this in the parenting manuals, did they?' she said. 'I don't think it sounds crazy. Everyone wants to feel valued, special, as if they're someone's one true love. That's why when you first meet someone it's so intoxicating, because they're not interested in anything but you, and vice versa . . . but it doesn't last. It can't. The kids come along or you just get used to one another, and you stop thinking about true love and start wondering if anyone else is ever going to put the washing away.' The champagne was finished now, so she poured herself a glass of water. 'It does my head in that Andrew and I are so busy going to work and keeping everyone clothed, clean and fed that we rarely look at each other properly.' She smiled, a faint flush appearing along her cheekbones. 'That's what sex is for. Like Amira said, it's not just the physical release, but that it becomes a . . . a refuge. It clears us a space that's separate from the family; it lets us be a couple again. There's nothing more erotic than not being mummy for twenty minutes, than locking the bedroom door and telling the boys they can't come in.'

Amira laughed. 'Good on you. Do you tell Macy too?'

Morag pulled a face. 'Oh, Macy would be horrified at the very idea of it. She thinks she owns sex, that she's the first person to ever discover it. I imagine every sixteen-year-old girl does.'

'I remember being like that,' Caro remarked wistfully, but Fiona barely heard her. Morag's words were echoing in her skull. *Refuge*. Sex wasn't a refuge in her marriage—sleep was, wine was, but sex? Not a chance. Had it ever been? Maybe, very early on, but those days were lost now, as out of reach as the size-ten jeans she'd been wearing the night she first met Todd. These days sex was combat, was about giving in; it was something she weighed up to decide if she could bear. It had been like that for years, but suddenly the thought made her incredibly sad. Once upon a time she couldn't keep her hands off him, would dissolve when he'd ring to tell her that he was on his way home and she should get in bed naked. If he did that now she'd probably just hang up. When had things changed? Was it when the kids were born, or when she realised he wasn't as good at running a business as he thought he was and she would have to go back to work? Was it when he put on weight, or when she did? Was it when his comments had started, the snide remarks about anything and everything—her arse, her cooking, her mother, her clothes?

God, she thought, Caro had no idea. Complaining because Alex adored his daughters? Try the opposite, try a husband who barely knew his was alive. Todd hardly spoke to Bronte. Neither, as a result, did Dom, following his father's lead in this as in so many other ways, the two of them ignoring her at dinner or changing the channel if they weren't interested in what she was watching on TV. And Bronte put up with it! Bronte just sat there and said nothing, or got up and went to her room. Fiona felt a sharp flash of anger at her daughter. It was no wonder she stooped. She had no backbone.

A stronger gust of wind stirred the tree branches above and blew Fiona's serviette from the table. She bent to retrieve it, her head pounding as she did so. It was time to stop drinking, to go to bed. She was drunk and worn out. She wouldn't feel so angry in the morning. And really, she couldn't just point the finger at Bronte, could she? She'd been complicit in things reaching this point. She'd let Todd get away with it too—with Bronte, but with herself as well—the barbed remarks, the subtle and not-so-subtle put-downs. Sometimes she fought back, met fire with fire, but mostly she was too tired. She worked so hard, she was so flat out keeping them afloat financially—not that Todd would ever admit that—that most nights when she got home she just wanted a drink, not an argument, wanted to ignore him until the alcohol kicked in and blurred his edges, made him more bearable. Besides, it wasn't as if he hit her or anything like that, and his tradie's hours meant he could do the after-school stint at home while she was still at the practice. Did that make it OK? Was that why she put up with it? That, and the alternative, the thought of starting again, having to move out and find somewhere to live, spending her weekends viewing grotty flats in dodgy suburbs miles from her friends . . .

A sudden fierce squall shook the frangipani petals from their branches and snuffed the candles into darkness. Caro's wine glass teetered, then fell to the ground, shattering; Fiona felt drops of rain strike her uncovered shoulders. There was the crash of thunder, then lightning illuminated their faces, simultaneously shocked and apprehensive.

In the midst of it all, Amira laughed.

'I was talking to Mason before dinner. He told me it was old Jabu who died—he used to live up here, but lately he's been over at La Djardarr Bay, across the other side of the peninsula. I reckon this might be his spirit passing through.'

Fiona's skin erupted in goosebumps, though the air was still warm. She glanced around apprehensively, thoroughly spooked. For all her earlier resentment, she couldn't help wishing that Todd was there.

Friday

Tess rolled over for at least the tenth time, trying to find a cool spot on her pillow. There wasn't one. The whole bed felt overheated, scalding, as if, like her, it might combust at any moment. Fuck Janey. She was supposed to be her best friend. What on earth had she done that for? Tess relived the moment yet again: Janey running towards them across the sand, her small mouth set tight; Janey producing the letter and reading out Callum's words in a mocking falsetto; Janey laughing and snatching the sheet of paper away from Tess when she tried to grab it. It was terrible, all of it, but what had hurt most was that laugh and the spiteful blue gleam in Janey's eyes when she saw she'd found her mark.

I should have hit her, Tess thought. *I should have stepped up and slapped that smirk off her face. I should have broken her nose.* Tia would have. Tia wouldn't have put up with that crap for a moment. But tears had threatened, and rather than compound her humiliation by breaking down she had fled for home instead.

They threatened again now, pushing against her aching eyeballs, welling in her throat. Tess sat up and turned on the light. There was no point trying to sleep; maybe reading would help, would shut down the scene replaying on a loop in her brain. She picked up *The Bell Jar* but couldn't bring herself to open it. She didn't want to hear about Esther's problems. She had enough of her own.

She set the book down again and lay on her back, staring at the ceiling. Try as she might, she couldn't shake the memory of Janey advancing across the beach, her fingernails hot pink against the white sheet of paper clutched in her hand. Even her gait had been different, Tess realised, so . . . *determined*, somehow. She and Janey had fought before—Janey was a high-maintenance friend and didn't bother hiding it if you'd somehow pissed her off—but this was different. In the past, whenever they'd been out of sorts with each other, Janey had simply stopped talking to her, never offering an explanation; she'd avoided their usual spot in the quadrangle or made a point of giggling with other girls whenever Tess was around. Then a week or so later she'd materialise at Tess's side again as if nothing had happened, flicking her hair and asking for some of Tess's chips. It had stung Tess the first time it occurred—in grade three, from memory—but she'd got used to it. Janey never sulked for long, and at least, as Janey herself had once remarked in a rare moment of candour, she always came back. Tess had come to see that the mood swings were just the price of being Janey's bestie.

This overt aggression was different, though. Was there any coming back from it? Tess got out of bed, dropped to her knees and pushed her arm between the mattress and the base, feeling around until she found the letter. It was pointless, she supposed, to still be hiding it here, but now she was hiding it from herself; she didn't want it anywhere in her room she might stumble across it and be reminded of its desecration. She unfolded it gingerly and smoothed it out on the fraying carpet. She'd stuck it back together with sticky tape, but it would never be the same. The tear went straight through Callum's words about the disco, rendering them almost unreadable.

Funny that it had been Janey who had given her the tape, thrusting it with the top section of the letter behind the screen door of Tess's house, before turning and walking away. After running back from the beach, Tess had been crying in her bedroom for an hour, but when she heard the door bang she went out to see if it was her mother, and recognised instead Janey's retreating back. Now she picked up the sticky tape from where she'd left it on the floor, rotating it in her fingers. On one side of the roll, *$3.70* was written in black marker. Janey must have gone to the community shop to buy it before she dropped it off with the other section of the letter. Tess almost laughed. The idiot, to spend that much. Amira was a primary school teacher; they had more gluesticks and sticky tape than they knew what to do with.

Tess hadn't said anything to Janey at dinner. Why should she? Janey hadn't said anything to *her*, just shoved her guilt offering behind the screen door without even having the guts to ring the bell. They had maintained their silence throughout the meal, Bronte glancing anxiously between them like a child whose parents are fighting; Macy sizing up the situation and ignoring all three of them, turning her attention to Amira instead. No doubt she thought they were being childish. They probably were, but Tess didn't care. She had a suspicion that it was caring what Macy thought that had started all this.

The front door opened and a light went on in the hall.

'Tess?' called her mother. 'Are you still awake?'

Tess snatched up the letter and pushed it back beneath the mattress, then scrambled into bed.

'I was just reading,' she called back.

Her mother's dark head appeared in the doorway. 'Pretty late to be reading. It's almost one. Aren't you tired?'

'I couldn't sleep,' Tess admitted.

'Any reason?' her mother asked gently.

Suddenly the tears were back again, and this time she couldn't fight them. 'Janey . . .' She gulped, then began sobbing in earnest. 'Janey's been a total bitch.'

Her mother was beside her in an instant, cradling Tess in her arms.

'Oh, baby,' she said, stroking her hair. 'I thought something was wrong tonight. I should have come back sooner, but I supposed you really were tired and wanted an early night. It's been a busy week.' She sighed. 'I'm sorry, Tess. Do you want to tell me about it?'

Tess shook her head. She did, she did want to, but then she'd have to explain the letter and Callum and why it all mattered so much. Her mother would understand, she knew that, but talking about it would change it somehow. It had been her secret, her own hidden treasure, something she hugged to herself at night or whenever she was alone. It was like the silver locket her grandmother had given her that she wore to school underneath her uniform in contravention of the 'no jewellery' rule. No one else knew it was there, but she did; she liked the way it rested, heavy and comforting, between her breasts.

'I'm sorry,' her mother said again. 'Janey's always been a bit . . . unpredictable, though, hasn't she?' She paused. 'OK, unpredictable's probably not the word. You're right. She's a bitch.'

Despite herself, Tess giggled. Her mother never made those sorts of judgements about anyone, at least not out loud.

'She is. She's a bitch on wheels. On steroids.' She snuggled in closer. Her mother smelled of frangipani, of sorbolene, which she used as a moisturiser, and just faintly tonight of red wine and lemongrass. Tess realised she was hungry. She'd hardly touched her dinner, she'd been so upset.

'Why don't you wash your face, get a glass of milk and come and hop into my bed?' her mother suggested, as if she could read her mind. 'There's a real wind tonight, and some rain too—did you hear it? We'll cuddle up and be cosy together.'

Tess hadn't slept with her mother in years. She had thought herself past that stage, that she'd outgrown it along with her soft toys. The idea, though, was surprisingly appealing. She was sick of lying here alone with only the memory of the afternoon's events for company. She reached up and kissed her mother's cheek. 'Thanks, Mum. I will. I'm just going to make some toast first.'

Amira carefully lifted Tess's arm off her chest and attempted to reposition it on Tess's side of the bed. The limb hovered for a moment but then came straight back, pinning her beneath it. Amira tried again, not so carefully this time, but the same thing happened. Tess lay spreadeagled on her back in the centre of the mattress, sound asleep. The sleep of a child, Amira thought, the same deep slumber Tess had often fallen into as a toddler—at the table, on the floor, even once, memorably, in the bath. Amira had let the plug out and still Tess hadn't woken, remained lolling against the chipped enamel as the water ebbed away, one flushed cheek resting on the soap dish.

Amira extricated herself and moved to the thin strip of mattress that Tess had left her. She'd forgotten all this, forgotten how to share a bed, both the comforts and the compromises. How long had it been since she'd slept a whole night with someone beside her, a fellow traveller on the road towards the day? She reached across and smoothed the hair from Tess's forehead. God, she was beautiful. She was so lucky to have her, her loving, thoughtful daughter, and not a snake like Janey. Whatever it was Janey had done to Tess, Amira wanted to kill her, though she'd probably have to stand in line for the privilege.

She felt her stomach contract as she remembered what Tess had told her as she drifted off to sleep. They'd been curled side by side, murmuring together in the dark—about their plans for tomorrow and how sore Caro's arm had looked—when Tess had said drowsily, 'Do you know what she did to Bronte?'

236

'Who?' Amira had asked. 'Janey? No. What?'

'She took a photo of her in the shower and put it on Facebook so anyone from school can see.'

'You're kidding,' Amira said. 'Was she wearing any clothes?'

'Muuum.' Tess had yawned and rolled over. 'I said she was in the shower. She was naked, but the picture stops at her stomach.'

'Does Bronte know?'

'No, she had her eyes closed. She's got no idea. Don't tell anyone,' she added in a reflexive burst of loyalty. 'Janey said she'll take it down.'

'And you've seen this picture?' Amira had asked, suddenly wide awake, but there had been no answer, just the rhythmic in-out of Tess's breath.

A faint light shone through the bedroom curtains. *The clouds must have cleared*, Amira thought, though her own mind hadn't. What should she do? Who did she owe her loyalty to: Tess, who'd asked her not to tell, or Caro, who really should be told? Daughter or friend . . . or Bronte, the daughter of a friend, who had the most at stake here? But should Amira even believe the story? She had no doubt that Tess did, but Janey had been prone to exaggeration—to outright lies, if it suited her—since first grade. Maybe Janey *had* taken the photo, maybe she'd even shown Tess, but who was to say she'd actually followed through and posted it online? Surely she wasn't that stupid, or that dangerous? Amira heaved herself up on her elbows. She could check now. There was no internet at the house, but she could take her laptop over to the school . . .

She sighed and lay back down. It wouldn't help. Tess was on Facebook, but Amira had never bothered with it. She didn't have the time or the interest—plus she trusted Tess, so she'd never felt the need. Yet what was it that all those glossy government-funded internet guides said, the ones she herself had parroted to classroomsful of parents perched uncomfortably on their children's seats? *Make sure you monitor your children online—that you know what they're doing and who they're talking to.* Some teacher she was. She couldn't even follow her own advice. And she *did* trust Tess, but she'd forgotten that that meant she had to trust everyone Tess was interacting with too. Amira groaned. She could probably find Facebook if she googled, but there was no way she could log in to see if Janey had really done what she'd said. She'd have to wait until morning and get Tess to find out.

And if Janey had done it, Amira thought, what then? Who did she confront? Something like that couldn't just be ignored. Friendships were such tricky things though. She and Caro had been close for years, but that wouldn't make it any easier to tell her what Janey was up to. Caro was such a proud and private person . . . It would probably only add to her anger, Amira reflected, to realise that not only had her daughter behaved badly but that one of her own friends had been the first to know about it. Then again, she'd be even angrier if she ever discovered that Amira had known about it and hadn't told her, just as Amira would be in the same situation. Should she challenge Janey directly, or was that out of line, given that the whole thing was actually none of Amira's business? Or maybe she could just tell Bronte—but then Bronte wouldn't know how to deal with it, so Fiona would have to know . . . The sheets tangled around her legs and she kicked them away irately. What a nightmare. Perhaps she should just pretend that Tess had never confided in her, keep them both right out of it.

The trouble was, she thought, that you loved your friends and you loved your children and you thought the two things were separate, would never impact on each other, but it didn't work out that way, not always. Like Tess's birthday party in grade two . . . The four of them—she, Caro, Morag and Fiona—had just about lived in each other's pockets back then when the kids were still small and Morag and Caro were at home with their toddlers and hadn't yet gone back to work. There were the Friday night drinks, of course, but all the other meet-ups too: twice a day at the school gate, the many play dates arranged at three thirty, the weekend barbecues or the lunchtimes spent doing tuckshop duty together. Their children had always attended each other's birthdays, but this year Tess was turning eight and had decided that boys had germs and she didn't want any at her party. Dutifully, Amira had left Callum and Finn off the invitation list, but when Morag found out she was so upset she barely spoke to Amira for weeks—Morag, who never got her knickers in a knot about anything. She'd feared she was being excluded from the group, she confessed later, somewhat sheepishly, and Amira sympathised, but what could she do? Tess had made her choice, and—for Amira at least—what Tess wanted would always come first.

She plumped up her pillow, determined to put the whole thing with Janey out of her mind and go to sleep. *Think about something else*, she told herself. The meals for next week, once everyone had gone back to Melbourne, or the herbs she kept meaning to plant in the community garden. Domestic planning always made her doze off . . . But suddenly her eyes flew open again. If Tess and Janey ever did stop being friends, dumped each other conclusively or just grew further apart, could she still be friends with Caro? A missed party invite was one thing, but this was quite another. Would it be too awful, too awkward to keep seeing Caro if their daughters didn't speak or, worse, actually loathed each other? Yet if this Facebook thing was true, Caro and Fiona would have to negotiate the same territory. God, and they'd thought toilet training was hard. They'd had no idea; pull-ups and puddles were nothing compared to dealing with teenage girls.

A memory came to her; something Mason had said. In traditional Aboriginal communities, if someone injured or aggrieved you the matter would often be dealt with using black law, not white, and justice would be meted out via payback. 'One fella hurts another or mistreats his woman, the elders bring him in front of everyone and get two strong men to hold him so he won't run away, then someone they've chosen spears him in the thigh. There's blood, but after that it's over.' Mason had laughed at her horrified face, but then grown serious again. 'It's finished that way, don't you see? Everything is balanced. Someone gave pain, they get pain back. Fellas witness payback and they feel right, they start again. It's better, often, than white man's way, draggin' it through the courts—our people don't have the money for that. Anyway, if they go to jail they often end up a lot worse off than being stabbed in the leg.' Fiona would laugh, but Amira *had* understood. She certainly wouldn't advocate for Janey to be speared, and yes, the whole concept was undeniably primitive, but in some basic way it made sense too. You give pain, you get it back, and everyone moves on, case closed. A line is drawn; an end is reached. Could she and her friends ever be like that with each other, so direct, no games? She didn't think so. The black way was unsophisticated and crude, but it was also somehow cleaner than theirs, and clean was appealing. She had a feeling that this whole photo thing was about to get messy.

—

'Macy—your shoes!' Bronte shouted. Macy looked down to see her black Doc Martens slowly sinking into the mangroves in which she stood, their yellow stitching already obscured by mud.

'Shit!' She abandoned the pokestick she'd only just worked, as instructed, down a crab hole, and attempted to pull her feet out of the ooze. At first she couldn't budge them, but finally one came up with a long, loud rasp and a fetid stench of rot.

'Pooh,' said Bronte, waving her hand in front of her nose.

'Macy, that's not very polite,' Mason rebuked, then winked at her to show he was kidding. She was tempted to shove her pokestick through his eye. One boot was out, but she couldn't free the other without placing the first back into the ooze. She stood there fuming for a moment, then leaned forward, grabbed a mangrove and hoisted herself into it, hoping its spindly limbs would take her weight. Her trapped foot came free almost immediately, clad in a sweaty black sock, but the Doc stayed where it was, now up to its eyelets in mud.

Macy gazed at it despairingly. Those boots had cost a fortune. Her mother wouldn't buy them for her—she wanted Macy to wear ballet flats and strappy sandals, for fuck's sake—so Macy had had to use some of the money she'd saved from busking. All that work, all that standing around on pavements while people sneered at you and threw in five cents if you were lucky, or spat if you weren't . . . all for her Docs to end up like this? She'd kill Amira. It had been her idea, of course. Amira couldn't stop being a teacher even when she was off duty. 'We're going mudcrabbing!' she'd announced at breakfast, before adding that the whole community was heading out to the mangroves to collect crabs for a feast that was being held tonight for that bloke who'd died. 'We'll join them!' she'd crowed. 'It'll be fun!' Some bloody fun, standing around in stinking muck while the Docs she'd scrimped and saved for met a sticky end. And in any case, being whiteys, they probably weren't even invited to the feast.

'Macy! Hey! Your stick's moving!' Tess hollered excitedly from where she was standing guard over another hole.

Macy glared at her uncomprehendingly. 'So?' 'It means you've got a crab,' Tess cried. 'Do you want me to get it for you?'

'No way.' Macy hesitated for a moment, then tugged off her remaining boot, wedged it in the mangrove she was clinging to and jumped down. The sandy mud soaked through her socks and sucked at her dress but she ignored it, focusing on getting to the pokestick before the creature lost interest. Slowly she eased it out of the hole, just as Mason had instructed, and was delighted to find a fat crab clinging to its end, one bright orange claw waving in agitation.

'He's a beauty!' Mason said, advancing towards her. She noticed that his feet were bare; everyone's were except those of them who'd come from Melbourne. 'Here.' Mason held out an arm. 'Pass your stick over and I'll tie him up for you. Don't want you losing a finger.' Macy did as she was told, then reached down and peeled off her socks, flinging them deep into the mangroves. It probably wasn't good for the environment, but they were so rancid after two days in the heat that surely they'd just dissolve or be mistaken by some scavenger creature for carrion. She wriggled her toes. The mud felt soothing, cool against the soles of her feet. Why on earth had she worn boots, she wondered, or even clothes for that matter? It wasn't yet lunchtime, but the heat was oppressive, a python enfolding her in its coils. Before she could change her mind she grasped the filthy hem of her long black dress and yanked it over her head, then balled up the fabric, found a clean spot and used it to rub all the make-up off her face.

'Whoa.' Mason grinned. 'So that's what you look like under all the war paint.'

Macy just stood there, enjoying the sensation of the air on her face and body, of suddenly feeling lighter, freed. Just as well she'd worn her bikini under her dress, in case they went for a swim later. She glanced around. It occurred to her that no one actually cared what she was wearing or whatever state-ment she was trying to make—they were all busy with their pokesticks, or trying to trap fish. It was a liberating notion. She took two steps forward and braced herself to wrench her

Doc from the mud, almost toppling backwards when it came free on the first try.

An hour and a half later she had managed to catch three more crabs, and was quietly singing Amy Winehouse's 'Rehab' to herself as she scouted for another hole. Poor Amy, Macy thought. She probably should have gone to rehab, as it turned out. It wasn't going to be like that for her when she was a big star. She'd be more careful. How stupid to work so hard and get so famous and then throw it all away . . . the applause, the flashbulbs, the money. Macy sighed. She couldn't wait for any of it—if only she didn't have to finish school and could get started now.

A shrill whistle disturbed her thoughts.

'Hey, you mob,' Mason called through the mangroves. 'That'll do. Bring everythin' you caught to the beach and we'll put it all together.'

Macy picked up her sullied Docs, knotted the laces together and slung them around her neck. Amy should have been sent here for rehab. You couldn't get into much trouble with no booze or drugs, and only crustacean-chasing for entertainment.

Most of their group were already on the beach by the time Macy arrived: Tess and Amira chatting by the water, Fiona and Morag sitting under the shelter, out of the sun, and Caro hovering admiringly around Mason. Three buckets of crabs sat at his feet, their claws tied with string. 'How come we never catch this many when we take the tourist groups out, eh?' laughed Mason, winking at Caro. Bronte flopped down on the sand, her pale skin glistening with sweat. 'How many did you get, Macy?'

'Four,' Macy said.

'That's fantastic!' Bronte exclaimed. 'I didn't get any. I felt kind of sorry for them, to be honest. My stick probably gave off negative vibes.'

Macy laughed. Bronte was alright. Tess too, now she'd taken a chill pill and was actually talking to them all again. It probably helped that Janey hadn't joined them this morning. Her mother had said she was too tired, but Macy would lay any money on her not wanting to damage her manicure.

'Say cheese,' said one of the community members, pulling out his phone to take a picture of the catch.

'Crabs, you mean.' Mason lifted one of the buckets of squirming shells in triumph.

'Hey,' Macy said. 'Why do you have a phone here? You can't get a signal.'

'You can if you go out on the point.' The man gestured to the rocks at the far end of the beach. 'You can pick it up from Wajarrgi, not that they know.'

'Cool,' said Macy. 'A bit of local knowledge, huh?'

Mason nodded seriously. 'Secret men's business.'

———

Thank God that was over. Morag handed back her pokestick, made the obligatory positive comments about the experience and headed towards her room before anyone could engage her in conversation. She'd only gone a few hundred metres before she had to sit down. She felt like crap: tired, lethargic, heavy. Was it because she'd had more than her customary glass or two of wine last night, or that she hadn't been for her run this morning? Probably both . . . The alarm had gone off, but for the first time since her pregnancies she'd ignored it and rolled over instead. It had taken her ages to fall back to sleep, and it seemed that as soon as she finally did, Amira was banging on the door, announcing that they were all going out to hunt for crabs. Morag didn't even like crab, but she'd dutifully got out of bed, applied sunscreen and joined the group.

At least they'd been in the shade, but that was the best she could say about it all. She'd never tell Amira, but she'd hated the whole thing from start to finish. She'd felt sorry for the crabs, ripped so abruptly from their snug silty homes; she'd thought she might pass out from the heat in the airless fug of the mangroves. Of course, it hadn't helped that she'd worn a long-sleeved top and full-length pants, being mindful of the sun. Almost everyone else had turned up in shorts and singlets, even Caro, who gamely prodded around in the mud with one arm wrapped in a bandage. She'd still looked good though, Morag thought with a twinge of jealousy.

Something tapped at her shoulder.

''Scuse me, missus—this yours?'

Morag jumped. An old Aboriginal woman was holding out her daypack, its black straps frayed.

'Sorry,' Morag said. 'You scared me. I was thinking about something else.' She reached for the pack. 'God, I didn't even realise I'd left it.'

'It was in the mangroves,' the woman said. 'Thought I better take it before the sea did.' She chuckled to herself. 'Tide's comin' in. Fish'd be nibblin' at it soon.'

'Thank you so much,' Morag said, embarrassed. 'I can't believe I was so stupid. I don't even remember taking it off.' She quickly checked inside: camera, iPod, water bottle, wallet . . . it was all there. A thought crossed her mind—should she offer the woman some money?

'I thought it was yours. I was watchin' you.'

Morag's head jerked up. 'Watching me? Why?'

The woman smiled. 'I was with my sisters. At first we were laughin' because you were stabbin' that stick so hard we thought you were tryin' to spear the crabs, not catch them.' She raised one hand and languidly waved it across her face to shoo away a fly. 'But then you looked sad, so we stopped.'

'Sad?' said Morag. 'I wasn't sad. Just tired. I didn't sleep well last night, and I'm not used to this weather.' She fumbled for her wallet. 'Here, can I give you a reward?'

The woman shook her head. 'No need.' She reached out and shyly touched the faded Saltire patch sewn to the front of the daypack. 'Is this your people?'

It had been there so long that Morag had almost stopped seeing it, but she studied it now: the midnight-blue background, the Saint Andrew's cross. She'd stitched it there years ago, before her first trip to Europe with some friends from university. Even as she worked the needle in and out of the canvas she'd known it was a bit naff proclaiming your identity in such a way, but it was the fashion back then, it was what you did when you were young and you travelled: you showed the world where you were from. Partly it was because you were proud, but maybe it was also so you'd remember to go back.

'Yes,' she said, still staring at the flag. The daypack had seen a lot of miles. Who would have thought when she first bought it for Paris that it would end up accompanying her here a quarter of a century later? 'It's from Scotland, where I was born. My mother still lives there, in Edinburgh. Australia's home now though,' she added with an effort.

'My daughter's away from me too,' the woman said. 'She lives in Adelaide. Might as well be Scotland for all the times I've seen her since she left.' She smiled. 'She has a good job, in a hospital. At least you've still got your girl, eh?'

'My girl?' Morag asked, confused, then realised that the woman must mean Macy. 'Oh, she's not . . .' She stopped. It was all too hard to explain, standing here in the red dirt with the midday sun stunning her senseless. What did it matter anyway? She supposed Macy was her girl while they were here. 'Yes,' she said simply.

The woman nodded approvingly. 'She did well. Caught some big crabs.'

Morag felt a foolish rush of pride. Macy *had* done well, better than anyone except Tess, and Tess was practically a local. It had been a pleasure to watch her—a pleasure, too, to see her out of her usual get-up, laughing with Bronte and Tess, content for once just to be a girl rather than a goth.

'They'll be good eating tonight.' The old woman lifted her hand and turned to go.

'Wait,' Morag called. 'Do you miss your daughter?'

The woman stopped and regarded her solemnly. 'Of course. Your blood is your blood.'

Morag swallowed. 'Do you talk to her? Not on the phone, I mean. In your head. I've heard that sometimes you can do that, your people . . .' She trailed off, embarrassed. All that humming yesterday had clearly unhinged her a little.

The woman's eyes danced. 'It's easier to get her on the phone. Or Hotmail. Your friend lets me use her computer.' She was still chuckling as she walked away.

Morag watched her go, flushed with humiliation. Of course she called her daughter. This was the twenty-first century, and probably even Telstra was more efficient than telepathy. It was just that sometimes, in the middle of the night, Morag woke and *knew* somehow that her mother was thinking of her, half a world away in her little flat in Trinity; *knew* that she was thinking of her with the ache of longing, with such an abundance of love that it telescoped the distance between them and spilled straight into her soul. *I'm here, Mum,* she'd reply in her head, and felt the answering relief, saw as clearly as if she'd been in the room her mother sit back in the chair with the doilies on the arms, a smile spreading across her face. *I'm here, Mum. I miss you. I love you.*

She wasn't hungover, Morag suddenly realised. She was homesick. For years she'd lived quite happily in Australia. She'd made her peace with it, she thought—this was where her husband was, her children, her future. Coming north, though, had shifted something. Broome and Kalangalla were so different, so foreign to her, that they magnified the strangeness of this continent, made it all seem new again. New and overwhelming and completely alien. Her mind went back to a home visit she'd done one winter's day over a decade earlier—Newhaven, she thought, or maybe North Leith. There was a hostel next door to the flat she was visiting. It was snowing, and a black-skinned family—refugees, she'd guessed, asylum seekers from North Africa—were standing in the garden with their pink-palmed hands out, catching the dirty flakes, a look of total bewilderment on each of their faces. That was her, she thought. That was how she was feeling right now.

⸻

The greys were coming through again. Caro peered more closely into the mirror, then reached for her tweezers. She'd have to make an appointment with Stefan as soon as she got back. She sighed. What she hated most about getting older was the constant maintenance: hair, nails, brows, make-up . . . She hadn't gone as far as Botox yet, but it was tempting. Janey could get out of bed, put on something she'd picked up from the floor, run a brush through her hair and look beautiful, but for Caro these days it took at least an hour of solid preparation just to achieve well-groomed. Beautiful she'd given up on.

Where was Janey anyway? she wondered. She hadn't seen her since before they'd all left to go mudcrabbing, when Janey was feigning sleep so she wouldn't have to come. Caro had thought about getting her up but then changed her mind. She still didn't know what had happened between the girls the previous day, and if they kept ignoring each other it would be awkward. They only had a day and a half left in Kalangalla, and she just wanted to enjoy the remaining time. Was that too much to ask? She leaned forward to yank a particularly recalcitrant grey from her temple, but just as she gripped it there was a knock at the door. It was Amira.

'You don't have to knock!' Caro smiled as she waved her friend into the room. 'You should have just come in.'

'I wanted to make sure you were alone,' Amira said. 'Is Janey here?'

'No,' Caro said. 'Why? What's up?'

Amira didn't answer straight away. She never did that, Caro thought. Like Fiona, she always said whatever was on her mind, though with more tact and care.

'Look, it's none of my business, I know that,' Amira began, 'but when Tess told me last night I couldn't stop thinking about it, and I know if I was you I'd want you to tell me, if that makes sense.'

'Tell me what?' Caro asked. There was something in Amira's voice that was making her uneasy.

Amira sighed. 'Janey put a photo of Bronte up on Facebook without Bronte knowing.'

Caro turned back to the mirror and picked up her tweezers, relieved. 'Is that all? The girls do that sort of thing all the time.'

'I know, but this was different.' Amira paused again. In the reflection, Caro watched her swallow, her throat shiny with sweat. 'It was a shot she'd taken of Bronte in the shower, naked from the waist up. Bronte didn't know about it,' she repeated.

'What?' Caro spun around. 'Bronte in the shower? What do you mean?'

'I don't know how it happened, but Janey must have crept in and taken it without Bronte noticing. I've no idea how long it's been on Facebook, but I'm guessing Janey uploaded it the day we were at Wajarrgi, when we had reception on our phones.' Amira took a step towards her and placed her hand on Caro's arm. 'I'm sorry, Caro. It's probably none of my business, as I said . . . I don't want to interfere, but I figured you'd want to know.'

Caro shook her off. 'Have you actually seen this picture?' she demanded.

'Well, no,' Amira faltered. 'But Tess has. Janey showed her. Tess was so upset about it she told me, late last night.'

Caro felt the familiar tightness in her chest; felt her hands balling into fists. It was only when a sharp stab of pain shot through her palm that she realised she was still clutching the tweezers. She dropped them to the floor. 'Last night . . . Something happened between the girls yesterday afternoon, didn't it? They were all so quiet at dinner. How do you know Tess isn't just trying to get back at Janey for something or other?'

'I don't,' Amira admitted. 'I don't know anything about what went on yesterday—Tess wouldn't tell me. But she wouldn't make this up, Caro. She's not a liar. She's not malicious.'

'And Janey is?' Caro cried. She had to sit down. She couldn't breathe properly. Feeling behind her for the bed, she sank down onto it.

'I don't know!' wailed Amira. There were tears in her eyes. 'I'm so sorry. I shouldn't have said anything. I asked Tess to show me the photo this morning so I could be sure—we went over to the school to use the computer there, but we couldn't log on, the internet was down. It happens sometimes when we have a storm, and there was all that wind and rain last night . . .'

Amira babbled on, but Caro wasn't listening. She stared at the ceiling, concentrating on getting the air in and out of her lungs, trying not to black out. Oh God, she thought, imagine having an attack here, when she'd kept them under control for so long. The first time she'd had one, a month or so after her mother's death, she'd thought that she was going to die too, that the giant hand squeezing her lungs would never let go. They'd stopped for a while as she'd grown older and met Alex, then reappeared when Janey was born. Even now she still couldn't look at any of Janey's baby photos without calling up that fog of her first months, the gut-clenching fear, the ever-present panic that she had no idea what she was doing and that she would somehow end up killing her child or having her taken from her . . .

'. . . So we went to the office, but they were in the same boat, of course.' Amira suddenly stopped, coming over to the bed. 'Are you OK?' she asked, her voice rising. 'Caro! Talk to me! Are you alright?'

Caro coughed and tried to nod. She couldn't speak, but her mind was racing. Could Janey have done that? Was it true? It couldn't be, but if it was . . . if it was she'd have to tell Fiona, face her scorn and her wrath. Janey would have to apologise to Bronte, of course, and delete the photo before anyone saw it . . . Caro moaned. The scholarship! There'd be no point even putting Janey's name down if anyone found out about this. Schools hated that sort of stuff. And Alex—what would he say? She'd let Janey get away with too much. The thought came unbidden, but she recognised the truth of it immediately.

She'd been lazy, stupid. She'd been blinded by Janey's looks, had trusted that her daughter was as smirchless inside as out.

Amira had rushed to the bathroom and returned with a glass of water. 'Here,' she said, thrusting it at Caro. 'Drink this. You'll feel better.'

The water was warm. Amira hadn't allowed the tap to run, but it probably wouldn't have made a difference anyway, given the heat outside. Caro sipped the tepid liquid, willing her heart rate back down, staring at the bedspread rather than looking at her friend. There was some Xanax in her handbag. She could ask Amira for it, but she didn't want her to know.

'Sorry,' she finally croaked. 'I just got a bit . . . upset.'

Amira reached forward and hugged her. When she drew back, her eyes were glistening again.

'You scared me. I'm sorry—I shouldn't have said anything until I was sure it was true. But we'll work it out, Caro, whatever's happened, OK? I promise. It's all going to be fine.'

Caro nodded. 'I need to talk to Janey.' Tentatively, she met Amira's gaze. 'Will you come with me?'

'Of course.' Amira squeezed her hand. 'Do you want to rest for a bit or shall we do it now?'

'Now,' Caro replied. 'I want to know what's going on.' As she stood up, still light-headed, she suddenly thought of her mother. How would she have managed this? What would she have done? But her mother had never had to face anything of the sort, had died long before her only child became a teenager. Maybe she'd been lucky.

The trick, Janey knew, was not to draw the smoke into your lungs. Inhale, but only a little, hold it in your mouth, then exhale. Easy. That way you could still look as if you were smoking without doing any of the damage. She snuck a peek at Macy, standing next to her leaning against the boab tree. Could she tell? Janey didn't think so. Macy was too intent on her own cigarette to be paying close attention to what Janey was doing; she was sucking at it as if it was oxygen and she hadn't breathed in a week.

'Fuck, that's better,' she said, blowing two fine lines of smoke out her nostrils. 'I've been hanging out for this ever since I got here. It's hard work getting away from Morag's eagle eyes.'

'Do you ever worry about it hurting your voice?' Janey asked. She tapped her cigarette into the dirt, then drew her foot across the ash, the red dust coating her toes like talcum powder.

'Nah,' said Macy. 'It'll make it better if anything. Huskier. Sexy.'

'Jaaaaaaaaaaaaney!' Her mother's voice drifted through the trees between their rooms and the beach. Macy glanced at her and quickly stubbed out her cigarette against the tree. Janey followed suit.

'That's your mum, isn't it?' said Macy. 'Bit unrefined for her, hollering like that.'

It *was* unlike her mother, Janey thought—as was the way Caro suddenly appeared, puffed and perspiring, in the clearing before them. A few metres behind her was Amira.

'Oh—Macy, hi,' said Caro. 'I need to talk to Janey. Would you be able to give us a few minutes?'

'Sure,' said Macy, rising to her feet, her cigarette butt concealed in her hand. 'I'll catch you later, Janey.' She sauntered away, white legs luminescent in the afternoon sun.

Caro waited until Macy had left, then abruptly turned on Janey, eyes blazing.

'Apparently you put a photo of Bronte on Facebook. A particularly nasty photo.'

Janey took a step back. Tess. That little sneak.

'Well?' her mother demanded, grabbing her by the wrist. 'Did you?'

'Ow!' Janey complained. Her mother's nails were biting into her skin. 'Let go!' She shook her arm free.

'Just tell me the truth,' she said.

For a second, Janey thought about denying it, then realised there wasn't any point. Tess must have told Amira, who was hovering like an avenging angel in the background, and Amira of course had had to tell her mother. For fuck's sake. Would it have been so hard for Tess to keep her mouth shut?

'It was just a joke,' she said. 'I was gonna take it down tomorrow when we get back to Broome.'

'Posting naked shots of your friends is your idea of a *joke*?' Caro's voice cracked on the last word. This was getting embarrassing.

'She's not naked,' Janey argued. 'It's just her tits. I've actually done her a favour by proving that she has some.'

Her mother's hand flew to her cheek so quickly that Janey didn't have a chance to duck. Amira winced as the slap rang out, resonating through the bush.

Janey's fingertips rose to her throbbing face as she stared at her mother.

'I can't believe you did that,' she said slowly.

'I could say the same about you,' replied Caro. 'How do you think Bronte will feel when she knows? Or Fiona, for God's sake. You've got to take it down. Do it now, so I can see that you've done it. I'm assuming you've got your phone on you.'

'Can't. There's no reception.' Janey shrugged, trying to play it cool. Her cheek hurt like buggery, but there was no way she was going to give her mother the satisfaction of seeing that.

Caro frowned, then quickly turned to Amira.

'This morning, during the mudcrabbing, one of the men said something about being able to pick up a signal here if you stood in the right place. Do you remember? Right at the end, when we were taking pictures of what we'd caught.'

'Sort of,' said Amira. 'I've never done it myself though.'

'It was somewhere on the beach, I think ... maybe the rocks. We could try and find it.'

'I'll ask Mason,' Amira said. 'He'll know.' She scuttled off, thighs jiggling.

'We'll meet you at the beach,' Caro called after her, seizing Janey's wrist again. 'Come on. You can help me look.'

Janey allowed herself to be dragged along through the scrub until their feet hit the sand.

'Mum,' she hissed. 'Let go. Stop it!'

Caro glared at her as if she might hit her again, and Janey raised her arm defensively.

'Don't,' she said hurriedly. 'I just wanted to say it's no biggie if I can't delete the photo today. No one here will see it anyway. I'll do it tomorrow, in Broome, like I said. Bronte and Fiona don't even know it exists. We don't have to tell them. I'll make sure Tess doesn't blab this time.'

Caro released her grip and stood there panting. A drop of sweat ran down her face, carving a track in her make-up. She wiped it away with the back of her hand and slowly sank to her haunches on the beach. Janey could tell she was tempted by the idea.

'It'll be fine, Mum,' she cajoled. 'Let's just go back and you can have a drink. I shouldn't have done it, OK, but I can fix it tomorrow. No one will ever know.'

Caro was still for a long minute; then she slowly shook her head. 'It's too late. All your friends back in Melbourne will have seen it by now.' She looked up at Janey, her blue eyes sad and faded; eyes, Janey realised, that were just like hers, only older, much older. 'I'm doing this for you, you know,' Caro said wearily. 'Yes, it's awful for Bronte, but the longer that picture stays up the worse *you* look, don't you get that? Do you want people knowing that you're a bitch?'

'Hellooooo!' Mason cried cheerfully, advancing towards them with Amira once again in tow.

Caro swiftly stood up, brushing the sand from her pants.

'Thank you for coming,' she said, beaming at him. 'We need to access the internet. It's a little bit urgent, did Amira tell you? If you can just find us the spot . . .'

'No problem,' said Mason. 'We'll have to go out on the point. How's the arm?'

Surprisingly strong, Janey thought, still shaken. What had her mother meant, *knowing* that you're a bitch? It was just a joke. Why didn't anyone get that?

'Much better, thanks.' Caro held it out for inspection even though it was wreathed in bandages. She gazed at it for a moment, then seemed to snap to. 'Come on,' she said. 'Janey, you go first. Hold the phone up so we can see when you've got a signal. Let's get this done quickly.'

Reluctantly, Janey walked towards the water, carrying her phone in front of her.

'Higher!' barked Caro. 'Right up.'

As she raised her arm she thought she heard Mason stifling a laugh. She hoped like hell nobody was filming her.

———

'You did *what*?'

Bronte's head swivelled automatically to seek out her mother, gauge her reaction, but her mum was staring at her lap and didn't look up. Bronte turned back to Janey. 'You took a photo of me, in the shower, without my permission, then you put it on Facebook?'

'She's taken it down now,' said Caro quickly, as if that made it all OK.

'But it was there, on Facebook, where everyone could see it!' Bronte could feel the blood coming to the boil beneath her skin, rising to the surface, staining her arms, her chest, her face. Oh God, what on earth must she have looked like in the photo? She tried to visualise it—her bony shoulders, her tiny breasts; the image was so awful she almost wept. 'How long was it up for?' she asked.

There was silence. 'Janey?' Caro eventually prompted.

'I'm not sure.' Janey shrugged. 'A couple of days, I guess.'

'A couple of *days*?' Bronte wailed.

The sound seemed to momentarily bring her mother out of her fog.

'This picture—can we see it?' Fiona asked.

'I don't have it anymore. I took it off Facebook, like Mum said, and I deleted it from my phone.' Janey pulled her mobile from her pocket and held it out. 'You can check if you like.'

'As if I've got the time to go through all your shit,' Fiona spat. 'It wouldn't prove anything anyway. Even if you did delete it you've probably already forwarded it to half your friends . . . of which I thought Bronte was one.' She shook her head. 'Lovely friend you turned out to be.'

'Fiona—' Caro began.

'Suit yourself, then,' Janey said and put her phone back in her lap.

Bronte clutched at the bedspread beneath her. She'd known something was going on the minute Caro and Janey had knocked at the door of the room she shared with her mother and asked if they could come in. Fiona had been napping but woke up when they knocked; because there were no chairs she motioned for them to sit on Bronte's bed. Bronte had closed her sketchbook—she was halfway through the new one now—and sat down apprehensively next to her mother.

'On Facebook . . . were there any comments?' she asked now, dreading the response but needing to know.

'A few,' Janey said. 'But I didn't have time to read them. Mum made me get rid of the whole post the moment we got reception.' She was lying, Bronte was sure of it. She had watched Janey wheedling her way out of things for years, and the signs were all there: the slightly widened eyes, the toss of the hair. Janey was a lifetime practitioner of the deceptive arts.

'I did,' Caro confirmed. The air-conditioner shuddered in its frame.

'But everyone will have already seen it.' Bronte could hear herself whining and felt any control she'd had over the situation slipping away from her. Her stomach heaved and knotted as if she'd swallowed poison. She'd been feeling crampy all day, she realised—gutsick, stricken. Maybe her body had known what Janey was up to before the rest of her did.

'Not necessarily,' Janey said unconvincingly. 'A lot of people are away on holidays, remember. They might be too busy, or not have wifi, like us.'

And that was meant to pacify her? Bronte glanced to her mother for support, but her mum had drifted off again. She had one arm cradled against her chest and was staring into space.

'Janey just meant it as a joke, but I'm sure she's learned her lesson now,' said Caro. 'Haven't you, Janey?'

'Yeah,' Janey mumbled.

Bronte was suddenly furious. A joke? Janey hadn't even said sorry. How did she get away with this stuff—not just once or twice, but again and again and again? Couldn't Caro *see*? And why didn't her own mother say anything or stick up for her? Wasn't she interested? Didn't she *care*?

'What's her punishment then?' she asked.

Caro looked taken aback. It was clear that the thought of punishment hadn't crossed her mind.

'Well, I suppose . . . I think . . . maybe I'll confiscate her phone until we're home again,' she ad-libbed.

What, for two whole days? Bronte thought. It was too much to bear, all of it: her humiliation, Janey's attitude, her mother's lack of interest, Caro's blindness. Rage swept through her, propelled her off the bed; she snatched Janey's phone from her lap and ran out the door, faster than she ever had in her life, sprinting madly towards the beach. She passed Morag, who stared after her, and Mason, sitting in the shade fixing a net, who called out, but she didn't stop. The rage drove her on and on, Janey's shrieks fading behind her, until she reached the white sand, lifted her arm high above her head and threw the phone as far out to sea as she could.

Fiona took another mouthful of wine and slipped her hand inside her singlet. The sun had gone down a few hours ago; no one could see what she was doing. No one would be interested anyway, caught up in their post-dinner conversations or thinking about retiring for the night. She eased her fingers under her bra, probing gently. Maybe she'd just imagined it . . . maybe it had been an ant bite, or a reaction to something she'd brushed against. Look at Caro—her arm was covered with angry red bumps. It seemed as if there was no end of ways to injure or inflame yourself up here.

Fiona's spirits rose for a moment, then plummeted as she found the lump again. Was she just imagining it or was it bigger than when she'd discovered it earlier that day, in the shower after mudcrabbing? She closed her eyes and tentatively palpated it, concentrating. It was bigger than a pea but smaller than a marble, and mobile rather than anchored in her flesh. Was that a good sign? She worked with seven doctors. She was always tuning out their conversations or telling them to stop talking shop in the lunchroom, but now she desperately tried to remember anything they might have said about breast lumps, anything at all. It was probably just a cyst, Fiona told herself, as she had in the shower, or something to do with starting menopause. She was forty-eight; the change must be close. Maybe it was related to her period, which was still going—she'd never noticed lumps before at that time of the month, but then she rarely examined her breasts. It was too boring, and they were so big and floppy that she'd once joked to Amira that she'd never be able to find a lump anyway—there'd have to be an aircraft carrier in there before she noticed anything. That didn't seem so funny now.

A biopsy, she thought, the moment she was back in Melbourne. That was what she needed. Maybe not Sunday, when her plane got in, but definitely first thing Monday morning, as soon as she arrived at work. Or maybe a mammogram . . . what did they do first? Her fingers sought the lump again, pressed down on it as if she could drive it right out of her body and into the dust at her feet, a still-pulsing morsel of blood and gristle to be tossed to the ever-hungry dogs skulking at the edges of the community. She'd slice her whole breast off now if she could, throw them that too.

Fiona lifted her glass to her mouth, then put it down again. There was a link between alcohol and cancer, wasn't there? Maybe she'd brought this on herself . . . but then there was a link between cancer and everything, pretty much. 'Calm down,' she muttered to herself. There was no point worrying about it now when nothing could be done. She needed to think about something else, anything.

She pulled her hand out of her top and looked around. Morag and Macy were deep in conversation at the far end of the table, Macy appearing more animated than Fiona had ever seen her before—though maybe that was because for once her face was free of her usual heavy make-up. Caro had risen from her seat and was scraping and stacking plates. Amira hadn't joined them for dinner, attending the community feast instead. Janey was nowhere to be seen—maybe she was down at the lagoon with a torch and a net, trying to find her phone—and Bronte and Tess were sitting side by side, heads almost touching as they talked.

Bronte. Christ. That was one way to distract herself. Fiona's jaw clenched. What a piece of work Janey was, what a first-class bitch. She'd finally revealed her true nature, hadn't she? Even Caro couldn't be sucked in by her any longer, surely. And what a way for it all to unfold: Tess tells Amira, Amira tells Caro, Caro tells Janey, Janey tells Bronte . . . it was like some fucked-up game of Chinese whispers. Women could be so pathetic, she thought, their own worst enemies. Sometimes she suspected they actually enjoyed being victims because it gave them something to talk about. If this whole sorry online saga had happened between men—not that it would *ever* happen between men—they would have sorted it out with fists, not endless chatter.

Still, she thought, Bronte had done alright. Better than alright—she'd been fabulous. Fiona couldn't quite believe it when Bronte had snatched that phone from Janey, and her surprise was mixed with pride. Bronte, who still stammered if Dom teased her, who'd carefully move spiders out of the kitchen rather than let Fiona kill them . . . Bronte had stood up to Janey. Caro had been aghast, but Fiona had quietly cheered her daughter on as she sprinted away. Who would have thought Bronte could run so fast, could leave state champion swimmer Janey in her wake? It must be those long legs of hers, Fiona mused. Nice to know they were good for something.

She settled back in her seat, enjoying the memory, and allowed herself a sip of wine—the damage was clearly done now, after all. She wished Amira had seen it. Too hard on Bronte, was she? Maybe, but Bronte was turning out OK if today was anything to go by. The problem was actually that most people were too soft, with their never-ending positive feedback and the affirmation workshop she'd had to attend at the clinic and all the awards they were forever giving out when Bronte was at primary school. Student of the week! Best helper! I can tie my shoelaces! Might as well hand out certificates for wiping their own arses. Her own mum had never gone in for any of that, had never lavished her with praise—quite the opposite—and it hadn't hurt Fiona. Sure, she and her mother didn't talk much, but that was normal at this age, wasn't it? They were grown women, they had their own lives. There was no need.

'Hey,' said Morag, sitting down beside her. Fiona noticed that Macy had moved to join Tess and Bronte, the three girls now sprawled out on the grass just beyond the table, their young limbs silver in the moonlight. 'Are you still with us? And Caro—the plates can wait. Come and have a drink before bed.'

Caro pulled out a chair, casting a wary glance at Fiona. They hadn't spoken since the phone incident.

'What a gorgeous night,' Morag remarked. She either had no idea about what had happened between Janey and Bronte or was choosing to ignore it, to smooth things over. Probably the latter, Fiona guessed. 'Though it's strange not having Amira with us. She's such a part of this place, isn't she? Watching her interact with everyone at mudcrabbing today—it's like she's been here for years.'

'A bit too involved, if you ask me,' said Fiona. 'Racing off to that corroboree, or whatever it is they're doing on the point. I mean, I know she works here and everything, but it's not as if she's actually one of them, is she? You know what I mean.'

'It's not a corroboree, Fiona,' Morag said mildly. 'It's a feast to honour the dead man's spirit and move it on. That's what Amira told me, anyway. I think it's wonderful that she attended, that she's welcomed there even though she's white. There should be more of it in Australia, from both sides.'

Fiona felt vaguely chastened. She fell silent, her hand once more drifting to her breast.

'It would've been nice to try some of those crabs,' Caro said. 'Do you think she'll bring any back for us?'

'Maybe,' said Morag. 'Hey—can you hear that?' At the same time, Macy suddenly sat up, inclining her head in the direction of the beach. The sound of voices drifted towards them, rising and falling in unison.

'Are they humming again?' Caro asked.

Morag shook her head. 'I don't think so. It's more like a song, but I can't make out the words.'

The ethereal melody rose between them, carried on the still night air, slipping across the lagoon and between the trees, encircling their table, the community. Goosebumps broke out along Fiona's arms; the skin on the back of her neck tingled. The singing reminded her of the didgeridoo she'd heard at Wajarrgi a few days ago: the ancient music somehow telling a whole story, infused with a whole history. It was unnerving and it was beautiful and she didn't understand it at all. She stared up at the stars, the same ones that had been there when this ancient land was new, and just then another, nearer singer joined in. It was Macy, her voice soaring in harmony with those by the water.

Saturday

It was only one night away, Amira told herself as she threw the overnight bag on the bed. She didn't need to take much. Her bathers, in case they stopped off at Cable Beach or she felt like a swim at The Mangrove; sunscreen, a hat and sunglasses, the holy trinity of accessories in the tropics; some clean undies; and something nice to wear out to dinner. Amira pushed her hair back from her face. *Nice.* If one of her students had written that she would have circled it in red and told them to use a more descriptive word: *beautiful, striking*, even *pretty*. She turned and peered into her wardrobe. The trouble was that she barely had anything pretty anymore. There was her fitted black dress with the beading around the neckline, but she'd already worn that at the Aarli Bar last Sunday. All the other summer gear she'd brought with her from Melbourne had long since faded or frayed, was either stained with pindan or baggy from overuse. Her clothes had gone into shock, she thought, assaulted by the UV, the humidity, even the antiperspirant she had to reapply every few hours. And she knew it didn't really matter—clothes up here were for purely functional purposes, not decorative—but she had wanted to make an effort tonight, their last together.

Amira sat down on the bed, her stomach clenching. Their last night. The hours were ticking away ... Right now her friends were in their rooms preparing to leave: gathering up their toiletries, shoving sarongs into suitcases, probably yelling at their daughters to hurry up. Soon they'd all load back into the troop carrier for the long drive down the bumpy red road to Broome, and this time tomorrow she'd be at the airport, preparing to wave them goodbye. She'd miss them. She'd miss the laughter and the sniping, she'd miss Caro's smile and Morag's dry wit and even Fiona's cynicism, she'd miss the simple ease of being with people who knew you, who got you, who were part of your history. But she didn't want to go with them. The realisation was abrupt, instinctive and shocking. She felt it race through her like an electric charge. She was glad she was only packing her bags for an overnight trip; she didn't envy her friends their return to the south. She could barely even picture Melbourne, she thought with a start. It wasn't real to her, not the way all this was—the sun and the sky and the ta-ta lizards sitting panting in the shade, waving one arm back and forth like wind-up toys.

She had thought she might be homesick after spending a week with her friends, but she wasn't. Oh, there were things she missed about Melbourne, no doubt about it: the lamb-shank pizza at Al Albero; not having to keep her armpits shaved all the time; being able to take her class on excursions. Amira smiled to herself as she folded a beach towel and placed it in her bag. To think how she used to grimace whenever an excursion was announced, immediately exhausted by the prospect of dragging her class around the zoo or the museum for what felt like the thousandth time, her temples pounding in anticipation of a day of constant headcounts and too much noise on the bus. How spoiled she'd been! What she'd give to be able to take her current students to the Bunjilaka Aboriginal Cultural Centre at the Melbourne Museum, or to show them an elephant or a chimpanzee. Most of the kids had rarely left the community in their lives; there were some who hadn't even seen Broome. She reached under her pillow for her nightie. It was one of the many frustrations of teaching up here: the isolation, the lack of resources—not so much in the classroom but in the community, in the day-to-day life going on outside the school. Kalangalla was beautiful, but it was limited. When she'd asked her year six students what they wanted to be when they grew up they'd told her nurses and teachers, or maybe working at Wajarrgi—all of which were fine aspirations, they really were, but no one had said *meteorologist* or *architect* or *chef*, as her class in Melbourne had done. And it wasn't that they weren't capable of dreaming or aspiring, Amira thought, crossing her room to get her bathers from the chest of drawers, it was that they didn't *know*. They had no idea those jobs existed, no notion of what their lives might be.

The bathers weren't in the drawer. Amira sighed. It got to her sometimes, just how much there was to do up here, but then that was why she'd come, wasn't it? For a challenge, and to make a difference. She was a good teacher, she knew she was, but there were lots of good teachers in the cities. People like her were needed in places like this. And she was getting somewhere, she truly felt she was, only it all took so much time . . . January was looming, and yet most days it seemed that she'd hardly got started. She'd have only just figured out these kids, this community, and then she too would be heading for the airport, like Fiona and Caro and Morag, her boab nuts wrapped carefully in newspaper for the journey, her work only half done.

Amira shut the drawer she'd been fossicking through and straightened up, squaring her shoulders. She wouldn't think about it now. She wouldn't ruin her last day with her friends fretting over things she couldn't change. And the bathers—they must still be on the line where she'd hung them to dry last night. After the comforting gloom of the house, the sunlight stung her eyes. Amira rubbed at them as she made her way to the old Hills hoists next to the communal laundry. Tess's would probably be there too, unless of course she was already in them, hadn't bothered changing after her regular morning swim. *Regular.* It still surprised Amira. Back home, Tess had all but given up any form of physical activity. She continued to play netball with Bronte and Janey on Saturday mornings but that was about it—otherwise her leisure time was given over to staring at the screen on her phone or laptop, going out shopping, or obsessing about her appearance. But now she went swimming every day and read more novels than Facebook updates. The move had definitely been worthwhile, even if it was going to be over too soon.

As she approached, she saw that Tia was at the line, hanging sheets, her back to Amira. Thank goodness for Tia. She'd been a great friend to Tess, had really helped her settle in. Amira was about to call out to her but then stopped. Halfway through her task, Tia had paused; she seemed to sway a little in the red dust, her hands going to her back. Standing like that, her belly thrust forward . . . Amira swallowed. No. She was seeing things. It wasn't possible. Tia was only fifteen, not much older than Tess—but that stance, that stomach . . .

'Tia,' she blurted, 'you're pregnant!'

Tia started and turned towards her, her face hostile. For a moment Amira thought she was going to deny it, but then the girl bent over the laundry basket, pulled out another sheet and silently pegged it to the line. Her ankles were swollen, Amira noticed; fingers too.

'Have you seen a doctor?' Amira asked. 'Have you had a scan? Do you know how far along you are?'

Tia shrugged, her hands dark against the white linen.

'It's Jago's baby, isn't it?' Amira persisted. 'Have you told him? You need to tell him. He'll have to be part of it, whatever you decide to do.'

'I told him the day you were all at Wajarrgi,' Tia replied sullenly, her back still to Amira. 'And there's nothing to decide. I think it's too late now anyway.'

'Oh, Tia.' Amira exhaled. 'You could have gone to university in another few years.'

'Still can.' Tia grunted, hauling a faded yellow blanket over the Hills hoist.

'How?' Amira said, her voice sharper than she intended.

'Leave the child back here, with your mum, who already has enough of her own to care for? Or take it with you and hope you can juggle work and study and looking after a toddler? That'll be fun.'

The basket was finally empty. Tia swung around, scowling.

'I'll manage. Who said I wanted to go to uni anyway? That was your idea, not mine. I like it here.'

'Oh, Tia,' Amira sighed again. She wasn't handling this well. 'What do your parents think? Your mum, Mason?'

'I haven't told them yet.' Tia wiped her palms down the front of her t-shirt, almost as if she was trying to smooth down her stomach, make it flat again. 'Mum had me young. She'll be fine.'

Maybe so, Amira thought, but Mason? Surely he'd be disappointed. Tia was a bright girl. She was one of the few her age who had what it took to make a life away from Kalangalla . . . but then Mason did too, and he was still here. Amira felt a headache rumbling into gear behind her temples. For all her love of it, she still didn't understand this place. Was the baby even an accident, as she had immediately assumed, or was it Tia's means of releasing herself from her own bright promise, ensuring she stayed with her people and on her land?

'Don't you tell them, anyway,' Tia said, walking away—Tia, who had always been so polite, so open, so giggly and uncomplicated. 'It's none of your business. You won't even be here by the time it's born.'

Amira watched her go until she disappeared into her home, then turned back herself. It wasn't until she reached her own front door that she realised she'd forgotten to get her bathers.

Bronte sat at the table where they'd had all their meals, toying with the food in front of her. She wasn't full, but she couldn't bring herself to eat any more. She was a bit over fish . . . fish for dinner, fish for lunch—there probably would have been fish for breakfast if she'd asked, sardines crumbled across her cornflakes or a side order of groper with her toast. Ugh. Every piece of fish she'd eaten had been freshly caught, expertly filleted, marinated in an ever-changing assortment of local herbs—but now all she wanted was a lamb chop or some carbonara. Funny how you could get so sick of something you liked if that was all that was offered every day. She wondered if it worked with people too. Did Tess ever get fed up of hanging out just with Tia and yearn for some variety, a whole noisy, heaving gang like she'd been part of in Melbourne? Against that, having one really close friend would be amazing. Someone who knew you and accepted you, who you could just relax and be yourself with rather than worrying if you'd said the wrong thing or were wearing the right clothes. She'd hoped it would happen when she moved to St Anne's, but she was still waiting . . .

'Bronte, it's not a bloody pet. Stop playing with it. Just hurry up and finish your lunch, can you—we still need to pack.' Her mother's voice cut through her thoughts. Bronte blushed, lifted a morsel of white flesh to her mouth and made herself swallow. She'd already packed, but her mum obviously hadn't realised that yet, their room was so littered with her own debris. Bronte would go and help her get it under control, then maybe there'd be time for one last quick look at the gallery before they left . . .

She pushed her plate away and stood up from the table. Something trickled down her leg—sweat, she thought—and she reached behind her to brush it off. Her hand came away red. Bronte thumped quickly back down into her seat. Tentatively, she examined her fingers in her lap. Blood, it looked like blood. She sat there, heart pounding, and felt a second trickle rolling down the other thigh. Under cover of the table she moved her hand into her shorts and found that her undies were wet to the touch, sticky and warm. Her mind raced. She wasn't hurt—she'd been fine all week, apart from those cramps yesterday . . . cramps. Oh God. What awful timing. She'd been dying for her period to finally start—she must be the last girl in her year at St Anne's to get it—but why here, and why now?

'Mum,' she called out, but Fiona was already walking away.

'Hurry up,' she repeated over her shoulder.

Bronte looked around. Only Janey and Macy were left at the table, the latter chewing slowly as she listened to her iPod, the former simply staring into space, uncharacteristically still with no phone to fiddle with. They hadn't spoken since Bronte had thrown it into the lagoon. Janey was probably avoiding her mother, Bronte supposed, but the thought gave her no pleasure. How could she get out of this? There was no way she was going to reveal her predicament to Janey and Macy, suffer their condescending sniggers—or, worse, stand up and have them gawp or laugh. Tess would know what to do, but she was nowhere in sight. Everyone else was preparing for their departure; Bronte had only lingered at the table herself because, unlike them, she was ready to go.

'*Mum!*' she cried again, voice wavering.

'I'm *busy*, Bronte!' her mother shouted back from their room thirty metres away. 'You should be too. *Hurry up.*'

Tears pricked at Bronte's eyes. The seat beneath her felt uncomfortably slick. How much blood was she losing? Was this normal? A sudden rage seized her. Her mother should be here for her now. Her mother should be reassuring her and taking care of her, but her mother—as usual—was too preoccupied with her own agenda. Bronte felt her skin grow hot, but with fury, for once, not embarrassment. She pushed back the chair, got to her feet and strode towards their room. Let everyone see, let them all laugh, what did it matter? She didn't care anymore.

'Bronte!' Janey exclaimed behind her. 'Your shorts . . . your legs . . .'

'I know,' Bronte snarled without looking back. 'Want to take a photo? You'll be able to post it tonight, once we're in Broome.'

Her mother had handed her a box of tampons. Bronte sat on the toilet holding one in her hand, the instruction leaflet in the other. She studied it closely, then tried again to insert the tampon, but it was hopeless. She didn't have a clue what she was doing, and everything was so messed with blood. She needed more than a tiny diagram to find the right spot. She needed a GPS.

There was a knock on the door.

'Bronte? It's Caro. Janey told me what happened.'

Bronte rolled her eyes. Of course she did.

'I hope you don't mind,' Caro went on, 'but I came over to see if I could help. I've got some wipes if you like, just in case you want to . . . clean up a bit. And I brought some pads. Your mum said she just had Meds.' The door opened a crack.

'Don't come in!' Bronte cried.

'I'm not going to,' Caro said. 'I just wanted to give you these.' A yellow packet fell to the floor. Bronte stared at it. *Sure and Natural.* She sniffed. Nothing about this felt particularly natural. 'And the wipes too,' Caro went on, pushing something else through the gap. 'Keep them both. I can get more in Broome if I need them. Hand me out your shorts and your undies. I'll rinse them and put them in a plastic bag. Your mum will pass in some clean ones. Now, do you know how to use the pads?'

'I'm sure I can work it out,' said Bronte.

Caro was still there when she emerged clean and changed, but somewhat awkwardly ten minutes later. How did women get used to this? She felt as if she had a mattress between her legs.

'Are you OK?' Caro asked. Behind her, Fiona leaned over the bed, struggling to do up her suitcase.

'I'm fine, thank you,' Bronte said stiffly. 'You can go now if you like.' Caro must still be feeling bad about yesterday, she thought, hanging around and washing her shorts. Still, she was glad that someone had. She couldn't have faced it.

'I wanted to see you,' Caro said. 'I wanted to say congratulations. You're a woman now.'

Fiona snorted, then pretended she'd coughed.

'It's a big deal,' Caro continued, ignoring Fiona. 'It really is, Bronte. Don't feel embarrassed. You should be proud.' Before Bronte realised what she was doing, Caro had wrapped her arms around her and pulled her close. 'Don't let anyone tell you differently.'

For the second time that hour, Bronte blinked away tears. A woman. She wondered if Ms Drummond would be able to tell when she went back to school, if she would notice immediately that Bronte had finally grown up. And then, because Caro had been so kind and was holding her so closely, she hugged her back.

Caro looked at her watch. It was the first time she'd checked it in days. She'd been a while with Bronte in the bathroom, but she still had time, as long as she was quick. Heavens knows, after the way Janey had behaved it was the least she could do, but she would have wanted to help out anyway. She genuinely liked Bronte. Loved her, maybe. The children that grew up alongside yours made their own place in your heart.

She'd send him something, Caro decided as she negotiated the track to the beach for the final time. She wanted to thank Mason somehow for all he'd done for her—for taking her out fishing and looking after her when she got stung; for helping her with that dreadful Facebook situation without asking any questions—but there was nothing here she wanted to buy for him. The store only seemed to stock junk food, and the beautiful crafts for sale at the gallery were nothing new to him. His wife Aki probably knocked them up between changing nappies. She felt a prickle of derision. They had so many children. Too many children. Maybe she could send him a gift voucher for a vasectomy clinic.

The water appeared between the trees, flashing blue and silver in the morning light. In the distance Caro could see Mason sitting out on the point, his legs dangling in the water, and was immediately ashamed of her bitchy thoughts. What did it matter to her how many kids he had? She'd never see him again after today; she'd get back to Melbourne and put something in the mail for him and that would be it. But what? Alcohol was out of the question, of course—a shame, when that was always the easiest option. Often she sent people hampers of the lovely foodstuffs Alex imported—stuffed olives, piquant cheeses, tiny biscuits as delicately and intricately constructed as the handmade lace he'd once brought back for her from the island of Burano—but she couldn't imagine Mason eating biscuits. They'd probably get broken in the post, anyway. She trudged on through the sand. A book? Clothes? A CD? She wasn't sure if he even listened to music . . . Western music, that was, not that funereal tune from last night.

Last night. Oh, that had been awkward. She could barely look at Fiona or Bronte—or her own daughter, for that matter. She probably shouldn't have slapped Janey—but God, she'd been furious. And scared, she admitted to herself. Mostly scared. Scared of what her own flesh and blood was capable of, scared of the gulf opening up between them and of the years that lay ahead. It would be a terrible thing to lose a child to cancer or an unfenced pool, but sometimes she wondered if it wasn't almost as bad losing them bit by bit, watching them turn their back on you and stride into the world. April still loved her forcefully, unconditionally, with a devotion that made Caro's heart contract. In April's eyes, her mother could do no wrong, was beautiful and competent and always, always right. Just the night before she'd come up here, Caro had gone into her youngest daughter's room to check that she hadn't kicked off her doona, and April had heard her, roused briefly, and mumbled, 'I love you, Mummy. You're so perfect for me,' before falling back to sleep. Tears welled in Caro's eyes as she remembered that moment. She missed April—but she missed Janey too, the Janey who used to happily chatter to her in the car as Caro drove her to and from squad, not hook herself up to her iPod and stare unseeingly out the window; the Janey who asked Caro's opinion on her outfits or told her what was happening with her friends. Children were a cruel trick. They shouldn't be allowed to grow up.

'Hello!' Mason waved as she picked her way over the rocks towards him. 'Headin' for the big smoke today?'

'No, Melbourne's tomorrow,' Caro replied, then caught herself. 'Oh—you mean Broome, don't you?'

'Broome's the big smoke to us.' He grinned.

Caro cleared a space among his fishing gear and sat down next to him. Barnacles bit into her thighs and bottom but she didn't get up. She didn't want him thinking she was soft. 'We're leaving soon,' she said. 'Amira's taking us somewhere to see a staircase, I think she called it, then the flight goes at eleven tomorrow.'

'The staircase to the moon,' Mason said. 'That must be the last one for the year. It never appears durin' the wet, you know. You're lucky you're around for it.'

Caro nodded dutifully. She didn't know, she had no idea. She didn't really care, to be honest. Amira had said that it was something to do with the mudflats, but she'd had her fill of mudflats after crabbing yesterday. 'Tess told me you'd be here. I came to thank you before we went.'

'Thank me? For what?'

'Your help yesterday with picking up the internet.' She felt sick at the memory of it, of standing on these very rocks silently praying for a signal, Janey glowering beside her, one cheek still stained red. 'And for when I got stung while we were fishing—for taking me back in again.'

Mason chuckled. 'I wasn't goin' to toss you overboard.'

'No, I know, but I interrupted your fishing,' said Caro, all too aware she was doing it again. 'I'd like to send you something from Melbourne, to show my gratitude. Maybe something that you can't get here. Is there anything you want?'

Mason slowly shook his head. 'I don't think so. I've got everythin' I need.' He adjusted his reel, then asked, 'Is it healin' OK?'

'I haven't looked,' Caro admitted. 'I'm not good with that sort of thing, but it feels fine. It's stopped throbbing. I'll have it checked by my GP when I get back to Melbourne, just to be sure.'

'Show me.' Mason gestured for her to give him her arm.

'It's fine,' Caro repeated. 'There's really no need . . .'

But Mason wasn't listening. Slowly, with infinite care, he had taken her forearm into his lap and released the silver clasp on the bandage. Then, starting at her wrist, he gently unwound it. It felt, Caro thought, like being undressed. She looked out to the horizon to try to distract herself; then she stared at her toenails, the varnish all chipped. Mason was peeling back the last layer now, his fingers deft and somehow tender. For a moment his dark skin rested against her pale flesh, and she had a sudden vision of the two of them in bed together, naked, black against white, curled around each other like a yin-yang symbol.

'Sorry—did that hurt?' asked Mason. 'You've got goose-bumps.' He bent over her arm. 'It's lookin' good. Healin' well. You're going to have a scar though.' Softly, he traced the raised red welt with one rough fingertip. Caro closed her eyes. She was being ridiculous, pathetic. She loved Alex; she would never dream of straying. 'A souvenir,' Mason went on. 'Somethin' to remind you of Kalangalla. Like a tattoo, only more original.'

Caro's head swum. It was the heat that was making her dizzy, surely, and the sleepless night fretting about Janey.

Mason looked up, stared into her eyes. 'You were lucky,' he pronounced. 'It could have been Irukandji—we're comin' up to their time of year. You could be dead right now. Remember that next time you get worried about somethin', it still beats bein' dead.'

Later, as she sat in the troop carrier bouncing along the road towards Broome, Caro turned the words over in her mind. Did Mason know how crippled she was by anxiety at times? Had he sensed that she was uptight when they were trying to access that Facebook picture? Perhaps Amira had told him about the panic attack she'd had beforehand. Caro knew she wouldn't have, though; Amira wasn't like that. He must just have guessed . . . or maybe he was speaking generally.

Caro smiled wryly to herself. She was doing exactly what he'd told her not to: worrying. But she wasn't going to worry anymore, she decided. Mason was right. She could be dead, yet she wasn't, and surely that outweighed everything else. A shot of pure happiness went through her, effervescent and fleeting, but intoxicating nonetheless. She wanted to laugh; she wanted to celebrate these final moments of the trip. As she loosened her seatbelt and leaned across the aisle to talk to Morag she realised something else: she had wanted to give Mason a gift, but he had handed her one instead.

———

Tess lay on her back, looking up through the palm trees and into the night sky. More stars were coming out, shyly poking their faces through the indigo shawl draped above her. Could she remember their names? The bright one was Venus—a planet, not a star, she corrected herself. Back at the end of the last wet, when the nights were warm enough to sleep outside with just a blanket, she'd camped out once or twice with Tia and her family on the beach at Kalangalla, and Mason had pointed out the constellations for them. Tess had no idea how he remembered them all—the sky up here was full of stars, bursting with them—but he'd shown them the Dreaming stars, as he called them, the emu and the serpent. They were different, he'd told her, from the ones she might have learned about at school. What the whitefella called Orion was actually Julpan, a canoe. Could she see it? There was the bow, and there was the stern, and the bright stars between them were two brothers who'd gone fishing, but one had eaten a fish that was forbidden by their law and so the sun had dragged the two boys and their canoe into the sky and beached them there . . . She'd wanted to ask him why the fish was forbidden, but she must have fallen asleep, lulled by the dance of his dark arms against the Milky Way. As soon as she was back she would do so, she resolved. And it was nearly the wet again. They could have another sleepout, lots of them, her and Tia and Mason and Aki and the tumbling little boys. Maybe her mother would come this time. She'd be interested in the canoe.

'Tess! Sit up! You're going to miss it all!' said Bronte.

Tess glanced across the bay. 'No, I'm not. It's not time yet.'

Bronte leaned over, her breath warm against Tess's ear. 'Have I got time to go to the toilet then?' she whispered.

'Sure,' Tess said. 'Are you OK? Do you need a hand?'

'I think I'm getting the hang of it,' Bronte said, then giggled and ran off.

Tess smiled. She'd never known anyone so happy to get her period, if that was indeed what had brought the colour to Bronte's cheeks. Ever since they'd left Kalangalla, through the jarring ride down the Cape Leveque road, a swim at Cable Beach, and then checking into The Mangrove, Bronte had been bright-eyed, chatty, animated. As they sat together on the back seat of the troop carrier she'd told Tess what had happened at lunch, but she'd turned it into the sort of story

Janey would have told, full of *Oh my Gods* and *I nearly died*, rather than the mortified silence Tess might have expected. What was even more surprising was that Janey had caught her mood. Since the furore over the Facebook thing, Janey had been sullen, uncommunicative, but on the trip back to town she'd started talking again. Not directly to Bronte, sure, just as Bronte still wouldn't directly acknowledge Janey, but both had joined in the same conversations with Tess and Macy. Maybe it was just because Janey was bored on the long trip without her phone . . . But even when they'd reached Cable Beach and everyone else had dashed into the surf Janey had simply laid out her towel and sat down on the sand next to Bronte, who didn't want to swim in her current condition. They hadn't talked to each other, but they hadn't tried to kill each other either.

Tess rolled onto her side and spotted Macy and Janey picking their way towards her through the groups of people who had gathered here on the back lawn of The Mangrove. Janey was carrying a jug of something and some glasses; Macy was tucking her lighter into her handbag.

'You got a good spot.' Macy sank down onto the blanket that Tess had laid out, her red sundress catching the light from the lanterns hung in the trees. Tess had expected her to revert to her goth garb once they reached the relative civilisation of Broome, but it appeared that for now Macy had banished the black.

'I've been here before. Most people go to Roebuck Bay park to see the staircase, but Mum and I think it's better here. Less crowded—and there's a bar. For the adults, I mean.'

Macy grinned and took the jug from Janey. 'Drink?' she offered. 'It's cider. No one bothered to check my age. Just tell your mum it's creaming soda if she asks.'

Tess glanced across at Amira, sitting a few feet away with Fiona, Caro and Morag, gesticulating and laughing. Her mother wouldn't ask. She'd pretty much stopped asking since they'd come up north, preferring to trust Tess not to do anything too stupid but to know that Amira would still help her if she did. It was a good policy. It was why they still liked each other.

'Hey, I think it's starting!' Janey cried, pointing out across the mangroves that fringed the water. Sure enough, there was a faint silver glimmer on the horizon.

Bronte squeezed herself next to Tess.

'Have I missed it? Did I miss it?' she asked.

'Relax,' said Tess. 'It's only just begun.' She held her breath as the full moon seemingly rose from the sea, a glowing orb, a golden balloon. As it slowly ascended, its light reflected off the exposed mudflats that stretched out before them, creating the illusion of a set of gilded stairs hanging in the sky.

'I can see it!' said Macy, forgetting for a moment to be cool. 'Can you, Janey?'

'It's amazing,' murmured Bronte. 'It almost looks as if you could climb right up into the moon . . . that you could sit on it, staring back at us.'

Tess felt her skin prickle. That was it, that was it exactly. *As if you could climb right up.* She'd have to remember that phrase for her letter to Callum. The letter. Just thinking of it made her warm. No more postcards—this was the real deal.

It was only half finished, stashed deep in her overnight bag, but tomorrow morning she was going to get up early, write another page or two, and then give it to Morag before she left. She didn't have any masking tape, but she trusted Morag. Morag wouldn't peek.

As the moon floated above them, rich and round, Tess composed her sentences in her mind. Callum would love this, she thought. Perhaps she might even suggest that one day he came and saw it with her.

———

Fiona peered through the gloom at the faces surrounding her, universally upturned in delight and awe, then looked at the sky again. Nup. She still didn't get it. A fat yellow moon—nice, but she'd seen full moons before—and a few fading bars of light below it. How could *this* be what everyone was in raptures over, the subject of all those tacky souvenirs she'd seen in town—fridge magnets, stubby holders, cheap jewellery? Maybe it was her—she'd never had the patience to wait for those 3D pictures to swim into view, after all. She tilted back her head and squinted hard, but all that came into focus was how itchy the sandfly bites were on her ankles and a nagging pain building behind her temples.

'Hey!' Warm liquid gushed across her foot, soaking her sandal and the hem of her taupe pants. When she looked down she thought for a moment it was blood, then realised she'd actually been splashed with red wine knocked over by the group sitting in front of them. The bottle rocked slightly at her feet, discharging its contents into the lawn.

'Hey!' she said again, louder this time, prodding the closest back with her dripping toes. They left a russet mark . . . Good. 'I think this is yours,' she said when a hippyish-looking woman turned around, and handed her the empty bottle. 'You spilled it all over me.'

'Oh—sorry,' the woman said, taking it from her. 'I didn't notice. We're all just so engrossed by the moon. Isn't it magical?'

'Yeah, magical,' grunted Fiona, holding her foot under her nose. 'So magical you fucking soaked me.' Amira laid a warning hand on her arm and Fiona shook it off.

'Serena,' said the woman to the person sitting next to her, 'Have you got any tissues with you? There's been a bit of an accident.'

'Don't bother,' said Fiona, standing up. 'Tissues aren't going to cut it. I'll need to go and wash these.'

Someone further back hissed at her to sit down, that she was blocking their view.

'Get stuffed,' she called out as she strode off. 'It looks better on the postcards anyway.'

Back in her hotel room, she took off the pants, ran some cold water in the basin and soaked the cuffs. The water bloomed red. 'Fuck it,' she said aloud. She hoped the stain would come out. She really liked those pants. They were the only ones she owned that made her arse look smaller than a pick-up truck. Fiona sat down on the bed. Now what? Get changed and go back out again . . . but for what? More of that stupid moon and the gawping tourists. She didn't have anything else to wear, anyway. Every other item of clothing she'd brought was befouled with red dust and encrusted with sweat. She was over this place, she really was. She couldn't wait to get on the plane tomorrow.

The door opened and Bronte stood there blinking in the light. 'I didn't know you were here,' she said. 'Are you OK?'

'Fine,' replied Fiona. 'Some idiot spilled wine all over my pants so I came back to rinse them. What about you?'

'I forgot my camera.' Bronte crossed to the small table between their single beds. 'I didn't think it would matter, but I had to come back and get it. The staircase is so—'

'Magical,' Fiona cut her off. 'Yeah, I know.'

Bronte picked up her camera and turned to leave again. 'Wait,' Fiona called. 'How are you going with all the . . . the pads and stuff? Are you managing OK?' She felt awkward. This wasn't the sort of conversation she usually had with Bronte.

'Yeah, I guess.' Bronte stared down at the carpet, her long hair falling over her face. 'I'm still a bit crampy though.'

'Grab some Naprosyn if you like. There's some in my toilet bag.'

'It's not that bad.' Bronte took a deep breath and looked up at Fiona. 'What does make me feel sick is that Facebook thing. I'm trying not to think about it, but every time I do I want to vomit.'

'Really?' Fiona asked, surprised. 'But you showed Janey—you got your own back. You took her phone and threw it into the sea!' She smiled at the memory, but Bronte's face grew pinched.

'That doesn't fix anything! Everyone I know will have seen that picture. It was up for two days!' She paused, breathing heavily. 'You don't get it, do you? You think if someone's mean to you you just be mean back and it's all square. But it's not, it's *not*! I've been totally humiliated and you don't care.'

'I do,' Fiona protested, uncomfortably aware that she was at a disadvantage. It was hard to convey authority clad only in a singlet and floral underpants. 'I wanted to see Janey cop it in the neck just as much as you did. Caro's way too soft on her, if you ask me.'

'It's not about Janey!' Bronte screamed. 'Will you stop going on about her? It's about me, your daughter! You barely even stood up for me—you kept looking out the window like you were thinking about something else. You should have dealt with it. You shouldn't have left it up to me. You're meant to be my mother.' Bronte's voice rose. She placed a hand on the doorknob. 'And when I get my period, you hand me a box of tampons and that's it? That's *it*? Caro had to come in and help me! You were useless—you were too busy folding your fucking clothes or something. Thanks a million.'

The sound of the door slamming rang in Fiona's ears. She sat down on the nearest bed. Should she go after Bronte? Her daughter had never sworn before, at least not in front of her. Bronte had never fought with her either, never raised her voice to her or questioned anything Fiona had done. Bronte was always so meek, so biddable, and that drove Fiona mad, but this was no improvement. She picked at the bedspread, trying to distract herself by concentrating on its florid tropical whorls. There was a taste of acid at the back of her throat. *Useless.* Had she been? But there was no point in mollycoddling, she'd always believed that. The world was a tough place, and the sooner you realised that and learned to deal with it the better. Useless, though. Did Bronte really think that? Was Caro a better mother than she was?

Her hand went to her breast, to the lump, working it between her fingers like a rosary. She sat there palpating it for five minutes, then got up and let the water out of the basin. A hairdryer. The room would have a hairdryer, maybe even an iron. Either would do. She'd wring out the cuffs, dry the pants as best she could, then go and find Bronte.

———

The cider was working. Macy sat back in her chair and enjoyed the warm glow spreading through her body, radiating out from her core to her fingers, her toes, even, she thought, her eyelashes. She blinked. Yes, definitely her eyelashes. They felt warm and sleepy, like the rest of her, so heavy that her eyes kept wanting to close. She gave in and let them. Thank goodness for alcohol. She'd bought the jug for all of them, but Bronte had wandered off somewhere and Tess had declined, so she and Janey had had no option but to drink it all themselves. Tess was crazy. She had no idea what she was missing. All day long Macy had felt a quiver in her stomach every time she thought about heading home the next morning: facing her mum, facing her dad, working out who the hell she had to screw to get back in the eisteddfod, but the cider had taken care of all that. Gone. Washed away. She'd kill for just one more glass, but there was no point asking Morag; her stepmother would spontaneously combust at the very idea.

Which was a bit hypocritical, given that she and her friends hadn't stopped knocking back the cocktails since they'd arrived at the restaurant after that staircase thing. Macy wondered if Morag had seen her and Janey with the jug between them on the lawn. She doubted it. Morag had been too busy taking photograph after photograph, gazing down her lens rather than paying any attention to what was right under her nose.

'Excuse me, are you finished?'

Macy opened her eyes to find a waitress hovering at her side clutching a tray. Embroidered on her blouse was some bright red lettering and an Oriental-looking character. *Matso's*, Macy read. That's right. That was the name of this place—Matso's. Matso's near The Mangrove. She began to giggle at the alliteration, but stopped when Bronte nudged her.

'Are you finished?' she said. 'It doesn't look like it.'

'No, I'm done,' said Macy, passing over her plate. 'I was full anyway.'

'I was just telling the others about the night markets up at Roebuck Bay,' Tess said, leaning across the table. 'They're only on on the nights of the staircase. Mum and I went last time we were down. They're really cool—lots of different food and craft, and sometimes they have a band.'

Macy had been drifting off again, but her ears pricked up at the last word.

'Cool,' she echoed. 'We should go.'

'I think everyone's pretty settled.' Bronte nodded towards the mothers, who were cackling uproariously at something one of them had said.

'By ourselves, I mean,' Macy said. 'Why would we want them anyway?'

'Mum,' Tess piped up, 'can we go to the night markets?' She had to repeat herself twice before Amira heard.

'I guess so,' Amira replied. She looked around at her friends. 'There are some markets up at the park at Roebuck Bay, about ten minutes from here. Tess and I have been before, and they're busy and well lit. What do you think?'

'Fine by me.' Fiona waved her glass dismissively in the air. 'Knock yourselves out. Embrace that local culture.'

Macy saw Caro and Morag exchange a look.

'Only if you stay together—don't talk to anyone else,' Caro said. 'And just to the markets, OK? No heading into town. Did you hear that, Janey?'

'Yeah,' Janey mumbled.

Macy pushed back her chair. The room tilted as she stood up, and she grabbed onto the table to steady herself, then pretended she was reaching for her bag.

'And be back by . . .' Morag checked her watch, 'ten?' she confirmed with Caro and Amira. 'It's not quite eight thirty now. That should give you enough time.'

'Plenty,' Amira agreed. 'Ten it is. And stay together, like Caro said.'

Already halfway out the door, Macy nodded without turning around.

She could hear it almost as soon as they were outside, a base line pulsating in the warm night air, lodging itself deep in her chest. A thrill went through her and she had the sudden urge to run, to find it, to hunt out its source and swallow it whole.

Now that they'd left the restaurant she felt more intoxicated, not less; high on the possibilities of the night, of finally being free of the adults.

'Slow down,' Janey complained. 'I'm getting a stitch.'

'Shouldn't have worn those heels then,' Bronte said. Janey pulled a face but didn't argue back. A gecko darted across the path in front of them, and suddenly there was the park, all floodlights and people, colour and noise, the moon, now fully risen, reduced once again to a minor role.

'I'm going to see the band,' Macy said, spotting a small stage that had been set up not far from the waterline, a hundred or so people crowded around it. It was pulling at her, she thought, reeling her in.

'Too loud for me,' said Janey. 'I need a Coke. That calamari was so spicy.'

'Your mum said we had to stay together,' Bronte said.

'But she won't know, will she?' Janey gave her a pointed look.

Tess shifted from one foot to the other, taking everything in. 'I'm not really interested in the band,' she said, 'but the markets aren't very big. We could meet up later. It's not as if anyone's going to get lost ... Last time I was here, Bronte, there was a guy tossing firesticks up and catching them in his mouth. Let's go look for him.'

Bronte hesitated. 'I don't know.'

'And there's a local woman who does these amazing screen prints of fish—barramundi and salmon,' Tess went on. 'They're just beautiful. They'd make a great present if you wanted to take something back for someone.'

'Really? They do sound good . . .' Bronte exhaled. 'OK, but we all meet at the stage at ten to ten. Don't forget.' She glanced at Janey and Macy, then allowed herself to be led away by Tess.

Maybe it was the cider, but it all seemed to happen in a blur. One minute Macy was pushing herself to the front of the crowd, singing along with the cover band; the next it seemed she was being beckoned up onto the stage and a microphone thrust into her hand. The lead singer smiled encouragingly at her, and she slipped into the song as easily as getting into bed.

'You're good,' he said in her ear as the final chords jangled to a halt. 'You've done this before, haven't you?' She nodded. 'I thought so. I could hear you from the audience. Our regular girl couldn't make it tonight. Do you want to stay for the rest of the set? It's mostly recent stuff, with a few oldies thrown in. You'll probably know most of the songs.'

It was that easy, that intuitive. She quickly lost track of the time—there was no time, there was only the music. The music, the crowd, the lights . . . She closed her eyes and felt it all swelling inside of her, becoming her, until she was nothing but one perfectly sustained note, her whole body ringing like a tuning fork. Just like sex and alcohol, performing got better the more she did it. The secret, she knew now, was to go with it, give in to it, let her own heartbeat slip away until all that was left was the rhythm . . .

'Macy! *Macy!*'

Bronte and Tess were standing right in front of the stage, frantically waving their arms. Shocked back to reality, Macy stumbled and missed a line. The lead guitarist shot her a look.

'Have you seen Janey?' Tess shouted over the music.

Macy shook her head and kept singing. Fuck it, she wasn't their babysitter. They were ruining her high.

'We can't find her anywhere,' Bronte called, then Tess pulled her away.

'Forget it,' Macy saw her mouth to Bronte. 'She's no help.' Just before they disappeared back into the night, Tess turned and pointed at her. 'Stay right there!' she yelled. 'We'll come back when we've got her.'

Macy closed her eyes once more and lifted the microphone to her lips. There was no problem with that. She wasn't going anywhere.

'Where are you taking me?' Janey asked as the boy led her by the hand along the beach.

'Somewhere private, mermaid,' he said. 'I want to have you all to myself.'

Janey giggled, though she could feel her heart pounding against her ribs as if she'd just swum one of her coach's ridiculous butterfly sets. It was excitement, she told herself. That was why she was so breathless.

'Shit!' said the boy, dropping her hand.

'What's the matter?' asked Janey.

'Stubbed my toe on something,' he said, hopping slightly. 'A rock, I think.'

As Janey's eyes adjusted to the darkness she saw that they had wandered off the sand and were walking on the edge of the mudflats, among rock pools and stony outcrops. The breeze shifted, and a stench of something rotten drifted past them from the mangroves.

'Ewww,' she said. 'Let's go back up onto the grass. We're far enough away from the markets. No one can see us now.'

'Keen, are you?' He grinned and reached for her hand once more.

She didn't answer, concentrating on picking her way out of the mudflats without getting her new sandals wet. Keen? Sort of, she supposed. She'd been both flattered and relieved when she'd run into the development squad at one of the many takeaway vans circling the night markets: flattered because the boy she'd met twice before had recognised and followed her, complimenting her so outrageously that she'd agreed to this private walk with him; relieved because at least now she had someone to hang around with, someone who wanted to be with her. It had felt strange wandering around the markets by herself. She hadn't liked being alone. She wasn't used to it—back home, people were always fighting to talk to her, sit next to her—but Macy, Tess and Bronte had acted as if they couldn't get rid of her quickly enough. A wave of loneliness washed over her; a lump rose in her throat. She forced it down, angry at herself for being so needy. She wasn't lonely, not one bit. She had the boy—who needed those girls? They were all idiots anyway. Macy, who thought she was so cool just because she wore black and could sing a bit; Bronte, that pathetic stick insect who'd ruined her phone; and Tess, who'd gone off and dobbed to her mummy about the Facebook photo. Didn't they get that it was just a joke? She wouldn't be emailing Tess again. She could rot up here for all Janey cared.

'Here we are, mermaid,' said the boy, pulling her down beside him onto the grass that ran along the edge of the beach. He shrugged off his polo shirt. 'You can lie on this.'

Lie? Janey felt a small tingle of panic. He'd said they were going for a walk. 'My name's actually Janey,' she said, stalling. 'What's yours?'

'Roo,' he said, slipping one arm around her.

'As in the animal?'

'As in Rupert, my grandfather. He was white, but my grandmother wasn't.' One broad hand slid along her shoulder and down towards her breast.

'Oh, that's interesting,' said Janey desperately. 'Where was she from?'

In reply Roo's mouth descended on hers. He had kissed her before, but this time, in the darkness, it was more of a shock, an invasion, and she felt herself freeze.

Roo drew back.

'What's the matter, mermaid? I thought you liked it last time.'

'I did—I do,' Janey protested. 'I just wasn't . . . ready, I guess.'

'We can go back if you like. I'm not going to make you.'

Janey fought the impulse to spring to her feet. Yes, they could go back, but to what? Roo would probably just join his mates again, and she'd have to hang around by herself until it was time to return to The Mangrove with the others. The loneliness rose again. She'd been on her own pretty much all day. Besides, she told herself, there was something romantic about being out on a beach with a handsome stranger. This was what she wanted, wasn't it? She'd been thinking about it, after all. And if so, how much better for it to happen here, under the stars, rather than in someone's parents' bedroom at a party with half her class hanging around outside? She took a deep breath, then leaned over and kissed him lightly on the lips.

'It's OK,' she said. 'I want to stay here.'

At first it was nice. Roo kissed her back, more slowly and less aggressively than he had at Wajarrgi, his arms around her strong and almost comforting. Janey wished they could stay like that, just kissing, but before she knew it his hands were on her stomach, sliding up underneath her top to cup her breasts, remove her bra, his calloused palms rough against her nipples. She shuddered, and he took it for arousal rather than discomfort, pushing her onto her back and rolling on top of her. Janey felt his penis hard against her stomach, and her eyes flew open. The moon seemed a long way away now. If only he'd just slow down a bit, she thought. He was going too quickly. She opened her mouth to ask him, but then closed it again. He'd think she was a baby, a scaredy-cat. She wanted him to boast about her to his friends, not laugh. Roo's hands moved lower, parting her inner thighs, and she gripped his shoulders, willing herself not to flinch.

'You like that, do you, mermaid?' he muttered against her neck.

Janey, my name's Janey, she wanted to say, but he was pushing up her skirt and pulling down her underwear and it was all happening too quickly. Roo paused and for a second she thought with relief that he'd changed his mind, but then she heard him fumbling with his shorts. Suddenly his full weight was back on her, suffocating her, and there was something hot and hard and very determined prodding between her legs.

'Do you have something?' she gasped, every cautionary tale she'd ever read in *Cosmo* flooding back to her. 'A condom?'

Roo groaned. 'I don't. I'll pull out though, OK? I promise.'

The prodding resumed, fierce and elemental, like the siege of a castle. Janey bit her lip, determined not to cry out. *This is your fault, Mum*, she found herself thinking. Her fault for slapping her, for calling her a bitch, for not being on her side; her fault that she'd been all alone at the markets and had had to go with Roo. This would show her. *I hope you're happy.* Then all of a sudden Roo broke through, was inside her. She was dry and it stung, his penis like a rasp, a chisel, something splitting her apart. She wriggled and tried to shove him away, but it was too late—he was thrusting now, forcing her against the tussocky grass that bit and scratched her where his shirt had ridden up.

'Stop!' she cried, but he shouted out 'Fuck!' at the same moment, spasmed, then went still. Janey lay back panting, grateful it was over.

'God, sorry, mermaid,' Roo moaned. 'I meant to pull out—I really did. You were just so tight I couldn't help myself. Fuck—pretty good, eh?'

A chill was spreading over Janey. 'What?' she asked. Without waiting for a reply, she pushed him off her with a mighty heave. Her hand went down between her legs. Something viscous and sticky was dribbling down her thigh.

'Oh, you arsehole,' she said. 'You complete and utter cunt. You promised!'

'Hey, it's a compliment, OK?' Roo lay on his back, his now-flaccid penis shrunken and shrivelled. 'You were so hot I couldn't stop—you should be proud . . . You can get that morning-after thingy anyway.'

Janey thought she might explode with fury. She hated him. She hated herself. She had to get away. Grabbing for her underwear, she leapt to her feet and sprinted down the beach, back towards the lights and safety of the night markets, legs pumping, mouth open, ran and ran and ran until suddenly something grabbed her by the foot and she was brought down, yelping, onto the cold, wet grit of the mudflats.

———

'They should be back by now.'

Morag checked her watch. Three minutes to eleven, just two minutes on from when she'd last consulted it. Amira had finally said out loud what Morag had been thinking, what Caro was clearly thinking, and maybe even Fiona too if she could be forced to admit it. For the previous half hour they'd all gamely acted as if nothing was wrong, that they were happily enjoying a last-night drink by the pool at The Mangrove, where they'd returned after finishing dinner, but slowly, inexorably, the conversation had dried up.

'Yes,' she sighed. The girls had been told to return by ten. They'd only gone three or four blocks away, at least according to Amira. Where the heck were they?

Fiona held up the sweating bottle marooned in the middle of the table. 'Drink?' she asked, then plonked it back down when no one responded. 'Oh, relax,' she chided. 'They've probably just lost track of the time. They're young. And it's their last night too. They'll be fine.'

Caro turned to Morag. 'Try ringing Macy again.'

Morag dutifully picked up her phone, entered the number and held it to her ear. *Please answer please answer please answer*, she chanted to herself, but the call went through to voicemail, as had all the previous calls. This time she hung up without leaving a message.

'Bugger,' said Caro. 'We should have realised that only one of them had a phone before we let them go. I just assumed . . .' Her voice trailed off.

Morag knew what she was thinking, that in this day and age everyone was immediately contactable all the time, but Bronte, it turned out, had never wanted a phone, while Tess had stopped using hers after moving to Kalangalla. 'There's no coverage, so she couldn't,' Amira had explained. 'I don't even know where it is now.' As for Janey, they all knew what had happened to her mobile.

'Well, it wasn't *my* idea,' Fiona said, pouring herself a drink. 'Cheers,' she added, holding the glass aloft. 'To our best-laid plans.'

'Oh, shut up,' Caro snapped. 'I didn't hear you protesting when Tess suggested it. You were only too happy to have Bronte off your hands for a couple of hours. Not that you even notice her when she's here.'

Fiona straightened in her seat, eyes sparkling. 'Glasshouses!'

she hooted. 'Because you're right on top of everything Janey's doing, aren't you?'

'OK,' said Amira, standing up. 'I'm sure everything's alright, but I'm going to go and look for them—then we can all enjoy what's left of the night without anyone getting their eyes scratched out.'

Fiona pretended to pout. 'I was only warming up. And she started it.'

Just then Morag saw some figures emerge from the shadows beyond the pool.

'Hey,' she cried. 'I think they're back.'

Each of the women turned to look, their heads swivelling like clowns in a sideshow game, but it wasn't all four girls, just Bronte and Tess. Spotting the women, Bronte broke into a run.

'Is Janey here?' she asked, pulling up at their table.

'No,' said Caro. 'She's meant to be with you.'

'We . . . um . . . separated,' Bronte admitted.

'What?' Morag said. 'You were meant to stay together! When? How long has it been since you saw her? And where's Macy?'

Tess joined her friend. 'It wasn't Bronte's fault,' she said. 'Macy wanted to sing—she got asked by this band—and we didn't want to spend all our time just hanging out there, so we agreed that we'd meet later.' She cast a look at Morag. 'She's still singing. We couldn't get her to come back.'

'And Janey—what about Janey?' Caro asked. One of her hands clutched the table; the other had gone straight to her throat.

'She said she needed a drink, so we told her the same as

Macy—meet at the stage at ten to ten.' Bronte hung her head as if anticipating the next question.

'You couldn't have just gone with her?' Caro didn't bother to hide the anger in her voice.

'I didn't feel much like being with her,' Bronte said, not meeting Caro's eyes. 'Sorry.' Morag thought she might start crying.

Tess put her arm around the taller girl.

'It's not Bronte's fault,' she said again. 'I talked her into it. And Janey was the one who didn't turn up—the rest of us were there. We've been looking for her for the past forty minutes.'

'Great. Just great,' erupted Caro. 'We ask you four to do one thing, just to stick together, and—'

'Come on, Caro, we'll go find her,' interrupted Amira, reaching for Caro's hand. 'She can't have got far. The markets aren't very big. Maybe she just got confused about where the stage was.'

'I doubt it,' said Bronte. 'It's really loud. You could find it with your eyes shut.' Tess elbowed her.

'I'll come too, to get Macy,' Morag said, rising from her seat.

'No, you stay here,' said Amira. 'We need someone to man the phones, and I don't trust her.' She cocked her head at Fiona, who had just drained her glass and was already reaching to fill it again. 'Seriously, Janey might turn up here while we're searching, then you can give us a ring and we'll come straight back.'

'With Macy,' Morag prompted.

'Yes, with Macy, of course. Thanks.' Amira shepherded Caro away into the night. 'We'll walk,' Morag heard her say. 'The markets aren't far, and you can never get a park there.

They're just so busy! I'm sure that's all it is.' She stopped abruptly and spun around. 'Bronte! Tess! You come with us and show us where you were meant to meet up. Morag will look after things here.'

Good old Morag, Morag thought as she watched them go. *Morag will look after things. Morag always does.* But who the hell was looking after Morag's child? Stepchild, she corrected herself. Not flesh, not blood, but still, somehow, her responsibility. It didn't seem fair. If anything happened to Macy Andrew and Janice would blame her, everyone would, even though she wasn't related to her and hadn't even wanted her here. Not that anyone seemed all that concerned about Macy—Amira hadn't even mentioned her when she set off on her rescue mission. Sure, Macy wasn't missing as such, not like Janey, but it wasn't as if she was tucked up safely in bed either. Who knew what had happened since Bronte and Tess had last seen her? The band might have finished and she might be wandering around lost, or backstage blowing a roadie . . . Why the hell hadn't she done what she was told to in the first place? None of this would've happened if the girls hadn't split up—and Macy was the oldest, so theoretically she should be the most responsible, the one you could trust. Hah! Morag could feel herself growing angrier and angrier. It wasn't like her, and the sensation was disquieting. She wanted to scream. She wanted to go for a run. She wanted to find Macy and shake her until her teeth chattered.

Fiona burped softly. 'Kids, hey,' she remarked from across the table. 'First you lose your figure, next you lose your social life, then you lose your mind. They're not worth it. I wish someone had told me.'

Despite her fury, Morag couldn't quite agree. Yes, having children was tiring, but Finn, Callum and Torran were infinitely precious to her; they were the sum of her days. As for Macy . . . with Macy it was different. Could anything ever come close to that bond of blood? Macy irritated and upset her more easily than her biological children; Macy always had a head start, somehow, in tipping her over the edge. Morag cared for Macy, she knew she did, even loved her on their good days—but that was just the point, wasn't it, that the love was more conditional, more limited than what she felt for the three boys who had been pulled wet and bloody from her own body. She wondered if every step-parent felt like this; she wondered if things would have been different if she'd known Macy since her birth rather than meeting her for the first time as an already cautious, already defensive seven-year-old. The problem, she thought, was that you chose to be a parent. The twins had been unplanned, but still she'd decided to go ahead, she'd chosen to keep them. No one ever chose to be a step-parent.

'Oh, I don't know,' she replied, straining to keep her tone light. 'It means you've got someone to look after you in your old age, at least.'

A shadow passed over Fiona's face. 'If you live that long.'

Morag picked up her phone. 'I'm going for a walk,' she said. 'I can't sit still at a time like this.'

Fiona hugged herself. 'You,' she said, 'can never sit still.'

Morag's mobile rang about ten minutes later, on her third circuit of the path between The Mangrove and Matso's. It was Amira, her words rushed. 'We've found Janey, but she's injured. We'll have to take her to hospital. I called for the ambulance, but there's only one in Broome and it's already out. Can you bring the troop carrier here? The keys are on the table next to my bed—the room should be open. Just head down the road from Matso's and keep going until you see the markets.' She drew in a shuddery breath. 'Oh God—Caro's freaking out. Can you hurry?'

'Calm down,' said Morag. 'It'll be OK. I'll get there as quickly as I can. Is Macy with you?'

Amira groaned. 'We haven't even looked for her yet . . . and I can't leave Janey, or Caro. We'll come back and find her as soon as we get Janey to hospital, I promise.'

A preternatural calm came over Morag.

'Are Janey's injuries life-threatening?' she asked. 'Is she bleeding? Can she breathe?'

'No, it's her ankle,' Amira said. 'It's badly broken. She's deathly pale and she screams every time someone tries to touch it.'

Morag made her decision.

'Don't touch it, just keep her as still as you can. I'll be there soon.'

Soon, she thought, but not straight away. No one else had bothered, no one else was looking out for Macy. She was damned if she wasn't going to go and find Macy first.

Sunday

'We'll keep going, yeah?'

The lead singer looked around at the other band members for confirmation. The guy on keyboards nodded; the drummer simply picked up his sticks, preparing for the next song.

'You too?' he asked Macy. 'It's the last night market for the year, before the wet sets in. We'll make hay while the moon shines.'

She hesitated. It was getting late—it must be after midnight, though she was too scared to look at her watch. The crowd had thinned, but there were still plenty of people left, faces raised expectantly to the stage.

'Sure,' she heard herself say. Stuff it. It wasn't as if she got a chance like this every day—to perform with a real live band. She'd had a couple of offers before, but her parents hadn't allowed it; in fact, the first time she'd asked her mother Janice had laughed and told her she was far too young to be up late at pubs and that she needed to concentrate on her schoolwork. It didn't seem to matter that the gigs were on Saturday nights, when she'd be out anyway, and that she'd sworn there was no way she'd be drinking (not a chance when she had a job to do, and anyway, the management would probably know she was underage); her mum had simply held up her hand in that supercilious way that indicated the topic was no longer open for discussion. It was infuriating. You got to sixteen and all the people who expected you to start acting like an adult wouldn't actually engage with you as such.

'"Sweet Home Alabama",' the guitarist hissed. 'D'you know that?'

Macy nodded, felt her hips sway in anticipation of the opening chords. It was an old song, but it always got people dancing. Years ago, when she was eight or nine and staying over at her father's one winter weekend, it had come on the radio while they were eating lunch and her dad had pulled Morag to her feet and twirled her around the room until they were both out of breath and giggling and the soup had gone cold. Morag. A prickle of guilt ran down Macy's spine. Morag had expected them back by ten . . . But Tess and Bronte must have told her where she was, Macy assured herself, so she wouldn't be worried. The other girls would have found Janey and headed back, probably ages ago now—and Macy was older than them, so surely she deserved to stay out a bit longer.

The guitarist grinned at her as they went into the chorus.

Home, she sang, feeling better, and she would go home, or to The Mangrove anyway, just as soon as they were finished. It would be a crime to stop now. The band was really good, so much better than that piss-poor one at school. Besides, her mother was always telling her to seize the moment, wasn't she? So here she was, seizing.

She threw back her head, harmonising. It was funny how easily the lyrics came to her, even when she had no idea what they meant. If only it was the same with the periodic table, or the cosine rule, or that soliloquy they'd had to learn from *Macbeth*. Why hadn't someone put *that* to music? It would have made it so much simpler. But nothing about school was simple, she'd accepted that now, and the thought of her final two years looming ahead filled her with terror. When she was little, in grade three, her mum had told her that it was just a matter of working hard and paying attention—that if she did both she'd be fine, that everything would come together like notes gliding up a scale, one flowing seamlessly into the next. But it never had, never, no matter how hard she tried. After the dyslexia was finally diagnosed a year or so later she'd hoped things might get better, but she was already too far behind and after a while she'd simply given up. She knew it upset her mother, who thought she was lazy, but it wasn't as if Macy had a choice. The song ended and the crowd applauded, someone wolf-whistling from towards the back. Macy tried to see if she could spot them and found herself staring straight at Morag.

'Oh, shit,' she murmured, pushing her mike back into its stand. 'I have to go,' she called to the band and started for the side of the stage, but Morag had beaten her there, was leaning up against it, waiting.

'I'm sorry,' Macy began, 'I know it's late, and you said to come back, but Bronte and Tess—'

Morag cut her off. 'You were amazing.'

Macy gulped in surprise.

'You just look so . . . at ease up there,' Morag continued. 'And your voice, with the music behind it, and the microphone—I mean, I've heard you sing before, of course, but not like that.'

'Really?' said Macy. The band had started their next number; she felt the throb of it roll across the stage towards her, engulf her.

'Look, I have to find the others,' Morag said. 'Janey's hurt, and I've brought the car to pick her up, but you can stay here if you like. It shouldn't take long. I'll come back. Do you want to do that?'

'Yes,' Macy breathed. 'Yes. I'll be here.'

———

She wished Janey would stop making that noise. As soon as the thought crossed her mind, Tess felt awful, but it was true. Janey was clearly badly hurt, her ankle splayed at an unnatural angle on the sand where they'd found her, and Tess did feel sorry for her—but still, that sound . . . It got inside your marrow, somehow; it set your teeth on edge. It reminded Tess of the time at Kalangalla when one of the dogs always hanging around the community had got its front paw impaled on a fishing hook; the dog had made the same unrelenting keening, a wail of distress. But it wouldn't let anyone try to help it, and in the end Mason had had to throw an old hessian sack over its head so he could hold it without getting bitten and work the hook back out. Janey was much the same, shouting at Amira to stop when Tess's mum had tried to examine her, though so far they hadn't had to use a sack on her. It was her cry that had enabled them to finally locate her, to pick their way along the darkened beach until they discovered her crumpled form, head thrown back, one long howl of pain emanating from her open mouth.

Tess squeezed Janey's hand, trying to make amends for her horrible thoughts.

'Mum will be back soon, I'm sure,' she said. 'She's gone to meet Morag, who's bringing the troop carrier so we can get you to the hospital.' Her mother had already told Janey that before she left ten minutes ago, but who knew what Janey was capable of taking in right now? Tess had a sudden idea. 'Do you want some water?' she asked, dropping her hand to feel through her bag. 'I've got a bottle in here somewhere.'

'No!' cried Caro, who was sitting on the wet sand, cradling Janey's head in her lap. 'Don't give her anything. She'll probably need surgery.'

'Oh. OK.' Tess snuck another look at Janey's ankle, then quickly turned away again. Even in the hazy moonlight it looked wrong enough to make Tess feel sick: Janey's whole foot was turned away from her leg as if trying to escape it. 'Do you want some then?' she asked Caro.

Caro just shook her head, continuing to stroke Janey's hair, now dark with sweat.

'What the hell was she even doing down here?' she muttered.

Tess didn't reply. She had no idea. At least Caro had pulled herself together now. It had been awful when they'd first come across Janey—Caro shrieking and falling to her knees, then gasping as if she was having an asthma attack. Tess herself had burst into tears, and even her own usually unflappable mother had squawked a bit before snapping out of it and calling Morag. Tess hated seeing adults lose it. They weren't meant to do that. Wasn't that the whole point of growing up, that you always knew exactly what to do? It had scared her to see Amira and Caro so confused and frightened. It had made her want to sprint back towards the lights of the markets and stay there until everything was sorted.

But of course she hadn't. Her mother had taken Bronte with her to meet Morag and told Tess to stay and look after her friend. That was exactly what she'd called her, *your friend*, as if she needed to remind Tess of the fact, as if Tess hadn't spent her entire childhood tagging after Janey. God, how she'd loved her, from the minute they'd first met at school, when Tess had been instantly entranced by Janey's golden hair—hair just like the princesses' in her storybooks, and so different to Tess's own. Loved her confidence too, loved that Janey always seemed to know exactly the right thing to do, say, wear, that she was in control of any situation she was part of—or appeared to be, anyway. Loved her into high school, where Tess had chosen French over German simply because that was what Janey was doing and she hated the idea of being separated from her for even four periods a week. Loved her right through year seven, and until they'd moved up here . . . but then something had shifted.

Tess studied Janey now—the other girl's eyes were closed, her whole face contorted in a grimace—and felt precisely nothing. Well, maybe not quite nothing . . . Pity for her, yes, for the agony she was clearly in, and a strange sort of fondness, a faded souvenir of almost a decade spent loving her so fiercely, but the love itself was gone. There'd been that awful scene with Callum's letter, of course, and then what she'd done to Bronte, but if she was honest with herself Tess knew it was more than that. It was the way Janey had sneered at Tess's new life from almost the moment she'd arrived in Kalangalla; it was her obsession with her phone and her looks; it was meeting Tia; and it was discovering who she, Tess, really was and being OK with that. Was this normal? All that emotion, all those years, and then nothing? Was this how her mother had fallen out of love with her father, and if so how could you ever trust love, how could you commit your life to anyone? She suddenly yearned for her mother's arms around her, to sit and talk with her until morning and have Amira sort it all out.

Footsteps sounded on the beach behind her. Tess swung around to see Bronte leading the way, Morag hot on her heels and Amira trailing in the distance.

'Oh, Janey!' Morag exclaimed, dropping to her knees beside her and reaching out to run one hand lightly over her swollen ankle. Janey had gone quiet in the previous minutes but screeched as soon as Morag touched her.

'Don't!' she cried. 'It hurts so much!'

'Sorry,' said Morag. 'I think it's broken.'

'Yeah, no shit,' mumbled Janey. Tess stifled a giggle and felt a flicker of her old admiration. Janey was tough, she'd give her that.

Amira finally joined them, puffing. 'We'll have to carry her,' she said. 'Tess and Bronte, you go either side of her—Janey, put your arms around their shoulders. Morag, you support her under the legs—I'll hold up the ankle.' She bent down to Janey, her voice dropping, and gently touched her cheek. 'I'm sorry, sweetheart, this is going to hurt, but you can't stay here. We'll do it as quickly as we can, OK?'

Janey nodded. Tess moved to where her mother had pointed. It felt good to be told what to do.

'On the count of three,' Amira said, stooping to take Janey's ankle. 'One, two . . . three.'

The scream that was ripped from Janey's throat as they picked her up sent bats in the mangroves spiralling into the air like inky clouds in the night sky.

'You yell, sweetheart,' Amira murmured as they lugged Janey along the sand. 'You yell as loudly as you like.'

⁓

Thankfully, the hospital was close to the beach. Once Janey and Caro had been taken to its tiny emergency department, Amira motioned Tess and Bronte back into the carrier. 'You two need to get some sleep,' she said. 'I'll drop you at The Mangrove, then come back here—Caro might need the company. Morag, you jump in too.'

Morag was already walking away, her bag over her shoulder. She slowed down but didn't stop.

'I'm going back to the markets for Macy,' she said. 'Remember her?'

'Shit,' Amira said, her hand going to her mouth. 'I'll give you a lift.'

'There's no need,' Morag replied, her pale legs disappearing into the night. 'I know where I'm going now.'

It was after one when they pulled up outside The Mangrove, but Tess could still hear music drifting across Roebuck Bay from the markets.

'Straight to bed,' Amira admonished as she drove away, heading back to the hospital.

'Fat chance,' Bronte whispered.

Tess snickered. 'When did you stop doing what you were told?'

Bronte shrugged. 'It's our last night together. Everyone else is still up—Morag, Macy, your mum, my mum, no doubt, definitely Caro and Janey. Why should we have to go to bed?'

Tess reached into the stand of frangipani trees growing along The Mangrove's driveway and plucked two blossoms. She tucked one behind her ear, then stood on tiptoe to do the same to Bronte.

'There,' she said, stepping back. 'You look like a local now. Let's go sit on the lawn near the bar for a bit. I'm not tired either.'

A frog croaked nearby and both girls jumped, grabbing each other.

'Some local,' Bronte giggled.

'Listen,' Tess said, 'all those sketches you've done while you've been up here—do you think I could have one? Something that will remind me of Kalangalla once Mum and I leave in summer.'

'You'd really like one?' Bronte asked shyly. 'They're not that good. You could always buy a postcard.'

'It's not the same,' Tess said. 'Your pictures are much better—and they're real. If you don't want to give any of them up, maybe I could send you a photo and you could draw one from that?'

'I'd love to,' said Bronte. 'Sort of like a commission.'

'I'll make you famous,' mused Tess. 'I'll show it to everyone. I'll put it on Facebook.' Then they looked at each other and burst out laughing.

——

She didn't want a drink. This had to be a first. The bottle still had about a third left in it, but since the others had left to search for Janey, then Morag had raced off in the troop carrier twenty minutes later, Fiona had suddenly gone off wine. It was bizarre. It had never happened before, as far as she knew—not even when she was pregnant, when she knew she was meant to give it up but only managed to last until the second trimester. Not that she was an alcoholic, she reassured herself. She *could* give up, she just didn't choose to. Anyone married to Todd would feel the same. And it wasn't as if her having the odd glass after dinner seemed to have done her kids any harm. It was meant to retard growth, wasn't it? So much for that. Bronte was a bloody giraffe.

She picked up her glass, but then set it down again. Maybe it was the heat. Wine didn't really work in this climate—it got warm too quickly. What she needed was a rum and Coke or a vodka and lime, something that you could fill with ice cubes. The bar was still open. She could hear the hum of conversation and clink of glassware from where she sat by the pool on the edge of the lawn. All she had to do was get up, take a few steps . . . yet she stayed where she was. Just the thought of a rum and Coke—the sticky cola coating her teeth, the calories that would go straight to her arse—made her feel sick. *I must be tired*, she thought. It had been a big week. She stared unseeingly over the water, wondering when Bronte would be back.

Useless. Fiona flinched. That word again. It kept popping back into her head, try as she might to distract herself. Fiona felt the resentment prickle in her gut. Useless was what her own mother was, not her. Useless wasn't going out to work every day, day after day, keeping the family afloat while her husband pissed around, pretending to run a business, and then still managing to put a meal on the table and keep the house halfway clean. Useless would have been just sitting back, as most women did, having their pedicures and their manicures and their lunch dates, not forever trying to soothe seven medical egos and manage a team of staff who seemed to spend half their days on Twitter rather than making appointments or filing the lab results. She wasn't useless!

Tears came to her eyes and Fiona brushed them away with the back of her hand. She really was tired, she realised—not from the trip, but from her own damn life. From the long hours and Todd's constant sniping, from the ever-present worry about whether they'd have enough to pay the mortgage that month, from the effort of keeping her constantly simmering anger from coming to the boil. And for what? She was probably going to die anyway. She was definitely going to die, she corrected herself, but possibly earlier than she'd expected. The thought gave her a perverse flash of pleasure. Good! Let's see how they all coped then. They'd soon realise she hadn't been so useless after all.

But just say she didn't die? Just say the lump was benign, or easily treated . . . She'd get out of hospital, go back to the practice, and nothing would change. Fiona sat up straight in her chair. It *had* to change. She saw that now. It drove her mad to watch Bronte being a victim—being picked on by Janey, afraid of her own shadow, always hiding behind that curtain of hair—but was she any better? She didn't creep around like Bronte, but then again she rarely stood up to Todd either, just put up with all his shit and then took out the way he made her feel on everyone else. On Bronte. Fiona swallowed. She wasn't much of a poster girl for the confident, hard-headed woman she was always harping at her daughter to become. And what about Dom? Her mind raced. What was her marriage teaching him—that it was OK to bag your wife, to deride as inferior every female you knew, to do no more than eat, grunt and fart at the dinner table, then piss off without clearing your plate or thanking the person who'd cooked your meal? God, no wonder Bronte scuttled out of the room as soon as Dom came in. He was turning out just like his father.

'Hey,' said Bronte, emerging from the shadows.

'You're back!' cried Fiona, surprised at the relief she felt.

'Oh, Tess and I have been back for ages,' Bronte said. 'We've just been lying over there on the lawn.'

The words stung. Back for ages, but she hadn't bothered

to come and find her mother, to say hello or tell Fiona what
was going on.

'Did you even know I was here?' Fiona asked, sounding
whiny even to her own ears.

'Yeah. I just assumed you wanted to be left alone.'

Bronte's hair was lit from behind by the moonlight, her
cheekbones thrown into sharp relief. She was beautiful,
Fiona thought. She was growing up. There wasn't much time
left. She had to make an effort, for Bronte's sake; she had
to break the cycle, be there for her. She didn't want them
ending up essentially estranged, as she had with her own
mother. And she needed Bronte, she thought with a sharp
stab of panic. Todd was the one who was useless; Dom was
heading that way. Who else did she have except her friends
and Bronte?

'Mum, are you listening to me?' Bronte said. 'I was telling
you that Janey, Caro and Amira are at the hospital, and Morag
went off to find Macy. Tess has gone to bed, but I just had an
idea. Can you do me a favour?'

Janey stared at the ceiling as her mother's footsteps receded
down the hospital corridor outside. There was a stain in one
corner, as if a vase of flowers had been knocked over and
the water had drained out. That was ridiculous though, she
chided herself. The drugs they'd given for the pain must be
fogging her mind. You didn't put flowers on the ceiling. It was
probably from the air-conditioning, or a tropical storm. She

made herself concentrate on the dark smudge. If she stared
at it long enough, maybe she'd wake up at home, in her own
bed with all her limbs still intact, and all of this would have
been a dream.

No chance. A trolley clattered past her room and she
jumped at the noise, then winced as pain shot through her
leg. She wondered dully what was wrong with it. She'd clearly
broken something—the radiographer had muttered 'Ouch' as
he inspected her X-rays—but how badly? Janey let her head
fall to the side, gazing now at the wall. It didn't matter. Her
ankle would mend. She wasn't so sure about the rest of her.

He'd fucked her. He'd fucked her and she'd let him, but
oh, how she wished she could take it all back now. She winced
again, remembering Roo's hands on her body, his tongue in
her mouth, his . . . thing between her legs. Ugh. Janey fought
the urge to vomit. She felt so dirty. She needed a shower. There
was sand in her hair, mud under her nails and Roo's semen
on her thighs. She hadn't even had a chance to pull her undies
back on, so intent had she been on getting away, and they
were balled up somewhere in her bag. She'd throw them in
the bin the first chance she got. She'd throw out her handbag
too, and all the other clothes she was wearing . . . anything
that might remind her of last night. Her skin crawled. She'd
thought having sex would change her somehow, transform
her, but she was just the same, only grubbier.

'Janey . . . hey . . . are you awake?'

She turned her head to the other side to find Bronte hesi-
tating in the doorway.

'Hey,' she replied weakly. 'Yeah. I guess.'

'Are you OK?' asked Bronte. 'Where's your mum?'

'She went off with Amira to talk to the doctor and fill in some forms. I think I need an operation.'

Bronte came into the room and seated herself gingerly on the edge of Janey's bed.

'Oh, that's awful. You poor thing. Does it hurt much? And you've got state champs coming up!'

Janey blinked. So she had. Funny how the thought hadn't even crossed her mind in the hours since the accident. Funny, too, how she couldn't care less. It was just swimming. It was just going up and down a pool and seeing who could do it the fastest. It didn't mean anything.

'I brought something for you.' Bronte reached into her pocket. 'I didn't know how long you were going to be in here, and I thought you could probably use something to take your mind off it all . . .' She held out an iPhone.

Janey stared at it, puzzled.

'It's my mum's,' said Bronte. 'She said you can borrow it. They have wi-fi here—I asked a nurse—so you can listen to music or watch some videos or even check your email. It'll be better than just lying around doing nothing.'

Tears came to Janey's eyes. 'Thank you,' she said. 'That's so nice.'

'Well, I knew you didn't have your own with you.' Bronte smiled shyly, ducking her head, then turned to examine Janey's ankle. 'Yow. It hurts just to look at that. How did you do it?'

Janey's shoulders heaved and she started to sob. Bronte's kindness had undone her.

'I went to the beach with a boy . . . the one I was with in the pool on the first night . . . and . . . and stuff happened and I was running away and I fell over a rock—'

'Oh God, Janey,' Bronte interrupted. 'Did he rape you? You have to tell someone.'

Janey shook her head, tears flying onto the sheets. Snot was pouring from her nose, but she was past caring what she looked like. 'It wasn't rape. I let him, but it hurt—and he said he was going to pull out but he didn't and now I'm terrified that I'm pregnant.' Her voice cracked. She couldn't stop crying. She wanted to go home. She wanted to die.

Bronte moved up the bed and wrapped her arms around Janey. 'The bastard. What an awful thing to do.' She rocked Janey gently back and forth as if she were a child. 'I could kill him . . . But I'm sure you're not pregnant. It hardly ever happens the first time. You'd be so unlucky.' She stopped and drew back without letting go of her, peering into Janey's eyes. 'Will you tell your mum?'

Janey shook her head again. She'd rather die. She'd already let her mother down enough by disobeying her instructions and breaking her ankle. All those hours of training wasted, all the money her parents had spent on squad fees and meet entries, all those five a.m. starts when her mother, who liked her sleep, had uncomplainingly got up and driven her to the pool. That was bad enough, but Caro would be even more devastated if she knew what else Janey had thrown away.

'I think she'd be OK, Janey, she really would. She's pretty good, your mum.' Bronte was silent for a moment, waiting for Janey to respond. When she didn't she gently pulled Janey back to her. 'Ok then, but you need to see a doctor when we get back to Melbourne. I'll come with you, if you like. I can organise it. Macy will know someone. And the morning-after pill—you've got a few days for that, and you don't need a prescription. I'm guessing you'll have to stay in bed for a while, but I could go to a chemist and ask for it, I suppose. They won't need to know it's not for me.'

Despite her fears, despite everything, Janey found her mouth twitching. She'd never even seen Bronte talking to a boy, yet here she was prepared to brazenly dupe a pharmacist for some emergency contraception.

'That sex-ed program at your school really is good, isn't it?' she snuffled.

'It is.' Bronte passed her the box of tissues next to the bed. 'I'm serious though. It will all be alright. I promise.'

Caro reappeared as Janey was blowing her nose.

'Janey, the doctor says—' she began, then broke off when she spotted Bronte. 'Oh, Bronte, I didn't know you were here. That was good of you to check on Janey.' She bent to smooth back the hair from Janey's face, then frowned. 'You've been crying!'

'She was a bit upset about her ankle,' Bronte said. 'They'll be able to fix it though, won't they?'

Caro nodded. 'They're going to operate tonight,' she said, studying Janey's face. 'That way they've said you can still fly home tomorrow, as long as everything goes well. It's not ideal, and you'll need lots of painkillers, but there's not another direct flight to Melbourne for another week—and I'd rather have you back there anyway, so I can get you checked by a specialist.'

'I'll go then,' said Bronte, standing up. 'Good luck, Janey.' She squeezed her hand. 'It will all be OK, remember? I'll see you in the morning.'

'Yeah,' Janey mumbled, then added, 'And thanks, Bronte. Thanks for everything.'

Caro watched as Bronte left the room.

'That was good of her,' she repeated. 'If I'd had to guess who'd be the first to come visit you . . .'

'I know,' said Janey.

'A nurse is going to give you a pre-op soon,' Caro said. She looked tired, Janey thought, the lines around her eyes longer and deeper. 'The doctor said he'd sedate you enough so you can sleep afterwards, through the rest of the night, which is good. When you wake up it will be time to go home.'

'Will you stay?' Janey asked, suddenly nervous. 'Here, I mean, in the hospital, not at The Mangrove.' She sniffed. 'I'm sorry about tonight. I know I mucked up. But I really want you to stay, Mum.'

'Of course I will,' her mother said, stroking her cheek. 'I'll be right here. I'm not going anywhere.'

———

'Here,' said Amira, handing her a polystyrene cup. 'White, with two sugars. That's how you take it, isn't it?'

Caro nodded. It wasn't—she'd cut back to one sugar—but there was no point telling Amira that now. 'Thank you for staying,' she said. 'You didn't have to. You must be exhausted after all the driving today.'

Amira sat down next to her, hands around her own cup. 'There's no way I'd leave you here alone. You wouldn't have left me if our situations were reversed, would you? And Fiona and Morag both wanted to come too, but I told them to stay with the girls.' She lifted her coffee to her mouth and blew on it, sending ripples across the cloudy surface. 'Anyway, I can catch up on my sleep tomorrow, once you're all gone. There won't be anything else to do.'

'It's been quite the week, hasn't it?' Caro shifted on the hard plastic chair, trying to get comfortable. When Janey had been wheeled into surgery Caro had asked to be directed to the waiting area, only to be told she was already in it: a dimly lit corridor opposite the nurses' station sporting four chairs, two dog-eared *Woman's Day*s and a vending machine humming to itself. Still, she could hardly complain. At least Janey hadn't broken her ankle in Kalangalla, where the doctor only visited weekly and there were certainly no operating facilities. It could have been worse, she told herself, and yet right now it was hard to feel that way.

'How long does the doctor think she'll be in plaster?' Amira asked.

'He said they won't know for sure until they've had a proper look at it, but at least a month to six weeks. She'll have to miss states, that means, and the district cross-country trials, which she always does well in.' Caro sighed. 'And I suppose she'll need crutches and rehab and I'll have to drive her to and from school . . .' She stopped, ashamed. 'Sorry. I'm not sounding like much of a mother, am I? I do feel sorry for Janey, of course I do, but I just keep thinking that this was all so avoidable. If they'd only stayed together, like we asked—why the hell did she have to go off by herself? It's infuriating.'

Amira nodded. 'You sound like a mother to me. I'm mad at them too—and did you see Morag's face when Bronte and Tess came back from the markets and she found out Macy wasn't with them either? I thought she was going to explode.' She ran her hands through her hair as if trying to tame it, then gave up. 'You can tell them what to do until you're blue in the face, but they still seem to think it's optional. Thank God I only teach primary kids.'

'But it's not just that she disobeyed me,' Caro said. 'What if the operation isn't a success? No offence, Amira, but we're not exactly at the cutting edge of medical practice here, and they said it was a bad break. Just say they can't fix it properly? What happens then? Just say Janey goes *lame*?' Her voice broke. The tightness was back, radiating from her sternum out across her chest and rib cage, pinioning her arms. It was as if she'd been grabbed from behind, she thought. It was like being abducted.

'I'm sure everything will be fine—' Amira began, laying a soothing hand on Caro's lap.

'But what if it's not?' Caro demanded. She was shaking, she was losing it, coffee slopping from the cup onto the floor. *Breathe*, she told herself. *Breathe* . . . Breathe, for God's sake. She sucked at the air, her vision beginning to swim.

Amira shot from her seat. 'I'll get a doctor,' she said.

'No!' exclaimed Caro. There it was—the oxygen finally rushing to her lungs, punching through, reinflating them. She gulped at it greedily, inhaling until the room stopped spinning and her pulse rate slowed. 'No,' she said again, more quietly this time. 'I'll be fine. It's all my fault anyway. I've spoiled her.'

'Oh, Caro,' Amira said, sinking back into her chair.

'Yes, I have,' Caro insisted. 'I've been too soft on her. I've always told her how beautiful and how clever she is, and now she believes it.' The words calmed her somehow, so she kept talking. 'I wanted her to be perfect, because it made me look good, so I acted as if she was. I knew she could be selfish, maybe even a bit cruel, but I told myself—and Alex—that she was just resourceful, determined. I thought that if I believed it enough I could make it true.' She felt her chest loosen, her head clear. *And I felt guilty*, she realised, *so I just gave in to her . . . Guilty that Alex was always away, that I worked much more than the other mothers, that I didn't even know how to be a proper mother. But how could I?* The rictus grin, the mouth hanging open . . . Caro screwed her eyes shut and willed the memory away.

Amira put her arm around her. 'I think you're being a bit hard on yourself. We're all making it up as we go along. And Janey will be fine, I know it—her ankle, and the rest of her too. They're teenagers. It's not terminal.'

Caro laughed, surprising herself. Talking to Amira had shifted something. She felt lighter, somehow, as if she was full of helium.

'You're a good mum,' Amira continued. 'You are. I know how much you love your girls, and what an amazing job you do looking after everyone, with Alex hardly home. He must be so proud of you.'

Was he? Caro wondered. She hoped so. She felt a sudden fierce longing for him. Strange, when she'd spent all week thinking about Mason; but Mason was just a fantasy, a holiday whimsy, and Alex was real, the father of her children. He was just as much their parent as she was, but she'd been doing all the work—and the worrying. They needed to start being a team. Maybe she needed to step back and get him more involved with his daughters. Maybe she needed to ditch work for a bit and go with him next time he headed off to Italy. Maria could mind the girls. She was clearly enjoying having April. *Ditch work*. The idea was delightfully transgressive, as novel as the thought of going to bed before stacking the dishwasher and straightening the cushions on the couch.

'Your colour looks better,' said Amira. 'Can you breathe OK now?'

In response, Caro drew in a long breath through her nose, feeling it sink into her lungs and make its way through her body, lighting up arteries and capillaries, causing alveoli to blossom like roses, and then just as slowly released it.

'I can,' she said, smiling. 'I can. It feels wonderful.'

———

'And for you?' the waitress asked.

Morag glanced once more at the menu. She was starving, even though she'd slept in and hadn't exercised. She'd had a fabulous night's sleep, actually—in contrast, it seemed, to everyone else.

'The same, I think—the Bircher muesli. With sourdough toast if you have it, and the scrambled eggs. And a latte, please—as hot as you can.'

The girl nodded and slipped her pad into her pocket before turning away.

'Thanks for this,' said Macy, sitting opposite her. 'It's nice.'

'It is,' agreed Morag, then didn't know what to say next. Nice, yes, but a bit awkward too. It was pretty much the only time they'd been alone together all trip, and certainly over a meal. It felt a bit like a first date. She wanted to be liked, to impress, but she'd probably just end up with oat flakes stuck between her teeth.

'I didn't think you'd be speaking to me after last night, never mind inviting me out for breakfast,' Macy continued.

Morag leaned back in her seat, staring up through the branches of the huge boab tree spreading above them. She hadn't even noticed it when she'd last been here, on the first night of the holiday, though they must have sat directly beneath it. That seemed like a lifetime ago now.

'I think I was just so glad to see you alive and well I was willing to forgive you anything,' she admitted. 'For a while there you had me imagining how I was going to break the news to Janice that I'd lost you.'

Macy laughed. 'That would have gone over well.'

'Yeah.' Morag felt her stomach tighten at the thought. 'I probably would have got your dad to do it, to be honest. It was his fault that you came here in the first place.' She stopped abruptly, embarrassed, her eyes darting across the table at Macy. 'I didn't mean it like that. I meant . . .'

'It's OK,' said Macy. 'It *was* his fault. And mine, for getting thrown out of the eisteddfod.'

'I can see now why you want to do it,' Morag said. 'You were really good last night. Seriously good. I'm not just saying that, either. I mean it.'

Their meals were set in front of them, followed by Morag's coffee. She vacillated for a moment, then picked up the sachet of sugar on the saucer and tore it open. Bugger it. It was her last day.

'Have you enjoyed it?' Macy asked, spooning yoghurt into her bowl. 'The trip, I mean. Having a break from everything.'

'I have,' Morag said. 'It's been wonderful to see Amira, of course, and to spend some time with Caro and Fiona, but this whole area has just blown me away. It's amazing, isn't it?' She gestured around her. 'The sky, the water, that moon we saw last night. It's so different to Melbourne. And I love Melbourne, it's great, but this has been like discovering another country. It probably sounds stupid, but it's made me realise just how foreign Australia still is to me, and how much I miss Scotland.' She paused. She shouldn't say anything—she still had to discuss it with Andrew . . . But what was there to discuss when her mind was made up? 'So much so that I'm going to go back.'

Macy's spoonful of cereal stopped halfway to her mouth. 'Hey? When? What about Dad and the boys?'

'Not for good,' Morag hurried to reassure her. 'Well, maybe, but not straight away . . . I've decided to go back over summer, our summer, for January at least. I haven't seen my mother in years, and she's not going to last forever. I want to spend some time with her, proper time, not just a week or two;

I want to see Edinburgh again.' Morag's hands were shaking, and she set her cup down on the table before she spilled it. It felt dangerous and daring to be saying this to Macy, to be making it real—to be putting her own needs first for once. It felt strange. It felt right. Her heartbeat pounded in her ears just like it did after a really good run.

'Wow,' Macy said. 'That's fantastic. It's huge! Will the boys go too?'

'No.' Morag shook her head. 'I doubt it. Too expensive—and too cold. Scotland in the dead of winter isn't for everyone. They'll be much better back here, with their friends and their surfboards, and that way I can just concentrate on Mum. Your dad can take some time off. Finn and Callum are old enough to be by themselves during the day anyway, and they probably prefer that. Torran's a bit trickier—maybe you could help out?' Her mind started ticking over. 'Or maybe . . .'

'Of course I can,' Macy said. 'What?'

'Maybe . . . maybe you could come over for a bit too? With me. It'll be your school holidays, and Edinburgh has this incredible live music scene—you could see lots of bands, maybe get some more experience.' Oh God, thought Morag. Had she really suggested that? Was she going to live to regret it? It was a crazy idea, but Macy, she now knew, needed to spread her wings too. Maybe they all needed to let her off the leash a little. Maybe they needed to stop worrying about what she couldn't do, and concentrate on what she could.

'Really?' asked Macy. Her face was lit up from inside—and it was her real face, thought Morag. Her stepdaughter wasn't wearing any make-up; hadn't reapplied it, in fact, since that morning in the mangroves. 'You'd really do that? You'd let me?'

'You'd have to behave—no staying out all night—and your parents would have to agree, of course,' said Morag, 'but if I told them I'd keep an eye on you . . . You could stay with us, in Mum's boxroom. She's got a camp bed. I'm not sure how comfortable it would be, and there wouldn't be a whole lot of space—'

'I'll hardly be there anyway,' Macy interjected, then rushed on, 'I mean, I'd be there when you told me to, duh, but I'd be out a lot too.'

'Don't say anything when we get back,' Morag cautioned. 'Let me bring it up. I'll have to work out how to do it.'

Macy grinned at her, her muesli forgotten. It was as if they were conspiring, Morag thought. Better, it was as if they were talking as adults for the first time.

'That would be incredible, Morag.' Macy reached across the table to squeeze her hand. 'Honestly. Thank you.'

Morag squeezed back. Macy's excitement had rekindled her own. She let her thoughts fly for a moment, imagined landing in Edinburgh, and then her first glimpse of the castle, of Princes Street, all lit up for Christmas, of the Balmoral Hotel with its enormous clock set two minutes fast so those heading for Waverley station didn't miss their trains . . . She imagined the taxi on the cobblestones, delivering her to her mother's home, imagined Margaret opening the door in delight and throwing her arms around her. It was funny, thought Morag. You spent all your teen years struggling to separate yourself from your mother, to distance yourself, but you never did, not really. Mothers were innate; they were part of you. One day Macy would know that too.

⎯⎯⎯⎯⎯⎯

Bronte angled her chair so that her calves were in the sun. She could enjoy it now, for the ten minutes or so she had left before Amira drove them to the airport. She'd been so careful all week to stay out of the sun—obsessive, almost—but surely even she couldn't get burnt in such a short time? And it did feel lovely warming her skin . . .

She picked up her sketchbook and flipped through the pages. Though she'd bought it at One Arm Point just three days earlier it was almost full, and she couldn't wait to show Ms Drummond what she'd done. This one, to set the scene, she thought, pausing at a drawing of the beach at Kalangalla just before sunset . . . And this one too, a few pages further on, where she'd attempted to depict the complex weave in one of the baskets at the gallery. It had made her wonder if the same effect could be replicated in fabric, maybe a kind of vest over a loose white shirt, both futuristic and primitive. Was that even possible? Her mind raced. She wasn't sure, but she wanted to find out. Perhaps if she drew it . . . That was how she worked her ideas out. Ms Drummond had taught her that, just to sit with her pencil on the page, to block all her usual self-censoring reflexes and let it move of its own volition, almost as if she was an eighteenth-century medium attempting to commune with spirits. It wasn't such a silly idea, Bronte thought. It *was* spiritual, the way inspiration seized you and moved through you, captured you, took you over.

She stood up from her seat by the pool and hurried the few steps back to her room. There was one page left in her sketchbook and still time to get something down before Amira hustled them into the troop carrier. She just needed some grey leads, her 2B and a 4B. She was definitely going to do fashion design next year, she decided as she walked. Her mother didn't want her to—she was pressuring her to choose something 'more practical', in her words, like typing or food tech—but for once Bronte was going to stand up to her. She could always learn to cook, or to type for that matter, but a whole year with Ms Drummond just to dream and draw . . .

She pushed open the door. Her mother was sitting on one of the beds, t-shirt puddled at her feet, her bare back still red and peeling and somehow vulnerable.

'Shit,' Fiona said, clasping her hands over her breasts as Bronte stepped into the room. 'Sorry,' said Bronte, quickly turning away. 'I thought you were packing.' Curiosity overcame her. 'What are you doing?'

Her mother sighed and reached for her t-shirt, then seemed to think better of it.

'I've got a lump,' she said.

Bronte didn't understand. 'A lump?'

'In my breast. Just near my armpit. I only found it the other day, while I was in the shower. I was seeing if it was still there.' Fiona looked up, face drawn. 'It is.'

'Oh God, Mum.' Bronte dropped her sketchbook and rushed over to her. 'Are you sure? How big?'

Her mother took Bronte's hand and placed it on the side of her breast. Something moved beneath Bronte's fingertips. A marble. An olive.

'Why didn't you tell me?' Bronte asked. Despite the lump, she didn't want to move her hand away. Her mother's skin was surprisingly soft, almost velvety. She gently shrugged off Bronte's hand and pulled on her top. 'I'll get it looked at when we're back in Melbourne. No point worrying about it until then.'

'That's bullshit,' Bronte said. 'You *are* worried.'

Fiona's head jerked up at the swearword. 'Language, Bronte,' she said, a smile flitting across her features. 'I should wash your mouth out.'

'You are though, aren't you?' Bronte was determined not to let it go. Sarcasm, deflection, cynicism—they were her mother's native tongue, and she was sick of it.

'Yeah,' said Fiona, her gaze dropping to her lap. 'Yeah. I am.'

'Oh, Mum.' Her mother wasn't much of a hugger, but Bronte threw her arms around her anyway. Too bad if it made her flinch. 'I'll come with you, when we get back. For the mammogram or the biopsy or whatever it is, OK?' The thought darted across her mind that she was going to be busy. She needed to look after Janey too. That was OK. She was up to it.

'You don't have to,' said Fiona.

'I know I don't have to, but I want to. I want to be with you. I'd want you to be there if it was me.'

She heard her mother swallow, then clear her throat. 'Thanks,' Fiona said, then paused and added quickly, 'And I'm sorry.'

'Sorry?' Bronte asked, pulling back. 'For what?'

Her mother couldn't meet her eyes. 'For . . . stuff. You know. For only having tampons.'

Bronte didn't know whether to laugh or cry. What a weird few hours it had been. All of a sudden, everybody seemed to be confiding in her—first Janey at the hospital, then Tess, who'd woken her up to talk about some news, now her mum. That never happened. It was strange, but it felt good.

'Are you ready?' Amira called from outside. 'We've got to go—we still have to collect Janey and Caro.'

'Coming!' yelled Bronte. She stood up, straightening her spine, throwing her shoulders back. Her mother would be fine, she told herself. She had to be. There was no option. But just to be sure, she wasn't going to let her out of her sight until she'd had that lump checked.

———

'Oh, I hate goodbyes,' said Caro, fanning herself with her boarding pass. 'I always cry. I think I'm about to start now.'

Fiona stretched her arms out in front of her, cracking her knuckles. 'That's probably because you've been up all night—and because you know who'll be fetching and carrying for Princess Janey for the next month.'

Amira glanced across to where Janey was slumped in a wheelchair, her left foot and ankle swathed in plaster and propped up in front of her. She didn't seem to have heard Fiona's statement. Good. Probably drugged to the eyeballs on codeine, poor kid.

'There's still half an hour until boarding,' Amira said. 'We don't have to start the goodbyes just yet.' She took a deep breath. 'Besides, I've got something to tell you all before you go. Tess and I . . . we've decided to stay.'

Morag was the first to respond. 'What do you mean, stay?' she asked, shifting on the plastic airport bench. 'You were already staying, weren't you, until January or so?'

'Yes,' said Amira, 'but I'm going to extend it for another year. Maybe even more—I'm not sure at this stage, but there's so much to be done up here and I feel as if I've only just got started. It's something I've been thinking about for a while . . . Tess and I talked about it last night after I got back from the hospital. I had to make sure she was OK with it first, but I'm pretty sure she is.'

Amira looked over at her daughter, who smiled.

'I love it here,' Tess said simply. 'And Mum said we'll fly down for Christmas anyway, so it's only a couple of months until we see you all again.'

Thank goodness for Tess. Amira hadn't realised quite how anxious she'd been until she'd finally worked up the courage to broach it with her daughter and felt the sweet relief when Tess had agreed, and with enthusiasm. True, she'd hesitated for a second, which was probably just her getting used to the idea, but then Amira had mentioned the trip home at Christmas, and suggested that maybe Tess could ask one or two of her Melbourne friends up to stay in the holidays next year, if their parents agreed. For a moment she'd been tempted to mention Tia too—it might have made Tess's decision even easier if she realised how much her new friend was going to need her—but that was Tia's news to give, Tia's situation to deal with. And it wasn't just about Tia, after all. Seeing her at the washing line yesterday, her stomach distended, had crystallised the decision in Amira's mind—Aki was already so busy with her four younger children that she wouldn't have much time to help out with a grandchild too, and Tia would need help. But it was more than that. It was what Tia represented that made Amira want to stay in Kalangalla: the chance to shape a young life, to influence and expand it, to extend the horizons and dreams and potential of the children she was educating. To improve literacy, yes, but lives as well. Was that absurd? Was she being naive? Probably, but she had to try. She'd had a taste of it, and now she couldn't let go.

'Tess told me about it this morning, and we were thinking . . . if you're coming down for Christmas anyway, maybe Tess could stay at our place for a few weeks after that, and fly back up before school starts?' Bronte suggested.

'I'd really love to—to be with Bronte, and to see all my old friends,' Tess said. 'Can I, Mum?'

Amira shrugged. 'Sure, if it's OK with Fiona.' Bronte herself hadn't checked with her mother, she noticed—Bronte, who always deferred to everyone.

Not that Fiona seemed concerned.

'Saint Amira of the Never-Never, huh?' She smirked. 'Our lady of the darkies.' She held up a hand before anyone could protest. 'I'm just joking. Much as you won't expect me to admit it, what you're doing is fantastic, Amira—and someone has to, to make up for people like me. Good on you for putting your money where your mouth is. We'll miss you.'

Amira blinked back her tears. She was as bad as Caro. 'You can all come visit again. Bring the rest of your families, if you like. The boys would love it here, Morag—April too, Caro.'

'I'll talk them into it over summer,' Tess said.

Janey shifted in her wheelchair, opening her eyes. 'I bet you will,' she muttered, but with a smile.

'How's your ankle?' asked Macy. 'Does it hurt?'

'Yeah,' said Janey, 'it throbs. The doctor gave me plenty of drugs though, and at least I'll get some sleep-ins over the next month. I won't be going back to squad for a bit.'

Amira turned to Caro. 'Does that bother you?' she asked quietly. 'She was doing so well.'

Caro pulled a face. 'If you'd told me at the start of the trip I'd have been devastated. But what can you do?' She exhaled. 'It is what it is. No point getting upset now. We'll just have to live with it.'

Maybe that was what Tia thought too, Amira reflected—or rather, *how* she thought. It had struck her previously that few of the Aborigines she'd met at Kalangalla and socialised or worked with were planners. They didn't think too much about next week or next year, just lived their lives as they unfolded. Sometimes it drove Amira nuts, and she'd caught herself wondering if they were simply passive by nature, or conditioned to be so by years of white rule, but now a new possibility occurred to her. Maybe they were just smart. If you didn't think too far ahead you didn't worry either. It wasn't such a bad way to be. She smiled to herself. Here she was with all her lofty ambitions for what she was going to do in the community—to inspire, to teach—but there was another reason she was staying as well. There was so much to learn.

When boarding was announced almost everyone got teary, not just Caro. The embraces, the goodbyes seemed to last forever, her three friends and their daughters lining up to hug her and thank her—but then suddenly they were gone, the departure lounge deserted save for a gecko scuttling up one corrugated wall and the ceiling fan turning lazily overhead. Amira stood with her arm around Tess, and they watched as the plane taxied away, sat for a few minutes, then roared into the air.

She felt strange, she thought as she started the troop carrier and pulled out onto Frederick Street: sad to see them all go, but happy too. Happy to be where she was. Tess sat beside her, humming a song by a local band that she'd first heard soon after they moved north. They crested Kennedy Hill and saw Roebuck Bay laid out before them, its turquoise waters sparkling under the sun. Tess sighed. 'I don't think I could ever get tired of that view.'

Amira nodded and reached briefly for her daughter's hand. 'Thank you,' she said.

'For what?' Tess turned to her, puzzled, then her face cleared. 'Oh,' she said, looking back out to the ochre earth, the blue sea. 'Oh, you're welcome.'

Amira eased her foot onto the brake. A quick stop at The Mangrove to collect their bags and have some lunch, then they had to get on the road to Kalangalla. It would be good to be back. She loved Fiona, Morag and Caro, but she was glad she wasn't on the plane with them. They still had a while yet to travel, but she was already home.

Acknowledgements

Fiction is the best way I know of telling the truth. With sincere and grateful thanks to those who helped me tell this one:

The wonderful women at Allen & Unwin and Curtis Brown: Jane Palfreyman, Pippa Masson, Siobhán Cantrill, Clara Finlay, Louise Cornegé and Grace Heifetz. Thank you all for your assistance, your support, your care and for being so damn good at your jobs.

Mrs Whitla (Beaumaris Primary School), Ms Walters (St Michael's Grammar School) and Mrs Drummond (Mentone Girls' Grammar School). Most people are lucky to have one life-changing teacher. I had three.

All those who welcomed, befriended and helped us out during our time in Broome, particularly the Thorns, the Stones, Greg Sutherland, the Banfields, Krim Benterrak, the Oggs, Toni and Richard Bourne, Miss Shioji, Sally and Rae at the Broome Library, Jodie Lynch, Wayne Lynch, the Bacons, the Millers, Shane Bilston, the Broome Barracudas, Broome SLSC and Yindi Newman.

My beloved family—Craig, Dec and Cam—for gecko hunting and frangipanis and the blow-up turtle and Sunday morning Nippers at Cable Beach; for those incredible trips across the Kimberley and up the coast via Ningaloo and Karajini; for breakfast at the Courthouse markets and threadfin salmon at the Aarli Bar; for Lombadina and Kooljaman and Middle Lagoon and Eco Beach; for painted boab nuts and Matso's on the deck; for turtles and manta rays and humpback whales and green tree frogs in the cisterns, for The Pigram Brothers and Tonchi and the flutestone and the camels going home along the beach at sunset. What an amazing year it was—thank you for talking me into it, Laddy.

And finally our dear friends Jane and Dan Magree, with such treasured memories of our trip together with the kids on the Dampier Peninsula, which is when I first started thinking about this book. So many laughs, such a happy week—thank you.